PENGUIN BOOKS

The Secret of Magic

'[A] riveting novel' *O, The Oprah Magazine*

'There are a million metaphors I could use to describe Deborah
Johnson's writing in *The Secret of Magic* – but all of them are
inadequate in conveying the ebb and flow of her phrasing or the
care in crafting her characters . . . If you liked *The Help*, you'll
love this one! . . . [T]he cadence of Johnson's writing is an
absolute joy . . . I can't think of any other recent book in which
I have so enjoyed an author's actual stringing-together-of-words'
Entertainment Weekly

'Johnson offers a completely engaging southern gothic with
unforgettable characters . . .' *Booklist*

'A work of masterful storytelling, telling truth with fiction in a
novel that comes alive with every word on the page. With as
many curves as there are branches on magnolia trees, this
novel will take you into the forest and leave a mark on you'
The Herald-Sun

'A spirited portrayal of the postwar South' *Publishers Weekly*

'[A] spellbinding novel of a young, female, black attorney
trying to earn justice for a murdered World War II hero'
San Antonio Express-News

'A passionate, nuanced drama about Southern race relations . . .
provocative' *Kirkus Reviews*, starred review

D0111692

'Get a copy of Deborah Johnson's *The Secret of Magic* [and] expect the unexpected . . . A disturbing, but fair, look at life in Mississippi and the South in a turbulent time that lasted far too long. We need to know about that history, however, to move forward' *The Oxford Eagle*

'I found this story about race, the South, our country, part history, part mystery – never disappointing. Like the South she tragically portrays, *The Secret of Magic* is a layered tale of the best and worst of our history, beautifully wrought by a master storyteller' Robert Hicks, *New York Times* bestselling author of *Widow of the South* and *A Separate Country*

ABOUT THE AUTHOR

Deborah Johnson lives and writes in Columbus, Mississippi, after having resided for many years in San Francisco and in Rome, Italy. She is the author of the novel *The Air Between Us*.

The Secret of Magic

DEBORAH JOHNSON

PENGUIN BOOKS

PENGUIN BOOKS

UK | USA | Canada | Ireland | Australia
India | New Zealand | South Africa

Penguin Books is part of the Penguin Random House group of companies
whose addresses can be found at global.penguinrandomhouse.com.

Penguin Random House
UK

First published in the United States of America by Amy Einhorn Books, Penguin Group (USA) 2014
Published in Great Britain by Penguin Books 2015

003

Set in Dante 11/13 pt
Typeset by Palimpsest Book Production Limited, Falkirk, Stirlingshire
Printed in Great Britain by Clays Ltd, St Ives plc

A CIP catalogue record for this book is available from the British Library

ISBN: 978-0-241-96893-2

www.greenpenguin.co.uk

For my grandfather Joe Howard Thurman
and his great-grandson
Matthew Thurman Schumaker,
with love

The Secret of Magic

I.

October 1945

Gotcha!

Joe Howard Wilson jerked and his hands went straight to his face, and then to his body, for his gun. Groping. Feeling. Saying his prayers. Checking to make sure that he was awake and what had happened in that forest in Italy, all the killing, was over. Checking to make sure it wasn't happening now.

'You all right, mister? Need any help?'

Did he need help?

He opened his eyes then, but he didn't turn them to the voice, didn't answer it, because it was a child's voice. Light, like L.C.'s voice had been in the dream. And Joe Howard didn't want to go back to the dream. Instead, he put a hand on the hard thing right in front of him and realized it was nothing more menacing than a window and that this window was on a courier bus and that this courier bus was passing through Alabama on its way to Mississippi, and that it carried him home.

Outside, it was coming on night. Twilight. 'The magic time,' his daddy called it, 'the make-a-wish moment between the dark and the light.'

And the dusk, the gritty Southern grayness of it, its harsh gathering, stopped Joe Howard from seeing out beyond the solitude of his own reflection, a soldier's reflection: dark hair, a trimmed mustache, eyes he didn't bother looking into, and farther down from them, the ghostly shadow of a khaki uniform, of lieutenant's bars and a medal. There was no brain, no blood, no bone, no friend called L. C. Hoover sprayed all over this Joe Howard Wilson – at least not anymore.

Other than that, it was already too dark to see much of anything, but Joe Howard didn't mind. This land wasn't foreign to him. It wasn't war. It wasn't Italy. He knew the ways of it, the slow progression of Alabama as it gave way to Mississippi. At its own pace, red clay soil gave place to black, trees grew greener, hills flattened themselves into plain and prairie, into delta.

'Mister?'

At last, Joe Howard turned to the boy. They'd been sitting side by side since the two of them had gotten on the bus together in Birmingham. He had promised the boy's mother to see to it that her child got safely to Revere, Mississippi, all in one piece. The boy's mama, who had worked at the Mobile Dry Docks during the war, was on her way out to Oakland, California, to see what the world might hold for her there. She was sending her son back to her parents in Macon, Mississippi, for what she called 'The Duration,' until, she told him, she could get herself established.

No way was she ever going back to Mississippi to live. No way was she going to have her son grow up there. Onto the front of his clean overalls, she had pinned a piece of sack paper with his name on it. Manasseh. 'Came straight out of the Bible. Revelations,' the boy had told Joe Howard. Below that came Manasseh's granddaddy's name, Preacher Charles A. Lacey, and his granddaddy's address, Short Cut Road, Macon, Mississippi. All of this neatly spelled out in looping capital letters. Manasseh still held tight on to the lard can that had once contained his lunch – a cold baked yam, some corn bread, a Ball jar of sweet tea that he'd offered to share. He was working on the stick of Juicy Fruit gum Joe Howard had given him as the bus pulled out of Birmingham. The taste must have long since been played out of it, but still the boy chewed on.

Manasseh had politely motioned Joe Howard to the window seat. His eyes rounded as he stared at Joe Howard's uniform, at his bars, at his medals. He didn't need to see out, he'd said. Joe Howard didn't tell him that when he was a boy, when he was this boy's age, he'd made this trip many times himself.

'I'm well,' Joe Howard said now, finally answering. He yawned, looked out the bus window again. He might know Alabama, but he didn't recognize a thing. 'Where are we?'

'Coming into someplace called Aliceville.'

'Aliceville?' Joe Howard thought he'd remember every little town they'd pass through going from Tuscaloosa to Revere. Carrollton, Gordo, Reform, Vernon, Mitchell, but he couldn't for the life of him place Aliceville in the mix.

'They said we had to make a detour. I heard the bus driver tell the white folks that.' The words lisped out of Manasseh's mouth through the space of two missing front teeth. Joe Howard didn't have much experience with children, but he guessed this boy must be about six. The same age he'd been in the dream he'd just had, and the same age L.C. had been in it. He knew that when he told his daddy this, his daddy would assure him, with grave wisdom, that sitting next to Manasseh had summoned poor, dead, blown-apart L.C. to his mind.

'Called him back.' His daddy, Willie Willie, would have nodded sagely as he said this. His daddy with his old-timey, magic ways.

Joe Howard looked past the boy now, to the front of the bus. The colored section was full, but there weren't that many white folks. No other uniforms, either. Since the war, Joe Howard noticed military uniforms as quickly as he noticed skin color, and as necessarily. Army, Navy, Army Air Corps, Marines – it didn't matter. They all made him feel safe. But there was no serviceman, no ex-serviceman, on this little interstate vehicle, making its slow way from east to west and south.

Instead, there was a young redheaded woman with two little boys. Twins, probably – at least they looked that way to Joe Howard. The driver took his eyes off the road and turned back to say something to her. She was right up at the very front of the bus, and so Joe Howard couldn't see her face, but the flow of her hair was pretty, the way she'd tied it back with a dusty pink bow, the way it danced around when she tossed her head. Joe Howard saw this but lowered his head, glanced quickly away. He did not want to be caught staring at a white woman.

3

Her children saw him, though, they watched him those look-alike, little twin boys, who had on identical shirts and brown short pants, gray sweaters. Without a word, now that they had his attention, they got up and started to the back of the bus, jostled side to side and against the seats by its movement. When they reached Joe Howard, they still didn't say anything, but they stared at his uniform, at the lieutenant's bars on it, at the medal, just like Manasseh had done. Then, together, they looked up into his face.

Joe Howard reached into his pocket and pulled out his yellow pack of Juicy Fruit. He offered each boy a stick and each took one. He thought their mother, who was looking back now, would call out to them, would stop them from taking something from a Negro. But she didn't.

It was the bus driver who shouted out. 'Hey, Henry! Hey, William!' Preening, Joe Howard thought, with the knowledge of their names. 'Come on back here!'

He watched the boys go to their mother, not to the man. He watched her lean each boy close to her and kiss his cheek, ruffle his hair. And he thought: I wonder what it would have been like to have a mother. But then, just as quickly, the thought was swallowed up by a burden of love for his daddy. That burden was always with him. Joe Howard said aloud, 'I got to call him. Let him know I'm close now, almost home.' His daddy was a good son of Mississippi, and, as such, he held Alabama at a distance but always in shadowed, distrustful view.

The first time Joe Howard had crossed the state line going east, he'd been maybe a little younger than Manasseh, five years old. His daddy had been driving the Cackle Crate then – probably he was still driving it now – and their green Ford pickup had been following a Ford pickup just like it, except for its brown color and its Alabama license plates. Revere was the last Mississippi town you went through before you got to Alabama, and the two of them, Joe Howard and his daddy, had been on their way to Tuscaloosa so that his daddy could buy him some new school shoes.

His daddy traded only where they let you come in, make your pick, try on what you wanted. Like a man. Like the *special* man Joe Howard would grow up to be – his daddy knew it! But there were no stores like this in Revere.

The truck they followed had had thirteen Confederate flags on it, if you counted all the decals. And Joe Howard had counted them. He knew all about the Stars and the Bars. Judge Calhoun had already brought him into Calhoun Place and shown him the flag that the judge's own granddaddy, Colonel Robert Millsaps Calhoun, had managed to scavenge out of the shambles that had been the Battle of Gettysburg. Sitting under that flag, teaching him how to read, Judge Calhoun had told Joe Howard about that great war, that righteous freedom-seeking war. His bourbon breath had been warm upon the names of General Nathan Bedford Forrest, and General Stephen Lee and General William Barksdale, warm upon battles lost at Vicksburg and Jackson and Shiloh – fought, actually, the judge assured Joe Howard, for the armaments and the train depot here in glorious Mississippi, right up there at Corinth – conjuring myths that beatified soldiers and made them heroes, and canonized their glorious lost cause.

'And not a black man among 'em. Not in any of the tales the judge might be telling. Not in anything he has to say. Not down here,' Joe Howard's daddy had whispered, tucked in tight beside him on their shuck-stuffed mattress, on their tiny bed at night. 'Don't worry about it, though. You'll be the first. You'll be in the *history* book. I'm seeing straight to that.'

So when Joe Howard had signed up at eight o'clock on the morning of December 8, 1941, for the Army, both his daddy and the judge had each thought he knew why, because of coming glory on the one side and past glory on the other.

But they'd both of them been wrong.

The bus lumbered off asphalt onto gravel and groaned to a stop. Again, Joe Howard looked out of his window, and this time the twilight had formed itself into a sign: ALICEVILLE, ALABAMA. That's when he remembered about Aliceville. There was a prisoner-of-war camp here, for Germans. He'd read about it, probably in *Stars and Stripes*. This was a good out-of-the-way place for something like that. Joe Howard pried down his window so that he could see the sign better and so that he could smell the earth and the trees. He squinted out but didn't see any trace of a camp. There were no low buildings, no barbed wire. Alabama wasn't like Italy, at least the Italy he knew, where every hill, every valley, every stretch of land had something man-made on it – a barn filled with straw, a stone house, a fence. Someplace that a German could easily hunker down behind, hide under. Until the time came to cry out:

Gotcha!

'You getting off?' he asked Manasseh.

Manasseh, carefully instructed by his mother, shook his young head.

'Not even to go to the bathroom?'

No, not even for that.

Joe Howard didn't feel much like getting off himself, but he had to call his daddy. He'd promised. Nowadays, these little inter-state buses took forever to get where they were going. They stopped where they wanted to, stringing little half-known towns in Alabama and Mississippi together like so many beads on a rosary chain. With first the fury of war and now the slow discharge of its dismantlement causing so many detours, there was no telling when a person would actually get where he was going. Even the printed schedules had started summarizing arrival times as 'around' and 'about.' But 'around' and 'about' were not good enough for his daddy. He'd want to know more precisely than this when Joe Howard would actually get to Revere.

'You call me when you get close, now, son. Let me know, because I want to be there at the station to greet you, and the Church wants to be there – Reverend Petty's bringing the Mothers. And all the folks . . . all the folks . . .'

His daddy's voice had choked up then, an amazement to Joe

6

Howard, who was used to thinking of his daddy's love for him as a force, capable of overcoming all obstacles, not as an emotion that might weaken him, might make him cry. So he'd said, a little too quickly, 'Last stop in Alabama, I'll call. I promise.'

So now he got up, walked off that bus, and went in an old-fashioned screen door under a turned-off electric sign that proclaimed: DR PEPPER – IT'S GOOD FOR YOU. He hadn't had a Dr Pepper in a while, and he'd grown up on them, on them and on RC Colas and on the treat of a honey bun when he worked in the fields. He thought about ordering one now, but there were no colored people in the bus depot, and his was the only military uniform. He decided it might be better to make his telephone call, get it over with, get back on the bus.

The air in the depot smelled just like everything Southern he remembered. Even inside, no matter where you were, there was always a hint of the earth and the things that died on it. You could not get away from the scent of things, from the richness of them, if you had lived, like he had lived, so near to the ground. Joe Howard couldn't quite make out exactly what track it was he was pulling in – maybe a deer passing, maybe the dead-end of the summer's kudzu decaying on the vine – but if his daddy were here he'd be able to call it out, to tell what it was that was tickling at their minds. Willie Willie knew all about the earth and its ways.

The telephone booth was up flush against the door. There was nothing written on it, at least that he could see, saying NO COLOREDS. He had a friend in Atlanta who, in an uncertain situation like this, always pulled out his gun and put it up on the telephone so that everybody could see it. He said there was nothing like a loaded revolver to help clarify things. Joe Howard had laughed right along with everybody else when he'd heard this – a bitter laugh. The laugh had been bitter for them all. But Joe Howard had packed his pistol – a service .45 – in his rucksack, and his rucksack was out there somewhere deep within the belly of the bus.

Nobody seemed to be paying him much attention and maybe,

even if there was a sign someplace that he'd missed, they might cut him some slack. He still wore his Army uniform, after all, and the war had just recently finished.

The way to reach his daddy hadn't changed for the whole of Joe Howard's life. He dialed the operator, passed the Calhoun number on to her – 1353W – and answered her question that, no, the call was not collect. He had money and, at her drawled instruction, dropped twenty cents' worth of nickels into their slot. He shut the cabin door.

Static at both ends, in Aliceville and in Revere. The fault of worn-out wiring and county systems too poor to change it out. It had been like this even before the war. Plus everything in their part of Mississippi still operated on a party line. By the time ancient Miss Betty Jo Hillman at the post office got the call through to Calhoun Place, at least three other households would have picked up and be listening in, too.

The telephone at home was black, heavy, and screw-mounted to the wall. Old-fashioned. And, like a lot in that house, once it was bought, it was expected to last. The Calhouns did not like change, and that instrument, as Miss Mary Pickett called it, had been in their kitchen for as long as Joe Howard could remember, since before Miss Mary Pickett's daddy, Judge Calhoun, and even her mama, Miss Eulalie, had died. The call rang through, and somebody would eventually answer, that new girl, Dinetta, Miss Mary Pickett had written him about or one of the help-out maids, maybe even his daddy. If he was lucky, it would be his daddy to answer. Joe Howard didn't feel like talking to anybody else.

Instead, the voice he heard was Miss Mary Pickett Calhoun herself shouting, 'Hello? Hello? Joe Howard, is that you? Hello?'

'Miss Mary Pickett?'

'Joe Howard? Is that you?'

For just a moment the static eased and she could have been right beside him, strong-voiced as ever, shouting her crystal-clear words right into his ear.

'It's me, Miss Mary Pickett,' then, just in case. 'Joe Howard.'

8

He said this though she had already called him by name so she knew who he was. 'Is my daddy there?'

'Sweet Jesus! Let me run on back outside and see if I can find him. Oh, Joe Howard, he's so excited you're coming home. Are you all right? Did those Germans . . . Did they . . . Did they do anything to you? Did they *hurt* you? It'd just about tear your daddy up if they did.'

Germans. Did they do anything to him? Did they *hurt* him? He wanted to tell her, 'Well, of course they have. We have battled. We have been at war.' He wanted to shout these words at her, but he couldn't do that.

And it didn't matter, because Miss Mary Pickett hadn't waited for his answer. She'd dropped the receiver and it bounced, on its electric cord, against the cream-colored walls of her kitchen. Joe Howard could *see* it. He was so close now. He was almost there.

He heard Miss Mary Pickett's high heels tapping against the black and white tiles of the kitchen floor, heard the back screen door slamming, heard her 'Willie Willie! Willie Willie! Come on in here quick!'

She'd be down the veranda steps now and among the raised flowerbeds in her backyard. She'd run along the path of her prize rosebushes, then around the back of the cottage. Her calls to his father grew fainter and fainter in Joe Howard's ear.

He reached into his pocket for a cigarette but discovered he'd left his Camels, like his pistol, somewhere back deep in the bus. The jukebox had switched over from Harry James to Benny Goodman. He recognized the band, but he'd been gone a long time and didn't recognize the song they were playing. Still, he started humming along. Something caught his eye – a uniform. Not a soldier, though, a policeman. Maybe. Joe Howard wasn't sure. He'd looked away too quickly. Policemen were like white women. He'd learned a long time ago not to let his eye linger on them, to ease his gaze right on away.

But Joe Howard was tired tonight. His eyes and his thoughts didn't skip forward as quickly as they might have. They slowed down. They moved back. Past the war, even, to the nights he'd walk the streets of Atlanta, going from Morehouse College to his job sweeping out the newsroom at *The Atlanta Journal* and then walk back from *The Atlanta Journal* to Morehouse College. After dark. Because after-dark work was the only kind of work he could find and still maintain the studies that Judge Calhoun was paying for and that his daddy was paying for and that Joe Howard was trying to keep up himself. The streetcars didn't run late and he didn't have a car and he didn't have any money. So he'd been forced onto the streets. Alone. Every night.

And every night he'd meet a policeman. Sometimes one, sometimes another. Maybe he'd seen them before; maybe they were strangers. It didn't matter. They all knew him. They all stopped him. They all said to him: 'Where you goin', nigger, to some whorehouse, out this late?' And he'd say, 'No.' And then, 'Sir.' It didn't matter what he said. Nobody was listening. This is just how they got around to saying what they really wanted to say, which was, 'Look here, nigger, you take off y'all's hat when you talk to a white man. Don't you know that, you ignorant coon?' He'd take it off. Then. Not until they told him to, but once they did tell him he'd do what they said. Every time. Because he had his daddy, his good daddy, who was back there in Revere, working hard and plotting and planning, so that his son could go on, get an education, get out of Mississippi, at least for a moment, and make something of himself in the wide world.

So Joe Howard would take off his hat to his daddy.

Once he had it off, the policeman would knock it into the dirt, sometimes with a billy club, sometimes with bare hands, and he'd be forced to bend down and pick it up from the street. He'd be let go then, with a curse and a 'nigger,' and he'd be free to continue on. They never really *hurt* him. They didn't even intend to *hurt* him. Joe Howard knew this, but as soon as his face was turned away from them, he'd start to cry. A man, a grown man, walking through the streets of a big city, crying like that, like a damn baby. Secret and shameful. But he couldn't help it. He hated those big-baby tears, and he hated himself for letting those stupid-ass white men get to him and for crying those rivers of tears.

Now, waiting for his daddy, Joe Howard cleared his throat, once, then twice. He was less than thirty miles from home and he had made it and his daddy had made it. They were both alive. They would see each other soon, and that was a blessed thing and a great one. In Italy, he was sure he'd never make it home.

Sometimes, when he was out on patrol, especially in the last months before the war ended, Joe Howard had been scared to death his daddy might die before he got back. He knew soldiers who had lost their mothers, lost their fathers, lost their wives, lost their children, even, while they were gone fighting. You never thought of that, but it happened. In foxholes, behind trees, in the bodies of dead animals and dead men, in the cratered earth, would hide the terrifying thought that he would somehow get back to Revere and that his daddy would be gone, that he'd never see his daddy again.

But Willie Willie was alive. Joe Howard heard him now, running up the back steps to the telephone, coming in from where he had been working – keeping up the garden, fixing things that broke down, telling his tall tales and his stories, driving Miss Mary Pickett, who couldn't drive, all over town in the old Calhoun Daimler. His daddy took up the receiver, breathing hard and shouting into it, just like Miss Mary Pickett had done.

'That you, son? You okay?'

'I'm well, Daddy.' He put the telephone receiver between his ear and his shoulder and reached, again, for a Camel before he remembered, again, that he didn't have one. 'It's taking longer than I thought. They got us caught over here in Aliceville.'

'*Aliceville?*' Willie Willie was plainly astonished. 'Why, son, Aliceville's not on the way home.'

'Close, though. Thirty, thirty-five miles. Maybe less. At least that's what they say.'

His daddy said, 'But it's an *unknown* way. Don't get yourself in any trouble. You know how folks are over in Alabama.'

Joe Howard laughed. They both laughed. This was their joke, talking about how things were over in Alabama, as though they weren't the same way in Mississippi, as though Alabama was a whole world away.

'I should be there in an hour, maybe less.'

'Just get here quick. Everybody's excited. They got your picture up all over Revere – at least all over the colored parts of it. Miss Mary Pickett's got hers laid out, too, up there in her office. She told me so herself. You know that snapshot she took of the two of us – you in your uniform and me right beside you? Well, she kept hold to it.'

'She did?'

Joe Howard didn't know whether he was pleased to hear this or not. Mostly not, he decided, because he knew the picture. Him all fresh in his new uniform and his daddy in old overalls, and they were leaning right into each other, holding on to each other like each was the only thing living that the other had left, which was true enough. And they were grinning, both of them. Hard. Except *grinning* wasn't really the right word. *Radiant* was better. Willie Willie and his son, Joe Howard Wilson, radiating love. Willie Willie looking prouder even than he had looked when Joe Howard had graduated from Morehouse College and the judge had sent him over to Atlanta – his first time in Georgia – on the Greyhound to see that blessed event.

Miss Mary Pickett had taken the picture and kept it to herself for some reason. She'd been going through a phase back then, still talking about writing a new book after that one about the forest and the old Mottley sisters, even after all the mischief that first one had caused. She'd told everybody who would listen that she'd soon be putting out another, was working on it, typing away on her old Corona. But Willie Willie said most of the time she was just out with her little Brownie camera snapping pictures, snapshots of the Negroes – in the fields, in their stores, on their porches, out and about wherever Miss Mary Pickett could find them. Nobody knew why. Nobody knew the reason for a lot of things she did, she just did them. And she could get away with doing whatever in the world she damn pleased, just like her daddy had before her, because their last name was Calhoun and that name had stood for something rock solid in Revere, Mississippi, for going on a hundred years.

'Proud of you,' his daddy said out of nowhere, in case the son somehow hadn't heard.

'Not much to be proud of,' said Joe Howard. He knew things that his daddy didn't. 'I only did what they told me to do.'

His daddy came right back on this. 'You did it good, though. Got yourself medalized.' Joe Howard grinned. His daddy was good at making up his own words. *"Lieutenant Joe Howard Wilson of Revere was awarded the Distinguished Service Cross for leading Negro troops to a decisive victory last April at the Battle of Castel Aghinolfi in Italy,"*' Willie Willie continued. 'That's what the *Afro-American* newspaper from down Jackson had to say about you. Miss Mary Pickett read it out to me and I told it out, word for word, to all the folks down at Stanley's Lookin' Good Barbershop myself. *"Lieutenant Wilson demonstrated exceptional bravery in helping to clear Italy from the Fascists and the Nazis when he did not and does not have the right to vote here in Mississippi, his natal state. Lieutenant Wilson is the son of Mr Willie Willie Wilson of Revere."* Course, they got my name wrong. Folks don't know us personally, they always do that.'

Willie Willie chuckled just like he had when Joe Howard was little and he'd told him story after story about the dark things that, for once, were the good and true things and that hid out in the magic woods and floated at night on the magic river. And, against all odds, somehow managed to triumph before *The End*.

So Joe Howard asked him, 'You been working out any more tales?' Shouting almost and hoping his daddy would shout, too, so he could hear him. The static was back again in force.

'Oh, a few. A few,' cried out Willie Willie. 'I'll tell you some once you get here. Real soon. But you watch out for yourself. Come straight home now! Watch out!'

This admonition was the last thing from his daddy that got through to Joe Howard distinctly before the crackling roiled up and took over the telephone lines.

'Daddy?'

Not wanting to hang up, listening hard, Joe Howard thought he heard something about ladybugs taking over the whole place, like usual. Ladybugs were a problem in Mississippi in deep autumn. They pestered on things and could be a complaint. Maybe Willie Willie said something about the winter coming on strong because the squirrels were taking over in the attic in his cottage. Getting ready. And maybe he said something about the cotton crop. Joe Howard thought he must surely have had something to say about the cotton crop. Everybody always had something to say about that. But he couldn't really hear now, so he couldn't be certain.

One last, 'I love you, Daddy' – probably useless, but called out just in case.

Joe Howard hung up the phone.

He walked out of the booth, looked around, and still nobody seemed to be paying him any attention. Nobody rushed him for being in the wrong not-for-coloreds place. His mind turned to Manasseh, waiting patiently on the bus, and the thought came that he might get him something, some candy. A few Sugar Daddys, maybe, or Red Hots. But he was still the only Negro inside the depot, and he decided it was probably better not to push his luck.

Joe Howard kept his eyes straight ahead as he climbed back onto the bus, but out of the corner of the left one he thought he saw somebody he knew. Somebody from Revere. He slowed his pace so he could study her without looking like he was doing it. He was almost sure she was a woman his daddy used to do odd jobs for once the cotton had been got in out at Magnolia Forest plantation and the household moved back into town. She had one child, a boy, about his age. Joe Howard recognized her because she was the only mama he'd ever known, even when he was little, who dyed her hair with Mrs Field's blue rinse. It always reminded him of a little piece of clear sky hovering over the cloud of her white face. Her name was Miss Anna Dale Buchanan, if he wasn't mistaken. But Joe Howard thought he *could* be mistaken. She was bent over a book, didn't see him. Her hair wasn't as bright as he remembered it, either. And she was a white woman. Joe Howard decided it was better not to speak.

Manasseh was still behind the sign that read COLORED ONLY, still behind the makeshift separating curtain, still there in his seat, still clutching his lard can, still wearing the pinned-on paper sign that gave him a name and a place in this world. He looked relieved when he saw Joe Howard, and the biblical solemnity of his face broke up in a smile.

Joe Howard smiled back.

'You know, I been out to Macon,' he said, settling into his seat once again. 'Lots of times. It's a nice place. You gonna like it. My daddy used to take me over there, to the forest. The Magnolia Forest – ever heard about that? It can be dead of winter everyplace else still in Mississippi, there's always gonna be at least some little speck of green. Grass peeking up through the snow in January. Full-bloomed bushes hiding out behind the skeletons of old oak and pecan trees. Christmas, and my daddy would take me out there, would point to the highest gray branch in the tree and say, "See that, son? That's mistletoe. Breathe on it. Sigh on it. Let it kiss you." You know what, Manasseh? I'd do just that. Blow a soft breath straight up and the mistletoe would come down to kiss it. It would float against my cheek and kiss me. Right there in Macon – that's what would happen.'

But Manasseh did not look convinced.

'And ladybugs. Everywhere you look, ladybugs. Did you know there's magic in a ladybug? One touches you – why, son, it's good luck.'

This, at last, was something Manasseh had heard before and remembered. He nodded. He smiled.

The bus started filling up again. Joe Howard saw the twin boys from before. He waved at them because it was safe to wave at white children, especially little boys. They looked at him shyly. One waved back. Their mother was still laughing with the driver but with a little less animation. Joe Howard wondered when the two of them would stop their flirting so the bus could get going again. He was looking down at his Longines, a little irritated, when he heard the driver say, 'Hey, well now. It took you long enough to get them. How all y'all doing?'

From the front of the bus there came a faint rustle. A movement and a shifting that seemed purposed to draw everyone's curious attention.

White men got on. There were a lot of them: five or six, from what Joe Howard could tell, but he couldn't see much from the back of the bus. Most of them were still in the well, and the courier heaved slightly under their weight. Manasseh perked up, curious now, too. He stopped chewing on his dead gum.

The first man was in a uniform Joe Howard knew was not military, but the man seemed to know the driver, to be on good terms with him. The two of them chuckled together for a moment. The driver introduced him to the mother of the twins. She said something and the uniformed man pointed to the other men behind him. The woman nodded as the men finished their climb and started down the aisle.

It was then that Joe Howard realized that the first of them was some part of the law. If not exactly a policeman, then close. Joe Howard started paying attention. The men he'd led into the bus and were now passing right through the white section and coming on into COLORED ONLY were prisoners. There were red *PW*s on their belts. When one of them turned around to whisper something to the man behind him, something that caused both of them to smile, Joe Howard saw a big *P* and a big *W* stenciled large as life on the back of his cotton-fleck shirt. What looked to be a deputy brought up the rear.

Germans, thought Joe Howard. *Prisoners of war.* Maybe about to go home, just like he was going home. Joe Howard settled back into his uncomfortable seat. He didn't see how these men had a thing in the world to do with him.

Until they stopped. Until he heard the guard say, 'You coloreds get on up. Give over these places to these here men.'

All around him Joe heard the slow shuffle of people gathering their things to move. A woman groaned to her feet behind him; across the way, an old black man reached for his pine cane. Even Manasseh, who had not budged even to go to the bathroom, started gathering his lard bucket together. Started shuffling. Started to obey.

Joe Howard could not believe it. *He could not believe it.*

'You want us to get up and give our places – that we paid for – to some German prisoners?'

The guard's face flared into a mottled map of angry affirmation. Could this be a black man talking back to *him*?

Yes, he damned well did want that. 'What I want,' he said, talking slow now, and loud, 'is for you niggers to get up and give these here places over to white men.'

When he said them, the words sounded as reasonable and as inevitable as the fact the sun would rise again in the east the next day. It was just simply the way things were, the way they had always been, the way they were always going to be.

L.C. calling out, 'Come on, Joe Howard! Catch up! Catch up!'

Joe Howard close behind him now. Running straight into the night forest.

'I'm not getting up,' he said, as he actually jumped to his feet and stood there, blocking the way with his uniform. 'And nobody else back here is getting up, either. Not for some Nazis.'

The other deputy came up from behind fast. He stared at Joe Howard, at his uniform, at his bars and his medals.

'Well, look-a-hear, Leroy,' he began, 'Maybe . . .'

Compromise was in his voice. But the man called Leroy was having none of it.

'I said move aside here, nigger. Give these white men your place.'

'And I said that I'm not moving, and neither is anybody else.'

Each word clear and distinct, and with the feel of his friend L.C.'s blood fresh on him again, the warm, iron smell of it, the sticky drained life. Joe Howard felt those always-near tears well up in him, threatening his eyes, threatening him, just like they had so long ago on the streets of Atlanta and just like they always would. It was the tears that told him that the war – his part in it, the long horror of it – hadn't changed one thing.

By now all the white folks had turned around and they were looking, too. Joe Howard saw the one he thought he knew, Miss Anna Dale. It *was* her. A prim lady in a lace collar, in a polka-dot dress, in a green hat with lilacs blooming on it. With a polished gold star pinned to her ample bosom. He saw all of that now. She stared at him with dark, deep eyes. Joe Howard heard her whisper, 'Oh, dear.'

Be careful!

Words, using his daddy's voice, slipped into his mind.

'Are you safe, son? Come on home safe!'

But Joe Howard had no use for those words. He closed his eyes. They disappeared.

He found his own words. 'Aren't these Germans? Aren't these Nazis?'

And even one of the Germans – light of hair, light of eye and skin, a stranger in this place – seemed anxious to help.

'It's okay. We can stand.' His words accented but still clear.

'You'll shut up if you know what's good for you, you lousy Kraut,' shouted Leroy. The German shut up.

And Joe Howard thought, clearly, distinctly: *Why the hell am I doing this?*

Manasseh, who in his short life had only left Mississippi to journey over into Alabama, knew what was coming next. He didn't need his mama to tell him. He shifted in his seat. Joe Howard had been nice to him. Manasseh *wanted* to get up. Joe Howard had to lay a heavy hand on his shoulder to keep him down. Things were just so much like always. The little colored boy getting up automatically, and the little white boys, ahead, just as automatically turning back to see what was going on but staying put.

Manasseh moved again, and Joe Howard looked down at him and he said – because he'd promised the boy's mama that he'd watch out for him – 'Everything's going to be all right. You'll see. Things are going to be different now. We just fought a war. *We* fought it, too – and that means nobody anymore's got the right to take our paid-for seats from us.'

He turned slightly and let his battle-sharpened gaze sweep on over the other Negroes – some already on their feet – on past them to the whites at the front where the woman had clustered her children close beside her. And where the bus driver had decided just what needed doing next.

He looked over at the mother of the twins, puffed up his chest, started back. Outside, the electric Dr Pepper sign still twinkled. Its brilliance flashed over the little depot and illuminated it with the purity of the Bethlehem star. But not all the lights on it worked, and Joe Howard heard the sizzle and crackle of currents trying to connect. He realized that he still was holding on to Manasseh, holding on to him too tightly. He might be hurting the boy. He relaxed his hand.

'I'm sorry,' he whispered. Manasseh from Revelations in the Bible nodded, but with that white bus driver lumbering back like thunder, he was too scared to look up at Joe Howard now.

The guard named Leroy said, 'You'll do what I say, boy . . .' creating a dangerous situation.

The driver drew close. His name, Johnny Ray Dean, was scripted in bright blue thread on his gray uniform. 'What's all this? I don't want no confusion.' His words were drawn out in a thick Alabama hill-country drawl and there was a glint in his eye that said he was aware of and happy that he had the redheaded woman's full attention once again. Happy that such a really pretty woman would see how good he was at solving nigger problems.

'There *is* no confusion,' said Leroy. 'This here boy's just got to let folks do what they been told to do.'

Joe Howard thought, *If this cracker calls me nigger one more time, I'm going to kill him. Kill him outright.*

Joe Howard said, 'And I have told this fucking white man I am not getting up out of my seat for some prisoner, for some goddamn German. For some goddamn fucking Nazi.'

He'd cussed now. Around him, all the old women, both colored and white, gasped.

Joe Howard said, 'I've had . . . My friends . . . The war . . .'

But what friends were left? They were all dead now. And these people – could they care about the war and what had happened to him there?

Around Joe Howard, the whole bus grew silent as a grave and the driver looked at him for a long moment. Eyes narrowed, fists bunched. Then he smiled. He opened up his mouth and he said, 'Hold on there, I don't want no trouble. There's another bus due in. It cleared out of Birmingham right after we left Tuscaloosa, a bare couple hours behind us. Why don't I see if I can get you and these here prisoners on that one, Leroy? Avoid all this confusion.' He said this even though the white part of the bus was half empty. But, of course, they would not put these German prisoners up there. Not with the white women. Not with the white children.

Johnny Ray Dean leaned in and whispered something to the guard, a few quick words that Joe Howard could not hear, and then added, 'I'll climb on down. Make the call myself.'

'Yeah, Leroy,' said the young deputy. 'Let him do that.'

Leroy paused over this, considered, though Joe Howard could tell this was only a ruse and that his mind was already made up.

Johnny Ray said, 'There's other ways to handle this; let this boy be for now. Just don't give me no more ruckus. GIs all coming home and they want everything they can get their hands on. I get trouble on this bus – somebody might think to give my route to one of them.'

Again, Leroy appeared to cogitate. 'Well, sir, you sure there's another bus coming?' Whatever the driver had whispered privately seemed to have calmed him down, made him stand tall again, at least for the moment. Still, there was face-saving to do.

'Oh, I'm sure,' said the driver. 'There be plenty of ways to skin a coon.'

The white men – all of them: guards, prisoners, and the driver – trooped to the front of the bus, the Americans whispering, the Germans behind them. The German who had spoken up earlier turned back. He caught Joe Howard's gaze and then quickly looked away. Joe Howard watched as all of them got off the bus. Johnny Ray climbed down with them. The blacks still had their seats, but Joe Howard felt like he always felt when he'd come out of a battle – that same strange alchemic mixture of relief and shame.

'Daddy wouldn't want me cussing,' he said out loud. His daddy wouldn't want him talking back to white men with guns, either, but there was no helping that now.

He made up his mind he was going to apologize to Manasseh; maybe even to some of the ladies, especially to that one who wore the gold star that told the world she had a son who'd been killed in the war. Maybe she might understand.

'Miss Anna Dale,' he whispered her name. Sure of it now.

Joe Howard sat back down again. He touched his face and his shirt and his arms and his hands, just as he'd done when he'd wakened from his nightmare, and found himself on this bus going home. He tried, but he could no longer see his face in the window. It had grown too dark for that.

Johnny Ray Dean climbed back on, the courier shifting under his weight, and the whole thing was over. He started up the engine, pulled out onto the asphalt road, but if he had thought he could win his maiden's admiration by swaggering back and taking control of things, he'd been much mistaken. He tried talking to her, and then after a silence tried again, but even Joe Howard could see she was no longer paying attention. She sat hugging

21

her children. Except for the flame of a match and the burning coal of a cigarette being smoked farther up, the bus rolled on, silent and dark.

It eased on down a road free of traffic, ambling along until it finally crossed the state line. Manasseh hadn't said a word since he'd first seen the Germans. Now Joe Howard remembered something – another tale, another legend from his daddy – and he bent close so that he could whisper it into the child's ear and comfort him with it.

'You see that sign – see how it says JEFFERSON-LEE COUNTY WELCOMES YOU? All white on green and pretty? And see the one stuck up behind it, WELCOME TO MISSISSIPPI? These two painted boards, coming one right after the other, mean you enter the county before you enter the state. Twenty feet between them, and those twenty feet are magic – because nothing owns it. Not Alabama. Not Mississippi. It's a special place. Free. That's what my daddy always said to me. And anything can happen on this magic land. My daddy told me if you make a wish here . . . If you make a quick wish here, why, the mistletoe might find you . . .'

It was in that place of magic that the Bonnie Blue Line interstate courier bus shuddered to an unscheduled stop. From his place in the back of it, Joe Howard saw Johnny Ray Dean crane his head to look at him and then slowly, slowly crank the bus door, opening it onto this special make-a-wish place.

Where Joe Howard heard voices. Where he saw men.

Where he blew his breath into heaven and let mistletoe float down from the sky to kiss him one last time upon the cheek.

2.

Regina Mary Robichard noticed the envelope as soon as she entered her office. Fat and cream-colored, it lay there among the business letters, newspapers, and circulars on her small desk. It looked out of place, like an invitation. Not just any invitation, either, but an opening to something she might actually like to attend. Later, it was the photograph within that envelope that would capture her attention, and keep it. But for now the envelope itself was enough.

She had come in on a Saturday with the idea of working for a few hours and then, since she was downtown, rewarding herself with a little shopping at Best & Co. or at Peck & Peck. There was a sale on hats at Gimbels, but she had a lot of hats and didn't really need more. She'd read about another good deal, this one for better suits, at May D&F and a new movie, *The Best Years of Our Lives*, which was playing at the Rialto in Times Square. She thought about taking that in as well. If she was lucky, all of this might keep her out of her new stepfather's house, and her mother – or, rather, her *parents* – would be asleep when she came in.

It was a legend in the family how Regina, when she was little, under six, would go up to a man – any man – who had come to hear one of her famous mother's famous speeches and say, 'Would you like to marry my mommy? Would you like to be my daddy?' Often the men she asked did not know how to take this. They'd duck. They'd turn away. Of course they all knew what had happened to Oscar Robichard, not that long ago in Omaha, Nebraska. They wouldn't have been there if they hadn't, and they were all sympathetic. But nobody wanted to be Regina's daddy. Nobody had wanted to marry her mother. Until now.

'Monday,' Regina said aloud, 'I've got to start looking for my own place.' *I've got a job now, and my own life. It's time.*

Behind her, she left the main door unlocked and opened a crack in case someone else came in, always a possibility on a Saturday here at the LDF, or the NAACP Legal Defense Fund, as it was more formally known. People worked late; they came in on weekends. There was always that much to do. Regina shared her space with three other lawyers, all of them men, one of them white. None of whom exactly relished having a woman in their midst. They never said this, not outright, but it was implied in their stories that stopped in mid-sentence, in laughter that abruptly died when she came into the room. She suspected that half the male lawyers thought she was here because her mother was Ida Jane Robichard, the other half because of the way that her father had died. They were all wrong. Regina knew she was here because she was *born* to be here, born to value the law and its order. With her history, who wouldn't? But this didn't stop her from sometimes feeling . . . well, strange.

Especially because she sat directly across from Edgar Morrison Moseley III ('But my friends call me Skip'), hired as a staff lawyer three weeks before she'd been, fully as ambitious as she was herself, and the nemesis of what she liked to call her 'legal life.' Skip had never been happy to have a woman in the office, a fact he made abundantly clear. Invariably, the women lawyers he talked about had something in common with Regina – 'Hey, she looked *exactly* like you look. Graduated Columbia, too. I was *astounded*' – and they all ended up in either a sad or bad way.

'War's over. Women need to do their duty, go back home and make babies. A woman working takes a job away from a family man.' This was his continual refrain, called out whenever he thought Regina might be listening. Once he'd actually lectured her to her face while they were having sandwiches and coffee at the Forty-second Street Automat. 'You need to get yourself married, settle down.' Ida Jane might have slugged him, but Regina didn't. She just made her excuses and caught a cab home.

'Why do you even *date* such a jerk?' Ida Jane had looked up from the piece she was writing, her brow still creased in concentration, splotches of fountain-pen ink dotting her hand.

'It wasn't a date, not really,' Regina answered. 'We'd worked late, decided to go out, that was all. Besides, Skip's got a right to his opinion. I just can't let his opinion interfere with my life.'

'Got to change some laws if you want to make sure *that* doesn't happen.' Ida Jane rolled her eyes, shook her head. 'But I guess that's why you're working over there at the Fund.'

Now Regina pulled off kid gloves and a veiled felt hat and put them on a wooden chair. She glanced from the small room in which she stood to a smaller room next to it, which was stacked floor to ceiling with alphabetized manila envelopes. This was her special place, the reason she'd come to work on such a sunny Saturday morning. 'Reggie's Realm,' the others called it, relieved that it was her responsibility and not theirs. These were her cases. Thousands of them, sent in by Negro servicemen who had been court-martialed or dishonorably discharged for doing what a white man had gotten away with doing or been slightly reprimanded for doing.

'My name is Legion,' Thurgood Marshall had said when he'd handed them over, while out of the corner of her eye Regina had seen Skip smirk. They were not considered a gift and had been assigned to her because she had been the last one hired, and could be the first one fired, if she wasn't careful. If she didn't keep her nose to the grindstone and work hard. But she had surprised herself by actually liking the cases – or 'the causes,' as she began calling them, though only to herself. She looked forward to opening each new envelope, reading through its depositions and briefs, getting to know men who had laid out their grievances in their own measured, carefully written-out words.

Still, the fat, cream-colored envelope beckoned her first.

She walked across the linoleum floor to take it into her hands, to weigh and measure it. Vellum, she thought, a good one. Being able to distinguish standard bond from good vellum was something that she knew how to do.

The writing on the envelope was in a spidery Palmer penmanship and addressed to Thurgood Marshall, Regina's boss. The name Thurgood Marshall had no *Mr* before it. There was no *Esquire* behind it. It had been sent to him care of something called the Negro Legal Office, 69 Fifth Avenue, New York 10, New York. The street address, at least, was correct. The fact that it had been mandated to Thurgood did not stop Regina from opening it. She had taken the New York State bar examination two weeks before and was waiting for the result. But before moving into a new position as staff attorney, she had clerked for Thurgood during her last year at Columbia Law, and she was used to opening anything that came to the office and was addressed to him. Even now, when he was out of town, which was often, the secretaries routinely brought his letters to her, and she went through everything that was not marked private. This envelope was not marked private.

The cleaning people had been in the night before, and the shades and windows had been opened to let in the fresh air. This far down Fifth Avenue there was little noise drifting up from the street on a Saturday morning, and from the other offices that surrounded theirs, even less. Not like Harlem, where she'd just come from and which, even at this early hour, was already alive to the full and syncopated rhythm of its day. For a moment, Regina just stood there, listening to the silence.

She looked for but could not find her letter opener, and so she used her fingertip to open the flap. This proved to be quite easy. The glue had been licked down only on the tip, but Regina's nail polish – Elizabeth Arden's Montezuma Red, worn patriotically during the war and still not abandoned – left a slender crimson wheal along the heavy ivory paper. Regina did not notice this. The envelope's contents, newspaper clippings, showered onto the tidy plane of her desk. She did not stop to study these. There was a snapshot as well, and she paused over it.

The photograph was of an old Negro man, his face ashy and worn, and gone not wrinkly but ropey in the way that black skin aged. He was smiling and holding on for dear life to a man younger than he was but who looked just like him. His son. The old man had on a white shirt that was carefully ironed but obviously threadbare. Regina could tell this even in black and white. His son was decked out in a splendid U.S. Army-issue uniform, clearly brand-new. Even though the two of them were looking into the camera, they were *beaming* at each other. She wondered, for a moment, where the mother was, then decided that, of course, the mother was the one who had taken the photograph. Who else could have captured such love? After a moment, Regina started reading.

And as she read, she took notes on a small stenographer's pad, a holdover habit from the many years she had spent at lectures in college and in law school, though she had decided that this particular practice was something she must give up. There were still so few women lawyers in the courts of New York that she was regularly taken for a stenographer, a secretary. Even that, she was told, was a huge step up in professional recognition for her, a pretty colored girl who dressed well. As Regina wrote, the sun moved to shadow her hand upon her words. She made two brief telephone calls from the shared phone on another lawyer's desk. At one point she went into a side office, riffled through the membership files, looking something up, and then returned to read and to write once again.

She was still at this when Thurgood came in. When he cleared his throat, she jumped. For a moment, as Regina looked up, she saw only the man in the snapshot, the soldier. His face haloed Thurgood's face. Regina slipped the snapshot into a pocket of her suit jacket instinctively, without knowing why.

'Hey, Reggie, what you doing here on such a fine Saturday afternoon?'

He was dressed casually in pleated twill trousers and a pocketed chambray shirt that was almost the same creamy color as the envelope. He carried a cardboard cup of coffee in one hand and a waxed-paper sack of Do-Rite Donuts in the other. The bag was chock-full, almost overflowing. Sweets were Thurgood's weakness. 'Want one?' He held the bag out to her.

Reggie shook her head. She was as careful about her weight as she was about most things. 'Afternoon?' she echoed, and glanced down at her watch. It was one o'clock. She'd gotten in before ten.

Thurgood answered his own question. 'I guess you came in to catch up on those.' He shook his head in comic commiseration and motioned with it to the case room.

Regina got up, stretched discreetly. 'Back so soon? We weren't expecting you until sometime next week.'

'I got in yesterday night. Late.'

'How was it?'

'Good. By which I mean the donations were good. What I had to tell the folks to get those donations – well, that was something else.'

There were so many cases, not even counting hers, that for a moment Regina had to stop, had to remember just exactly which one had formed the basis of the LDF's latest appeal. Then it came to her. A white family in rural Oklahoma had been murdered, their house burned down round about them. A colored man had been accused of the crime. He was simple, in the polite and colloquial implication of that word *simple*. This translated that the colored man 'wasn't all there.' He also happened to be crippled, with a badly misshapen and withered right arm and right leg. And he was known to be gentle, kind to ladies and to children. The white family – a husband and wife, their three little girls – had been tied up, tortured, individually slaughtered. The woman's breasts had been sliced off. The little girls – well, nobody could bear to write down what had been done to them. But even the white woman's grieving father could not believe the colored man had done this. How could he have? Even physically? The father repeated this over and over again. Other white people agreed with him, but not many. At least out loud. Theirs was a small community where everybody knew everybody else.

None of this mattered. There was an election coming up, and the man people actually believed had done the murder was white.

Whites could vote. Blacks could not. Everything came down to this in the end.

Still, the blacks weren't going down without a fight.

The Fund was called on and took up the case. The accused man's name was Tom Studdard. He was tried, found guilty, and sentenced to the electric chair. He had no idea what had happened to him or what was about to happen to him. Nor was Thurgood able to explain it, not with any satisfaction. He had a hard enough time trying to explain it to himself. All these hopeless cases, one right after the other, were starting to wear.

'Have you heard anything?' she asked.

'I didn't need to hear anything. I was still there yesterday when they fried him,' Thurgood said, then added, 'We had used up all our appeals.'

'Oh,' she said. 'I didn't know.'

For a second, tears threatened, but Regina shook her head. Willed them back. She'd never get on here if she got emotional, and she knew it. And getting on here was important to her.

Thurgood lingered in the doorway, saying nothing. Regina decided he might be just too damn drained to move on, and she wanted him to move on. Just a little. She needed to get back to the letter, figure out what she wanted to do with it before she shared it with him.

But she'd been brought up to be polite, to respect her elders, so she asked, 'How's Buster?' Buster was Thurgood's wife.

'Buster's fine. Tired of me being gone so much. Tired of me being tired.' He let his voice trail, and the trailing was not quite a sigh. 'How are your folks – your mama and your new daddy?' He chuckled at this. 'Dr Sam and Ida Jane. Who would have thought it?'

Regina sure hadn't. She glanced away, toward the window. 'Great. They're doing well. They're happy.' But she sounded as guarded as Thurgood had sounded when he'd talked about his wife.

Thurgood knew both Samuel and Ida Jane Robichard

Robinson well. Regina's stepfather was the Marshalls' doctor. Ida Jane – well, she was Ida Jane. A heroine.

'Fine people,' said Thurgood. He smiled, like everybody seemed to when they talked about Regina's mama. 'Glad they found each other at last. What your mama went through when they killed your natural daddy.' Then he stopped talking, looked over at Regina. 'What's that you got in your hand?'

She did, indeed, have something in her hand. The envelope. She jumped, and the jump made her feel guilty. At least she thought it did. Like she was doing something she should, perhaps, not be doing when actually what she was doing was fine. It was what she wanted to do, or, rather, what she wanted *him* to do, that might annoy Thurgood. That might make him mad.

She said, 'This came for you.' She held the envelope out to him.

He shook his head slightly, a weary man who had stopped to say hello and did not want to be faced with more problems. 'Is it important?'

'I think so.' Reggie considered. 'I think it could be.'

'Then bring it on back. Coffee's getting cold. I need to catch up.' Thurgood, all business now.

He set off briskly down the short hallway that led to his cluttered office, and she followed, leaving her hat and her purse and her gloves where they lay but clutching the envelope. She had quickly managed to stuff the clippings back in, but the whole thing, bulging at its sides, was no longer as pristine, as pure-looking, as when she'd first seen it that morning.

Thurgood's private office was on the north side of the Fund's general offices, and so not as brightly lit by sun as hers had been, and it was cooler. Regina felt the difference right away.

With his bag of doughnuts, Thurgood motioned for her to sit in one of the green leather client chairs in front of his desk, and then he took the other. He stared at her, sipping his coffee as she reached into the envelope and handed over the letter.

He pulled a pair of glasses from his shirt pocket and began to read, his whole head moving from side to side, like a blood-hound's, sniffing words across the page.

While he read, Regina looked around. Thurgood's office was almost exactly as it had been two years ago when she'd first come into it, wanting the job as his clerk so badly that her heart was thumping against the ribs in her chest and her knees knocked together – phenomena she'd encountered before only in books. A woman in a position like this was practically unheard of. She was terrified, too, because Thurgood Marshall knew her mother and knew about her father. But Thurgood never mentioned Oscar Robichard and what had happened to him in 1919 in Omaha, Nebraska, on a day as bright as this one was and as filled with promise. Regina took this as a quiet kindness from someone who, too, knew the meaning of loss.

The office had been chaotic then and still was, with open law books laid out helter-skelter, and with briefs piling haphazardly up the walls. Regina, apprehensive and even frightened, had still loved the space, much like she idolized the man, already a legend. The messiness, the ghost lingerings of way too many smoked-to-the nub cigarettes, the muffled urgency in the noises that reached them through the closed door, the rhythm of a thousand cases, a hundred appeals, even the faint scent of Thurgood, his Glo Mo Glo hair oil, his Old Spice aftershave – all of this had pulled her, like magic, into the pulse and the heart of a bloodstream. Her pulse, her heart, her bloodstream. She recognized its beating right away.

The first thing he'd said, even before he'd gone through her carefully typed-out résumé, was, 'Regina Mary Robichard? That's a bit long. Mind if I call you Reggie?'

She hadn't minded a bit. She loved the new name, wondered why nobody had ever thought to call her that before.

He'd then launched into tale after tale about the Fund, telling her what they were working on, his careful choice of words making her understand even more fully how important that work was. Important *man's* work, that's what she was hearing, because that's what people had been telling her all her life. Only Ida Jane had said, 'Baby, you can make it.' And Reggie had made it – at least this far. Now, listening to Thurgood, Regina felt her knees stop shaking, her heart stop beating, and she was already thinking, *There is just no way I'm going to get this,* when Thurgood said, 'When can you start?'

'Today. This very minute.' She'd been way too excited to even think about trying to sound cool.

This was her first lesson with Thurgood. You couldn't always tell what he was thinking from what he was saying. She'd come to see this as a very lawyerly trait. Later, she'd also learn how much he respected women. His mother had been the first Negro woman to earn a degree at Columbia Teachers College. When he'd needed money for school she'd not hesitated to sell both her engagement and her wedding rings to get it.

Now he looked up and at her over the white line of the letter and began to read it aloud:

> *I would like you to come down to Revere, Mississippi, to investigate the death of Joe Howard Wilson, a veteran recently and honorably discharged with the rank of lieutenant from the United States Army. His family, and most especially his father, Willie Willie, has worked for my own family for years. Willie Willie has expressed to me his wish to have this unfortunate incident investigated by a Negro. I thought it best to choose a Negro from outside the state of Mississippi. I imagine you are far too busy in New York to find time to attend to this matter, but should you choose to concern yourself, I will agree to pay all the attendant expenses.*
>
> *Sincerely,*
> *Mary Pickett Calhoun*
> *(M. P. Calhoun)*

Thurgood said, 'Doesn't sound too enthusiastic. A little luke-warm. Not like she really expects us to do anything.'

'Or wants us to,' agreed Reggie. 'It's strange. Why would she write in the first place? There's no salutation. Did you notice?'

Thurgood had noticed. 'Since she seems to be asking for our assistance, she probably thought it best not to start right out with "boy."' He stretched a little, and the old chair creaked beneath his weight.

'It doesn't sound to me like she's really *asking* for anything. I don't get the feeling of a "please."'

'A woman like that' – Thurgood waved the embossed letter paper – 'living like she does in the backwaters of Mississippi . . . Believe me, she's not used to associating the word *Negro* with the word *Please*.'

Again, he bent close, 'Hey, I think I know that name.'

'You do.' Regina kept her voice even. 'At least you know about him.'

'Her,' corrected Thurgood automatically. He looked up, squinted. 'Is that the writer, or somebody just named the same?'

'It's her, all right. I checked. Did you read the book?'

Thurgood shook his head. 'Too busy. But I know all about it. Everybody does. It's damn famous, or at least it was. Made the front page of *The New York Times*.'

Regina nodded. 'It was called *The Secret of Magic* and it's still in print. It came out about fifteen years ago. I read it then. As I remember, it created quite the sensation. She wrote about a colored man. His name was . . . Lemon. Daddy Lemon. And Lemon wasn't an Uncle Tom. He wasn't an Uncle Remus, either, but, like him, he had his legends and his tales. He knew about the people who tell them, too. He knew about the land, and his land was Mississippi. He had hold of its secrets and its magic.'

'Voodoo?' Thurgood raised an eyebrow, rolled a comic's eye. Regina wanted to laugh, but she didn't. Her laughter might quake. It might show just how nervous she was, and how eager. That wouldn't be good.

Instead, she said, 'That's what people think first when they put together Negroes and magic, something dark. Magic was different in M. P. Calhoun's book. Lemon was a good man, but he knew all about dancing rabbits. He knew about toothache trees. And he knew about two old ladies who lived in a big white house stuck out in the middle of the forest. Colored ladies.' She thought for a moment. 'The Mottley sisters. Peach and Sister. They had a brother, too. Or they did have. Once upon a time.'

She was talking too quickly. She forced herself to slow down. 'The brother's actual name was Luther, but in *The Secret of Magic* he was known as Luther the Disappeared. I can't remember why now. Maybe I'll look it up. Folks said his sister murdered him, then hid his body out in someplace called the Magnolia Forest. And there were these three children, and they knew Daddy Lemon and they wanted to *find out* about this murder. Two boys, one girl. Two white, one black. I guess that was part of the scandal, the mixing up of these children. It's not how we think of the South. It's certainly not how the South thinks of itself. But I guess the unsolved murder played its part as well. In the book's popularity, I mean.'

'You *guess*?' Thurgood wrinkled his forehead, pulled his glasses back up to it. 'A children's book with killing in it?'

'His – ' She stopped and corrected herself. '*Her* novel was *about* children, and I read it first when I was a child. But it wasn't really *for* us. I wouldn't say that.'

'You sure know a lot about it.'

Regina had the grace to blush. 'Some I remembered. I called over to the public library, and they told me the rest.'

How could she explain *The Secret of Magic* to Thurgood, all it had meant to her and the spell it had cast? How she had lain, night after night, in her young girl's bed, curled up under blankets and quilts. Her hand clutching tight to a heavy aluminum flashlight. Her eyes racing words across the page. Her heart rat-tat-tatting against her ribs. Her mind desperate to find out what happened next.

Three children. A dead man. A wide-open forest.

Now Regina wondered if she still had it. She wondered if it

had been packed up, like everything else, like her mother had been, like she had been, and carted to their new home, Dr Sam's brownstone, smack in the middle of Harlem's lovely Edgecombe Avenue.

'It was a very *involving* novel,' she said to Thurgood.

She realized how pompous she sounded when he threw back his head and laughed. And this time she laughed with him, tentatively at first, and then until tears started. The laughter was a relief.

'Did Ida Jane get involved with it?' Thurgood wanted to know. 'The book, I mean.'

Regina shook her head. 'Early on, M. P. Calhoun calls Lemon, her hero, a "black Nimrod." Mama didn't care that Nimrod was in the Bible, even though I told her it was. She said it was a demeaning and antiquated way of describing a colored man and she had no intention of continuing on with any book in which that word was used. You know how she is.'

Again, the laughter. 'Sounds like Ida Jane. But *you* did read it.'

'I read everything back then, even cereal boxes, and Mama always kept huge piles of books for her and for me. Library books, mostly – that's all we could afford – but when I heard about this one, I wanted it right away. It took me a month to save up, but I got it. I read it straight through first, then immediately took it up again and reread a little each day. I did that for a long time.'

'It certainly caused a ruckus. Murder and Mayhem. Threatened Miscegenation.' Thurgood's eyes twinkled. 'A wonder M. P. Calhoun didn't see herself in trouble, living in Mississippi and writing stuff like that. Such a sensation . . . I wonder why it never got out she was a woman before?'

'Maybe timing,' speculated Regina. 'As I recall, *Magic* came out in the spring of 1929 – I was maybe eight – no, nine. Six months later the stock market fell, then came the Depression. After that was the war. All of this could have moved her out of the limelight, if that's what she wanted. Still, who knows? I imagine that book made a lot of money for her. Everybody in my school was reading it back then, and mine was a Catholic school, so most of the kids in it were white. As I remember, it was banned in six of the old cotton states, including her own, and banning always seems to help sales. People get curious. I imagine M. P. Calhoun wouldn't have actually *needed* to produce another. And it seems like she didn't.'

Thurgood cocked his head.

Regina said, 'I called Walter Winchell's office over at the *Daily Mirror*. Somebody was there on a Saturday. With a gossip column like his, turns out Saturday's their biggest day. This somebody called out to somebody else and came back saying that after that first book, M. P. Calhoun never wrote another word. Or at least another one that's been published. She seems to have just disappeared into thin air. Of course they said "he," as in "he disappeared." I didn't correct them.'

'Why not?'

'Lots of people read that *Magic* book. There might still be a curiosity about him – about *her*. A curiosity that, maybe, she wouldn't welcome. I thought it best not to put Winchell's office on the scent – at least not yet.'

Curiosity got the better of Thurgood for a moment. 'Well, who did it? That book murder, I mean.'

'You never find out,' said Regina, thinking quickly back. 'They get close, but the children – they're in the forest all alone. At night. Next thing you know, the sheriff turns up and maybe a parent or two.'

'How'd they find them, the children? How'd the parents know where to look?'

It was hard to remember all of it now, but at least some of it was coming back to her.

'Daddy Lemon,' said Regina. 'I think he knew where they were and alerted somebody.'

'See, what did I tell you?' exclaimed Thurgood, triumphant. 'Your mama was right. Sidling up to white folks like that . . . That man was nothing but an Uncle Tom hiding himself out behind a Daddy Lemon face.'

It wasn't like that. But Regina thought the better part of valor at this moment might be to let the matter slide.

'Interesting,' said Thurgood.

But there were a lot of interesting things in this life, and probably a good many of them were waiting for him on this desk right now. He'd already stuck his reading glasses on his forehead. Now he reached a hand up to pull them all the way off.

'The thing is,' Regina said quickly, 'you know about Joe Howard Wilson, too.'

She took up the envelope, pulled out the newspaper clippings, and asked, 'May I?' When Thurgood nodded, she walked over to his desk, cleared a small space, and laid out the slurry of articles that had accompanied M. P. Calhoun's cryptic communication.

She had numbered everything, except the note itself, with the same deep blue ink with which she had written on her letter paper. But foolscap was not vellum. Ink bled into the cheap paper like blood flowed into veins. It sieved into snatches snipped from the *Afro-American* out of Thurgood's hometown of Baltimore; *The Negro Voice* from Tulsa, Oklahoma; Pittsburgh's *Courier*; three differently dated issues of Jackson, Mississippi's *Black Leader*; and four of the Revere, Mississippi, *Fair Dealer*. This last was printed on the thinnest paper of all. Altogether, there were nine separate stories. Regina had counted. She laid them out in chronological order. Their emboldened headlines reminded her of the beginning outlines of a novel, a tale.

'Negro papers. We'll print on anything,' said Thurgood. He glanced over at the vellum envelope. 'Not like M. P. Calhoun.'

He'd put his glasses back on his nose and come up beside her. He took the top clipping, held it high. Even though the light was dim, they could see the whole of his office through it – chairs, books, unfinished legal briefs. And not just vague outlines but colors, too, everything captured by the black-and-white tragedy of what had happened to Lieutenant Joe Howard Wilson on his way home from war.

The clipping he held was from *The Chicago Defender*. It was dated January 15, 1946, almost ten months earlier, and was bylined by one Charles John Steptoe. Everybody at the Fund knew who Charles John Steptoe was, and a fortunate few actually knew him, although Regina didn't. He was a journalist famed for flamboyant folksiness and for what he himself immodestly called 'a certain grandiloquent way with a word.' His specialty was the nascent area of Negro civil rights.

Thurgood said, 'Lots of folks from Mississippi in Chicago now. Black people been going up there since before the Great Flood of '27; by now it's taken on almost the magnetic appeal of a Promised Land. *The Defender* sells a lot of papers when it prints a Mississippi story. Folks want to keep up with what's happening in their hometown. Let's read what Mr Steptoe has to say for himself.'

OUTRAGE

Revere, Mississippi, January 1946

The illustrious product of a one-room Rosenwald Colored Children's School in Revere, Mississippi, Joe Howard Wilson went on to the Revere Colored High School (two rooms this time), and from there to a private Negro institute in North Carolina. He graduated Morehouse College in Atlanta with Honors at the age of 19. It was Judge Charles Pickett Calhoun, his father's employer, who reportedly paid for this stellar education. I call it 'stellar' because I am a proud Morehouse Man myself.

Lt. Wilson participated in ROTC in college and, fulfilling his patriotic duty, signed up early in the war for the Army. It goes without saying that he served in a segregated unit, as all units for our colored soldiers were segregated and still are. Trained in Alabama, he was sent to Italy, where he distinguished himself and rapidly rose to the rank of 1st lieutenant.

He received the Distinguished Service Cross for heroism at the Battle of Castel Aghinolfi, where many of the men in his platoon were killed, including his best friend, L. C. Hoover, with whom he had roomed at Morehouse. Lt. Wilson was honorably discharged from the Army just after V.E. Day. Still in his decorated uniform, he landed in New York and took a train straight from there to Richmond, another to Atlanta, and then yet another from Atlanta to Birmingham, Alabama. In Birmingham he boarded a Bonnie Blue Line interstate bus ultimately bound for Aberdeen, Mississippi. He got off it once in Tuscaloosa and again in Aliceville, where he made a call home to his father on the public telephone because he had promised to do this. Lt. Wilson paid for the call himself. Aliceville is some thirty miles from Revere, Mississippi, just over the state line. After making that call, Joe Howard got back on that bus, rode off in it. And disappeared . . . for two weeks.

Eventually his body was found floating facedown in the Tombigbee River. My sources tell me it was obvious this decorated war hero had been beaten and perhaps tortured before his body was dumped. Naturally, there was an outcry. But the coroner of Jefferson-Lee County said the body'd been in the water too long for him to make what he called 'anything near a determination as to cause of death.' Said he couldn't be certain. And the judge had all kinds of excuses why it took him so long to pull together a grand jury. If there was no cause of death, then how could a grand jury decide that an actual crime had been committed? And if a crime hadn't been committed, then how could it indict anybody for committing that crime?

And that, my friends, was the sad end of that.

Other clippings told much the same tale.

Negro Veteran Found Floating in the Tombigbee River!

Decorated Veteran Murdered!
Foul Play!

1946 AND CAN THIS CRIME GO UNPUNISHED – EVEN IN MISSISSIPPI?

The Revere Fair Dealer demanded to know this in twenty four point bold type.

'I guess it can,' said Thurgood. He stared at her.

Regina stared back. They were both thinking of her father, of Oscar Robichard, of what had happened to him, and she knew it. 'There's nothing about lynching in any of this. It seems like Joe Howard was beaten to death, then thrown in the river. That's what I read.' This distinction was important to her. She thought of the picture in her pocket – the old colored man and the young colored man, leaning close in to each other, smiling. She lowered her hand into her jacket and ran her fingers along the snapshot's jagged edge. Her face hardened. She didn't want what had happened to her daddy to have happened to this young man. And what had happened to her mama and to her, the 'survivors' – she didn't want this to have happened to Joe Howard's proudly beaming daddy. More than anything else, she didn't want that.

'Not hanged,' she repeated. 'Beaten.'

A breeze rattled the shade at the window. Regina loosened her grip on the snapshot. Eased her fingers away, aching and stiff.

'Only two articles more,' she said, and her voice was steady, her tone a lawyer's balanced one.

The first of these had been clipped from something called *The Revere Times Commercial*. The news stock was good. No *Negro*, no *Afro-American*, no *Colored*, no *Black* in the title. It was not one of theirs. The *Times Commercial* seemed to be a general-interest newspaper owned, edited, and published by, they read, one Mister Jackson E. Blodgett. The *Mister* had not been left to conjecture. It had been fully spelled out and writ large just beneath the masthead.

'Thinks well of himself,' said Thurgood, 'but I never heard of him.'

From the looks of it, this particular piece of news had found a home deep within the recorded comings and goings of Revere, Mississippi. The small one-inch-by-one-inch notice had been attached onto the newspaper's title page with a single straight pin. It looked like something you actually might find hidden in the forgotten back end of a paper, dropped in among ads for twenty-five-cent housedresses at Kresge's and church notices and a sale on children's shoes at the local TG&Y. Mary Pickett Calhoun had used her blue ink to underline the date.

> The Jefferson-Lee County Grand Jury, called in this State of Mississippi, ruled January 18, 1946, that the Negro whose body was found floating in the Tombigbee River last October met with the adventure of an accident and was drowned.

'So they called one after all.' Thurgood paused. 'I wouldn't have expected that, not in Mississippi. Why, I wonder? Now, that's intriguing.'

This time it was Regina's turn to ask why.

'Because the judge must have called the grand jury back into special session,' said Thurgood. 'There's no mention here of any other case and nothing about the mundane things they handle at their regular call-ups, two, three times a year – stuff like jail upkeep and forest fire prevention and what's going on with the tax sessions. There's no mention of any of that here.'

Regina said, 'Do you think this is about Lieutenant Wilson?'

Her boss whistled through his teeth. 'Who else? First thing you got to learn about down there is they don't ever call a colored person by his rightful name in a white newspaper. Most they ever write is "auntie" or "uncle" – and that's just when some old auntie and uncle's perfected living a perfect God-Fearing, and especially White-Folk-Fearing, life. This is surely Joe Howard Wilson they're talking about. Why else would that Calhoun dame have included it? Dates match up, too. He disappeared off that bus in October 1945. The grand jury came back January 1946. That makes sense. What doesn't make sense is why this is all being sent to us now, so long after the fact. If this M. P. Calhoun cared so much, why didn't she get in touch back when we might actually have been able to do something?'

Regina said, 'There's one more. It's the last.'

This, too, was from *The Revere Times Commercial*. It had been front-page news on October 8, 1946, just the week before. Both Regina and Thurgood bent close to read about a fire in some-place called the Bottoms. The house – 'destroyed beyond knowing' – had belonged to a Mr Jackson Blodgett, whose official residence was listed as 600 Main Street in Revere, where he lived with his wife, Mae Louise Wynne Blodgett, and his twenty-three-year-old son, Wynne Vardaman Blodgett. The burned structure had been something called a 'home place.' Neither Thurgood nor Regina had any idea what a home place was.

But for whatever reason, its blazing seemed to have caused quite a stir. The fire department had been called out, and the police and the sheriff, even though the flames themselves had been quickly extinguished. Not a total loss, the *Times Commercial* reassured its readership. For his part, *Mister* Blodgett expressed nothing but praise for the efficient carrying out of duty on the part of all concerned. He and his wife would be eternally grate-ful, he added, in print. Indeed, a barbecue had been hastily organized for the firemen – all volunteer – the policemen, the sheriff, his deputies, their wives, and their children at what appeared to be yet another Blodgett residence, 'Magnolia Forest, their magnificent plantation on the Black Prairie.'

Regina looked up. 'Magnolia Forest? That's in *The Secret of Magic*.'

'Hey, look at this,' Thurgood said. He pointed to a half-page ad, taped to Joe Howard's small notice.

VOTE
NATHAN BEDFORD FORREST 'BED' DUVAL V
DISTRICT COURT JUDGE
PLACE 1
A NAME KNOWN AND TRUSTED IN REVERE FOR YEARS

'I wonder if it's just a coincidence,' Thurgood said, 'this being included.'

'Why?'

'Strange she'd send a political advert along when she could have just as easily omitted it. Especially since she doesn't seem that interested in our actually *coming* at all.'

Regina reached over to pick up the vellum envelope again and there was a ladybug on it, fat and speckled. Maybe it had crept out of the letter. She thought she'd actually seen it doing this – just barely, out of the corner of her eye. But could this be possible? The ladybug made her think again of M. P. Calhoun's book, *The Secret of Magic*, with its hidden portal forest, with its cunning, dark animals, with those two old, old ladies who lived there alone, with the brother who had once lived with them, and with those three children who had set out to find him. Or what was left of him. Regina watched as the ladybug spread its wings, trying them out in the stillness of Thurgood's office. She moved her hand away very slowly, and closed her eyes. When she opened them again, the ladybug had disappeared.

'I want to go there.'

Shocking words. Shocking even to Regina. This was not what she had planned to say to Thurgood as she read, as she telephoned, as she hid the snapshot deep, deep within her pocket. She had told herself that she wanted *him* to go – Thurgood, whose very presence in Mississippi would confer the integrity of the Fund itself on this just cause. Thurgood *should* go.

Yet . . .

'Please let me go. I think I can . . .' But what was it exactly she thought she could do that Thurgood couldn't do – and better?

'Do they have a branch there?' He meant an NAACP branch.

'Not that I know of. I looked. We're not showing one on our lists.'

'Makes sense,' said Thurgood. 'NAACP's not very welcome in Mississippi. White folks down there call us subversive. Say we're a communist front. Any black folks want to join . . . they have to be totally independent of the whites. That means *economically* independent, and there aren't too many of those around. Not yet. But I was thinking, if they had one, maybe this M. P. Calhoun belongs.'

'A *white* woman?' Regina's eyes opened wide. 'Who wrote a *book*?'

'Why not?' said Thurgood but he was grinning. 'You were wrong about her being a woman in the first place. To keep that much of a secret from the rest of the world for years? M. P. Calhoun might turn out to be just full of surprises. Besides, we have a lot of white members, and not only here in New York. Just thought I'd ask. It might be an explanation.'

He wanted her to say, 'An explanation for what?' But she didn't. Instead, she repeated, 'I want to go.' Her voice stronger now. In case he hadn't heard her. In case she hadn't heard herself.

But Thurgood had heard. 'I figured that. All this attention for a letter and a bunch of clippings on a Saturday afternoon when you got the courts-martial room to handle.' He fished in his pocket for a cigarette. 'Surely you must realize that. The Fund doesn't have . . .'

'She said she'd pay.'

'. . . any *interest* in this matter, which, incidentally – as I've already pointed out, but I'll do it again – is not even a case, because the Jefferson-Lee County Grand Jury did not see fit to make it one. When they *did* have a case, when they fished that poor fellow out of the river, then maybe we could have done something. Maybe. But nobody called on us back then. Not even the Negroes in Revere called on us.' He paused, raised his free hand, waved smoke away in dismissal. 'And they could have. We get calls from Mississippi all the time. There's some feisty folks down there. If they had wanted us, they would have found some way to get in touch.'

'M. P. Calhoun got in touch.'

'A white woman? A white woman who once wrote an old-timey, stereotypical novel? Please!'

'You said you never even read the book,' said Regina.

'I didn't have to read it. It was famous. Plus, you're the one said Nimrod. You're the one said it had dancing bears.'

'Dancing rabbits. It's a folk tale. And M. P. Calhoun certainly must think there's something to this. She's laid a case out for us.'

'Somebody works for her for slave wages. She wants to keep him happy.'

'That may well be. That might be her reason for wanting us to come.' Regina paused. 'It doesn't have to be our reason for going.'

'And,' added Thurgood, on a tear now, 'if it's so important to her, why didn't she write when we could have done something.'

'Maybe she has,' said Regina. 'Maybe she'd got some new evidence. Maybe something's changed. We won't know unless we go down there and find out.'

Thurgood did not look convinced.

So Regina repeated the magical words: 'She said she'd pay expenses.'

'It's not about the money,' he shot back, 'so you can quit going on about that. It's the *time*. You know how I feel about these individual cases. So many, one right after the other. We're drowning in them.'

'This one's different.'

'Reggie, you've been here two years now. You know there's not a one of them different, except in the fact that each is usually worse than the last. What they share in common is that they take us away from the *law*, from changing it. That's the only thing ever going to make a difference.' There was a warning in his voice.

Regina braced herself for the torrent she knew was about to break over her.

'I have said many times now,' Thurgood thundered, 'that in order to change – I mean really *effect* this country, we have got to move on to changing the law, not trying all the individual cases that break it. Things like *Plessy v. Ferguson* – separate but equal – that has got to go. It's a farce. Separate is never equal. Once they can legally separate us out, they make us second-class. As they keep us separated, they can keep us second-class forever. What we've got to spend our time on now is getting the schools integrated, getting public facilities that we are helping to support with our taxes integrated . . .'

He had wound himself up good and, lawyer that he was, it would take him a long time to wind down. And Regina had heard all this before, especially since the end of the war. 'Effect the legislation' had become the Fund's battle cry. She stopped listening to the main argument. In her mind, she was already mapping out the appeal.

So busy was she with this that she barely heard the murmur of his: 'Why is this so important to you?'

But her answer came quickly. It lived in her heart and on the tip of her tongue. 'Justice,' she said, 'if not for this man, at least for his family. M. P. Calhoun seems to think we can get it. At least she's willing to give us a chance. You can't just kill a man and that's that.'

Short. Simple. He would either let her go or he wouldn't. Around them, the room held its breath.

Thurgood looked at her, nothing on his face. He reached for another Camel, his Ronson lighter, a fresh ashtray. He flared the cigarette to life.

'There's more to it than what you're saying. I don't know if you realize that yet yourself, but you soon will. Mississippi will enlighten you, and, believe me, she's a great teacher. Maybe the greatest teacher of all.' He smiled then, and the brightness dazzled her and blazed the weariness and the years from his face. 'Oh, for the unmitigated zeal of young lawyers! Now, tell me, you ever actually been to the South? I know your mama's from Louisiana – she ever take you there?'

Regina shook her head, eager now. 'Never. She said once that south Harlem was plenty south enough for her. She said she doesn't have a thing against it, and she's gone there herself. With her talks, I mean. The South didn't kill Daddy. It was the North did that.'

Thurgood said, 'It's different from what you think it's going to be. It's better and it's worse. Still, it might be useful for you to get on there and get the feel of it.' He seemed to consider. 'We've got something coming up in the public schools in Jackson. Maybe even early next year. You could be helping out with that, so it could be good for you to get a feel for Mississippi. Way things are going, these days we might all could use some of that.'

She thought: *He's letting me go.* But the elation and the triumph of it, what she should have been feeling – her own first real case! – was shadowed by that unexpected mention of her daddy.

Thurgood was still speaking: 'Two weeks – three, tops – down there should tell what M. P. Calhoun knows or suspects, whether there's anything to it. The answer's probably here someplace.' He gestured toward the clippings. 'Hiding out in plain sight.'

'Might take a month,' said Regina, on a roll now herself, but she was pleased enough with the two or three weeks.

'I said three weeks *tops*. No longer. You've got those courts-martial to get through. How're they going, anyway?'

'Nothing new. It all takes time. You know how slow the government can be.'

Thurgood knew all about the slowness of government. 'Especially when it wants to be. What about the bar exam? When will you hear?'

'Not for another week or so.'

He nodded. 'Call me every day – or, at the very least, once a week. Collect. And don't look at me like that. I'm not singling you out. I'd make the men do it, too – Skip and the rest of them. I need to keep up with things. By the way – want Skip to go down there with you? The South can be tricky.'

Regina bristled. No, she didn't need anybody – especially Skip, who'd want nothing more than to best her at this. She could handle things herself and she told Thurgood this.

He nodded. 'Well, it's a damn shame what happened – to that soldier, to his daddy. To your daddy.' Regina stood still as a statue, like she had learned to do a long time ago whenever her father's name came up. Most of the time, if she stayed quiet people would just stop talking about him, and she *wanted* them to stop talking about him because talking about him hurt. You had to do some thing about it; that's what Ida Jane had always told her. You couldn't just *talk* about it. Talking didn't do one damn bit of good.

But for the first time, Thurgood seemed determined to talk about Oscar Robichard. 'When someone dies as young as your daddy, as this Joe Howard Wilson – horrible, brutal deaths – that's all about them that tends to get remembered. The way they laughed and what made them angry, the way they moved and the way they talked. The *humanness* of them, all that's forgotten. How they died becomes how they live on. Maybe, going down with a fresh eye, you can find something out. Maybe.'

He had made a decision, and he seemed, if not happy, then at least relieved by it. 'Buster's right. I'm away too much. Plus, as it turns out, this M. P. Calhoun is a white woman, and there's always the chance, once she gets over the fact that you're a woman, too, she might actually say more to you than she would have to me.'

Regina wanted to believe this.

'Know how you're going to get there?'

'I thought,' she said, talking right off the top of her head, 'I might take the bus. That one Joe Howard Wilson took, that Bonnie Blue Line. Catch the train from Penn Station down to Birmingham and then go west from there, just like he did.'

'Better take a pillow with you, then.'

'A pillow?'

'Oh, you'll understand once you try finding some comfort in the COLORED ONLY section on a long-distance bus in the South.' He glanced at his desk and waved her away in dismissal. 'Go on home, now. Rest up. You're gonna need it. And say hello to Sam and Ida Jane for me. Give them my best.'

The Secret of Magic. *Daddy Lemon. The Mottley sisters and the mystery of their disappeared brother. Three children running into a forest. Now M. P. Calhoun herself/himself and Joe Howard Wilson – all beckoning to her. It was as though they were all right there. Whispering among themselves. Urging her on.*

Sunlight shafted through the office door they had left cracked, into that dark, quiet office, and the dust dancing on it seemed to Regina, with her lawyer's eye and a mind that was not normally given over to fancy, like a sliver of road. Maybe it wasn't yellow brick, but it was leading her somewhere.

She thanked Thurgood once again, nodded goodbye.

She walked out of his office.

She walked into M. P. Calhoun's book.

Three children running into a forest, that's how *The Secret of Magic* began. And the children's names were Collie, and Jack, and Booker. Regina had to think hard to remember the first two, but Booker's popped right to mind. It was almost as though he had been hiding out there all along, tucked away in some hidden fold of memory. In all the books she'd read when she was little, and she'd read many – the Nancy Drews, the Hardy Boys, the Bobbsey Twins, Five Little Peppers; the list went on and on – Booker was the first person she'd come across, with his smart little black self, who reminded her of people she actually knew, of her mother, and of herself.

She'd went straight back home after the meeting with Thurgood, thinking so deeply about what she was going to do, about the snapshot in her pocket, about M. P. Calhoun and *The Secret of Magic*, that she almost missed her subway stop, barely made it off in time.

She walked up Edgecombe Avenue, through the sedate row of apartment buildings and brownstones that marched along each side of the pavement, their crisp awnings and still-bright October geraniums announcing to the world what a *nice* place this was to live. Across the street at number 409 the sun caught a flicker at one of the second-floor windows. Regina looked up. She caught sight of a woman standing in front of the Venetian blind and carefully removing a forgotten blue star that hung at the glass. They'd been everywhere in Harlem during the war; you couldn't walk anywhere without seeing at least one. A blue star meant you had a child in active service; a gold one meant they weren't coming home. But the stars had almost vanished now. Regina couldn't recall the last time, before now, that she'd noticed one.

War fought. War won. War over. The woman disappeared from the window. Behind her the Venetian blind snapped back into place.

Regina turned and looked up past the sign that read DR SAMUEL JAMES ROBINSON, GENERAL MEDICINE at the ground flour of the brownstone, then on up the stairs that led into his – their – home.

When she opened the door, she heard them laughing. She recognized Dr Sam's deep boom right away. Then she heard her mother's voice and it was clear and pure, like what Regina imagined a mountain stream might sound like as it rushed against the last of winter's ice. She stopped, listened. Ida Jane sounded happy, and Regina had never really pictured her mother as happy. She'd thought – still thought – of her as strong and fierce, like a hero in an action comic. And not Lois Lane, either, the sidekick, but Superman herself. Regina stood there, in the darkness of the shadows, as the laughter washed over her again, and she marveled.

Dr Sam had done this? It wasn't that Regina didn't know him. Actually, she had known him all her life. In fact, he'd brought her into her life when her mother fled east after her daddy was killed. And Dr Sam had been there ever since. A round, dark-skinned, competent man, he had sent Ida Jane clients for her little dressmaking business. He'd encouraged her to apply downtown at Hattie Carnegie, where she'd gotten that good seamstress job. What a godsend that had turned out to be! It had supported the two of them, mother and daughter, so that Regina could prepare herself at Catholic school and Hunter College and Columbia Law, while Ida Jane worked days and spent her nights propelling her own mission – which was to enact the anti-lynching laws.

'It's not right that folks get away with what they do.' These were the first grown-up words Regina recalled her mother saying to her.

When she was little, sometimes Regina wondered if Hattie Carnegie and the other ladies Ida Jane worked with downtown even knew anything at all about her mother's other life, knew that she was famous in it. She wondered if they knew about the speeches her mother gave at nights and on the weekends, about the pamphlets she wrote and the endless letters. Sometimes Regina wondered if the people where she worked even realized that Ida Jane was Negro. She had high yellow skin and light hair. She had light eyes, too, that were liable to snap out at you for no reason, at least no reason that most people understood. Many white people mistook Ida Jane for white, a mistake that had probably caused the death of Regina's father three months before she was born.

Ida Jane and Dr Sam hadn't heard her come in. Regina stood and listened to them for a moment, mostly to the low, peaceful mingling of their voices, their sentences punctuated by a sigh, a silence, sometimes more of that laughter. Regina, who was slightly bemused by her mother's happiness – so sudden, or at least it seemed that way to her – and maybe a little frightened by its implications, nonetheless smiled at the sound. And then she went looking for the book.

She found it in Dr Sam's attic, among a pile of boxes all neatly stenciled with her name, REGINA MARY, and then the word PERSONAL. Ida Jane's work. Regina herself had been too busy with her studies for the bar exam, with her duties at the Fund, to take care of the move. So Ida Jane had taken care of it, like she'd taken care of so many other things in her daughter's life.

Just the two of us. We've got to stick together.

Regina had the feeling this would change soon, and if it hadn't already, it should. Ida Jane had a life of her own now. Regina thought she'd go looking for a spot for herself, her own little apartment, once she returned from Mississippi. Voices echoed up to her, footsteps moving in tandem across the polished wood floor from the living room to the kitchen. Yes, find her own place. When she got back, that's what she'd do.

She weaved slightly on the novel motion of this thought and felt a little seasick, but the sensation was not altogether unpleasant.

She riffled through and found *The Secret of Magic* in the third box she searched. It still wore its original dusty pink jacket, the one with the three children on it, carefully preserved. She picked it up, ran her fingers along the spine, over the letters and the words of its title, over M. P. Calhoun's name. It had been years since she'd last seen it, but when she pulled the book out, it fell open in her hands and she read:

> *The children had always heard that the Mottley sisters were witches,*
> *at least that the youngest, Peach, was. Collie Collington especially*
> *had heard this, because this was the sort of thing she listened for.*
> *You couldn't say the word 'witch' around her without her paying*
> *attention. She had a nose for anything out of the ordinary, anything*
> *other people might not want to get into or explore. Of course the*
> *children all knew about Peach and her pies and her unfortunate*
> *sister, Sister. But when Collie heard that Peach Mottley had killed her*
> *brother, Luther, with nothing more than words strung together and a*
> *bad look, she called the others – Jack and Booker – together. And the*
> *three of them set off into the woods.*

A murder, thought Regina. Just like now there is a murder. For the first time she wondered if there might be a thread between the two. But you couldn't *assume* this. One of the things Thurgood always reminded them was: *'Assume* makes an ass out of *u* and *me.'*

When Ida Jane called out that dinner was ready, Regina had to force herself to stop reading. She slipped the book into her purse just as she'd earlier slipped the snapshot into her pocket. Two talismans. Together, they made her feel ready to go.

Early the next morning, Regina Mary Robichard started out from Penn Station on the Burlington Southern Star. She had thought of a list of things she should do on the journey and had written them out in her neat, precise hand.

   – *Go through the letter from M.P.C. again.*

Reread the newspaper clippings.
- *Write out questions for Mr Willie Willie Wilson and for M.P.C.*
- *Grand jury???*

She'd underlined this last one twice and then starred it. She only had two weeks if she wanted to make this case, three weeks at the outside. Still, with all this to do and a new land before her, the train hadn't left the station before she'd dug out her copy of M. P. Calhoun's book.

This time she started on page one.

I just know for a sad fact, after the events of last summer, nothing more's bound to happen to me in this life. Therefore I, Collie Collington, age 11, originally from Mississippi but exiled now to boarding school in Holy Virginia (the very heartbeat of the Confederacy) have decided it's time to write my memoir. I have chosen, after this brief introduction, to do this in third person because, believe me, I don't feel like myself anymore. But I swear to heaven – something my poor dear dead mama would kill me for doing – everything you're going to read about really happened. It all happened. Some of it's still going on. Yet what I'm putting together right here is a novel.

It was novel, after all, that someone like her, brought up 'lady-like and proper, taught to always keep my knees together and my mouth shut,' should even think about writing a book.

After that brief introduction and true to her word, Collie Collington hid herself within a change of grammatical voice. *She* did this. *She* did that. But mostly *she* hated Virginia, pined night and day for Mississippi . . . its forests, its fields, its wide-open spaces, its new history, its ancient ways. A place named for a river so mammoth it was known as the Father of Waters.

Bad as she missed Mississippi, Collie missed her friends more. A boy named Jack and a colored child called Booker. She and Jack the same age, Booker a little younger. Two whites, one black. Two boys, one girl. One rich, two poor. You wouldn't think they had a thing in common, but they did, and it was, in Collie's words, a 'deepened sensibility' brought on by the fact that all three of their mothers were dead. It was Daddy Lemon who whispered that this made them special. Made them see, he assured them, things that maybe other people might miss.

And the reason they couldn't see them was because they didn't know enough to realize when something wasn't there. But 'his children' did know the ache of missing the missing. Yes, they sure did. 'He's the only one,' wrote Collie, 'in my experience, able to make different seem better, or leastwise as good as.'

That's what Daddy Lemon always told them, at least he told this to Collie and Booker. It was Collie who went on to tell it to Jack because she told *everything* to Jack. Had a schoolgirl's crush on him, at least that's what Regina, a schoolgirl herself, had thought. And Collie had made sure Jack knew first thing when Daddy Lemon gave them the idea of forming themselves into the Dancing Rabbit Magic Club.

The deep wood and what lay within it was what Daddy Lemon wanted his children to know. The good-luck properties in a buck-eye. The healing and the numbing that came from a piece of a toothache tree when your mouth was acting up. He showed them how to tell the difference between a natural hillock and a built-up Indian mound. Showed them fish scales, old as Jesus, that he'd found on a rock under the trestle bridge that spanned the river. He taught them to tell golden alexanders from butterweed and ox-eyed daisies – rough, wild flowers rarely spoken of at the Revere Garden Club, whose sacred meetings Collie, like her mother before her, was forced to attend. And the moons – harvest in autumn, beaver in winter, blue when two moons showed up in a month. Once, he called them outside, made them look straight up at that beaver moon – dead of night, if they'd known, their parents would have killed them – made them look straight up at the fat winter moon.

Until that last summer. Those three children going deeper and deeper into the forest, sometimes with Daddy Lemon, sometimes without. Until one day Collie whispered, 'I heard Miss Betty DeLean Mayhew talking about a murder. I heard her say something about a witch.'

And with that, the magic ended and the mystery and the troubled times began.

Regina read all this, thinking with each sentence she'd put the book down. But a sentence became a paragraph, which flowed on into a page, two pages, a chapter, more. She was still deep within it when the train shuddered to a halt in Richmond, Virginia, where cars were added.

They were old cars, and they were rickety. Regina, looking out, could tell this right away. A white man came up to her and handed her a new ticket. She was told, matter-of-factly, that she'd have to give up her seat, get off, move herself and her belongings to the rear. The man did not remove his hat when he spoke to her and he called her 'girl,' but he did smile and he had a nice, bright, friendly smile, nothing malicious about it. Regina was not upset at first. In fact, she felt slightly ennobled. She had expected this. After all, the South and its Jim Crow laws had to start somewhere, and where better than Richmond, the seat of the old Confederacy?

She did what she was supposed to do and climbed down from the train onto the platform where her things had been off-loaded. She'd brought a lot with her. A hatbox, a makeup case, a Pullman big as a trunk. All of this in matching Hartmann brown tweed that had been given to her by Dr Sam's sister and her husband as a law school graduation gift.

All around her, the races fluttered like birds in separate migration, white folks toward the clean, new cars near the engine and colored folks to the dilapidation that brought up the rear. Everybody chatting away and nobody anxious or angry, at least not that Reggie could tell. She had thought she might have a problem down here with the language, with its cadence, with its various dialects, with – as Dr Sam would say – its patois. Instead, she found she understood every word that was being said around her.

It was just that none of them helped her one bit. So there she stood, like a dividing boulder, still fresh and perky in pearls, a hat, white gloves, and a ladylike suit but having not the faintest idea how she was supposed to transport herself and all she had with her from where she was to where she was supposed to be.

She, cracker-jack at hailing a cab in the city, tried calling out, 'Sir!' tried a 'Here, please!' and met no response from the busy porters, or were they red caps? It didn't matter what you called them. They were all black. While around her white folks were calling out for boys (grown black men) to help them, and the boys (grown black men) were doing just that.

A conductor cried out, 'All aboard!' and she jumped.

Scared now, and frantic not to miss this train, which would be a disaster, and scolding herself – *Did I really need all this?* – Regina tucked her briefcase under one arm and her purse under the other. Then she juggled the makeup case and the hatbox into one hand. The hatbox fell, tumbling down onto the platform, rolling over. *Oh, God, would it crash open? Would her brassieres fall out and even – heaven forbid! – her panties?* In front of these people! She chased the bag down, barely catching it with a long reach that tore the strap loose on her rayon slip and dug the stays of her latex girdle into her sides.

She had grabbed the makeup case again and the hatbox and was yanking at the huge Pullman's short leather handle, thinking she'd drag it along, when she heard a low murmur.

'Here, ma'am. Let me help you out with that.'

And there he was, a savior, a miracle materializing right beside her in the form of a Negro red cap who didn't look up. He gathered her things, tucking them under his arms, lifting them by the handles, managing them, and he started off quickly, running almost, under the load. Regina could barely keep up with him. All around them, people were calling out – *Boy, here! Boy, there!* – but he kept going. And he kept his head down.

In two minutes it was over. Regina was on the train again and her luggage loaded, situated around her on the rusting tin floor at the end of the COLORED ONLY car. That's when the red cap looked up, so close to her now that she could see his eyes, the wink in them, the brown irises the exact same color as his brown skin. For a second she thought she could see herself mirrored in them – a little thing, frightened and alone.

Regina wanted to cry, she was that thankful. But tears were an embarrassment. Where would they get her? She quickly looked down, fumbled into her purse. Searching for a tip, because this was the way, in New York, you showed you were grateful. When she glanced up again, the porter was already halfway down the platform, calling out to a stout white man, 'Here, sir, let me help you out with that.' He'd left Regina clutching onto her gratitude and the galvanized steel of a railing as the train lurched forward, pulled onward by the magnet of the South.

Regina had turned back to the door with the big, flaking COLORED ONLY painted on it when, out of the corner of her eye, she caught sight of the newsboys. Her train was speeding up; had she blinked, she might have missed them. But she didn't blink.

She knew who they were by the cotton satchels they carried, by the megaphone one had by his side. Boys like this were every-where in New York.

There were five of them – three whites, two black, all hun-kered together at a deserted end of the station, their papers forgotten, their hands and their arms flapping furiously, shooting craps. A shout of laughter, and a black boy clapped a white one on the back. Regina winced. She'd thought there'd be a fight for sure over this, or maybe even a lynching, but there wasn't. Only a white man, a conductor, it looked like, put his hands on his hips and shouted, 'Y'all . . .' Regina couldn't hear more than that, but immediately all the boys stopped their playing, picked up their papers, ran off in different directions. Once they separated, they didn't look back. Regina stood, clutching onto the rattling door, stared at them, frowning but intent, like you might look at a mirage or a vision, watching until they disappeared.

*

Once past Richmond, the land itself grew darker and richer. And blacker and blacker, black people everywhere. Not just in their own place, a separate place, like what she had expected, but *everyplace*. There didn't seem a place where there was one without the other. She'd be looking at some black people and see a white person walk by in the background or, looking at a group of whites, she'd catch the shadow of a black – and there seemed to be just as many black people as there were white. Sometimes there were more. This was nothing at all like Harlem, Manhattan, New York itself, where the races rarely mingled – a place that Regina always thought of as a slow, smoldering white candle with a burning black wick. She tried but could not think of a metaphor for this new land, which was, after all, part and parcel of her own land. But it was too early, the juxtaposition of this life still too new.

Sometimes, Regina thought, she was farther from New York than the trains and then the Bonnie Blue bus could possibly have taken her. Even the air was different, the way it wrapped itself around her when she stepped out onto the platform at some small-town station, the way its dense, lush moisture seeped through her pores. And the fragrance of it! And the color! All the mixture of shades and gradations that shimmered through, and that wasn't *just* skin color but included skin color along with everything else. Regina thought about all of this as she sat on hard train benches, as she remembered that red cap at Richmond, as she read through M. P. Calhoun's book once again, as she stole the picture of Joe Howard Wilson and his daddy out of her pocket to study it. As she stared out upon the land, first with interest and then with growing anticipation, through cracked train windows and then cracked bus windows in the COLORED ONLY sections of both. As she took in the South for the first time through a mottling of grit and of dirt.

One full day and a half after leaving New York City, Regina got to her feet on the Bonnie Blue Line interstate bus. She picked up her pillow, a ruffled and smocked pink-satin dainty, from the hard wooden seat. For the tenth time in as many hours she thanked God for Thurgood Marshall, who had told her to bring it. She gathered up her gloves, her hat, her briefcase, and her pocket-book. She smoothed down the wool of her skirt. Once all this was done, she started the long walk that led from the back of the bus to the way out at the front.

She still carried the snapshot of Joe Howard Wilson and his daddy, Willie Willie, in the pocket of her suit jacket. The suit was a new one, brown, not the gray she had worn to the office on Saturday, but she had transferred the picture from that jacket pocket to this one. She hadn't shown it to Thurgood, hadn't shown it to anyone. It was her secret, and she wanted the picture handy. She liked looking at it. Why? She couldn't say.

A small Negro child dressed in patched overalls maneuvered her bags out, one by one, from deep within the underbelly of the bus. He was huffing. This time Regina had her change handy. When she handed over a bright, shiny quarter, he smiled.

It was colder here than what she'd left behind in New York. A few degrees, but she felt them and they surprised her. Wasn't the South supposed to be warmer than the North? She pulled her jacket tighter, put her gloved hands in its pockets, felt the picture. She teetered a bit on the high heels of her alligator pumps as the parking lot's gravel gave way a little beneath them. She looked around. Men, maybe six of them, sat still as a tableau near the splintery ticket window of the unpainted depot. White men. Regina kept track of them out of the corner of her eye. Ida Jane always said, 'You got to watch white folks every single minute.' Regina had been doing just that for all of her life.

And was still doing it when she heard one bird call, and then another. She didn't have the faintest idea what kind of birds they were, but she thought the sound they made was wonderful, trebly and rich and alive. But where were they? When she looked up, there was a circling of lush green trees, radiating off in every direction, as far as her eye could see, with no break in them. The trees, thick and close, rising darkly on low hills, and mapping a forest. Regina wondered if this was the place, or something like it, that had stirred M. P. Calhoun to write her book. The thought made her shiver, and she wondered what Mary Pickett must be like, living in this spot that must be so Southern, and yet smelled of pitch pine and loam, was cuddled by hills and not planed into fields of cotton, was cold and not warm. Regina reached up with her gloved hand and brushed away a swarm of gnats from her face. When she brought her hand down again, she saw the lone Negro man.

Mr Willie Willie.

She recognized him from that snapshot safe in her pocket, from the smile that irradiated him as he looked over at his uniformed son. He was grinning that way now, with a rascal's face full of mischief, shaking his head. Looking at her and at the same time tossing something into the sky, a small bright something that caught at the light. Regina decided he must already have figured her for the New York lawyer, and realized that this lawyer was not the anticipated Thurgood Marshall. But she had expected that. She took a deep breath, ready to face up to the displeasure she knew would be coming once people realized *she* was here and *Thurgood* was not, and marched over to Willie Willie with her hand stuck out.

He came toward her, across the small gravel patch where the bus had stopped, where its engine had started to rattle and settle, looking like a man who wanted to be introduced.

Impressive, she thought, dark-skinned, clean-shaven, trim and small. And old, much older than he looked in the snapshot, and changed from it, too, from that time. But even as he drew nearer, Regina couldn't make out just exactly what it was that was different about him. How could she recognize him as one man but know he was now another?

Maybe, for one thing, he had dressed in a chauffeur's uniform, not the overalls he had on in the picture. If she looked closely enough, Regina imagined she could see herself reflected in the smooth, sharp lines of its gray stiffness. Her mother, Ida Jane, had once told her that you could tell a lot about a man by the way he closed up his shirt, by whether he buttoned it right to the top or not, by the way his pants were creased, and by the way his clothes hung straight or they didn't. Regina wondered what Willie Willie's sharp folds and lined-up, buttoned-up buttons were telling her now.

Crack!

Something snapped behind her, a brisk, hollow, no-nonsense sound. Automatically, Regina, the smile still on her face, turned back to it, toward the depot and the men lounging against its dilapidated walls. She saw the knife right away. She saw the white man holding it. He was talking to the driver of her bus, both of them looking over at her, not even pretending not to, the driver whispering something in the man's ear. He was sitting under a bare electric bulb, the light from it shining into his thick gold hair, brightening every strand of it, making it look as thick and luscious as a summer wheat field. A young man, she thought, too young to be wasting his life whittling wood on a bus depot porch, which was what he was doing. Her eye traveled from the man to the knife in his hand. It looked like a bowie, but then again, she had to admit, all knives that weren't near a kitchen looked like bowies to her. She was no expert. Her personal experience of them was limited to matinee Westerns at the Roxie. Shavings from the wood fell like delicate tracings onto the rough planks of the flooring, into the rusted can that lay toppled by his side, onto his tight blue jeans. Blue jeans were workman's clothes, loose and baggy. Regina had never seen them fitted close to a man's body until now.

He was staring at her. There were a good twenty feet of gravel lot between them. She was too far away to see the color of his eyes, but she knew they were lasers, and she felt those eyes watch her in the same level way she knew her own were watching him. She did not like white men, was frightened of them, really. It was smart to be frightened of white men. Still, she continued to stare.

Willie Willie said, 'You the lawyer?'

She whirled back to him. He had taken off his uniform cap and held it in his hand.

Reggie nodded. 'Regina Mary Robichard.'

Someone snickered behind her. Low, but she heard it. Was meant to hear it, at least that's what she thought.

'R. M. Robichard, *Esquire*,' Willie Willie said. 'Can't forget that last part. Miss Mary Pickett read it off to me from that telegram you sent down here – or maybe it was Thurgood Marshall sent it down here – saying when the lawyer would come.' He made a great show of looking around. 'Miss Mary Pickett was expecting a *him*. And, truth told, a Thurgood Marshall him at that. She's gonna pitch quite a fit when she sees she got herself a her.' His eyes twinkled. 'That your stuff? I'm Willie Willie.'

She wanted to say, *I'd know you anywhere.* But didn't.

'Pleased to meet you, Mr Wilson.' And she was; relieved, too. Regina took off her glove and held out her hand.

'I'm no Wilson – my son's the only Wilson,' said Willie Willie as he took it. His own hand was rough and warm as it enveloped hers. 'But I *am* the one who changed his name to a real patronymic.' He looked slyly over at Regina as his tongue rolled, syllabic, through the word. Regina barely knew its meaning, and she wondered who had taught it to Mr Willie Willie.

'It was the judge,' he said.

Regina, embarrassed, thought for a second she'd spoken aloud but then changed her mind as Willie Willie continued, 'He arranged the changing himself and took me over to the courthouse to do it.'

'The judge?'

'Judge Calhoun. Miss Mary Pickett's ex-daddy. "Ex" now because he's been such a long time dead. Those your things there?'

She nodded.

He nodded with her.

'Looks to me like you're planning a stay.'

'It depends,' said Regina, all business now, and anxious to get started because there was so much to do and so little time in which to do it. 'Mr Marshall sent me down to begin a preliminary investigation. That seems to be what Miss Calhoun wanted, what *you* wanted. I've got a couple of weeks, that's all. After that – I guess Mr Marshall will decide.'

'I didn't have nothing to do with you coming. Let me make that clear from the beginning. All this here' – he made a wide gesture that took her in, along with her luggage – 'all this was Miss Mary Pickett's idea. One I imagine she'll be regretting soon enough.'

'Then why did she ask us to come?'

Willie Willie seemed to consider. 'Probably because she thought you *wouldn't* come. Not really. Thurgood Marshall, all the way to Revere, Mississippi? And him all busy, as he is? That wasn't likely. Still, at least she could say she did her best.'

'Her best?'

'She read it out to me,' he said. 'That letter. Sent me over to the post office with it, made me mail it myself so I'd know it'd gone out.'

He hadn't answered her question, so Regina insisted. 'But why? Why would that matter?'

'I imagine she wanted to keep me happy,' he said after a while. 'To keep me quiet. To keep me . . .'

Regina waited, but there was nothing more after that.

Willie Willie strolled over, hoisted up her bags, and carried them back as easily as the red cap had carried them in Richmond. When she offered to help him, he brushed her aside. Instinctively, she knew this was about her, his wanting to help her, but it was also about the men on the depot porch. They had stopped what they were doing, their checker games, their whittling, to stare at him, saying nothing to one another, all movement suspended. Watching him. Just as the young blond one still watched her. And, like her, Willie Willie stared right back at them, passing much closer to that little porch than he needed to, than perhaps he had a right to do. Above them another bright sign, FILL UP AT BILLUPS – ALL YOU CAN EAT SATURDAYS, BEST FOOD IN TOWN, flickered to sudden electrified life.

Willie Willie walked past Regina, standing straight, not appearing to be winded by his load. Without a word, she fell in step beside him. She was relieved that he was here, that she was safe beside him. She turned away from the others, didn't look back.

'Miss Mary Pickett got a room for you at the Queen City Hotel, or at least she got that room for Thurgood Marshall.' His voice rose up in marvelous imitation. ' "Stay dressed up in your uniform now, Willie Willie. Take that Thurgood Marshall over to the Queen City. Tell him we can meet together tomorrow. Tell him what to expect" – as though Thurgood Marshall don't know what to expect in Mississippi.' Willie Willie shook his head. 'But she won't want to be putting you there once she sees you and knows you're a lady. That wouldn't be right, since she's the one asked you here. Maybe I should just carry you straight on over to the home place first. See what she wants to do.' He gave Regina a sharp, quick glance. 'Not many lady lawyers down here, at least not white ones. No colored ones at all that I know of. Barely any colored men. Tom Raspberry, maybe – but that's a whole 'nother story. For him, lawyering's something he makes up as he goes along.'

'There aren't many of us in New York, either. Women lawyers, I mean.' Willie Willie might not be winded, but Regina was.

'Then why did that Thurgood Marshall pick you to send?'

'Because I wanted to come. I asked to come. So he let me. He's busy, you know.'

A chuckle from Willie Willie. 'That's what she was counting on, that he'd be too busy to come. I knew that right off, soon as she told me what she was up to. She sure didn't expect him to have a *team* behind him up there at that Negro Defense Office, I'll bet you that.'

There was another snigger from the porch, this time louder than before. Regina forced herself not to look over, but Willie

Willie did. She could tell he was looking straight at them as he said to her, 'Why would anybody want to come here?'

Because of the photograph Mary Pickett Calhoun sent, the snapshot of you and your son, the family-ness of it, and of course what had happened to my own family, to my own father. I came to get us some justice. I came to meet M. P. Calhoun. Those were the words on the tip of her tongue. But how could she say them? Already reason after reason, and Thurgood had said there'd be more.

'I don't know.' She looked down at her purse, considering. 'Maybe I thought this case might help me to get on. As a lawyer, I mean. It might.'

He looked at her. 'I've always been one to let a person go on. That's how I raised my boy, and he *did* go on. He was aiming to be a proper lawyer just like you are. Maybe a judge someday, like Judge Calhoun. Who knows? If they hadn't killed him . . . If he'd moved up north . . . It could have happened.'

Regina looked over at him. His face had turned flint hard. She thought she could easily have blazed up a match on it.

Their eyes met. 'Bad things go on in the North, too,' she said softly. 'You better believe it. But maybe we can get us some justice.'

'Maybe,' said Willie Willie. 'Maybe you can. One thing for certain, you're here now, and I guess that's what matters.'

His eyes were still on her, and there was a glint in them – was it hate or was it hope? Regina couldn't tell.

4.

They stopped at a truck, a battered green Ford pickup that might as well have been sporting a sign that proclaimed it MADE BEFORE THE WAR. It was certainly polished and tidy, but not, Regina thought, something you wore a uniform to drive.

Again, Willie Willie seemed to read her mind.

'This was another problem for Miss Mary Pickett.' And maybe it had been for Mary Pickett, but Willie Willie sure looked like he was enjoying himself. 'She the one *determined* to have Thurgood Marshall and nobody less. But it wouldn't do to dress me up and send me to fetch him in her car, in the old Daimler, the *family's* car. Known and recognized. Me sent to drive a colored person as a bona fide passenger in it? God forbid! So she dressed me up, all right, but she sent me around in my own truck. Thought that would be good enough. It was her way of accommodating her Calhoun good manners to the way things actually are.'

He piled Regina's bags into the open bed, tied them on, helped her inside, then jumped up himself. The truck cab smelled of cigarette smoke and peppermint buttercream patties, the milky green kind that came wrapped in waxed paper. Regina loved those candies; they were her favorite. Their sweet smell was the first clear thing she'd been able to recognize in this new, strange place. She relaxed a little into the cracked leather seat. Though she wanted to, she didn't look back one last time at those white men.

Willie Willie turned the single key in the ignition and steered the truck out onto a deserted two-lane blacktop. But there was an overhang of streetlights, and it was in their glimmer that Regina saw the medal for the first time.

'Is that Lieutenant Wilson's?' With the words out, for some reason Regina held her breath.

'That's his, all right,' said Willie Willie.

He kept his eyes straight ahead; he didn't look at Regina, but his knuckles had gone dead white at the wheel. 'I went looking after they drug him up. He was under that trestle bridge spans the Tombigbee, the one the white youngsters swing off of in the summertime. But that wasn't where they killed him. I knew that. I knew what I was dealing with here, the kind of folks. So I followed the river, went looking, went hunting, every day, into the night. Until I found the place where they'd done it.'

'How did you know?'

'Because I found his medal. He's my son, he knew I'd come looking, so he left it for me . . .' Willie Willie paused, cleared his throat. 'He left me something else too, an *identifying* something.'

'And what was that?' Regina kept her voice low, but she perked right up.

'A personal something. Nothing that would signify to you.'

He didn't say a word after that. He kept his eyes straight ahead, and Regina decided to let him be. For now at least. Lawyer or not, something in her balked at pushing this man who was still so obviously grieving. *What would Thurgood do? He'd come back to this later, after his client had gotten a chance to know him better. To trust him.* At least that's what she thought, so she kept her hands clasped firmly in her lap so they wouldn't reach out to him, wouldn't try to pat him on the shoulder, so that their fluttering movement wouldn't cause her mouth to open and erupt with a stream of trite words. He didn't look like the sort of man who'd want an unknown woman to see him weep. No matter what he said, he was probably just as disappointed that she wasn't Thurgood Marshall as Mary Pickett Calhoun soon would be.

'We are going to find out who did this,' said Regina. 'Folks just can't be allowed to get away with murder.'

Willie Willie looked straight ahead, his gaze on the ribbon of road as it wound its way through a dark forest. 'Some people do,' he said. 'Get away with murder, I mean. Happens every day of the year.'

She opened her mouth, the question already rising, Did Mr Willie Willie really know who'd gotten away with *this* murder, the killing of his son? Despite what she'd just decided, words rose in her throat. *Do you know?* But before she could get them out, she heard what her New York-trained ear heard as the staccato crack of a backfire. Then another. Where were they coming from? Regina looked quickly, but their truck was the only vehicle moving along the long, deserted ribbon of road.

'Bullets. Night hunters,' said Willie Willie. He lit a cigarette, and it flashed bright in the gloom. 'Not quite the season for it yet, but we got ourselves a big buck running wild. Now, don't you let your city self start ooohing and aaahing and crooning on about Bambi. This here one's a destructive son of a gun – eating away at the crops, kicking down the fences. Folks almost killing themselves trying to dodge him when he's looking to jump himself over the road.' A pause. A whisper. 'Like he is now.'

She might easily have missed him. If Willie Willie hadn't slowed the truck, she would have. They rattled nearer as the deer remained motionless, blending into the twilight, shadowed by the darkness of the trees. Suspended in that slight space where the reach of the forest almost, but not quite, touched the road.

Regina caught her breath as she looked at him, let it out on a pleased sigh. 'I've never been near a deer before.'

'A *buck*,' corrected Willie Willie.

Regina nodded. 'Only in books – I mean, that's where I saw them. And movies, too . . . Bambi, like you said . . . things like that. I never knew they grew this big.'

'Big,' repeated Willie Willie. 'That old thing there, he's king of this place.'

Again, Willie Willie gentled the brakes, slowed his old truck to a creep, and they passed so close that they almost caressed it. Regina felt she had just to reach her fingers through the lowered window and they would touch the tip of his nose. As they passed by, the buck's eyes followed them, stared after them. They reminded Regina of the bus driver, those white men at the depot, the way their eyes watched, and she was glad they were behind her. Glad she sat in this snug truck with Willie Willie.

Another shot rang out in the near distance. Regina looked back as the buck leaped over the road behind them, barely missing the truck, disappearing into a rustle of trees.

'They never gonna catch him, making all that ruckus,' said Willie Willie. He curled his lip with contempt. 'Men firing like that – they must be new to town, new to Revere. Not boys I took out with me into the forest. *Those* boys would know that this here's not just your ordinary animal. He's smart as they are. Eventually going to get what he's after. Right now, he's just biding his time.'

Something in the way the words snapped out of him caught Regina's attention. She kept her face straight ahead, but her eyes sidled toward him.

'Mr Willie . . .' she began cautiously.

But he'd not stopped talking. 'This is my truck, but I drive the Daimler, too. The Daimler belonged to Judge Calhoun. It's owned by Miss Mary Pickett now, though, 'cause the judge, he's long dead. But I think I told you that already. Killed off, he was, by a Calhoun writing something caused a scandal. You know about that book?'

'I read it,' Regina said, 'a long time ago, when I was a kid. But I found my copy. I brought it with me.'

A chuckle from Willie Willie. 'Did you, now? Miss Mary Pickett'll sure put her name in it for you if you tell her that. And even though she won't act like it, she'll be tickled pink. She says folks have forgotten all about that book, but they haven't. How could they? We are talking *scandal* here. Banned outright, it was, by the legislature down there in Jackson. And not just here, either. It's a book still outlawed in all the old cotton states. That's what I heard. I'm not telling who told me.' He winked. 'Too hot for folks to handle, I imagine. The black boy, Booker, was too smart. The black man, Daddy Lemon – well, Daddy Lemon was just himself. What you might call a card. The Calhouns are a fine old family. Respected. But there's lots of folks think Miss Mary Pickett wrote what she wrote for revenge.'

'Revenge?'

'Ohhhh, yes,' sang out Willie Willie in a storied crescendo that promised a sure denouement. 'Revenge because her daddy wouldn't let her marry Jackie Earle Blodgett, or Jackson Blodgett, as he calls himself now.'

Regina shook her head; she didn't quite understand it. 'How would writing her book be revenge against that?'

'Well, if Miss Mary Pickett didn't write you nothing about it – and really why should she, her sending off a business letter and all? – I guess I'm going to have to fill you in myself.' Willie Willie chuckled, a low, deep roll of a sound. 'The two of them, she and Jackson Blodgett, or *Jackie Earle* Blodgett, as he was back then, ran on over to Gordo, Alabama, right after she turned fifteen. Called themselves getting married. Her daddy was hot behind, with me at the wheel of the Daimler of course. Calhouns and Picketts never could drive for nothing. There was a whole passel of Mississippi state troopers flaring right behind us. Judge Calhoun had the clout, and he'd put in a call. Thing was, I was the one informed the judge in the first place. I was the one knew all about it. Miss Mary Pickett had told me herself. She'd *confided* in me how much she was crazy about that boy. And she sure was. Crazy about him, I mean.'

Like Collie had been for Jack in her book.

'Now, I loved me some Miss Mary Pickett. I'd known her all her life, just like I'd known her daddy before her. She knew her forest – Magnolia Forest, with its small creatures and its magic. And shooting – why, once you got her shooting she was good as any man. Took down most any critter she aimed for.'

Regina had never heard being good with a gun described as a virtue, but Willie Willie obviously thought that it was, and so she bobbed her head because that's what he was doing. *Nod along to get along,* she thought. But she'd never liked blood, and the idea of someone killing 'critters' roiled her stomach, made her very glad she'd not eaten since lunch.

Willie Willie wasn't finished. He took a puff of his cigarette, and the smoke from it briefly clouded the cab of the truck. 'The judge and I grew up together on Magnolia Forest. That's the old Calhoun place out deep in the county. Their old cotton place, so I knew my duty.'

'Your duty?' Again, Regina felt a prickle of resentment that this man whose picture she carried in her pocket, whose son had been killed – that a man like this could be so easily taken in, think that he was important to these white people.

'My duty, and not just to the judge. To her, too. Oh, yes.' Willie Willie nodded. 'We caught up with them on the steps of the Gordo Twilight Inn Hotel in "a nick of time," as the judge put it. He got them annulled for what he called non-consummation. What he called, "before the fact." Even though I imagine it was way after the fact, if you take my meaning.' He shook his head, but his face had softened and his eyes had gone dreamy. Like his mind was looking back at the something that now made his lips smile. After a moment he continued, 'Miss Mary Pickett was motherless. She was wayward. And she and Jackie Earle Blodgett had been sneaking around together since the day her mama died.' He sighed. He raised his head toward heaven – but not so far toward heaven that Regina couldn't catch the twinkle in his eye. He looked expectant, like he might want her to say something. But what could she say – yet? Still, she was more eager than ever to meet the great, and perhaps scandalous, M. P. Calhoun.

And a part of Regina – the no-nonsense lawyer part – wondered why on earth Willie Willie would expect Mary Pickett to put all that in a business letter, but another part of her was already falling into the magic of Mr Willie Willie's tale-telling voice that pulled her into his story, made her want to hear what happened next. She heard herself saying, 'Why didn't they just try again, Jackie Earle and Mary Pickett? Later.'

'Because she got sent away.'

'To school in Virginia? Just like in the book?'

'Just like it.'

'Then what happened?'

'Next thing we knew – and believe me, everybody in this town was paying attention – Miss Mae Louise Wynne turned up expectant. Jackie Earle Blodgett ended up marrying *her*. And this time it took. At least for *Miss Mae Louise* it took, but maybe a little less for our boy Mr Jackie Earle.'

Regina may have been new at interrogation, but she already knew when to keep quiet and let her client talk.

'When Miss Mary Pickett got back down here, flowers started arriving, regular as clockwork, every year on her birthday and at Christmas. The biggest box of chocolates you ever wanted to see on Valentine's Day. Nothing signed, but in a town this size, this prone to gossip . . . No doubt in anybody's mind who was doing the sending. Everything aboveboard, mind you, everybody smiling in each other's faces – at least until lately.'

Now, *this* was something to ask about. She remembered that the Blodgett house, their 'home place,' had been burned down. That his father's newspaper had said, practically insistent, Wynne Blodgett was away when it happened. Reading again, on the train, it had struck her as odd that a newspaper article describing a fire would have been so explicit about the whereabouts of someone who wasn't even there. She wanted to ask him about this, but before she could, the truck turned a sharp corner, and there was the river, a big bear of a thing, lumbering along its slow brown path.

'That's where they brought up Joe Howard,' whispered Willie Willie so softly that he could have been in church. 'See that trestle bridge there? See that rope swing hanging from it? That's the exact spot. Little white children play off that rope in the summertime, and the older ones, too. Teenagers. Joe Howard washed up right under there, like he was coming home to me. Killed in Alabama but come home to Mississippi in the end.'

Regina rolled her window down, leaned out. The air outside the truck was so thick you could lick it. It blew at her hair, almost catching it in an overhang of live oaks. But by the time she turned back there was no more river; it, too, had disappeared behind the trees as the blacktop curved and broadened, and, with a magician's flourish, pushed past the last curtain of wild woods that ushered them into Revere.

'Main Street,' said Willie Willie softly.

Nothing much to it. She thought she could see almost to the end of it from this, its beginning. A long row of hanging lights marched straight ahead, over a street carved from the forest. Around her were low frame houses, some painted, most not, some with other tiny huts – *outhouses?* – behind them.

But then, immediately, came the big houses. One right after the other, almost on top of one another, brick ones with black trim, white columned antebellums, Victorian gingerbread fronting at least twenty rooms, some that had obviously started out as cottages and been added onto and then added onto again. Regina had no idea what she'd expected this small town to look like, but it sure wasn't this.

She gestured to one of the largest. 'Shouldn't this be out on a plantation somewhere?'

'White folks,' said Willie Willie, 'thought it would be better if they all stuck together. Back in the old days, that is. So the men, they built city houses for their wives and their children. Used to be the old families lived on Main. Now the cotton's mostly gone, people from here leaving close behind it. I've heard tell there's more Revere folks living in Memphis than we got staying on here. Most of what you see been broke up into apartments now.'

Regina barely heard him. She was captivated – no, not exactly captivated. *Appalled* might be better – by the sight in front of her.

It was a brick confection of a house on the left-hand side of the street, with six fat, wedding-cake white columns standing at attention along its front veranda, a skeleton of new construction attached to both sides, a line of clipped boxwood leading up to its door. Guarding all this, at the curb, was a black-faced stone Negro boy dressed in a bright red stone shirt and with huge red smiling lips, bugged eyes, his white-nailed hands clutched tight an electrified lantern, the light inside it already lit.

'Oh, my God!' she cried. Disgusted.

'Draws attention to itself, don't it? I imagine it's meant to, that black boy. Keeps people planted squarely in their place. Shows what you think of them. Got stuff like that up north?'

'All over,' said Regina. 'All over. You get used to seeing things, but you never get used to the feeling. It – I don't know – it *hurts* every time.'

'It does, don't it? Makes you mad, too. I can tell.'

Willie Willie seemed to be sizing her up. Regina didn't know why she thought this, but she did, and she was embarrassed that she'd allowed herself to be so easily read. She turned to the house again. 'Who lives there?'

'Mayhew sisters used to. Mayhews were one of the best families in these parts. Now the place belongs to Jackson Blodgett.'

'Mary Pickett's ex-husband?'

'One in the same. Though I imagine it's his wife, Miss Mae Louise, done the place up like that, put that stone pickaninny out front of it along with all the rest of that too-muchness. Once she got her hands on it.' Again, he fluted up his voice, this time obviously imitating the present Mrs Blodgett. ' "My daddy is a gentleman planter from over Carroll County, Alabama." When everybody knows there's no such thing as a plantation in Carroll County. Land's way too hilly. Only thing grows over there is moonshine and blood feuds and snake-charming religions. And *that's* what she's related to.'

Regina had to laugh.

Willie Willie looked over at her. He waved his hand out once, like a windshield wiper meant to clear away Mae Louise Blodgett and her kinfolk. 'But Revere – we built up ourselves a pretty place here. Don't you think?'

'It's pretty.' Said grudgingly, but at least it was said.

'We look nice because the big war didn't take us out,' he said. 'Federals wanted to burn the whole place down in the winter of '64, but General Nathan Bedford Forrest and his Sixty-fifth Artillery stopped them cold. That makes him a hero to half the white folks in town. Forrest is the one started the Klan up in Mississippi. That makes him a hero to the other half.'

'I can imagine,' said Regina. She thought back to the house they'd just passed. She thought to that awful stone black boy at the curb.

Willie Willie winked. 'I just bet you can. They have their history. We have ours. You can't always tell the difference between the white families and the black. I mean, as far as names go. Same spelling a lot of the time; there's nothing anybody can do about that. But the pronunciation changes, and sometimes a letter here and there. Black Hairstons are pronounced like it's spelled. White Hairstons are Har-stons. You're a *Bill*-ups if you're white and a Bill-*ups* if you're black. A white one-*t* Motley or a black two-*t* Mottley. Black Golsons. White Gholsons. Once you know what you're listening for, the race is always in how things are said.'

'Really?'

Again, Willie Willie nodded. 'You'll soon see that for yourself.'

She was happy he'd said it, like he wanted her to stay. That might count for something with Mary Pickett. Now that they were getting closer, Regina realized she was still scared she might be sent away. But she'd got this far, got through Thurgood, got through Richmond, survived the Bonnie Blue Line in one piece. Surely, Regina thought, she could get through a little old Southern white lady, too.

'Riverview's over there. Mr Pick Calhoun still owns that, just barely. He's Miss Mary Pickett's cousin three times removed. And right beside it, that burned-out place with the seedlings taking over? That's Stream Run, or it used to be.' Willie Willie pointed out the window, going on with his guided tour, obviously proud of his town, which was a wonder to Regina. It looked nice, all right, like she'd told him, but how could you be *pleased* with a place like this, built up on slave labor? How could you like living here, feel it was yours? Still, Willie Willie seemed to. He said, 'All the other Calhouns lost everything in the Depressing. Picketts, too, and their McGraw cousins. Don't know what any of them would have done without Miss Mary Pickett. They don't, either, since she took all them in. She managed to hold on to Calhoun Place, you know, because of her book, so she just filled it up with all kinds of kin. There were cousins in all the bedrooms, folks in the basement. A whole family of Eastman relations appeared out of nowhere and were stuck up in the attic. All their land gone . . . She'd already lost Magnolia Forest herself. You know about that place, now, don't you?'

'From *The Secret of Magic*,' said Regina. 'But I thought she made it up.'

'Oh, it's real enough, both the forest itself and the plantation named for it. Miss Mary Pickett owned them both, along with Calhoun Place, or she used to. The Depressing took the cotton, and when they lost the cotton the next thing to go was the land. Down here, that's what they call the natural progression.'

The truck picked up speed; the houses gave way. They were down to business now, and shops lined both sides of the street. Regina ticked off the Dew Point Flower Shop, a TG&Y, the Silke Shoppe, Eppler's Downtown Department Store, Robinson's Shoes, the Make It New Paint Store, a Woolworth's, a Kresge's. Shipley Do-Nuts. Thurgood, she thought, would feel right at home. All this enterprise suggested to Regina that Revere might be larger than she'd assumed, in New York, that it would be. Maybe it wasn't really just another sleepy little Southern town. She was wondering how this might affect things and feeling just a little bit of hope that it might affect them positively – Mary Pickett Calhoun had written to the Fund, after all – when she looked over and there was the courthouse.

At least Regina thought it was the courthouse because it was surrounded by a square, it had a statue of a young soldier leaning against a bayonet, it had a granite memorial with finely chiseled names she could not read from where she sat, a beautifully tended laurel wreath. It looked like any county courthouse at first. Except for the banner. A blood-red background. Blue bars. A cascade of white stars. Everything that made up the Stars and Stripes she was used to – but arranged nothing like it at all.

'Is that the *Confederate* flag?'

Even as she said it, she couldn't believe it. She poked her head out the window again, turned back to look.

'That's it all right,' said Willie Willie. 'Old Glory. The Stars and the Bars. The Battle Flag, at least that's what it's called.'

'Doesn't matter what you call it. It's illegal to fly that over any government building.' She bristled, then remembered where she was and said with a bit less conviction, 'It must be.'

Willie Willie looked over at her.

'Nothing illegal about it. It's how things are done. That's the same place I went to get justice for Joe Howard. Now you're gonna try your hand there.' He pushed a whistle through his teeth, noncommittal. 'We'll see what happens.'

'We *will* see,' said Regina. She kept her voice bright, but she turned back to the flag, watched as the breeze lifted it a little, as it seemed to wave her away. Or challenge her. Yes, the challenge was in it.

Think you're up to me? That's what we'll see.

'Why didn't you leave?' she blurted.

Willie Willie looked straight ahead, past the houses, to the forest. She realized there was love on his face. He could have been looking at Joe Howard. 'I stay because this here is my home,' he said. Then his eyes narrowed, a curtain over his feelings. 'We're almost there.'

Two more short blocks, another hard right. Willie Willie pulled up next to a long brick driveway and a white columned house. Discreet, but a mansion, really, big enough to dominate the street.

'This here is where Miss Mary Pickett lives. I used to live here, too. Out back.' He motioned with his head into the darkness.

'Not in the out-back house, though. We got indoor plumbing. We're modern here. Miss Mary Pickett even put it in my place. Before I left.'

'You've left here?'

But Willie Willie didn't answer. He reached behind the truck's sun visor and pulled out his pack of Camels, then pointed to a small wrought-iron sign that proclaimed

CALHOUN PLACE
A.D. 1835

'Built way before anything else you've seen yet, and built better,' he said. 'When I was a boy, my own granddaddy used to take me around the outside. Showed me the columns he'd helped his own daddy work on. Told me you have to gradually grow each one a trifle bit bigger around the middle, then bring it back in again – that is, if you want to make it look just right. A true straight column's just an illusion. He did the floors in the house, too, carved them out of river oak. Worked cotton fields in summer, worked building Calhoun Place in the winter. All this happened back in slavery times.'

'Your grandfather was a slave for the Calhouns?' Regina hadn't really thought of this before. But this house, what Willie Willie said about it and even its beauty, made slavery stark and real to her, not something she'd just read about in a book.

'Sure he was,' said Willie Willie. 'My own granddaddy and the granddaddies of half the other colored folks here in Revere. We, most of us, been here a mighty long time, longer than many of the white folks. This here's the oldest part of the town, nearer the forest than anywhere else, and nearer the river. Remember that spot I pointed you to? Where they drug Joe Howard out of the water? Well, it's right down there, at the bottom of that deep decline. The way the road is, it loops you around the trees, gets you confused. Jackie Earle Blodgett's place is here, too. The Folly, his old home place that burned down.'

The truck settled in with a rattle and a purr. 'Wait here. I'll just be a minute.' Willie Willie opened his door, put his shiny shoes down on the sidewalk's broken pavement. 'I better go on in the back and prepare Miss Mary Pickett. She's in there, and looks like Jack Blodgett's with her.' He nodded to a dark Buick, badly parked, more in the street than to the side of it. Calhoun Place might look like it owned the sidewalk, but this big car gave the impression it owned everything else.

'Good thing there doesn't appear to be much traffic,' Regina said, but she wondered what to make of this, what Willie Willie thought about Jackson Blodgett's car being parked here at Miss Calhoun's and if it were here often. She thought about the early marriage and the continuing flowers and the Valentine choco-lates. Innocent-sounding enough, at least when Willie Willie was the one telling the story. But Regina couldn't help wondering what Mae Louise Blodgett thought about all this.

'Why would he . . .' Regina began, but Willie Willie was already strolling away, around toward the back of the house. In another minute, she heard the slamming of a screen door.

No use waiting in the truck. So Regina climbed out. Her legs were shaking. A surprise, but she decided it was from being cooped up for so long on trains and buses. From what she could tell, the street was deserted; at least there weren't any people around. It was full dark now, too, with just a few streetlights strung overhead and Calhoun Place itself lit only in fits and starts. She tried stretching a little to see if she could glimpse anything through one of the windows but there were too many lace cur-tains and heavy draperies for that. A pity. She was more curious than she cared to admit about what might be hiding there. Why, this was M. P. Calhoun's real house! It might have modeled the gorgeous Collington house in *The Secret of Magic*. But Regina realized suddenly that even if she managed to sneak a look inside, she had no idea what to expect. Not one thing in the book had really occurred in the house. Collie had run out of it; the others had run past it. On their way to the forest, to the river – the places where things really happened, at least in M. P. Calhoun's book. Still, Regina couldn't help herself. She stood on tiptoes, inched a little closer. This might be her only chance to look inside a real antebellum mansion. *Tara* brought to life . . .

The squeak made her jump back, set her guilty heart racing. *Oh, God, they've seen me! Somebody's letting out the dogs!*

She'd heard all about Southerners and their dogs. It seemed every lawyer in the Fund came back north with a story.

But then there came another squeak. Followed quickly by another. A chattering, really, and something in their spiky repetition made her calm down, let her catch sight of the mailbox.

At least Regina thought the noise was coming from the mailbox, but there was a lot of it for such a small space. Close now, right up on it, she bent down. And looked squarely into the eyes of a bluebird. At least she *thought* it was a bluebird – she was from the city, she couldn't be sure – surrounded by his family of bluebirds, staring at her as she was staring at them, and showing absolutely no signs of fright or intimidation. Instead, they chattered on, angry and insistent, acting like she was the intruder and they were the *owners* of the mailbox they found themselves in.

Must be white bluebirds, she thought. But at least they weren't dogs.

She wondered how long they'd been there and how the Calhoun household got its mail, since the birds seemed so irritably territorial. Her answer was tied to a string that ran down and ended at a red-painted aluminum lunch bucket that had one word, MAIL, scripted out in bright yellow crayon on its side. Regina recognized the flourish of M. P. Calhoun's perfect Palmer penmanship hand.

What must she be like – a woman who would put together something like this, go to this much trouble for a bird? Regina had heard almost as many horror stories about Southern women – how sugary-sweet they could be, and how ornery – as she had heard about mean Southern dogs.

Willie Willie came from around the back of the house, and he was grinning. Regina wasn't as reassured by this as she once might have been. She'd already found out Willie Willie could smile for strange reasons. Regina straightened up. And as she did, she caught a movement, and maybe a soft snuffle in the street shadows beyond the blue Buick. Something she'd missed. A donkey? Latched onto a wagon? Here in *town*?

She squinted closer but didn't have time to tell because Willie Willie was saying, 'Miss Mary Pickett is as ready to meet you as she's ever gonna be. She said, "Good God! Fetch her on up to the back porch. I imagine I'll have to figure out something." ' Again, the high lilt of his imitation. 'She didn't look happy.'

But Willie Willie *did* look happy, and suddenly his smile exploded into laughter. 'You not been here no time, but already you managed to stir up some stuff.'

5.

She'd always pictured M. P. Calhoun as an old man, round and kindly. Someone with a lap made for holding children. Someone who would fill them up with story after story.

The brittle reality: dressed in dark silk and what looked to be heirloom pearls, holding on to a cocktail glass with one hand and a lighted cigarette with the other, her hair turned rosy at its edges from the backlight of her door, and younger than what Regina had visualized. Forty years old. Tops.

'You are not at all what I expected,' said Mary Pickett Calhoun, 'I imagine you already know that.'

'Yes,' began Regina, 'but . . .'

'A deception. Is this how you all run things at that Negro Fund up there in New York?'

With the way Mary Pickett spoke, the precisely drawled clip of her words, Regina thought it best to shut up. If she opened her mouth, she could easily make things worse.

'Tomorrow,' snapped out the great author. 'I'll be sending you right back where you came from. First thing.'

They were standing at the back door, Mary Pickett squarely between Regina and whatever lay within.

All this was, quite frankly, a shock. But Regina knew it was a shock she'd best quickly get over. Standing on the back veranda steps, she was too far away to make out the color of Mary Pickett's eyes, but she couldn't miss the flash in them. If looks could kill, Regina knew she'd be a goner for certain.

'*And* I don't see any sign of Thurgood Marshall.' Mary Pickett looked all around with wide-eyed exaggeration, even though Regina was fairly certain Willie Willie had already informed her that Thurgood was still in New York.

'He's not with me. I am here by myself,' answered Regina.

'So it would appear.'

Regina had forgotten Willie Willie, but he spoke up from behind her now. 'Miss Mary Pickett, I don't think you been properly introduced. This here's Miss Regina Mary Robichard. She was the R. M. Robichard in that telegram, just like you was the M. P. Calhoun in your book.'

They both turned to look at him, Regina with her mouth open, not knowing what to expect. This was Mississippi, after all, where Negroes were supposed to keep their mouths shut if they knew what was good for them. Anything could happen if they didn't, most of it bad.

But if Mary Pickett was shocked, she didn't show it. She swiveled back to Regina again, all business. 'Willie Willie has said you may stay in his place. In the cottage. For the night.' She made a vague gesture toward something in the dark behind Regina's left shoulder. 'He pretty much lives out in Magnolia Forest now anyhow, don't you, Willie Willie? He's a nimrod, you know, way the best in Jefferson-Lee County. Hunting's pretty much all he does nowadays.'

Mary Pickett looked out for a moment, and even though Regina could not see her eyes, she knew that they had sought out Willie Willie's. She wondered what they were saying to him. She wondered what his eyes were answering back.

'The cottage will do for the night,' continued Miss Mary Pickett briskly. 'He'll take you over, get you settled. I imagine you've missed your supper. I'll send out a sandwich and some milk. Tomorrow morning . . . Well, Dinetta brings out breakfast at eight. I'll expect you to be prompt.'

'I will be,' said Regina, almost giddy with relief that she hadn't been summarily carted off to the Queen City Hotel. She was still right here, right near Mary Pickett, and she had a whole night ahead of her to figure out how to stay put.

Without another word, Mary Pickett turned back to her house, banged the screen door shut behind her. There had been no sign of Jackson Blodgett, no mention of his name – and Regina had been looking and listening hard for him. But there was a movement now at the kitchen window. A strange flash of color, of bright red and of gold, that couldn't *possibly* be him.

Regina said, 'Smells like Miss Calhoun might be baking some kind of pie.'

'She don't cook. You coming?' said Willie Willie. He'd pulled up a kerosene lamp from the side of the porch, lit it, held it high.

Regina turned, hurried down the stairs. She looked back at the window one last time, but the shade had been pulled down tight as a drum and the brilliant incandescence that had been at it and the smell of pie were both gone.

Willie Willie's 'cottage' turned out to be about twenty feet from the main house, partially hidden from it by trees and flowers that, in the darkness, were only vague, dark forms and rich scents. Regina doubted that, even in broad daylight, she could have named them anyway. Ahead of her, Willie Willie opened a door. He switched on a light.

Regina had immediately translated Mary Pickett's 'cottage' into 'cabin,' some hardscrabble shelter left over from slavery days. And Willie Willie's place was certainly simple. It just wasn't as crude as she'd thought it would be. A couch, two chairs, an end table, a desk in a tidy cream-painted room. Maybe not much, but enough. A small bump led down to an attached kitchen; railed steps beside her lifted to something above.

A much nicer place than what she'd expected him to have. Indoor plumbing, even. She remembered the outhouses she'd seen on her way in.

'There's sheets and towels in that shelf off the bathroom. Got my own refrigerator here, but it's empty. Like Miss Mary Pickett said, she'll be sending somebody over any minute with your supper. I'll get your bags and carry them up.'

He had stood just inside the door and was out again before Regina could thank him. Strange, she thought, since this was his

home. She'd imagine he'd want to look around, make sure everything was like he'd left it. But then again, she decided, maybe he
already had, before he'd come to get her. Not that she spent
much time thinking about Willie Willie. She had other things on
her mind. Her feet were killing her and her girdle was itching;
even the peacock feather on her hat was starting to droop. She
blew at it, found a switch, turned on a light.

Once upstairs, she saw the bathroom door right away, a sly,
wide-open gape leading to a Promised Land that just might
include a tub. She kicked off her shoes, peeled off her gloves and
her hat, all the time making straight for it. Thank God for indoor
plumbing!

There was a tub. She went right to it, pulled back the plastic
curtain . . . and screamed. At the biggest roach she'd ever seen in
her life. Big as a mouse. In fact, heaven help her, it might actually
be a mouse.

'Honey, ain't nothing but a little ol' palmetto bug. How can it
hurt you?' From downstairs floated up a woman's voice – deep, rich,
mellow as molasses – that was not Mary Pickett's voice, and certainly not Willie Willie's voice. 'He's more scared of you than you
be of him. All you got to do is pick him up, put him out the window.
That's where he come from. That's where he wants to go back.'

Pick him up? Put him out the window? By myself?

'Ma'am . . .' What was it Mary Pickett had called her? Dinetta?
'Miss Dinetta . . .'

'Just go right on over to him. He's not gonna bite. Pick him up!
Let him go!' That woman again, and then the unmistakable click
of a closing front door.

No help for it now; either that bug had to go or she did. Regina
started looking around for anything, a roll of toilet paper, maybe –
something to pick the bug up with and not touch it. The window
was already open. She was grateful for that.

Regina woke to a wild chirping of birds. At least she thought they
were birds at first. It took a closed-eyed second for her to realize

86

that what she heard was meowing, not chirping. Kittens. This noisy, this early? But at least they'd roused her.

She opened her eyes to bright sunlight in a strange room in a strange house in a strange place. Still, she recognized where she was right away, and what lay before her. Eyes wide open now, she jumped out of bed, found the luggage Willie Willie had left outside the door, and fished through it for her robe. Then she went looking around.

Willie Willie's place consisted of two rooms, stacked one on top of the other, with a kitchen added on to the back of the downstairs and a tiny bathroom tacked up on top of that. Except for a few odd, threadbare pieces that had presumably been handed down from the big house – a dull gold damask couch, the curlicue iron bed, two red brocaded easy chairs – the rest of the furniture looked handmade. The rooms smelled cedarwood and Ivory soap and pitch pine, and neglect. All in order but covered in dust, as though Willie Willie had been gone from his house a lot longer than Mary Pickett had said.

Regina dressed, came downstairs, went over to the lace-curtained window. It was still bright and early, but across the way Calhoun Place was already a hive of activity. As she watched, Mary Pickett carried out toast holders and a big silver tray. Behind her, close as a shadow, marched a little black girl dressed up in a white uniform, red socks and scuffed shoes, holding tight on to a tray with two porcelain teapots, two cups, and two saucers.

'Could that be *Dinetta*?' wondered Regina, remembering the rich voice that had called up to her from this very same room last night. She couldn't imagine that much power being forced out of such a little-girl body. Why, this child looked like she should still be in grammar school. Regina made up her mind to point this fact out to Mary Pickett as soon as she decently could.

Regina watched Mary Pickett poke out her lips, study the china, shake her head, take it back into the kitchen and bring back some more. She and Dinetta dragged out Chippendale chairs, put them across from each other at a large white wicker table. Slowly it started to dawn on Regina that all this preparation might be for her. If so, then Willie Willie had been right and her presence was going to be one continuous social quagmire for M. P. Calhoun, an unknown place where she'd have to carefully seek out traction and mind every new step.

Mary Pickett strode purposely in and out, got so sweaty from her exertions that the bun at the nape of her neck started to unravel. Curls of hair had broken loose and surrounded her face like little russet question marks. A few of them drooped down onto her shoulders – calling Regina's attention to Mary Pickett's cardigan sweater. It was a camel-colored cashmere with a row of exquisite pearl buttons. Probably bought, if recollection served Regina correctly, last season at Best. She knew this because she had one just like it. And she'd brought it with her.

Abandoning the window, she ran up the steep steps to the small room she had slept in, pulled out the sweater, put it on, checked herself in the mirror over the bathroom sink, walked back down the stairs, and on out the door. Her step, as she crossed the brick drive leading from the cottage to its big house, was springy.

She thought she looked a little better in the sweater than Mary Pickett did. What with her sensible shoes, her hair coming loose, a white lace blouse and her constant veranda-arranging, Miss Calhoun had started to come a little undone.

'Good morning,' Regina called out, waving.

'Good morning.' Mary Pickett's eyes narrowed as she took in Regina – one long glance that stopped for a slow beat at the sweater – but all she said was, 'Won't you have a seat?'

Cool as a cucumber, thought Regina, and she wondered if there was ever anything that might get through to this woman, anything that might shake her up. There didn't seem to be, because after the seat, the novelist offered toast, tea, and a pregnant silence.

Regina didn't mind. She hadn't figured out what to say anyway, and she was content for the moment to just look around, get some bearings, and the first thing her eyes really lighted on was Mary Pickett herself. Why, behind all that sharp brittleness, she's actually quite pretty. Huge doe eyes, thick, rich hair, skin as white and translucent as a good Minton china cup. The two of them were out on Miss Mary Pickett's back veranda, the same one Regina had been led to the night before, and it was lovely. It had a green planked floor and a blue-painted ceiling that had been spotted over with bright, white cumulus clouds. Regina remembered, from reading Mary Pickett's novel, that the green and the blue were supposed to confuse mosquitoes in summer and keep them away. Daddy Lemon had said this. Regina, in New York, had thought this only an illustration of the magic in the book, but, looking around her now, she decided this must be something in which M. P. Calhoun truly believed.

Finally, Mary Pickett said, 'I trust you slept well.'

'Very nicely,' said Regina.

'I heard you had a little . . . visitor.' She looked down, but Regina didn't miss a lip twitch that could only be glee.

'You mean that little ol' palmetto bug? Why, he was nothing.'

Mary Pickett raised her eyes. They were a rich earth brown. 'Really?' A long, slow drawl. 'I imagine that's what you made of him. Nothing. What'd you do . . . flush him down the drain?'

'Actually, I picked him up with a piece of cardboard and put him out the window. I thought that would be best. Not to kill him, I mean.'

'You can't kill a palmetto bug, putting him down a drain,' Mary Pickett said with a smirk. 'A flushing drain's his natural habitation. How'd you like the cottage?'

'I liked it,' said Regina.

Mary Pickett flashed out what looked like a genuine smile. 'It's Willie Willie's. I fixed it up for him myself. Not what you were expecting, was it? The *cottage*, that is.'

'I didn't know what to expect,' said Regina honestly. 'I imagine you didn't, either.'

They looked at each other. They both knew what she meant.

It was clear that Mary Pickett had been plainly amazed by Regina the night before, and she was still astonished. She didn't try to hide it. Every time she glanced over, her eyebrows canted upward and she automatically started shaking her head. Regina saw this, but she pretended not to. She didn't want to make things easier for Mary Pickett, or more difficult for Willie Willie or for herself, by starting off on the wrong foot. So she said, 'I realize that I'm not the person you were expecting, but as I'm sure you can well understand, Mr Marshall himself is always quite busy . . .'

Mary Pickett brushed a fly away from a silver bowl of blood-orange marmalade. The dish was polished bright as a mirror, the marmalade so thick it kept a spoon straight up, standing at attention. Mary Pickett let her gaze roam to a row of enormous pink roses. She said not a word. She did not look at Regina, who continued gamely on.

'He chose me as the most qualified to replace him. I have experience with ex-GIs, with their civil rights cases. Surely since you were the one who wrote for our help, it cannot be my race that matters. You seemed to know you were calling on the NAACP.' Regina paused. 'Is it my gender?'

' "Is it my gender?" ' mimicked Miss Mary Pickett. She swirled a small cyclone of sugar into her tea. 'I asked specifically for Thurgood Marshall. You do not look like Thurgood Marshall to *me*. Much, much too young, for one thing. The way life is here . . . how could you possibly understand?'

'Understand what?'

But there was no answer to this.

'Believe me, Miss Calhoun,' continued Regina, 'Mr Marshall is extremely sorry that he could not come himself. He understands the gravity of the situation. We all do.'

This caught Mary Pickett's attention. 'Really?' she said. 'And what exactly *is* the gravity, as you so neatly phrase it, of this situation?'

'Why, that justice for Joe Howard Wilson has not been served.

You want us – me – to find evidence that will persuade a grand jury to reopen the case.'

'Oh,' said Mary Pickett, considering, 'is that what you think? Well, you're wrong. And had you informed me who you were before you got here, you would have saved me a great deal of money and you and your office some time. Soon as we're finished here, I'll have somebody haul you back down to the Bonnie Blue depot. The bus will take you far as Birmingham. You can catch a train north from there. I'm sorry, but this is a serious matter. Life and death. I need someone with Thurgood Marshall's experience. I need *expertise*.'

'That's not what Mr Willie Willie told me. It's not why he said you wanted us here.'

'Really?' Mary Pickett's eyes were steady over the rim of her cup, but Regina could tell from the flicker in them that she'd made an impression.

'Really,' she echoed. 'In fact, he thinks the only reason you sent for us was that you thought we wouldn't actually come. But we did come. I'm here.'

'Indeed,' said Mary Pickett. 'You are.'

She had a beautiful voice, slow, rich, and deep, a voice that thoroughly frosted its phrases and laid them out like so many caramel cakes. A little too sweet for Regina's taste. It was probably something, she decided, best imbibed by small, sparing dose. Mary Pickett poured more tea for herself then turned the handle so her guest could pour for herself. *God forbid she should serve a Negro!* Regina reached down and started swirling sugar into her own teacup. Which was chipped. Both Regina and Mary Pickett noticed this at the exact same moment. Regina's lip curved upward in triumph.

I may not be what you expected, but you are exactly what I expected, her smile said.

'I am sorry,' said Mary Pickett, blushing. 'This was not done with intention.'

She looked like she meant it. And much to Regina's amazement, she snatched up the cup, rushed into the house, and returned with another. Perfect, this time.

But this show of good manners changed nothing else. Settled back into her seat, Mary Pickett appeared, once again, ready for battle. 'This is Mississippi, and this is a boy's – a young man's – death we're talking about, and the life of a man who has worked for me for years. There's nothing someone like you can do for us down here. You'll only get in the way. You'll make things difficult.'

'Difficult?'

'As though they're not already awful enough,' said Mary Pickett. 'In a killing way.'

'But Miss Calhoun, Lieutenant Wilson is already dead.'

'It's not Joe Howard I'm worried about,' said Mary Pickett. 'It's Willie Willie. I'm afraid he's going to get himself killed. Do you know what I'm saying?'

Lynched.

Regina nodded. She knew what Mary Pickett was saying.

'Because he won't give up,' continued Mary Pickett. 'He says he will, but he won't. I thought once I wrote up to y'all and he saw – '

'Why?' Bad manners to interrupt, but Regina did it anyway. 'I mean, why won't Mr Willie Willie give up?'

'Why?' repeated Mary Pickett. 'Honey, "why" is the history of this place. It's the only question we ever ask, and it's the one never gets answered.'

Soft music played into the silence left by her words. Slow and sad. Negro. Gospel, maybe. Regina thought it must be filtering out from a radio nearby. She couldn't be certain, couldn't identify the tune. But Mary Pickett sure knew it, and she was humming along. Suddenly, Regina thought, *Why this is* M. P. Calhoun *sitting across from me at this table. I'm drinking tea with one of my favorite authors. It's me here!* And she allowed herself to be *thrilled* by this fact – but just for a moment.

Then she said, 'You send me away now, Mr Willie Willie'll

know he was right about you. That you were . . . I don't know . . . maybe bluffing.' She stopped, searching for the right words. 'Though I can't imagine what he thinks would much matter. He's just another black man works for you, after all.'

It was a calculated risk. Regina held her breath as Mary Pickett looked over a sea of flowers to the small out-built cottage. When her head swiveled slowly back, the humming stopped. And Regina knew she had Mary Pickett's full attention.

'Continue.'

'I was thinking,' Regina said after a minute, 'that I might pay a call on the district attorney. Nathan Bedford Duval V, at least that's the name in the clippings you sent. He's the one asked the judge to call up a grand jury – '

'Why on earth would you do that?' This time it was Mary Pickett who interrupted. 'Bed's already done more than he was called on to do. Worked hard at it, but he never came up with a thing. You ask me, some no-account bad boys got on that bus, took Joe Howard off. They were over there, across the state line in Carroll County when it happened, weren't they? Everybody knows Alabama's just full up, one end to the other, with troublesome folks.'

'How'd you hear that?' said Regina. 'I mean, how did you hear that those men actually got on the bus in Alabama?'

'Because I just know.' Mary Pickett stopped. She seemed to realize she'd admitted to knowing too much.

Like what was on the secret grand jury docket. But Regina slid past this, at least for the moment.

'And why?' she prompted.

Mary Pickett looked wary. 'Why what?'

'*Why* would the men get on the bus in the first place? Why would they just, out the blue, decide to stop the bus and . . . I don't know . . . take him off? Aliceville, Alabama, was mentioned in those clippings you sent us. It was his last stop, and something must have happened there. Something that got Joe Howard killed – or was the excuse for him getting killed. There has to be a link, and it seems to me the district attorney would be the most

93

likely place to start in order to find it. He seemed to have been active in putting the case together. The newspapers talked about him, not about the sheriff. Once I have some idea what was presented, I'll know what we need to find out to get him to reopen proceedings. Unless, of course, you think I should speak directly to the circuit court judge.'

'Judge's out with his dogs,' Mary Pickett snapped out. 'It's bird season.'

'When will he be back? Tonight?'

Mary Pickett looked at Regina like she was crazy. 'I said Judge Timms's gone *bird* hunting. He takes his dogs out once a year because, in his words, "They just love it to death." If you're lucky, he'll be back here right about Thanksgiving. But I don't imagine you plan on staying that long?'

'No,' said Regina. 'I think we can clear things up before then. Look, maybe the district attorney knows how to get in touch with him. He might get the judge to release the grand jury findings.'

'You won't find a thing in it.'

'With all due respect, Miss Calhoun, I think I should be the one to make that decision. Isn't that why you sent for someone from the Fund – so that Mr Willie Willie would have a responsible lawyer?'

Mary Pickett regarded her. 'Maybe.'

She reached for her toast. 'That's a nice skirt you got on.'

Something in her tone sent a warning, but Regina said, 'Thank you. My mother made it. She's a dressmaker.'

Now Mary Pickett was looking right at her. 'Ida Jane Robichard. Isn't that your mother? The anti-lynching crusader? I put the whole thing together myself last night. I recognized the *patronymic* right away when I saw it on the telegram y'all sent down. Robichard's not that common a name, even down this close to Louisiana. I thought you might be related.'

For a moment the only sounds were those of a bee buzzing, a bird chirping, the tires of one lone vehicle traveling slowly up a nearby road. That's all, as Regina sat reeling at the idea that this Southern white woman would be talking in her drawled voice of Ida Jane; that Mary Pickett would even know of her at all. A surprise. Almost a violation. Regina hoped to God the shock didn't show on her face.

'Yes,' she said. 'I am related.'

'Your mother, I imagine. You look like her. Pretty.' And then, to Regina's unasked question, 'I've seen pictures of her. Willie Willie gets the Negro newspapers, and I read from them. Sometimes. Your mother's all through them. She's famous. A firebrand. A martyr.'

'No,' said Regina, a little too quickly. 'She's not that.'

'Don't make a martyr out of yourself.' How many times had Ida Jane drummed that into her. *'Martyrs are dead folks. And dead folks can't get the job done.'*

'My mother doesn't think of herself that way. She doesn't think of herself at all. It's the injustice that matters.'

'But your father was, wasn't he? A martyr, I mean. I imagine it's given you a great deal to live up to.' Mary Pickett sighed. 'Well, one way or the other, we've all got to live up to something. It's a shared burden, nothing particularly racial about it.'

Regina sat still as stone, her mouth chiseled into one tight line so thin it hurt her cheeks to draw it in. Who did Mary Pickett think she was, talking so glibly about Ida Jane and Oscar Robichard? *Smug* even that she had known their names. Regina wondered how a woman, so white and so privileged, could possibly think she knew anything at all about what it meant to be them.

Mary Pickett swiveled slowly toward her, and not just with her head this time but with the whole of her body, with her careful sweater, and her lace blouse that hid the wink of good matching pearls. She moved no closer, but Regina caught a brief trace of her perfume, and it was a surprise, more opulent than she would have thought, deeper. Sexier.

And Regina knew it. Shalimar. By Guerlain.

Mary Pickett said, 'You are ambitious. A lady lawyer. Deter-mined to get ahead.'

'Determined to help Mr Willie Willie,' corrected Regina. 'As I presume you are yourself.'

'Yes,' said Mary Pickett, as the lines of her face gravitated upward. It was a small smile, but it worked a wonder on her face, lightened it up. 'Helping my Willie Willie – that's what I know to do best.'

'*Your* Willie Willie?'

'Yes, mine.'

Regina opened her mouth, then quickly shut it again. She wanted to ask just what Mary Pickett meant by that word 'mine'? Did she think of Willie Willie as a possession, like her big house or her big foreign car that sat beside it? Something that made up what could be considered the gracious Calhoun life? Or was there more to it than that? Regina thought there might be.

A breeze caught at the late roses and fire geraniums, brushed against carefully trimmed hedges and through low-hanging branches along the tree-lined lane that Regina had hurried through that morning on her way to Mary Pickett's great house. The move-ment drew Regina's attention down its short distance, straight to Mr Willie Willie's cottage, where she had slept last night.

'He doesn't trust people,' Mary Pickett was saying. 'He might act like he does, but he doesn't. I'm talking about Willie Willie. I'm talking about white people. That's the only thing about him that doesn't have anything to do with Joe Howard. Willie Willie hasn't trusted white people in years. Doesn't like us, either. Doesn't even pretend to anymore. It all started with Daddy.'

Regina turned back from the cottage. 'Your father?'

'My daddy was the circuit judge for this county. He was that before I was born and will be that long after I've died, even though he's been dead himself now for many a good year. His picture's over in the courthouse, and the brass plaque under it still announces that's what he is. Present tense. No dates. You will find that the past is still very much alive down here.'

You will find . . . Future tense. This did not have the ring of being sent away in it. She tried not to smile as Mary Pickett continued.

'Daddy's the one actually taught Joe Howard to read and to write. He did this when Joe Howard was little, a teeny-weensy boy. Daddy's the first one told Willie Willie that he had himself a special son, that Joe Howard was going to grow up to *be* something. At least once he got out of the South.'

She paused. Considered. 'Of course, now I think about it, Willie Willie probably already knew this. He's quick as all get out, so he's the one made sure *Daddy* knew just how smart Joe Howard was. I wouldn't put it past him. In sly ways, that's how he'd do it. He always could read Daddy like a book. He had to, in order to make a way. And he, too, was always ambitious, not for himself but for Joe Howard. Sounds good, doesn't it? Wanting your son to go on, to be better than you were? I imagine, though, it could be a weight. Especially if you were like Joe Howard. Gentle, like he was. Loving his daddy like he did. Now, my own daddy was . . .'

Regina thought she'd say 'a dreamer.'

'. . . a drinker.' Mary Pickett clipped the word out. 'A bitter man. Just like Willie Willie's got bitter . . .' She let her voice trail off.

'You think Mr Willie Willie's got no reason to be bitter?'

Mary Pickett fielded a brief, significant glance toward the cottage. 'You think he's got reason?'

'Miss Calhoun, the *world* thinks Mr Willie's got reason – even without what happened to his son.'

Something flashed behind Mary Pickett's eyes and then died there. Its movement made Regina think to the way the pigeons on the ledge outside her bedroom window in Harlem fluttered early in the morning, almost in slow motion, when first they began to stir.

Mary Pickett said, 'Well, maybe.'

Well, maybe. Indeed!

Regina wanted to reach both hands right across that carefully laid table and shake this woman until she woke her right up.

'You know,' said Mary Pickett, 'when I was a child, I worshipped Willie Willie. He didn't have to do that much – just spend some time with me. My mama was always sick. My daddy was busy. Willie Willie taught me things, taught all of us things. With him, there was always something new to learn. Something secret and magic. It made me feel special to think that Willie Willie belonged to *me*. I can remember being five years old and telling everybody who would listen that he was my natural daddy. Feeble as she was, you can sure bet my mama put a quick end to talk like that.' Mary Pickett narrowed her already thin lips. 'Did he tell you how he changed Joe Howard's name to Wilson?'

'He told me he did it.'

'But did he tell you *how*?'

Regina shook her head as Mary Pickett nodded hers. 'I imagine he didn't. Too busy gossiping about me.' She sidled a quick glance over to Regina, who blushed. Mary Pickett continued, triumphant, 'I knew it! Talking about when I got married. That would be Willie Willie. Wanting you to look someplace other than at him. It's the secret of magic, known by the great Houdini himself. That's what Willie Willie always told me. Distract folks. Get them to look where you want them to look.

'Welllll' – Mary Pickett dragged the word out – 'like I said, Daddy was the circuit judge here. He had his office at the courthouse, right where Judge Timms is now. Daddy had known Willie Willie since – I don't know – forever. Willie Willie was born on our place out at Magnolia Forest. His own granddaddy had been a sl— ' She stopped, darted a quick glance over at Regina. 'He'd worked out there for my great granddaddy. Calhouns have been Jefferson-Lee County a long time, and the Willies have been here just as long. They came, all of them, down from Pickett County, Carolina, together. Negro and white.'

Mary Pickett looked down, then quickly up again. She said, 'I think things began to change that summer when Joe Howard turned eight. Something happened . . . Willie Willie decided a boy like his boy – with potential, with the interest of my daddy, who was going to help him – a boy like that needed a proper patronymic. At least, that's what Willie Willie called it. I was twelve years older than Joe Howard and had what you might call a fine education, but I didn't know what that word *patronymic* meant myself. Had to look it up. Daddy knew, though, and I thought he'd bust open the way he got so tickled by Willie Willie saying that. But he made sure that Willie Willie got what he wanted. Took him over to the courthouse himself, walked him right in – a black man there to get some legal rights that didn't have a thing to do with jail time. It was odd. Folks talked. And that was the whole point of it – folks talking. To this day, I still haven't figured out what it was my daddy wanted more – to help Joe Howard or just stir things up. Because if Daddy stirred things up enough, he could keep people looking at where he wanted them to look – which was at race – and keep them from seeing what was actually going on . . .'

Mary Pickett hesitated. Maybe it was dawning on her, Regina thought, that she might be saying too much. She half expected her to stop, but Mary Pickett went right on. She was obviously not a woman who listened to reason, even her own. 'Which was that he was drinking and my mama was dead and Picketts and Calhouns were steadily losing their land hand over fist to the Mississippi Commerce and Agriculture Bank. All the old families . . . fading out fast.'

Regina leaned closer, drawn into the rich, strong scent of Mary Pickett's perfume and the smell of the roses from the silver loving cup on the breakfast table and this piece of the story of Willie Willie and Joe Howard, a story that she was eager to learn.

Mary Pickett drew a wide arc with her hand, bright red nails flashing sunlight. 'Everything going, going, gone – or at least most of it. How can I phrase it . . . Daddy *willing* people to think, "Well, will you look at that Charles Calhoun. What a hoot! What a card!" Dressing Willie Willie up. Taking him over to the courthouse.

Protecting him, in a manner of speaking, and doing just enough for him that folks here might be slightly scandalized . . .'

'But not enough that they would feel threatened.'

'No, Daddy couldn't have that. He needed the judgeship, the little money it paid him, and it was elected. Willie Willie knew this. He was also smart enough to know he was being used by my daddy, but he would have done anything that would help Joe Howard to get out of this place, move on, get going, make something of himself.'

At first, as she listened, Regina could not figure out why Mary Pickett was doing all this talking and confiding, until finally it struck her that maybe the whole thing was, for Mary Pickett, like being on a long-distance bus. Because on a long-distance bus you could pour out to the stranger next to you things you wouldn't tell your own mother. Folks sitting next to you on something like that – they're not real people. *Just like I'm not a real person to her. The next time the bus stops, she thinks I'll be gone.* Regina rooted herself a little deeper into her Chippendale chair. She had not the least intention of going anywhere.

Mary Pickett had a pack of Chesterfields on the table, and she lit one up now. It must finally have struck her what she was saying and to whom.

'My daddy was a *good* man,' she said. Her words came out on a plume of smoke. 'Just like all of us here in Revere are good people – at least up to a point.'

Her voice lost some of its trilling languor. Regina wondered if a little bit of it had been put on for her benefit – 'This is how all y'all think we all talk down here' – and if the great author wasn't, perhaps, laughing at her some, underneath. But she couldn't tell, not from what Mary Pickett was saying.

'A good man. He had influence, and he used it. All these years and the Klan never marched in Revere, never got a foothold here. It marched in the North, though, all through it. It marched in Nebraska, where your daddy was killed.' She looked dead at Regina. 'Daddy protected our people.'

Just exactly who Mary Pickett meant by 'our people,' Regina could not tell. Just like she hadn't been able to tell what she'd meant by that 'mine.' They were mysterious words, perhaps even offensive. Regina put her napkin down, pushed back in her fine-wood indoor chair from the rattan table and got up.

'Miss Calhoun,' she said. 'I believe it's time I got going. Will Mr Duval be at the courthouse? I need to get started with the investigation.'

'Ah – Nancy Drew.'

No, Collie Collington. In your book.

That's what Regina wanted to say. She had thought about telling Mary Pickett that she'd read *The Secret of Magic*, that she actually had her old, worn copy with her, that she had searched for it and found it and brought it down from New York and that it lay on the nightstand by her bed in the cottage. She decided against this, even though she had the feeling that it would be a pleasure, after all this time, for Mary Pickett to hear that her novel was still read, that it held its place in a life and that it was loved. Willie Willie had told Regina so himself.

No, she couldn't say all this. So she clamped her jaw shut and said nothing.

Mary Pickett stubbed her cigarette into a crystal ashtray. Light danced on her face when she looked up. 'Bed Duval won't be at the courthouse. Not this time of day. Not in Revere. Serving justice isn't a full-time occupation here. He'll be in his office, though, the one he shares with his daddy. It's at Sixth Street and Second Avenue. On the corner. Wait a minute. I'll point it out.'

She disappeared into her house, the screen door slamming behind her. When she came out she had on a felt-and-feather hat and she was pulling on her gloves. She'd been gone only a minute, but that had been enough time for her to change her sweater. This new one was the dark color of a storm cloud. The buttons on it were muted as well, and Mary Pickett had obscured her eyes behind a pair of sunglasses framed in yellow tortoiseshell.

'The thing you got to know about Revere,' she trilled out, as they set out along the side of the house, her voice a perfect imitation of Willie Willie imitating her, 'is that the whole town is laid out on a grid – north to south avenues, east to west streets. All numbered, except for Main Street, which should be First Street, but isn't. And, of course, what should be Second Avenue is actually College Street. If you remember all this and keep people placed where they belong, you won't get lost and you'll keep yourself out of trouble.'

She walked along with calm deliberation as she said all this, brushing against a bush whose flowers were, perhaps, a little past their prime. Petals rained onto Mary Pickett's shoulders and onto the smoothly clipped perfection of the lawn. The air around them was so still and so thick that Regina was able to catch their petal fragrance as they tumbled past her, hear them as they touched the grass.

'What *are* they?' Regina thought she'd never seen a flower so fat and ripe, so beautiful.

Mary Pickett smiled. 'That, my dear,' she said, drawling out the words, slow, wicked, and delicious, 'is the *Confederate* rose.'

6.

Regina started off, alone, toward the courthouse. The sidewalk she traveled along was rutted from one end to the other. And of course they'd all been this way in the book. *Magnolia roots glaring up through the rugged pavement, looking for all the world like eyes on top of a scary ol' alligator head. An alligator head that was just waiting there, quiet as Sunday, to trip you up, to bite you hard, and to call out 'Gotcha!'*

But nobody or nothing was going to get Regina. She was determined. She'd watch her step, all right.

'Turn right. You can't miss the Duval place. It's in front of the courthouse. Mind what I said about that grid.' That's what Mary Pickett had told her as she passed her through the gate and then left her. Regina had to shake her head. She thought, *All that – Mary Pickett's changed sweater, her hat, her gloves, her dark glasses – put on for a two-minute appearance on a deserted mid-morning street.* Everything so different from *The Secret of Magic,* and M. P. Calhoun, too, so unlike the kindly old man Regina had pictured.

But at least the courthouse was right where Mary Pickett had said it would be – a two-story red brick building with white-painted trim. Regina saw it loom up straight in front of her, plain as day in the morning light. And with a soldier standing guard right beside it. A *granite* soldier, clutching a stone rifle and with stone eyes that seemed to pick out Regina and follow her down the street. The War Memorial. Beneath his feet a plaque, its bright brass turned verdigris by humid air and time. She was too far away to read it. She didn't know if she'd want to even if she could. There'd be no black name on it, of that she was certain. Not with that Confederate flag flapping overhead.

This wasn't a flag you came upon often in New York, and if

you did usually it was buried deep someplace in a book. Or else, once in a while, you'd see it on the front page of some daily, grimly sinister in a black-and-white photograph, surrounded by men who thought it best to hide who they were behind pointed hats and long, plain sheets. But no matter where she saw it, the Confederate flag remained an object of caution. Certainly not something Thurgood or the other lawyers at the Fund would think to bring back as a sweet Southern memento. Yet here, in Revere, Mississippi, the Stars and the Bars reigned supreme.

'And not just anywhere,' whispered Regina, 'but over the damn courthouse.'

Perhaps not the best of omens as it fluttered over a square that was filling up with white people, going into the courthouse or coming out again, folks who stopped to chat with one another on its broad steps. It waved over a black man, busily snapping his shining rag over the shoes of a portly white man, both of them deep in conversation, over what looked to Regina from this distance like a one-page racing form. The white man shook his head, stabbed the air with a forefinger. The black man, shook his head, mumbled, 'Uhm. Uhm. Uhm.'

But they looked helpful enough, at least the black one did, and Regina was heading in their direction, her perkiest smile at the ready, a polite 'Excuse me, sir, is the Duval law office near here?' rising to her lips. When she noticed the woman. Or rather, being Ida Jane Robichard's daughter, when she noticed the woman's jaunty felt hat. A cloche that looked for all the world like a chipper red sailboat; feathered, veiled, facing optimistically forward, and bobbing along on a carefully straightened, darkly perfect, wave of marceled hair.

That's a really nice hat, thought Regina, surprised a little by the fact that the woman who wore it was Negro.

And she looked serene, too, looked sprightly, as she made her slow way down the main street. It didn't seem to be easy going. One hand steered a white wicker baby buggy while the other clutched what looked to be a three-year-old boy.

His mother – because surely she was the mother – had to wheel around the uneven sidewalk paving and dodge tree roots that poked up through the asphalt, just like they did on Mary Pickett's street. And her little boy was a handful. Lively. He clamped his arms to his sides, told his mother, and anybody else within earshot, that he was too old now to hold hands. He and the woman looked just alike. Same big eyes. Same high cheekbones and coffee coloring. Not a white child. And Regina wondered what this woman's husband must do for a living that she was able to dress smartly and walk about with her own children on the sidewalks of Revere, Mississippi, in the middle of a fine, bright day.

The carriage lost its balance, nicked against the curb, shifted. Inside it, a baby started to cry. The woman looked like she might need some help. Regina started toward her. But then she stopped. Men were coming down the street, straight toward the woman, and they were closer than she was.

White men, dressed in shirt sleeves and ties, their suit coats slung over their shoulders. They had hats on their heads and they were talking, busy with what they were saying, and they didn't appear to notice the woman and her children on the sidewalk. Even though she was coming straight toward them. Even though the child still loudly protested that he was way too old to hold hands. And the baby crying . . . How could they miss all that?

But they sure seemed to.

The woman kept her eyes studiously down; kept them on the buggy, on her recalcitrant three-year-old son, on the pavement, on her shoes. But she must have seen the men, must have been paying attention to them all along. Because as Regina watched, she deftly maneuvered her baby carriage and herself and her boy, all together, off and into the street, leaving the white men to own the sidewalk. Only after they'd passed did she climb back up where she'd been and go on like before – except for one difference. Her little boy stopped protesting. He followed his mother's example and lowered his eyes to the ground.

Regina could not believe it. She *could not believe it* – except, of course, she could. It's why she was here, wasn't it? Bad behavior taken for granted, ending in murder and who knew what else. What she didn't understand, though, was the scintilla of her anger – a sharp, bright shard of it – that splintered off from the rage she felt toward those men and trailed that Negro mother.

She thought of Ida Jane, all the hard work, all the fiery speeches.

'You don't stand up for yourself first, ain't nobody in this world going to stand up for you.'

Bed Duval's office, too, turned out to be exactly where Mary Pickett had said it would be, catty-corner and across from the courthouse. It was in a one-story brick building hugged up between the Moffett's Dry Goods Store (COFFINS $5, MADE WHILE U WAIT) and another squat structure with a simple LAWYERS CHEAP (LAND ISSUES), green paint on a white sandwich-board sign. The Duval office was different from both these. More impressive. You couldn't miss it if you tried. Twin windows glared out onto the sidewalk. One read NATHAN BEDFORD FORREST DUVAL V, ATTORNEY-AT-LAW in gold-edged black letters, the other said NATHAN BEDFORD FORREST DUVAL V, ATTORNEY-AT-LAW AND DISTRICT ATTORNEY. The two windows were separated by a worn red door.

Regina opened it. Stepped inside, where everything was dusty and dim. It took a few seconds of real concentration before her eyes were able to focus. When they did, she found herself in a cramped, unadorned room, staring at a good-sized wooden partner's desk stuck like a sentry post right in its middle. Behind which sat a precise little white woman, her back pulled up to attention, ramrod straight.

'What you want?' Said in a husky voice that seemed redolent of some deep, strong substance, either good liquor or bad cigarettes.

Regina took a deep breath, plastered a smile on her face, strode over, her hand held out.

'I am Regina Mary Robichard,' she said. 'And I would like to speak with the district attorney for a moment. I'm sorry I don't have an appointment.'

'About what?' said the woman. Maybe more curious than actively hostile, but with nothing about her that indicated *May I help you?* either. Regina drew her hand back.

The woman had on a blue linen suit with a piece of white lace pinned, corsage-like, to its shoulder, hair gray as gunmetal, lipstick bright as fire. Sixty years old if she was a day. A gold sign perched on her desk proclaimed her as Miss Tutwiler. Which was a relief to Regina. Not a full day in town yet and already she'd noticed a subtle social distinction between somebody you called Miss Mary Pickett or someone you addressed as Miss Calhoun. *Miss Tutwiler*, spelled out, left no room for equivocation. This was further emphasized by a crisp THE RECEPTIONIST written beneath.

A model of secretarial perfection but . . . It was early. And Miss Tutwiler, maybe, a trifle inattentive. She'd passed over a pin curl. Smack in the middle of her forehead, the steel bobby pin in it winked out from surrounding corkscrew curls like a third eye. Regina wondered if she should point this out, if that would be the polite thing to do. But Miss Tutwiler's scowling face did not seem to welcome a warning.

So Regina repeated, 'Mr Duval. I'd like to see him, if you don't mind.'

'Well, I certainly *do* mind, and I'm sure he would, too,' said Miss Tutwiler. 'If he were in, but he isn't. Nobody here now but me.'

Just then the telephone jingled. Without taking her eyes off Regina, Miss Tutwiler reached down and picked it right up. 'Well, good morning to you, too, Mr Blodgett,' she sang out bright as a bird into the Bakelite receiver. 'He sure is. I'll get him right on.' She punched a button on her desk. Regina heard the echo of a buzzer behind a closed door.

'What you want?' This from a man's voice, a deep rumble that sounded decidedly like Miss Tutwiler's did – same accent, same brine.

'Mr Jackson Blodgett on the horn for you, Forrest.' Then she turned back to Regina, her small eyes narrow, a decided smirk on her tight little lips. 'What, you still here?'

Laughter echoed out from behind the closed door. *Two* men there. Right behind it. Obviously 'Forrest' was one; she wondered about the other. Could it be Bed Duval?

Regina drew herself up, ready for battle. But then she remembered the Confederate flag. She could almost hear it snapping just outside the office window. This was not the place, nor the moment, to get righteous, not if she wanted to help Mr Willie Willie.

'If you don't mind, I'll wait.'

'Outside,' Miss Tutwiler said matter-of-factly. 'No place for your kind to lollygag around in here.'

Regina glanced pointedly over at six empty straight-back chairs that were lined up like lemmings around the walls, old *Saturday Evening Posts* sprinkled on tables beside them.

Miss Tutwiler saw where she was looking, shook her head. 'You gonna wait outside or I'm gonna call the police. Those are your options. Choice is up to you.'

Well, wasn't this what Regina had expected? She headed toward the door but paused with her hand on the knob and turned around to face the righteous Miss Tutwiler.

Should she or shouldn't she?

She decided she should.

'Oh, by the way,' said Regina Mary Robichard, Esquire, all innocence. 'I thought you might like to know, you missed a bobby pin. Unfortunately, it's sticking right out in the front of your head. Normally I wouldn't think to mention it, but – it just *ruins* your appearance.' She drawled the words out, slow and easy, and hoped she sounded Southern. Like this was said by a Negro who *belonged* here.

Miss Tutwiler's hand flew up. It had a life of its own, she couldn't stop it. The surprised 'Oh!' of her mouth almost exactly matching the metal errant 'Oh' of the bobby-pinned curl on her head. Regina turned away quickly. She didn't want Miss Tutwiler to see the twitch of her own wicked smile.

But outside, in the sunlight, her triumph lasted all of thirty seconds. That was the amount of time it took her to realize she was, again, back on the street. She blinked into the bright sunlight and turned back to the door she was certain closed her off from Bed Duval. In there with his father . . . Well, the both of them would have to come out sooner or later. She'd just sit down and wait.

Trouble was, she didn't know where to sit, or even if she *could* sit. Sitting didn't seem to be racially designated, unlike the drinking fountains in front of the courthouse, which she could easily see from the Duval office steps. WHITES ONLY read the sign over clean, snowy porcelain; COLORED over the rusting spigot right next to it. But the wrought-iron benches that lined the square – who got to sit on them and where? They didn't have anything written on them, no signs. Maybe they didn't need to. They were already filled with old white men deep in animated conversation, with hatted and gloved ladies batting at the still air with palm-leaf fans. There were no Negroes sitting anywhere.

But, sitting or not, everybody – black and white – turned to look at her. Regina saw what she now thought of as the Tutwiler 'O' distorting the features of many a face. Fans ceased fanning; men stopped their talking on the bench. The only person not staring at her was the shoeshine man. *He* was looking down, paying strict attention to every pair of scuffed boots that shuffled past. Regina felt almost as sorry for him as she did for herself. She'd become a spectacle, something she didn't like and wasn't used to being. Who, in New York, stood out on the street? But there was no help for it here, not that Regina could see. She was never going to get into a courtroom with this case unless she found out what had happened with it in a courtroom already. She opened up her purse, pulled out a clean white lace handkerchief – glad she'd brought a few of them with her; they might come in handy – laid it out on the step, and sat herself down. Behind her, the Duval law office remained silent, shut up tight as a tick. Nobody went into it. Nobody came out.

Soon as she was settled, she wanted water, but she dreaded that spigot. She wanted a bathroom, but she dreaded that, too. Who knew where it might be? And even when she found it, what would it be like? She also started sincerely regretting the beige cashmere sweater. It had seemed such a good, heaven-sent way to tweak Mary Pickett's pride this morning, but Regina was burning up in it now. Still, she couldn't pull it off, and she knew it, not when she was sitting on concrete steps, waiting to see the district attorney. *That* wouldn't look professional at all.

She was thinking all this as the wagon pulled up, so close that Regina could hear the crackle of ice melting through the straw that lined its bed, so close she could smell the sharp odor of mule and dusty plank and water-saturated hay stubble. So close she could make out the heady, unmistakable aroma of fresh-from-the-oven peach pie.

Just like what she'd smelled last night, at Mary Pickett's. The wagon seemed familiar, too. And maybe even the mule – or was it a donkey? Who knew? Certainly not Regina, but she perked up. She looked over.

A woman climbed down from the wagon seat – *jumped* down, really – her little black boots hitting the asphalt with a sharp, hollow click. The woman was short and round and looked like a biscuit. Both her skin and her hair that same color, so similar you had to stare hard at her forehead to see where one ended and the other began. She wore a long yellow dress that was stamped all over with tiny, faded pink flowers, with pin tucks and smocking pulling in the waist. It was a riot of a dress, something that seemed created for a late-afternoon tea dance. Ida Jane would have known for sure, but Regina didn't need her mother's sharp dressmaker's eye to see that this costume had certainly not been made to wear on the dusty streets of Revere, Mississippi, at ten o'clock on a weekday morning. Nor, probably, had it been made for this biscuit woman, at least not originally. If you looked closely, and Regina did look closely, you could see that the dress was threadbare at its hem and at the ends of its long sleeves. That it was faded almost white at its armpits; that it was old and that the woman who wore it was old, too – which came as a shock to Regina. She certainly hadn't seemed like an old woman when she'd jumped down from her seat, when she lapped the mule's reins around the hitching post that – *in 1946!* – was still embedded in the street. No, when she did all this, the woman moved with a grace that was ageless as air.

Not looking right or left, the woman walked to the back of her wagon, opened a safe, lifted out four pies, and balanced them down the length of one arm. They were peach pies, golden brown, with lattice crusts thick with the dark ooze of amber fruit juice. Now Regina was convinced this was what she'd smelled at Mary Pickett's last night. She leaned forward, curious.

The woman crossed the street, still balancing the pies, strolled down past the courthouse, speaking to no one, not nodding. But, like Regina, she'd been noticed.

A man called out, 'Hey, Peach? Come into town to get away from the haints out there in the forest? Your brother, maybe? Waiting to call out "boo"? Waiting to get his hands on you, to snatch you baldheaded if he can? Kill you like you killed him? Hey, don't you hear me talking to you, Peach?'

Peach?

There was a Peach in *The Secret of Magic*. Regina narrowed her eyes, looked across the street again, closely this time. The man talking was the one she'd seen last night at the depot, the blond one, the one who'd been playing with the knife. And once again there were other men with him. Three of them. Young. Able-bodied. Ought-to-be-working guys. All white. But here they were, sprawled on a bench, taking the sun at the courthouse. As Regina watched, Knife Man – that's how she thought of him – stuck out his leg, like he meant to trip the woman as she passed. The others guffawed, but the woman stepped deftly around him, curled her lip, went on about her business. While the men catcalled after her, she walked calmly through a door Regina hadn't noticed before but that opened onto something called the Old Jail Café.

Walked through the *front* door, and this was important. It encouraged Regina, who was still thirsty and was starting to get hungry as well. If that woman could walk through that front door, then so could she. Regina got up. She gathered her things and followed the woman to the Old Jail Café. Which was a busy place, people going in and out. Not maybe a lot of them this time of day, but enough. All of them white.

But that woman had been colored, and *she* was inside. Regina had seen her go in. Surely this must mean that the Old Jail Café was a place where Negroes could enter, where Negroes could get themselves something to eat?

Still, something made Regina hesitate. She went up to the window, tried peering around and through the whitewashed letters. But she could see nothing, not really. The sun had angled behind her. It bounced off the dust on the glass, made it opaque. Which meant she couldn't see race. Were there black people inside? She glanced furtively around one last time to make sure she hadn't made a mistake, that this was where that mysterious colored woman had disappeared. It had to be. Except for the door of the courthouse, there was no other. Regina took a deep breath and walked inside.

After a lifetime spent in New York, Regina recognized a diner when she saw one. Red vinyl-topped stools, a chipped white counter, a ringing brass cash register, huge and old-fashioned. Yet . . . she stayed close to the door, her hand never leaving the mesh of the screen, brushing against it to make sure, just in case, that she had a clear way out of here. But the familiarity of the diner smell reassured her. She looked around.

Along the wall there were six small tables, two with people at them. She was looking hard at these people, trying to see if any of them were black – which they weren't – and holding on to the door and looking around for a waitress, and deciding whether or not she should ease out again into the street, pretend she'd never come in here – *Where was that Negro woman? The one they called Peach?* – doing all this at once, when her eyes eased up the wall behind the tables. And she saw the pictures.

Not pictures really. Photographs. Black-and-whites, like the little snapshot of Willie Willie and Joe Howard that she had in her skirt pocket right now. But these had been enlarged, and maybe a tad too much. They were grainy and strung one after the other along the wall by a pyramid of baling wire. And they were a curiosity, nothing to her.

At least at first.

Then she moved a little closer, *edged* closer, really. *Still*, they were nothing – men clustered around a wood platform. Men standing puffed up and tall like they'd done their duty with honor, some smoking, some smiling, all of them looking like they were proud of themselves. But what were they doing? Regina saw two dangling legs, a pillowcase thrown over a head.

What they were doing was lynching folks up.

Daddy. My daddy.

She wanted to but couldn't look away. It was as though the photographs pulled her to them, fascinated her, just like the one of Willie Willie and Joe Howard had done. Close up now, she saw the stars she'd missed before and she realized the men weren't part of the Klan but sheriffs and deputy sheriffs. And what they were doing wasn't called lynching, it was called hanging, because what they were doing was carrying out the law.

'Hangings. Hangings. Hangings.' Regina whispered the word over and over again, as though the saying of it made all the difference. And for a moment it did, at least to her it did. It allowed her to take in air again and to breathe.

'You! Get out of here!' A waitress in a red gingham dress barreled toward her, a pencil in her hand, a grease-splattered short-order cook right behind.

'Get out! Get out! Get out!' Then, 'Nigger!' An afterthought. Called out for good measure.

Miss Tutwiler all over again. Except this time charging forward, quill at the ready, wild as a boar.

But Regina didn't mind. She *wanted* out.

She ran through the door, back across the street – and there was the woman. The biscuit-colored woman with the bright clothes and the pies, the one Regina had followed into the Old Jail Café. Now she was sitting on the concrete step in front of the Duval office. She had a basket on her lap and was calmly regarding Regina's progress through the narrow squint of what Regina now realized was her one good eye.

Not exactly a friendly face, but a Negro one and familiar. Regina homed toward it like a bee to a hive.

She stopped, too breathless to speak, but that didn't matter. The woman was talking, and Regina recognized the voice, had heard it echoing up from Willie Willie's living room last night.

'Ain't nothing but a little ol' palmetto bug. How can it hurt you?'

Now it was saying, 'Honey, don't you let those poor crackers get to you. Mess they cook over there – you wouldn't want to eat it, anyway.' And, 'You must be the lawyer Willie Willie kindly told me about. And that Miss Mary Pickett told me about, too, though maybe less kindly. My name's Peach. Peach Mottley. I bake pies. Do laundry, too, but that's a different story. I live way out there in Magnolia Forest. But then you must know all about me. Willie Willie said you read Miss Mary Pickett's book.'

'Miss Mary Pickett's book?' Regina echoed. So she'd heard that knife man right. Regina sat down. 'Peach Mottley . . . The one who killed her brother, Luther?'

'*Might* have killed him. But I guess, after all this time, it's the same.' Peach shook her head when she said this and lifted her lips into something that just *might* have been a smile.

Regina couldn't help herself. Lawyer or not, she reached out a tentative hand to make certain that this woman was real.

Peach chuckled.

'I'm solid, all right. Just as solid as that courthouse standing over there. Old as it, too, I reckon.'

Her smile deepened, and when it did, Regina noticed a deep scar on the woman's face that welted down from her ear to her lips. Three of her front side teeth were missing as well. Regina wondered what had happened to her, and if it had been an accident. In the book Luther had been violent, had been scary. But Regina knew she couldn't ask, just as she couldn't ask Peach if she dyed her hair, either, though sitting this close to her, Regina clearly saw the white roots. An old woman, a scarred woman, but if Peach was self-conscious about any of this, it sure didn't show. And Lord – did she smell good! Like herbs in a garden and spices in a cake. Like sunshine and lavender. Like Central Park after a good spring rain.

Regina said, 'She wrote a book about you and used your own name in it?'

'Why wouldn't she?' Peach looked incredulous. 'It's my story, isn't it? Not much made up.'

'But . . .' Regina wondered how she could put this. 'It's about murder.'

'Ah, murder,' said Peach. 'Isn't that why you're here?'

'To find out who killed Lieutenant Wilson.'

Peach shook her head sadly. 'Honey, everybody in this town knows the answer to that. You'll learn it, too. That is, if you stick around long enough and the answer don't kill you.'

The square hushed around them. They could have been the only ones in it. The knife man, the one who'd tried to trip Peach – he and his friends gone now. Disappeared.

'Who killed him?' It was a whisper from Regina but . . . what did she mean? Who killed Joe Howard? Who killed Luther Mottley? And who was this woman, come out of a book and talking to her?

'Will you tell me?'

When Regina said this, Peach looked over, squinted slightly as though all she wanted to do was take in part of Regina and leave the rest of her out.

'Maybe I could tell you, but I won't, and for the same reason

115

nobody else is going to tell you, either. And believe me, everybody knows who did this, but ain't nobody gonna come right out and say it. They're just gonna keep inventing little diversions, conjuring down folks like you from New York, hoping time will heal a scab over the sore spot. Hoping Willie Willie will forget – which he won't. Or decide to leave well enough alone – which he might. He *trusts* Miss Mary Pickett, good or bad, always has. But all this magic thinking and wishing not gonna do one bit of good. Something like this, the races involved, the only way it goes is from bad to worse. Me, I passed by my worst a long time ago. I don't want to go back to it. No, no, no. Can't go back.'

But there must have been something about Regina that arrested Peach, because the scar on her face suddenly gathered up to her eyes again as she smiled.

'Tell you what I can do, though, for you, and that's lay out a trail. You know, like Hansel and Gretel into the woods. Ask Miss Mary Pickett about that colored boy sat next to Joe Howard on the Bonnie Blue. His name's Manasseh Lacey. He won't count for nothing in the law, that child, but at least your knowing about him will show you found *something* out. To Miss Mary Pickett, that is. She'll know you mean business. She'll think you might just find out something else. Then once that's established, ask her about Miss Anna Dale Buchanan. She's a white lady. And you can believe ol' Peach on this one. Mrs Buchanan is the reason you're here.'

7.

The Mottley sisters, Peach and Sister, baked their pies and their cakes early most mornings, in the out-back brick kitchen that their daddy had built. The cakes stayed the same – lane, coconut, and a very rich Lady Baltimore were their specialties – but they changed their pie making with the season: peach in the summer and fall, pear in the winter. Sweet potato was the only one they made all year long.

Luther, their brother, carried the pies into town to his store, where he sold them. Actually, it was the sisters' store, too. Their daddy had left it to all three of them. But that wasn't something Luther liked brought up, and so the sisters didn't bring it up. Luther could be mean if you crossed him. He could beat you up.

'Didn't I have my own life in New Orleans? Didn't Daddy call me back to godforsaken Mississippi to take care of the godforsaken pair of you two?'

This wasn't exactly what had happened, why exactly he'd come back home. But after two months of his being there, the sisters knew enough about Luther not to cross him, to get on with life and just do what he said.

So they baked the sweet potato only once a month even though they could have sold out every day, if they'd wanted to. But the once-a-month way was how things were done back then, or else how Luther had wanted them done. The way things were done or the way Luther wanted them done – to the sisters it became the same thing.

There was something about Luther that didn't want folks to have what they wanted. He'd always been sly like that, even before his daddy called him home to take up the store and his sisters. Luther called this his 'exclusive way of doing things.' Peach and Sister called it something else.

Were these the exact words? Regina didn't know for sure, but she'd just read them, or something very much like them, in *The*

Secret of Magic, and so she knew they were close enough. The idea was, anyway.

And the idea was that . . . good heavens! There was a real Peach Mottley! She existed. She hadn't just been made up in a book. And if *she* was real, what else was real? Were Collie and Jack and Booker real? Was Daddy Lemon real? Could he be – Willie Willie? This thought struck Regina as a tingle up her arm. But it also made sense.

If there were a monster in the story, it had sure been Luther Mottley. But Luther Mottley had ended up dead, or 'disappeared,' as M. P. Calhoun had so delicately put it, while making sure her meaning was abundantly clear. How he'd got 'disappeared' nobody knew. At least in the book they didn't. And by *The End*, the children who'd gone looking for him, or what remained of him, never found out the answer because by then they had other things on their minds. Just as there were other things on Regina's mind now, as she hurried quickly along the rut-filled sidewalks that led back to Calhoun Place.

'His name's Manasseh Lacey,' she said, breathless by the time she got to Mary Pickett. 'He was sitting next to Joe Howard on the bus. You know, that last night.'

'A colored boy?'

Regina colored herself. 'Yes. A Negro.' As if that made any difference, though she was coming to realize that it might.

'How old?'

'Maybe ten.'

'And who told you about him?'

'Peach.' Then deliberately, 'Miss Peach Mottley. Like in your book.'

Mary Pickett had been standing on her back veranda, busily arranging champagne-colored roses in twin blue-and-white vases. She cocked her head to one side, pursed her lips, made a slight adjustment. Only then did she look up.

'I knew you'd read it,' said M. P. Calhoun, considering Regina in the same practiced way she had just considered her flowers. 'You had that *Magic* look about you. I can always tell someone's read my book first time I meet them. Dinetta! Come on out here!'

Please. Dinetta, *please.* You say *please* to the people who work for you. Regina so wanted to correct Mary Pickett's bad manners, but she held herself back. Because, please or no please, the screen door flew open and there was Dinetta coming on out.

Up close, she looked even younger than Regina had suspected, thirteen years old at the most. Way too young to be wearing a too-big gray uniform and too-small run-down oxfords – the little toe cut out of them; she must have wide feet – and no socks. Working when she should still be in school, thought Regina. She made up her mind once again, to have a little discussion about this with Mary Pickett soon as she could. Just not right this minute.

Mary Pickett said, 'Dinetta, take these on in the house. Put them in the morning parlor.'

Dinetta nodded, said not a word as she, careful not to look in Regina's direction, slipped back into the house once again.

Mary Pickett turned back to Regina. A fly buzzed close. She waved it away. 'Talking to a colored child, that's not gonna help you.'

'What *will* help me, Miss Calhoun?'

'Nothing,' said Mary Pickett.

'Then why am I here?'

'I already *told* you that,' replied Mary Pickett, like she could have been talking to a child. A servant. A slave. 'To *conciliate* Willie Willie. I want him to realize I'm doing everything I can to help him out, and I am. But my willingness to help's not going to change any outcome. Joe Howard, bless his heart, is dead, but Bed Duval's not, and he's got a tricky election coming up. Everybody hates Judge Timms, at least behind his back they do. Folks all say he's corrupt and a slacker, but when it comes down to it, they vote for him just the same. All his years in office – Judge Timms's built up a lot of connections. He can make life miserable for you if he wants to. Bed's already stuck his neck out, calling up that grand jury in the first place. His daddy's not going to let him do more.'

A grown man, and his daddy *won't let him?* But Regina Mary Robichard, Esquire, let this pass.

Instead, she said, 'But Peach told me Manasseh was sitting right by Joe Howard when those men took him off the bus. She won't tell me how she knows this, at least not yet, but I'm sure that child saw something that could identify them, something that will help us.' Regina considered. 'Or perhaps I should say, something that will help me.'

'That's even worse,' said Mary Pickett. 'And could be worse for him – that child – most of all. His people won't let him talk to you. I already told Peach that.'

'Then you knew about him.' Regina's voice pitched so low she barely heard it herself.

'Of course I knew about him. This is *my* town, isn't it?' said Mary Pickett.

Mine again, thought Regina. *Does this woman think she owns every single thing in sight?*

But Mary Pickett was still going on. 'Most nights after she's finished delivering, Peach'll stop off before she heads back out to the forest. She was here, right there in the kitchen, when you arrived last night.'

'She told me that. She said she was the one who came over to the cottage.'

'Indeed, she was,' said Mary Pickett. 'Telling you what to do about that palmetto bug . . . That would be Peach, all right.'

'Okay. I can understand about Manasseh Lacey and how talking to him would be dangerous for him,' said Regina. She exaggerated her shoulders, up and down, into a shrug. 'But what about Anna Dale Buchanan?'

You had to give it to Mary Pickett, she was a master at holding on to her feelings. She wasn't about to give anything away. A little tightening of the lips, a little loss of color, that was all.

'I imagine it was Peach told you about her, too.'

'Only because she assumed you already had. From what Miss Peach said, Anna Dale Buchanan is the reason I'm here.'

Without a word, Mary Pickett turned back to her flowers. Only after a moment of concentrated arranging did she deign to look up again. 'She lives across Main Street, over on Southside. She came to me about a month ago, after Jackson put that snippet in the paper about the grand jury. It was just a little thing and I don't know why he did it, but it got her attention. You see, she was on that bus with Joe Howard.' Mary Pickett paused. 'And she's white.'

'That's what Miss Peach told me. I'd like to speak with Miss – or is it Mrs? – Buchanan.'

'Mrs. She's a widow. Had an only son, but he got himself killed off in the war.'

'I'm sorry,' said Regina, but she was eager. 'How can I reach her? Is there something . . . I don't know . . . a telephone book?'

'A telephone book in Revere? For what?'

'So I can get her address. I need to talk to her.'

'You don't need her address. I'll take you over there myself.'

'*Take* me?'

'It's only right.'

Now, this was a surprise, but Regina recovered. 'When can we go? Later on today?'

'I'm busy today.'

'Tomorrow, then? In the morning?'

Mary Pickett had started sweeping gardening detritus from the veranda table into a paper grocery shopping bag at her feet. Now she stood up, tall as Regina, and for a minute they looked at each other eye to eye. 'Tomorrow. I'll come for you when I'm ready. Wait for me in the cottage. I'll get there early as I can.' Then, with the slightest lowering of her eyelids, 'Mornings I always work.'

Work? At what? A new book? M. P. Calhoun writing again after all these years? And she, Regina Mary Robichard, the first to know it, at least the first in New York. For a moment this eclipsed everything else in her mind and she thought briefly of calling Walter Winchell's office and sharing the news. Surely they'd be interested, and it might come in handy someday to have Walter Winchell owe you a favor. But then Regina realized Mary Pickett hadn't actually said she was working on a new book. She'd just said she was working. Rich as she was, painting her toenails red could have evolved itself into a full-time occupation. Besides, it had been a long time now – really, who cared? *Regina* sure didn't. Anyway, that's what she told herself the next morning as she got up.

After the helter-skelter formalities of that first day, Mary Pickett must have decided Regina was fully capable of taking the rest of her meals in the cottage. Alone. When she got downstairs there was a napkin-covered silver tray waiting for her but no sign of Dinetta. She must have slipped in and gone. Regina felt a tiny stab of disappointment. She wanted to get Dinetta alone, talk to her. Maybe even fire her up. Certainly she would have asked about school, where it was and why she wasn't in it. And she might even have hedged around and asked something about Peach Mottley, about the murder – not of Joe Howard but that older one. The one of Luther Mottley, the one that had never been solved. Was this part of Mary Pickett's book true, too – like Peach had been and maybe Willie Willie – or was it made up? This last thought frightened Regina, made her catch her breath – that a story could end without having an ending. That something real could be turned into fiction and then just allowed to disappear.

But her little talk with Dinetta wasn't going to happen, at least not this morning. Regina lifted the napkin. There were eggs, grits, ham, biscuits, toast, bacon, two kinds of jam – one straw-berry, one quince; each carefully denoted by Mary Pickett – a bowl of fruit ambrosia, milk thick as cream, cream thick as but-ter, coffee, tea, a small glass of orange juice. A whole day's worth of food! A week's worth! Regina ate the toast plain, drank the coffee black – her usual breakfast. Then she carried the rest out into the kitchen, put it away into an electrified and humming Frigidaire refrigerator.

Back once again in the little parlor, she settled down to wait. And wait. Toward eleven, she got restless, thought of trying her luck again at Bed Duval's but then decided against it. Mary Pickett might come over while she was gone, and if Regina wasn't there . . . why, her chances of being able to talk with Anna Dale Buchanan might be . . . *Gone with the Wind*. And Regina knew she needed that interview, needed its direction. The clock was ticking and, so far, Anna Dale Buchanan was the only lead she had found.

So Regina remained where she was, glum but determined, looking out through the lace curtains at Willie Willie's window, straight over at the back veranda on Calhoun Place, busy as ever. She watched a parade walk up the steps, go in the screen door, come back out again. Laundry people and dry-cleaning people, the milk man, the egg man, a dressed-up woman carrying a potted flower plant ('Mary Pickett, you in there? Come on out, see what Betty's girl sent me down from Memphis!'), a Negro toting in vegetables from a mule wagon that looked identical to Peach's, or so Regina thought. But, of course, she was no expert. Nobody but the black man bothered to knock, and absolutely nobody paid the least bit of attention to the bell.

And all the time with a key left right there in the lock, unused and maybe unusable. It winked at Regina, made her look over at the cottage door to notice for the first time that there wasn't even a keyhole in it, much less a key. Had she ever slept in a room before, she wondered, without being able to be safely closed in?

It wasn't until about eleven that things quieted down. Regina, still at the window, busy now scratching notes into a Big Chief pad, was struck by the silence and looked out. Willie Willie was there. He and Mary Pickett were sitting on the steps, side by side, a newspaper between them. Dinetta, with a tea towel in her hand, hovered nearby, not really working. Even from a distance, Regina could see that. As she watched, Mary Pickett pointed something out on the page to Willie Willie, and he laughed and she laughed, and Dinetta giggled. Amazing to Regina that the three of them could be laughing together like that.

Regina hadn't seen Willie Willie since he'd dropped her off that first night, but she'd thought he'd come over – secretly, she'd thought this – if for no other reason than to see how she was making out with the case. But he hadn't, and he wasn't now. He was with Mary Pickett. Regina, touching the fragile, old lace at the window, moving it aside just a little, gazed over at them – and felt more alone than she ever had felt before in her life.

Promptly at one, Mary Pickett knocked at the cottage door. She was clearly herself again, her no-nonsense Miss Calhoun self. No 'You-hoo! How you doing?' about her and certainly no more laughter. She had on a suit, hat, kid gloves, her sunglasses. Around her shoulders were draped two dead foxes, sewn together, with their heads still on them, as was the fashion, and with beady eyes that never let Regina out of their sight. Mary Pickett, all business now, carried a trim little crocodile purse.

'Regina?' Rhyming it with *vagina*. 'You ready?'

Regina was ready. She'd been watching. She followed Mary Pickett out into the driveway, toward her museum piece of a car. Regina found she had to hurry to keep up. As it turned out, Mary Pickett had a surprisingly long stride.

But she was no driver. Willie Willie had already told Regina this, and he'd been right. This fact became apparent even before Mary Pickett turned her key in the ignition. Made evident by the fact that she did not see the key, even though it had been left right there, plain as day, in the ignition.

'Now, where in heaven's name . . .' Mary Pickett looked everywhere but the right place. Regina was the one who pointed it out.

She did this from the backseat of the Daimler, where Mary Pickett had placed her, isolated amid splendors of polished mahogany, plush gray velvet, a portable silver drinks caddy, a partially opened partition window. The whole thing struck Regina as highly luxurious. Not a New York kind of luxury, exactly – the car was too old for that, its glory a little age worn, the air inside it faintly clouded with dust – but still, in its way, rather charming.

This pleasant realization remained with Regina for exactly two minutes, which was the time it took for Mary Pickett to turn the key in the ignition and lurch her car out into the street. Which was, thankfully, deserted. As were most of the others she went up or came down. Regina had already noticed how few cars there were on the roads of Revere, Mississippi. It was 1946, she'd thought, and still more wagons than automobiles out and about. Now, holding on to the safety strap for dear life, she was grateful for that.

Not that Mary Pickett seemed to notice. She sailed serenely onward, screeching her tires around the corner onto Fifth Street, killing the engine altogether as she started up again from a stop sign on Main, Mary Pickett waving away at every living soul she passed. Animated again. Calling out, 'Hey there, how you doing?' A few times adding, 'What you know good?'

Nice, thought Regina, *folksy*. But why would such a famous woman want to hide out here? The place she'd been born, yes – but what was the attraction?

The street sign clanged red as they turned off Main Street. Mary Pickett stuck her arm straight out into the traffic. Regina took this to be the sign that she intended to turn left. But they had stopped right next to the stern brick façade of the Mississippi Commerce and Agriculture Bank. Jackson Blodgett's bank. Regina, staring at it, banged her head against the window as Mary Pickett once again careened forward.

'You hurt?' she called out. But she didn't look back.

Finally – or so it seemed to Regina – they stopped on a street that could have been . . . anywhere, Corona, Queens, or Flushing. At least anywhere in America where modest wood and stucco houses were separated from one another by reasonable lawns and well-maintained fences. A place straight out of Norman Rockwell, where tire swings hung from the low branches of elm trees and where baby blankets were scattered like yellow and blue and pink confetti on top of trimmed grass. The compact tidiness of this neighborhood, its ordinariness, came as a relief to Regina. Even though it was different from Manhattan, and way different from Harlem, *The Saturday Evening Post* had made places like this and the people who lived in them seem familiar, like you might know them. This comforting thought buoyed Regina, and she scrambled out of the backseat of the Daimler on a current of hope.

'I guess I'm not much for driving,' said Mary Pickett, 'like I told you. Willie Willie did all the driving for me and my daddy. That and a whole bunch else.'

Not that Regina was complaining, glad as she was to have arrived safely in one piece.

'Did you know her? Miss Anna Dale, I mean, before she called you about what happened on the bus.'

Mary Pickett had started up the sidewalk, but she turned back now, frowning sharply. 'It's *Mrs* Buchanan. And the reason she's *Mrs* Buchanan is that I never even knew this woman existed until she showed up two weeks ago at my front door.'

'That surprises me,' Regina said. 'A town this small – you don't know everybody in it?'

Mary Pickett stretched up taller, bolstered by what appeared to be a healthy dose of civic pride. 'Revere is home to twenty thousand souls. I don't imagine you know twenty thousand people in New York City, do you, Regina?' Still rhyming it with *vagina*.

Regina-Vagina shook her head no, she did not know twenty thousand people in New York City.

This seemed to mollify Mary Pickett. 'Then, as you might say, I rest my case. Actually, I'd never even heard tell of her, if you can imagine. She just called up over to my house one day and said she'd read about what happened to Joe Howard in the *Times Commercial*.'

'Funny,' said Regina. 'I don't recall the *Times Commercial* mentioning his name, at least not in that clipping you sent.'

'They didn't. But Willie Willie had worked for her. That's what she said, odd jobs now and then. He did that once in a while, after the cotton was in and we came back into town from Magnolia Forest. I guess Willie Willie must have brought Joe Howard with him. Anyway, Mrs Buchanan knew who he was. She said she knew what had happened to him, too.'

'But why didn't she go to the sheriff? I mean, wouldn't that be the first place you'd go?'

'She did go to the sheriff,' said Mary Pickett, looking funny. 'But I imagine she'll tell you all about that herself.'

With that, she reached into her purse and brought out a slip of white paper. She looked at it, took off her sunglasses, peered up again, her eyes searching street numbers. Finally, she pointed to a gate.

'That's it,' she said, 'Two-twenty-five Fourth Avenue.'

Fourth Avenue was a street that still smelled more of spring than autumn and, like Mary Pickett's garden, was alive with flowers everywhere. Regina had always thought of fall flowers – when she thought of them at all – as without significant scent. Chrysanthemums, late daisies, geraniums, nothing perfumey about any of them, at least not the ones you got at a florist's in New York. But even this late in October the scent of flowers filled the air, filled the street, filled the neighborhood here in Revere. Regina reached over to a prickly hedge and touched one, a small bright white thing, hoping Mary Pickett wouldn't turn around to see her do it.

What is this? Regina crushed the bloom gently in her fingers and then brought them quickly to her nose. *Heaven.*

'Sweet olive,' Mary Pickett called out. She'd stopped. Looked back. 'It grows wild here, like a weed. Comes from the forest.'

She was standing in front of a morning glory – Regina didn't have to ask about this; she recognized it from a lithograph she'd once seen in a book – trained around an arbor curved over the wicket. When Mary Pickett opened it, there was no squeak. She started off first, but by the time they got to the door itself, Regina had taken the lead. Excitement flooded her forward. Anna Dale Buchanan had been on that Bonnie Blue bus. She had seen Joe Howard. She knew, or could know, what exactly had happened to him.

Regina peeled off her gloves. One fluttered from her hand, landed on the ground.

'Nervous?' Mary Pickett asked, with a smug grin. 'Nothing to be worried about with Mrs Buchanan. She's the one called you here.'

Not me really who called you, but her. Because once she got in touch with me, came over, I had to send that letter to New York. There was no getting out of it. Willie Willie had seen her. He knew what she said. But, of course, Mary Pickett felt no need to re-mention that now.

Instead, she pointed.

The gold star in the front window of Anna Dale Buchanan's bungalow was real, officially and appropriately fringed and sent to her by a grateful government.

'I know you've got to ask your questions,' said Mary Pickett sternly. 'But remember, this woman has suffered a loss.'

Regina bristled. *Southerners must think they're the only ones been raised with good manners!* But Mary Pickett didn't seem to be paying her any more attention. She knocked once, softly. While they waited for the door to open, Regina looked around, expecting that things would be here like they had been for her at Calhoun Place. That there would be a tray laid out on the front porch, or maybe on the back, that had been made up specially and where they would all eat, very politely, because a colored person was here.

Thinking all this as Anna Dale Buchanan swung open her door. She said, 'Miss Calhoun. I am honored.' She held out a hand, and then she turned to Regina.

'And you must be Miss Robichard.' The welcoming hand stretched out again. Regina took it. Then Mrs Buchanan said, 'Both of y'all, please do come in.'

This was the first time Regina'd been called by her last name since she'd got to Revere, and definitely the first time a white person had placed a *Miss* before anything to do with her. She looked over at Mary Pickett. Her face had frozen into a careful, blank mask.

Anna Dale was older than Regina had expected her to be, so old that it was hard to picture her as a soldier's mother. The way her hair fluffed around her head, the simple black dress with its cream battenburg lace collar, the brooch of fresh violets pinned over her heart, laced up black brogues, all this made Mrs Buchanan look as worn and comfortable as one of her horsehair sofas. Still, not the sort of woman Regina would ever have imagined offering her a seat in the living room, not in Revere, Mississippi. But that's exactly what Mrs Buchanan was doing.

'Tea?' said Mrs Buchanan. She'd already laid it out and made it look special. Crisp linens, polished silver, not a speck of tarnish or dust anywhere. Regina had an idea what all this meant. A Calhoun in the house! The walls practically sang it.

'Yes, please,' said Regina and Mary Pickett together.

Behind Mrs Buchanan, on the white mantel, marched a row of studio photographs. Regina counted six of them, the telling of a life. They started with a gurgling, white-gowned baby and a serious-looking couple – older parents, perhaps, that's how they looked, the father already bald. After that, one picture followed another. The baby grew into a child, then a boy and as his expression changed, his smile grew brighter. After the fourth photograph, the father disappeared, but the boy, now a young man, smiled on through his high school graduation right up to his Marine uniform and the end.

Anna Dale said, 'When you lose a son like that, it makes you start thinking. Things that seemed so important before, the way things just are, you find out maybe they're not that way anymore. Or shouldn't be.' Then, 'Would either of you care for something to eat? I have a nice date cake in the pantry.'

A polite no was on the tip of Regina's tongue, but Mary Pickett spoke first.

'Why, that's mighty nice of you, Mrs Buchanan, to offer. I do declare, just yesterday my friend Lucille Pendercross absolutely *raved* to me about your date cake, said it was the best she'd ever eaten. She told me she won one at the last Episcopal Women's Bazaar and that her family was *lucky* there was any piece left for their supper. She'd liked it that much.'

Regina's brow furrowed. *Hadn't Mary Pickett said she'd never heard of Anna Dale until less than a month ago?* But Mrs Buchanan's cheeks glowed a pleased pastel. 'My goodness. Mrs Pendercross said all that?'

'Yes, indeed she did. Why, did you know . . .'

After that, Mrs Buchanan poured tea for them, sliced cake. And the cake was really good. A marvel. Meringue-topped, rich, fruit-and-walnut-filled.

'Delicious,' Regina said as she put her plate on the table, ready to get down to business.

But Mary Pickett had already launched into a polite little story about the various notable cakes she remembered, who had made them, what was in them, where the recipe came from, and how much money at raffle each had brought in. Listening, Regina had to stop herself from fidgeting in her seat.

What about Joe Howard? What about the murder?

In the end, Anna Dale was the one to bring him up.

She wiped her mouth with a tea napkin, looked straight over at Regina, and said, 'I was on that bus with Joe Howard Wilson. I saw what happened.'

Regina sat forward, reached into her purse for a pen, her note-book. Hoping she kept the amazement off her face. *At last! Something!*

'On the bus with him?'

Anna Dale nodded. She put her cup and saucer down onto a small round table, rattling them both.

'You are certain it was Joe Howard Wilson you saw?' Regina asked, just to make sure.

And of course Mrs Buchanan was certain. Joe Howard had come over often with Willie Willie to help out with chores after her husband had died. Joe Howard had played with her boy, Butch.

'My son hunted with him and with his daddy. They all did. Bed Duval. The others. Willie Willie knows Magnolia Forest backwards and forwards. With him leading them, the boys could find things – strange plants, Indian relics, Choctaw and Natchez – that nobody suspected even were there. Deer and boar, too. Once even a bear. Wild this and wild that. I can't remember all the strange names Willie Willie gave to things. But Butch did. He

remembered everything. He always said those days with Willie
Willie out in the forest . . . Those days were some of the happiest
in his life.' She stopped. Sighed. 'So, yes, I knew Joe Howard
when I saw him. When I got on there in Tuscaloosa, I knew right
off it was him on that bus.'

'Did you speak to him?'

A quick glance at Mary Pickett. Regina thought, *What am I
missing here?* Anna Dale said, 'No, I didn't do that. I wouldn't
have. It was a short trip, Tuscaloosa to Revere. He was sitting . . .'
Mrs Buchanan squirmed slightly in her seat, but then she lifted
her chin, and now her eyes never left Regina's as she continued,
'Well . . . where he was sitting. In the colored section. I thought
I'd be able to talk to him, ask after him and his people, once the
bus got here.'

'May I ask,' said Regina, 'why you'd gone to Alabama? I don't
want to seem impertinent, but . . .'

'You're not impertinent. I'd gone over to visit my sister in Tuscaloosa,' said Anna Dale. She'd been sitting rigidly in her chair
but now she eased back into it, 'and I was coming back home on
the Bonnie Blue. They took a different route than they normally
did, stopped the bus in Aliceville, where they kept all those German POWs. That's where the trouble started – in Aliceville.'

Anna Dale Buchanan told it all. How she'd seen Joe Howard
first when he got on the bus in Tuscaloosa, the medals, how he'd
got off, got on again in Aliceville, the prisoners, the little colored
boy who was sitting beside him . . .

Regina thought, *That must be Manasseh, the child Peach told me
about.*

'. . . And two other little boys – white ones. Twins, it looked
like. Their mother knew the bus driver, at least she talked to him
like they already knew each other. I don't know where she got
off. Maybe here. By the time I got to Revere I was so flustered.
Too flustered. I wasn't paying attention. By then, you know,
they'd taken Joe Howard off.'

Regina writing all of this down, her fountain pen leaking ink, but she didn't open her purse to forage for another. It might distract Anna Dale Buchanan, and she didn't want her to stop thinking, to stop talking, to lose the thread of her tale.

'*Who* took him off?'

'Men,' said Anna Dale.

'White men?' Regina's voice was barely a whisper.

Anna Dale nodded. 'Oh, yes, they were white.'

'Did you recognize them, *any* of them?'

Another quick glance at Mary Pickett, who had gone pale as marble, hands folded in her lap, for once not saying a word. 'No. I'm sorry, I didn't,' said Anna Dale, then, 'Not really.'

Not *really*? What did that mean? But Regina decided she'd go into this later.

'How many were there?'

'Five. Six. Maybe more. It was hard to tell. Some of them stayed outside.'

Regina went back. 'Not their faces . . . But did you recognize anything else?'

A pause, then, 'Shoes. One of them had on a mighty nice pair of boots for someone . . . Well, for someone like that.'

Regina had no idea what 'like that' meant, so she asked.

'Bad folks. That . . . element. No account. Masks on their faces.'

'Masks? As in the Klan?'

'Maybe. Or maybe they just wanted to puff themselves up, pretend they were in something strikes fear like the Klan.'

'But why would they do that?'

'I don't know . . . Maybe they were just . . . jealous.'

'Jealous?' said Regina, completely dumbfounded.

'Men are coming home with medals on them, talking about veterans' rights. Black men coming back like that.' Again, Anna Dale hesitated. 'Some white men, they're not used to that. You know the type. They do what they've always done under the circumstances.'

'So they *were* in the Klan?'

'No. No, not really.' Mrs Buchanan was getting flustered again. 'But masked. Not with *sheeting*, though, flour sacks.' As if this made a difference. 'With holes cut out but not lining up, if you know what I mean. Eyes weren't always where they should be, noses, either. Like things had been put together real quick.'

'And you? What about you? How did you feel? What did you see?'

'Well.' Anna Dale sighed. 'I was appalled. The whole thing was a shock, even Joe Howard's part in it. Like I told you, he cussed. But soon as I got off the bus, I went straight to Rand Connelly. He's the sheriff. He knows me. His granddaddy and my daddy used to small farm near each other out there in the county. I told him Willie Willie's boy had been taken off the bus at the state line. That part of Alabama – it's home to some rascally types. I told Rand he'd better start looking for Joe Howard before some-body did something we'd all regret.'

'Did he – the sheriff, I mean – ask you if you knew any of those people? I'm talking about the ones who took Lieutenant Wilson off the bus?'

'I told him I had my suspicions.'

This was new. Regina looked up.

'Suspicions?'

'It was those shoes. Nobody has hand-tooled boots like that here, not normal people. Mississippi's a poor state. And then' – the room tensed up around them; Regina could *feel* Anna Dale not looking at Mary Pickett – 'there was the car.'

'The car?'

'A blue Buick. Parked off the side of the road. They hid them-selves, but they didn't think to hide that.' Anna Dale shook her head. *Carroll County folks.*

A blue Buick parked by the side of Mary Pickett's house. Jackson Blodgett's car. That's what Willie Willie had told. But Jackson Blodgett involved in something like this – a rich man who still sent flowers and candy to Mary Pickett? Who had been married to her? Surely that made no sense.

Regina said, 'But you didn't see a face, so you couldn't be certain.'

Anna Dale's lips tightened. 'That's what the sheriff said when I told him. "Now, Miss Anna Dale, you didn't really see much, and you wouldn't want to libel somebody, now, would you?"'

'Mrs Buchanan, but once you'd talked to him, what happened?'

'He told his deputy to put me in that little Ford patrol car they got and carry me home.'

Regina decided to try again. 'I mean, Mrs Buchanan, what did he do about Joe Howard?'

Anna Dale Buchanan shook her head. 'I just told you – he had his deputy put me in the car and carry me home. That's what he did. The sheriff – Rand Connelly's his name, but I imagine I already told you that. Anyway, he didn't speak a word about Joe Howard. Didn't ask me one question. When the deputy took me to the car, I looked back and saw Rand leave the jailhouse. I saw him take off down the street.'

'Do you have any idea where he was going?

'I don't *know* where he was going,' said Anna Dale. 'He didn't tell me. But I imagine, given the direction he turned in, he was on his way to the *Times Commercial* building down Main, and if he was on his way there, he meant to see Jackson Blodgett.'

Regina looked up. The ink smudged on her finger had taken on the irregular smear of a bruise. 'It's been a year. What made you decide to tell all this to Miss Mary Pickett now? I assume you did tell her everything you've just told me.'

Anna Dale hazarded a brief glance at Mary Pickett, who nodded. Barely discernable, but Regina caught it.

'I did,' said Mrs Buchanan.

'Then why come forward now?'

'I read in the *Times Commercial* about the grand jury, and I knew they were writing about Joe Howard. There wasn't that much, just a thimble full of information, but it was him, all right. And I knew they – the sheriff, and probably the district attorney – knew I'd been on that bus, but nobody had called me to testify, nothing like that. I thought the whole thing had just been, maybe, forgotten. That's usually what happens. In those cases.' Anna Dale stopped, coughed discreetly. 'But when I found out it hadn't, I thought it best to get in touch with Miss Calhoun.'

'You called Miss Calhoun before you checked what the district attorney knew, or didn't know?'

'Willie Willie *works* for Miss Calhoun.'

'No, he doesn't. Not anymore.'

'Well, he used to. As far back as anybody can remember, he always worked for her, for the Calhouns. That makes her responsible,' said Mrs Buchanan, as though this explained everything. 'Besides, by the time I told her, I'd already tried telling the others. They knew all about me. The sheriff did; that means the rest of them did as well. But no one cared what I had to say. They didn't want an eyewitness. Honey . . .' She shook her head. 'Weren't you listening at all?'

Yes, Regina had been listening and listening hard. She followed Mary Pickett out into the hallway thinking that she probably wouldn't call Thurgood with this. It was still too early, everything nebulous. But she would find a way to get in to the district attorney. Something had made him ask for a grand jury investigation, and something had made Judge Timms call one. In Mississippi. Where 'those cases' were never prosecuted. So she'd try again at Bed Duval's office. And there were those children – the two white ones with their mother, the little black boy who had sat next to Joe Howard. Mary Pickett had pooh-poohed the idea that he'd be any help. But Mary Pickett had already shown a marked tendency to want to hide a lot of what she knew. Even now, standing in the hallway, her hand had beaten Mrs Buchanan's to the front doorknob, as she tried ever so hard to be extra-polite through clenched teeth. *Lovely cake. Wonderful tea. Hope to see you again shortly. Thanks so much for your help.* Mary Pickett desperate to get out of there. Regina could tell.

But maybe Anna Dale couldn't. She excused herself – 'For just a second. If you don't mind.'

Anna Dale hadn't quite turned her back before Mary Pickett wiped the smile from her face. There wasn't much to see in the small hallway – a table, a Dresden shepherdess lamp, a Blue Boy reproduction near the stairway – but Mary Pickett did her best with what she had. Everything got a thorough scrutiny, her full attention. You'd have thought she was in the Louvre.

Regina wasn't fooled. Cool as a cucumber, she thought, or at least that's what Mary Pickett was trying to be, but she was no noir heroine, no Veronica Lake or Gene Tierney. Mary Pickett's face was far too open for that. It gave things away – maybe not everything, but enough. And there had been something about that car. *Something* about it had surprised her, had shocked her, even. Regina could think of only two things. Either Mary Pickett had known about that car and hadn't wanted Regina to know about it or else what she'd heard had been a disagreeable revelation to Mary Pickett as well. Easy enough to find out which, though. A simple call to Mrs Buchanan, a private one, following up, should tell her what she needed to know.

When Anna Dale came back she was clutching a copy of *The Secret of Magic*. It was just like the one Regina herself owned, a first edition. She recognized it right away as Anna Dale held it out to Mary Pickett.

'Miss Calhoun, if you wouldn't mind? Of course, I couldn't get it here in Mississippi, the banning and all.' Mrs Buchanan's cheeks turned rosy as she said this. 'I had a cousin send me a copy from a nephew stationed at the Presidio in San Francisco. I wonder if I might get you to affix your name to it?'

'Why, I'd be right honored, Mrs Buchanan,' said Mary Pickett, a bit rosy herself as she searched in her purse for a pen. The tension had disappeared off her face. If anything, she looked faintly amused, as she flourished a tidy BEST WISHES! M. P. CALHOUN onto the flyleaf.

'Thank you so much,' whispered Anna Dale. 'I don't know what's wrong with those folks down Jackson. Yours was just a *feisty* book. I loved it. Just loved it. Those children. That mischief. That Jack. He reminded me so much of my Butch.'

They were out on the sidewalk now, Mary Pickett and Regina, each tapping along briskly to her side of the car.

Mary Pickett looked down a street where people were pretending not to look back at her, at them. 'It was kind of her to talk to you, kind and maybe a little foolhardy. She'll lose friends anybody finds out about it, that's for sure. And don't for one minute think it's going to make a tinker's damn worth of difference to Bed, to any of them. To the way things will work out in the end. Do you hear me?'

Mary Pickett talking and talking.

Regina nodded. She heard her. And she had questions, too, she wanted to ask. About Jackson Blodgett. About that blue Buick. About that little colored boy, and the white ones, too, for that matter. But these could wait. Anna Dale Buchanan, with her covert copy of *The Secret of Magic*, had seeded something in Regina, the first faint hint of an idea.

By the time they reached Calhoun Place again, the idea had grown into a full-out plan. Regina hurried up the stairs in the cottage to the bedroom and her own copy of *The Secret of Magic*, which was still on the little blue-painted bed table where it had been laid. As she snatched it up and saw a parcel. Brown-wrapped, string-tied, it lay stark against the worn chenille spread. Left on the pillow so it couldn't be missed. Regina reached out for it and, as she did, looked quickly around to see if whoever had left it might still be there. She felt her flesh crawl, couldn't tell if this came from fear – or anticipation.

But no one was there with her. Not a sound from the cottage except its own creaking, so she reached over, undid the simple bow of twine, pulled back the wrapping, saw the shirt for the first time. Again, she glanced around, and again she saw no one. She wondered who had put this package here, how this shirt – dazzling as snow against the brown earth color of its packaging – how exactly it had gotten here and what it might mean. Frowning, she lifted it up, shook it out. It had been so heavily starched that there was a crinkling sound and some few flakes floated away when she did this, falling from the creases along which it had been folded. Creases so crisp they looked like they had been carefully ironed in to stay. She'd seen lots of white shirts since she'd come to Revere. A long-sleeved white shirt seemed to be the uniform of the Southern male, black or white. But this one was different. She saw that right away. The fabric better. The detailing more precise. The buttons silver – or at least silvery. Whatever they were, they were bright.

Only one thing wrong with it, but this one thing was glaring. There was a button missing, the third one down from the top. It had been lost someplace, somehow, and not replaced and the loss was made glaring by the two rust-colored splotches that had taken its place. Hardly bigger than quarters, they were free-form and jagged, and reminded Regina of a child's finger painting. But not *quite*. She had no idea what they were. Regina leaned closer, smelled Fab detergent and bleach. Clean smells. Still, the shirt wasn't exactly what she would call clean, not with the free-form of those smudges on it. Frowning, she lifted the shirt closer. That's when the note fell out.

It had been hiding within that brown paper parcel, maybe wrapped up in the shirt itself, surely concealed by it. The paper it was written on was old, yellowed by age and dried out by it, with embossed pink and blue roses along three of its sides. Everything in the pale colors that brought to mind fading. Especially since they framed words that were stark black with new ink, but as clear and forceful as Mary Pickett could have written out in her perfect Palmer penmanship hand.

Hide Me.

8.

Next morning, Regina showed up so early at the Duval law offices that even Miss Tutwiler had yet to arrive. Eight o'clock sharp. She heard the courthouse bell pealing. The door was unlocked, as she had suspected it would be, so Regina went directly in and perched lightly on the edge of the waiting-room chair nearest the desk.

She was still there when Miss Tutwiler came in through the back. The receptionist whistled – 'I'll Be Seeing You,' something they'd played all the time when the war was on – as she opened the shades, picked the mail from under the slot. Only when Miss Tutwiler straightened up – 'Oh, Sweet Jesus. My poor back!' – did she catch sight of Regina . . .

'You again!' she exclaimed, mouth widening, eyes narrowing; this morning all her pin curls carefully undone. 'You better haul your butt on off that chair and out that door, and I do mean right this minute. I already told you once. I'm not studying to tell you again!'

Naturally, Regina Mary Robichard, Esquire, no longer quite so fresh from New York, had expected this reception. She said, 'When the district attorney gets in, please tell him I'd like to see him. I'll be waiting for him out front.'

With that, she nodded politely and stepped back into the sunshine, where she noted with satisfaction that the square was filling up. *The more, the merrier*, she thought grimly, anticipating what was to come.

Last night, watching out for palmetto bugs, she'd searched until she found what she thought might be a safe hiding place for the shirt, which was hard in a cottage that had no built-in closets and no bureaus or wardrobes with drawers. Finally, she discovered what she thought might be at least a good enough place behind an old barkcloth curtain – green palm leaves fronting a tan background – that covered the lower pipes under the kitchen sink and hid Dutch Maid cleanser, and a box of Ivory Flakes detergent, bottles of lye and Three Seal ammonia and, way in the back, a sack full of rags. She stuffed the shirt in the middle of these. Not the best hiding place maybe, but at least *something*.

It never entered Regina's mind that she might not actually hide the shirt, that she might show it to someone. There was something about the urgency of that *Hide Me* note that made her do exactly as it said. What else could she have done, anyway? Ask Dinetta or Willie Willie? Mary Pickett? *Any of you leave a stray shirt on my bed? Whose is it? What's it mean?* No, *Hide Me* said enough. For now. Whoever had put it there would come forth, would give her more instructions or more facts, of this Regina was certain. Just like she was sure this shirt had something to do with Joe Howard, with her investigation into his death. How important it was, she had no way of knowing – not yet, anyway. And maybe it was nothing, not crucial at all. Maybe it was what it pretended to be, a child's finger painting on a clean white shirt. But she'd hide it anyway and not mention it until it was mentioned – as it would be, and probably sooner rather than later, by the person who had come in her door, come up the stairs, put it on her bed.

But first there was something else that needed doing, and she found what she needed for it under Willie Willie's stained porcelain sink as well – a wicker basket, a blue vinyl-covered thermos. She'd washed them both, filled the thermos with water, put it into the basket beside the pillow Thurgood had warned her she'd need. Then she'd put in the book.

Now, hustled summarily out of the office, and sitting once again on the Duvals' front steps, she pulled out *The Secret of Magic*, a novel still very much banned in Mississippi, or so Anna Dale Buchanan had said. Regina had forgotten her handkerchief here the day before, and it had disappeared, so she pulled out another, settled herself, looked around, started to read:

They were at the very edge of the forest now, but they'd found the right path. Collie was sure of this, and she told them so. It was later than they thought it would be, though. The daytime peepers had stopped their chatter, and the hooty owls were whooing deep down in the woods. This licking close to the river, anything could happen. Good or bad, you never knew which.

'Come on, Booker. Hurry up! You scairt?'

Jack calling out. Collie laughing.

Regina was used to seeing the dusty pink cover of the book in New York – the two blond white children running toward a distant forest, but with Booker turned back, his face captured by the moment. Booker with his dark skin, his devilish expression, his wide-open eyes. A face that hinted at something, never quite gave it away. Yesterday at Anna Dale's, Regina had thought for the first time how this cover might play in Mississippi, the *scandal* of it. Above all, there was the arch of the prominent title and the author's name, M. P. Calhoun, printed big as you please. In front of the Duval office, people walking past slowed when they read this. Both the square and the street hushed.

'Get on in here!' Miss Tutwiler banged open the door. She stuck her head out, shook it with such force that those folks looking would know she was only doing her duty – and that she'd soon have a tale to share with anybody who might care to listen. *Uppity New York Nigra. There she sat, bold as you please!* 'The district attorney said he'd see you. Five minutes. No more.' Miss Tutwiler no longer called him Bed, at least not to Regina Robichard.

Regina sprang to her feet, smoothed down the skirt of her suit. She reached to put the book away into her basket, but Miss Tutwiler was quick as greased lightning. 'Better hand that over. Reading a banned something is *illegal* in the state of Mississippi.

Mr Duval could get himself in a heap of trouble letting you bring that in here.'

Regina gave her the book. Then, immensely satisfied, she followed Miss Tutwiler in through the Duval front door.

The front door – because there was obviously a back one, and it was the back one people must use when they came here. Regina realized this right away. Nobody had passed around her, but the reception area was full. Two white-shirted men on straight-back chairs, staring at Regina through the smoke of their cigarettes, a young woman in a polka-dot dress looking up from a tattered copy of *Look* magazine. Miss Tutwiler sailed through the midst of them, the book's front cover held tight against her prim, buttoned-up bosom. But no one paid the least bit of attention to Miss Tutwiler, not with Regina striding through there.

Miss Tutwiler opened a stout oak door. 'She's here.'

Regina skirted around her and walked in.

She didn't know what she'd expected but whatever it was, it had not included this many people – a young white man, an even younger white woman with a notebook in her hand, an older black man. All of them reverently grouped around the central motif of an aw-shucks country lawyer in his ah-shucks country office, a spittoon on conspicuous display right beside the mahogany desk in case anybody failed to get the *Hey, now I'm just one of y'all* message. Linen suit, dun-colored and a little too light for the season, flourished bow tie, round red face, a vandyke beard so scrupulous neat that Van Dyck himself might have trimmed it – and sharp little eyes that followed Regina's every movement like twin razor blades.

Was this Bed Duval? From what Mary Pickett said, Regina had expected someone younger. She held out her hand to him anyway. 'Thank you for seeing me, Mr District Attorney. My name is Regina Robichard. I am an attorney with . . .'

'Everybody knows who you are, Missy.' The words rumbled out from the man at the desk, cascading against Regina with the force of glass marbles.

He didn't take her hand, didn't look at it, even, and after a moment Regina pulled it back. She cleared her throat.

'I represent Mr Willie Willie in the wrongful death of his son, Lieutenant Joe Howard Wilson. I am here at the behest of Miss Mary Pickett Calhoun.' She added this last for good measure.

'We also know why you're here.' This from the woman. Like Mary Pickett, she had a high, trilling voice; like Miss Tutwiler, she was dressed in dark blue with lace trim.

Nobody had introduced themselves, but Regina flashed a bright smile. 'Are you the stenographer? Would you mind taking notes?'

A current sizzled through the room. Instantly, Regina realized she'd said something wrong. Mighty wrong. That is, if the woman's stony face was any indication, and there was certainly nothing aw-shucksy about the sitting man now.

'Girl,' he barked, his voice pitched so low Regina heard the tick of a clock through it. It sounded like a death knell. 'This here lady is my daughter. And you better treat her with respect if you know what's good for you. Mrs Marjorie Duval Tisdale is a lawyer, come up from Jackson to help her brother get elected judge. Mrs Tisdale is a graduate of the University of Mississippi School of the Law, as is her brother and her daddy and her daddy's daddy before that. And she, Missy, is a proud member of the Mississippi bar.'

'I am so sorry,' Regina said, and she meant it. She wanted to tell this woman how the same thing happened to her in New York all the time, that people were continually taking her for something she wasn't, asking her to take notes, wondering aloud where her steno pad was, so she understood how this woman felt, the frustration. But nobody in this room seemed like they'd want to hear that. So she repeated, 'I'm sorry.'

The black man smirked, Not as sorry as you gonna be, and, for the first time, Regina looked closely over at him. He had on a dark suit and dark tie. Something deliberately chosen not to be noticed, like an undertaker's clothes, she thought. She wondered who he was, but she'd learned a lesson. She'd wait to find out. What was it Thurgood said? '*Assume* makes an *ass* out of *u* and *me*.' Well, she had assumed about Marjorie Tisdale and made an ass of herself. She turned back to the man at the desk.

'I'm here to see about looking through the grand jury report on Joe Howard Wilson's death.' She added, 'If I may.'

'DA can't do that,' said the black man, quick as you please.

'That's enough, Tom.' The older man scowled, waved a hand at him, and then turned back to Regina. 'What did you say your name was again?'

I thought you said you knew. But aloud she said, 'Regina Robichard. I am . . .'

'Let me introduce you here, Regina. Now my name is Forrest Duval. This is my son, Bed. He's a Nathan Bedford Forrest Duval, too. The *fifth*, to be exact. Bed's his nickname, and he's district attorney. My daughter – I imagine you know who she is now. Not likely ever to forget it again. And that there colored man's Tom Raspberry.' No explanation as to who Tom Raspberry was or what he was doing here. 'And like Mrs Tisdale said, we know just who you are. *What* you are, too – and what you aren't, Regina. Like, for instance, the fact you haven't passed over any bar yet. Bar, as in the New York State bar.'

What did that have to do with anything?

'I graduated from Co— from law school this spring.' She thought it best not to mention Columbia, try to stir it into a pot that seemed already filled to the brim with University of Mississippi pride. 'But I have taken the bar exam.'

Forrest Duval swiveled his large head like a lighthouse from his daughter to his son. 'That place, that *Nigra* place, she comes from in New York . . . Why, I imagine it's lousy with lawyers. But all they found to send down here is a teeny-tiny, itsy-bitsy little lawyerette. That don't sound to me like they're serious about our Willie Willie. More like they want to use him for a publicity stunt. The more they can show how bad things are in Mississippi, the more money it brings in for them.'

Tut. Tut. Tut.

'Mr Duval . . .' began an indignant Regina. But the arrow had hit home. The Fund did need money. It always had, and she imagined it always would. 'I've got new information. A woman. A white woman. She saw what happened on that Bonnie Blue bus.'

'What you think? We don't know about her, too?' said Forrest.

His son cut in. 'Why don't you tell us what exactly it is you want?'

Regina turned to him. He was in a white shirt, no jacket, with his tie loose at the neck and his shirt sleeves rolled up. He looked like those men she'd seen walk right past that woman struggling with her child and her baby buggy. He *could* have been one of them, Regina thought. White men looked pretty much the same to her. Not bad-looking, maybe about Joe Howard's age, or the age Joe Howard would have been. She wondered if he'd been in the service. A nice enough face, pleasant, even, but with the same sharp gray eyes as his daddy – eyes that were beaded in on her now.

'I'd like to see the grand jury records. I need to see what they say.'

This time the quick look passed from the judge to his daughter. Their lips pursed together at the same time.

'Something you should know, if you haven't already been told,' said Forrest, 'and that is, judgeships are elected here, and taking on a rascal like Ezekial Timms would be a tough business, even at the best of times. But my boy's moving up. Got to. And he's already stuck his neck out enough on this Joe Howard thing, asking for a grand jury in the first place. I warned him not to get involved. Something like that – you just asking for trouble. Told him it wouldn't do one bit of good, and it didn't.'

All this said for Regina's benefit in Forrest Duval's best better-watch-it-little-lady voice.

Marjorie Tisdale looked over at her brother, both eyebrows knit into one dark slash. She opened her mouth, then shut it again, lips pressed tight. Regina wondered what she had been about to say – this woman who was a lawyer like she herself was, who might understand things, since, without a doubt, she'd been discriminated against herself. What woman lawyer hadn't been? But Regina never found out what Marjorie Tisdale was thinking, because Forrest Duval started pontificating again.

'My son can't help you. The grand jury already turned in its findings. Ain't nothing going to get those folks to change their minds. Tom Raspberry, now . . .' Without turning around, Duval punched a finger toward the black man behind him. 'He's the one handles our colored problems, been handling them for years.' Duval smiled, and his face lit up with mischief. 'You got anything else to say, take your tail over to Catfish Alley. See him.'

Take your tail, indeed! Regina started seething. She was dying to tell Forrest Duval what he could do with his own tail, but how could she?

Instead, she said, 'Thank you for your time,' and turned to the door.

When she opened it up, Miss Tutwiler almost tumbled right in. But the receptionist managed to recover her balance quickly enough to step Regina smartly through the reception room and out onto the sidewalk again. This time when the wooden door to the Duval law offices closed behind her, its click was decisive.

Regina looked down. All her things were still on the step where she'd left them – basket, thermos, pink pillow, her briefcase, her purse. And *The Secret of Magic* was there, as well. It lay on top of everything, neatly arranged beneath a brown paper bag. Miss Tutwiler's work. No doubt about that.

Gathering it all together, Regina started wondering what she ought to do next. Maybe she should go see Tom Raspberry like Forrest Duval had told her. He was a black man, after all; he might help her. Certainly, she wasn't getting very far with the whites. And he'd been there with the Duvals in their office. Which meant he might know what the Duvals knew.

She crossed the street and was halfway down the block when

she heard someone's, 'Hey, there!' But who would be calling her? She kept on going. Then she heard, 'Regina! Hold up!' Regina/ Vagina again. Would these Southerners ever learn how to pronounce her name right?

But she turned back anyway, and there was Bed Duval, and a stocky white man striding along beside him. She waited. Wary. The memory of that woman stepping children into street traffic so white men could pass still fresh in her mind.

'You're a mighty fast walker,' Bed said, hurrying up. Words, Regina thought, used to buy himself a little time. But he didn't seem to need time. He got right to the point.

'I'm sorry about all that back there.'

'Sorry?' She studied him for a second. Fair-haired like his sister, rumble-voiced like his daddy. Maybe trying to be his own man, she decided, but resembling them both.

'Daddy just wanted to save you a whole lot of trouble.'

Oh, God, she thought, another you-got-to-understand-the-way-things-are-down-here lecture from somebody like Mary Pickett who always acted as though she was from 'here' in ways she wanted to be and 'not from here' in ways that she didn't. But Regina had already stopped. Now she might as well listen. He was still the district attorney, after all.

'Nothing in that grand jury file's gonna help you. The whole thing – the convening – was over in fifteen good minutes. Not a serious witness called except for the coroner. I know. I was there.'

Regina caught that qualifying word *serious*, wondered what it meant.

'Maybe,' she said, 'if I could speak to the circuit court judge . . . ? He's the one holds the grand jury docket.'

'You want to talk to Judge *Timms*?' Bed looked around to the uniformed man beside him, whom he'd not introduced. *The sheriff?* Regina couldn't tell. Both men shook their heads. Both men chuckled. Bed Duval lowered his voice. 'He's the one I'm running against, and there's no ornerier man in all Mississippi. You being new here, let me tell you a story. He's been on the bench thirty years now, and I'm his first major challenge. I'm also fresh back from the war, and he's not happy about that, either. He thinks I've brought in new ways. And he's got his supporters, people he's been doing favors for, for a very long time. One day, one of these men – a moonshining owner of one of those little honky-tonks out deep in the county – sidled up to him and said, "Judge, a bunch of us been watching over that young Duval. There's talk he wants to do you out of your Your Honorship." Then just like that, "Want us to kill him?" The person who told me this said Judge Timms shook his head. Said, "Charlie Bob, now, you know killing's against the law." A significant pause. "But if you did happen to shoot him, mind – I mean, if it just happened, an accident maybe – why, you sure can count on getting a fair trial in my court." '

The only reason Regina laughed was because Bed was laughing and the man beside him was laughing, making it seem like being jolly was the thing to do. Finally, she said, 'You make Revere sound lawless as the Wild West.'

Bed quieted down. 'In some ways, I imagine it is. Oh, don't let the softness of our accents fool you. It's an eye for an eye down here.'

People were staring at them now, and Regina's load was getting heavier by the minute. Neither man offered to give her a hand, take any of it from her, which didn't surprise her. She decided to come to the point. 'Why'd you do it, then? I mean, if you weren't going to see it through. Why'd you get Judge Timms to call up a grand jury in the first place? It must not have been easy. Especially when it was pulled back into special session.'

She saw the reaction to her question in his eyes, saw their pupils close in reflex against it. It took him a moment to answer. The other man, his thumbs through his belt loop, said not a word. Then from Bed, 'Judge Calhoun and my daddy and Willie Willie all grew up shooting together. Joe Howard and I used to hunt out in Magnolia Forest. With his daddy. My own daddy came out with us, too.' He paused. 'At first, I didn't even recognize him when they drug him up out of that water. Joe Howard. When I saw what they'd done. The *indecency* of it . . .' Bed Duval's voice trailed off.

Why, he wants me to say it's okay, thought Regina. *He wants me to say, 'Well, you're a good person. You did what you could. What more was there to do? It's not your fault.'*

But she had no intention of saying any of that.

'You thought what happened to him might bear investigating . . . Just not right away.'

Now Bed's eyes snapped with the same better-watch-it-little-lady snap that his daddy had thrown her way.

'Yesterday,' said Regina. 'I met with Mrs Buchanan. You know, the lady we talked about back at your office. She saw Joe Howard taken off that bus, she was on it, and she went right around to tell the sheriff all about it when the bus got into Revere. Now, the sheriff, he wasn't that interested. She hadn't seen faces, you see, Mrs Buchanan. But she had seen a car. A blue Buick. Brand-new, she said. Don't see many of them in Revere do you, Mr Duval?'

She saw him glance around, at the hitched mule wagons, the pickups, the few dusty Fords parked on the square. A quick look, but old Forrest Duval wouldn't have chanced it. He'd never have taken his eyes off Regina. Watching her. Assessing. But this man was young, a young lawyer. *Nothing to be scared of.* That's what she said to herself.

What she said to Bed Duval was, 'Maybe you might want to talk to Mrs Buchanan. Some afternoon. I can tell you she makes a marvelous date cake. But, of course, you already know that. Since, like you said, you and your daddy and the sheriff and Mr Willie Willie and Joe Howard . . . the whole darn town it seems like . . . spent so much time together hunting deer in the forest. So bucolic. Makes all northeast Mississippi sound just like one big happy racial family.'

A *new* young lawyer, she thought again, maybe wanting to do the right thing, but still fueled by bravado and not much else. She knew the type, all right. You bet she did.

She nodded to both men, then turned, started off.

'Can I give you a little advice?' She hadn't heard this voice before, but she knew it belonged to the other man, the man to whom she had not been introduced. *Purposely* not introduced, she thought, as she turned back to him. Makes things scarier that way. Still, she was surprised that Bed Duval had left them, was already halfway down the street. She and the man faced each other, two worn-up squares of city sidewalk between them. He was the sheriff. She saw his star now. He said, 'You're new down here. Don't know how things work. Watch your step. And if I was you, I'd pay a call on Tom Raspberry. Like Bed's daddy told you to.'

His voice wasn't kind but it wasn't mean either.

'Thank you,' she said, as she started on her way yet again.

Regina wasn't aware just when Willie Willie came up, only that he was suddenly there and right in step beside her, reaching out his hand. Next thing she knew, he was taking all the things she'd been carrying. A relief.

'See those there,' he said, bending close to her and pointing to three solitary orangey-red flowers sprouting up on the mani-cured perfection of the courthouse lawn.

Regina nodded.

'Know what they are?'

This time she shook her head. She'd never seen anything like them before.

'Why, they're wild things. Spider lilies,' Willie Willie whispered close to her ear. 'They sprout up like that, full blown, overnight. You couldn't cultivate them if you wanted to, because they're on a mission. They come out specially to tell us when seasons be changing. When summer's all over and winter's nigh here.'

'Really?' said Regina. *Flowers, not only with names but with legends.* 'You know things like that?'

'That,' answered Willie Willie solemnly, 'and a whole lot more. For instance, I know you met Miss Peach Mottley. She told me all about it. Thinks you're smart. Thinks you might be able to *do* something. She wants me to bring you out to her place, back there in the Magnolia Forest. Wants to have a nice talk with you. That's what she said. There's a lot you can learn in the forest, a lot she can teach you. It's all out there, the whole story, and I'll take you right to it – that is, if you can be persuaded to go.'

'Maybe,' said Regina, 'but this case . . . You know, my work . . .'

Willie Willie cocked his head, regarded her. 'I'll tell her you'll come. You're ready. Might learn something useful.' He didn't exactly whisper, but he looked around and dipped his head when he said this. 'Saw you reading Miss Mary Pickett's book out in public, for all the world to see. I recognized the cover. Saw you go into the Duval law office. Saw you come out.' He fell in step beside her, and they walked beneath an overarch of elm trees that shaded the sidewalk. 'Saw Mr Bed follow you out onto the street, bringing the sheriff with him. Now, *that* was a wonder.'

'Rand Connelly?'

'The sheriff. Mr Bed have anything to say for himself?'

'Nothing useful. The sheriff told me I needed to see Tom Raspberry. They *all* told me that, or at least intimated it.'

Willie Willie nodded. 'Those white-folk Duvals – they think they got Tom Raspberry in their pocket. And maybe they do have. Still, it might be worth your while to go on over to Catfish Alley, pay him a visit, hear what he has to say. Him being a lawyer and all.' Willie Willie nodded sagely. Sunlight, filtered through the hanging treetops, fell like lace on his face.

This surprised Regina. 'Nobody said anything about him being a lawyer.' She thought for a second and then said, 'Well, maybe you did before, but he didn't say anything about it himself.'

'Well, that's what he is. At least, that's what he calls himself to us colored folks. An *attorney*-at-law. Written bold as brass on that plate-glass window outside his spanky new building. But he wouldn't want to be seen putting on airs in front of Mr Forrest. He'd get himself slapped down in a minute. That's the nature of things. A colored lawyer in Revere got to piece together a living just like an old woman pieces a quilt, a stitch at a time. He can't just put together a practice out of whole cloth. Lots of Tom Raspberry's piecing involves the Duvals. He lends them his eyes and his ears when they need them. His mouth, too, saying what white folks think needs to be said.'

Regina's step picked up. This was the first time she'd been close – physically close – to Willie Willie since she'd gotten to Revere. And he was telling her something, giving her information that might be of some help. Because he believed in her, thought she might actually be able to do something? She sure hoped so. Without thinking, she canted her head toward his, the same angle as Joe Howard's head in the snapshot she still had in a pocket. She smiled at him, too, just like Joe Howard had done. Willie Willie was tossing something in his hand, catching it again. Up down. Up down. Just like he'd done at the bus depot. Something glittery and tiny, bright as a new dime. It caught at the sun.

Willie Willie said, 'I wish my boy could have been here to see you. He would have busted out laughing, just like I did. I was watching that old lady Tutwiler gawping at you out the window while you were reading that *Magic* book,' he said. 'The whole sight of it was so *rich*. Shook them all up, that much is certain. Not that I think there's any hope of getting law court justice for Joe Howard in Mississippi . . .'

Regina stopped. Turned to him. 'What other kind of justice is there?'

'I don't know. The homemade kind.' He looked off to the distance, to the forest. 'The kind you do for yourself.'

'No!' Regina surprised herself, how strong her voice sounded. 'If you don't get what you want – what you need – under the law, then you really don't get it at all. It can always be taken from you and then the bad folks can do what they want to, and they can do it again and again.'

'Maybe,' said Willie Willie, 'it'll be like that someday. Or maybe Peach is right. You're the one to do it now. Time's gonna show, and we'll see.'

'Not much time,' said Regina. For a moment, she had the sensation that he might reach over and ruffle the hair on her head. Like she was a child. But she wasn't a child. She was his lawyer. And she thought maybe she might ask him about Anna Dale Buchanan – had Willie Willie known about her, like Mary Pickett had and even Peach had? And the sheriff and Bed Duval as well? Maybe the awareness of who she was and what she knew and how this might matter came to each of them at different times – after all, Anna Dale had just called on Mary Pickett when she'd read about the grand jury findings in the *Times Commercial* less than a month ago – but they all knew now. *Surely* Willie Willie would know as well. Was that why the old Blodgett house had been burned, and was Willie Willie behind that? The timing made sense, but nothing else did. A black man – doing something like that in Mississippi and still alive, walking beside her right here on the street? And the shirt, had he been the one to put it on her pillow, to write *Hide Me* on that slip of yellowed notepaper? This gentle man, tossing into the air his small bit of glitter – could he have done that?

She thought of him as she'd last seen him on the back veranda with Mary Pickett and Dinetta, Mary Pickett reading from a spread-out newspaper, the two of them shaking their heads, laughing. Surely Mary Pickett had told him something as important as Anna Dale Buchanan's visit? But Willie Willie had never mentioned her to Regina. In fact, he hadn't said anything to her about Joe Howard's actual death, who he thought might have killed him, how he thought it had happened. Strange. She opened her mouth to ask him about it, the words forming as they rounded the corner. But then she saw Calhoun Place. With a blue Buick parked out in front of it. Maybe the same one that had been sitting there the night she arrived. Maybe the same car that Anna Dale Buchanan had seen. Regina didn't know, not yet, but the car pulled at her like a magnet.

'Is that . . . ?' She turned back to Willie Willie, who was no longer there. He had just vanished, leaving her briefcase and her basket and her book piled neatly under a privet hedge at the side of the road. She wondered where he'd gone, *why* he'd disappeared so suddenly – but for only a moment. Because standing right ahead of her, leaning against that blue Buick, was the same man with blond hair who had stared at her from the porch of the bus depot the day she arrived, the same man who had teased Peach on the courthouse square. She was certain it was.

He wasn't looking at her now, though, not like he had that first day. His eyes were searching out something else, something behind her. Something that caused him to frown. She swiveled back and saw nothing, only the spot where Willie Willie had disappeared.

The Secret of Magic. *Booker and Daddy Lemon alone at the edge of the forest. Daddy Lemon saying, 'You go deep down in there, son – deep enough, past the loblolly and the woody plants and the trumpet vines – you'll find the place where life turns itself upside down and the dark things are the good things and they win out in the end.'*

'Hey, Regina.' The man at the car whispered her name, and she turned to him.

He still wore crisped-out jeans and shirt like he'd worn at the depot. But it was his shoes Regina was most interested in now. She looked down. She noticed. They were boots. Hand-tooled, polished crocodile, they stuck out from the turned-back cuffs of his pants legs like two long, dark tongues.

Good boots. A big blue car. Everything Anna Dale Buchanan had said, but *something* was missing. A man like this – why would he kill?

He said, 'Name's Wynne Blodgett.'

And she nodded. 'I know who you are.' She pieced a little together. 'You're Jackson Blodgett's son.'

'That's me, all right,' he said, chest puffed up. Proud to be who he was. 'He's around back somewhere. Said he'd got something to do, probably for Mary Pickett. But what I've got is for *you*.'

Holding something lacy and white out to her. Her handkerchief, the one she'd left yesterday on the Duval stoop.

She stopped right in front of him, at most three feet away, but she didn't reach out her hand.

He smiled at her. 'I saw you leave it. I thought you might need it again. Sometime.'

'That was nice of you.'

'I'm a nice guy.' Then, 'You gonna come get it?'

She stepped forward, and he shifted, brought his hand back a little so she had to move closer, then moved it once more and drew her closer again. She knew the game they were playing, cat and mouse. She reached over, careful not to touch him, but when she took the handkerchief his fingers brushed against hers and every single horror story she'd ever heard about white men and black women flooded immediately to the very tip-top of her mind.

But she said, 'Thank you. That was kind of you to pick it up.'

'Hey, there,' Wynne said, lips slashing upward into a clown's bright grin. 'Weren't you listening? I already told you I'm a nice guy.'

Mary Pickett was in her back garden, pruning her rosebushes. *Chop-chop-chop.* Jackson Blodgett, whose son and whose car were so conspicuously present, was nowhere in sight. Mary Pickett had on a heavy tweed skirt and an old straw hat, almost as big as an umbrella, eyes hiding out behind her dark glasses. But she knew Regina was there.

'Yoo-hoo! Yoo-hoo!'

Who talks like that? But she walked toward Mary Pickett anyway. 'I saw Jackson Blodgett's son out front.'

Mary Pickett stopped her clipping. She reached up and pulled her sunglasses down. The eyes above them narrowed, cool as cat's-eye marbles. 'Yes. Wynne.'

'He said his father was back here. With you. I'd like to talk with him if he is.'

Regina met Mary Pickett's cool gaze with one of her own. Mary Pickett considered. 'He's around.' And then, 'He's got an old home place near here, burned out now. One of those clippings I sent you talked about it. He might probably have gone down to check on things there.'

The Folly. That's what Willie Willie had called the Blodgett place. He'd waved a hand toward it the night she'd arrived.

'If you see him, would you tell him I'd like to speak with him? Please?'

She started on toward the cottage, but Mary Pickett's soft voice trailed her down. 'You call up north yet? Fill that Thurgood Marshall in on how much progress you made . . .' She paused. 'If any?'

Regina hesitated, turned back. 'I didn't see a telephone in the . . .'

'Right there in the kitchen,' said Mary Pickett, motioning with her big Chinese-looking hat. 'Go on in.'

'Not right now,' Regina said. This came out a little too quickly.

'What? Not got much to report?' Mary Pickett drawled the words out, each syllable taking up the space of two. 'Well, I'm sure you will have. Before your time here runs out. Just go on into the kitchen anytime you want to. I'll tell Dinetta. Keep in mind, though, it's a party line. Half Revere's on it, which means everything you say will be all over town in fifteen minutes. At most. Like you reading my book on the Duval office steps. Believe the *whole* town knows about that by now.'

'I needed to speak to the district attorney,' said Regina.

'You could have spoken with him yesterday, if you'd asked for my help. One call from me – that's all it would have taken. You could have gone straight on in.'

'Through the back door?'

'*Everybody* goes in that way over at Duval's, didn't you notice?' said Mary Pickett, eyes now twinkly bright. 'The back door for you is just the way things are. But your pride's not the point, is it? You're here to help me with Willie Willie. That's why I called you down.'

'But I *came*,' said Regina, 'to find out who killed Joe Howard Wilson. To get him some justice.'

'It's the same difference.'

Regina said nothing to this. A bee buzzed through a potted geranium on a pedestal at Mary Pickett's elbow. She seemed to pay it a great deal of attention. 'Did you enjoy it? My book, I mean. I suppose I should ask you that.'

'Yes,' Regina said, then, 'Very much.'

'Ah.' Mary Pickett's word was short, not drawn out with pleasure. She reached into the pocket of her skirt and pulled out a pack of Chesterfield cigarettes, put one in her mouth but didn't light it. She looked back at Regina instead and said, 'Then you know.'

'Know what?' Regina moved closer, drawn like a pin to the magnet of Mary Pickett's word, *know*. For the first time she thought Mary Pickett might actually be useful, that she might be more than just a proper Southern woman helping a colored man-servant because of some old-timey sense of noblesse oblige. Or of guilt. But then, who wouldn't feel guilty about slavery, about those separate water fountains, about the Confederate flag standing guard over the courthouse door, about that woman guiding her children into the street? About this house, even, built up on slave labor? And about Lieutenant Joe Howard Wilson taken off a bus and beaten to death.

Mary Pickett struck a match to the cigarette, drew deeply on it, exhaled. Caught in the strong crosswind of her exhalation, a bee changed its mind about the attractiveness of the geranium and took flight. Mary Pickett looked over at Regina, her eyes narrow behind a cloud of smoke.

'About Willie Willie.' Another deep draw on the cigarette as Mary Pickett seemed to consider. 'My daddy and Willie Willie grew up together.'

'They were friends? You told me that already.'

Mary Pickett shook her head. The straw hat bobbed. 'You're young, and you're not from here. My daddy and Willie Willie weren't friends. They couldn't be. Friendship is something eye to eye, between equals. Daddy and Willie Willie were *friendly*. Or, rather, Daddy was friendly to Willie Willie – but it was Daddy always in control. Still . . . it's hard to explain their relationship, one to the other.'

'Not so hard,' shot back Regina. 'Your daddy stayed in the big house. Willie Willie lived in the old slave shack out back.'

Mary Pickett folded her arms across her chest. Shut down, that's what she did. First her eyes, then the whole of her face.

'Well, Regina, why don't you haul yourself on over to your own shack and wait for Mr Blodgett there? I'll ring the quittin' time bell for you when he gets here.' The words drawled out, slower than ever – if that were possible.

Regina rolled her eyes. Grimaced. *Quittin' time bell, indeed!*

Without another word, Regina started off toward Willie Willie's, her high-heeled shoes clicking like Dorothy's as she made her way along her own yellow brick road.

9.

Years later, when she thought back to those days in Revere, Regina would always remember Jackson Blodgett as a smile that illuminated Mary Pickett's face. A presence that seemed to actually slow her down, make her look like she was moving through honey, that softened the lines around her mouth and chiseled light from the cold marble of her eyes. It's funny, Regina thought, how just a little movement of the mouth could do all that. No matter how much else would happen, what else would change about him in her eyes, Regina would always remember Mary Pickett's illumination as part of what made up Jackson, too.

Regina was sitting at the desk, staring at them through the lace at Willie Willie's window. They were standing in Mary Pickett's late flowering garden, near the veranda, and standing close. As Regina watched, Jackson reached up and touched a wisp of Mary Pickett's hair.

'Gosh,' whispered Regina to herself, 'I thought Willie Willie said all that was over a long time ago.'

But it was plain to see that it wasn't.

'Regina! That you peeking out over there? Why don't you come on over and meet Mr Blodgett like you wanted?' said Mary Pickett, triumph smooth as a mint julep lacing her voice. *You spying, bad-mannered, no-account Yankee – I'm looking right at you!*

Regina jumped, blushed. *Caught in the act*, but she headed out the door anyway.

Even from a distance, it was obvious that Jackson Blodgett was no matinee idol. Wynne was the handsome one, and he didn't look like his father. Jackson's hair was dark where Wynne's was light, and his shoes were dusty, unlike his son's, like he used them to tramp through his small town's streets. Jackson had on a blue serge suit and held a gray felt hat in his hands. The suit was natty, something Thurgood might have chosen, but the effect wasn't at all the same. Jackson's didn't fit him right. It was a little too wide around his body, a little too short in the sleeves. Something he might have admired on a rack but that needed a tailor. Still, there was something appealing about him – nothing that Regina could put her finger on, not what she'd expected, but there anyway. She thought of Wynne, so beautiful, so sharply and expensively dressed. She wondered just what it might mean to a man like Jackson Blodgett – once poor as dirt, at least that's what she'd heard – to have a son so Movietone perfect as that.

Her eyes traveled from Jackson to Mary Pickett. She wondered what the two of them had been like when they were younger, when they'd run off together. She wondered what they'd looked like when they got married and been caught on the steps of that hotel in Gordo, Alabama, in what Willie Willie had called 'a nick of time.' The young lovers were older now, settled. It was hard for Regina to imagine either of them doing anything rash. Yet here was Mary Pickett just a wee bit flustered and Jackson Blodgett looking – well, glad to be back.

'Mr Jackson Blodgett,' said Mary Pickett primly, but she'd turned rosy. *Was this Mary Pickett actually blushing?* 'May I present to you Regina Mary Robichard. Regina is from New York.'

A great deal was said in that simple introduction, none of it missed by Regina Mary Robichard of New York. She'd been presented to Jackson Blodgett like he was royalty, rather than the other way around. And Mr Jackson was *Mr* Jackson, but there'd been no courtesy title, no Miss or Mrs, not even a 'This here's our Lady Lawyer,' at least for a colored woman down here in the South.

'Good to meet you,' said Jackson Blodgett with a hearty nod that somehow or other seemed a cue to Dinetta. She slipped out through the screen door, childlike, skinny as ever, and carrying a silver tray with two cups, two saucers, two crystal glasses, two decanters – one marked SHERRY – two cloth napkins, and one very large piece of cake.

'Good afternoon, Mr Jackson. How you doin'?' The girl stood there beaming, all teeth, trying hard not to stare over at Regina – this strange black woman from the North – but not quite succeeding. A darted look here, a darted look there, before she disappeared back behind the kitchen door.

It was Mary Pickett who, after a moment, leaned over and picked up a cup and saucer and poured coffee – nothing else – into it. She reached Jackson a fork and the cake. Through all of this moving, all this shifting and pouring, she said not one word. She also did not look at Jack Blodgett, and he was not looking at her.

But they didn't go up to the big rattan table. He and Mary Pickett settled on the porch steps side by side, Jackson propping his shoulder against one of the newel posts. Regina hadn't noticed before that the paint was peeling on the Calhoun banister, but when Jackson sat next to it, she did. He took a sip of his coffee. Mary Pickett did not touch hers. No one offered anything to Regina, who was left standing on the bright green lawn.

Jackson said, 'This your first time in Mississippi, Regina?'

She nodded. 'My first time.'

'You enjoyin' yourself?' And then, before she could answer, 'But of course you aren't. How could you be? You got *business* here.'

Mary Pickett reached for the sherry bottle, poured herself a drink.

Jackson sadly shook his head. 'Haven't had a chance to see much of the town, have you, and Revere is such a lovely place. Not burned down by the Federals. Grant thought it was too pretty to torch. You'll like it once you get to know it.'

'Oh?' said Regina politely.

'Miss Mary Pickett here tells me she called you down here to investigate what happened to Joe Howard.' Jackson sipped his coffee. 'And that's a good thing to do, a *noble* thing to do – if Joe Howard had been killed. But he *wasn't* killed. Now, Willie Willie, he's simple. He makes up things in his mind, and what he makes up isn't always the truth. But the law *is* the truth. You know that, you're an officer of it. And the law said that Joe Howard Wilson's death was an accident.'

He was looking at her now, his face earnest, his eyes shrewd. 'Now, I'm not saying Joe Howard wasn't taken off that bus, 'cause he was. We all know that. But maybe folks – okay, *white* folks, let's be honest here – thought they had their reasons. I heard he'd refused to do what he'd been told to do. I heard he cussed in front of the ladies. My own son – Wynne. You met him? Why, he'd sure get a whuppin' from me for pulling a stunt like that. But' – and here a sigh from Mary Pickett's once-husband – 'who knows what happened to Joe Howard, with the war and all? Sometimes all that hero talk can go to their heads. Soldiers, I mean. They start to believe what they been hearing. Maybe somebody wanted to remind him he was home now, remind him a good Southern boy needs to be minding his manners. So . . . they took him off the bus. They roughed him up. Maybe. A bit. Maybe tried to teach him a lesson for his own good. Once that was done, they would have let him go. They sure would have done that. But . . . What can I say? Joe Howard was disoriented. He got himself lost out there in Magnolia Forest. Fell into the Tombigbee. That makes sense, at least to my way of thinking.'

So what had happened to Joe Howard was his own fault. If he'd just acted like a good boy in the first place, he'd still be alive, none of this would have happened. That's what Jackson Blodgett was selling, but Regina wasn't buying.

She said, 'You seem to know a lot about it.'

'It's a small town.' Jackson's blink was so shallow she almost missed it. 'You hear things.'

'Maybe,' she said, unconsciously echoing his word, 'but it would be a help if I could actually see the coroner's report.'

Jackson reached over to put his cup and saucer on the tray. It was only half empty. Regina saw his quick look to Mary Pickett, the clear *no* in the slight shake of his head.

Nothing to lose, Regina decided to gamble. 'And the grand

jury docket. They might help me prove what you're saying. At the very least, it'll stop any discussion. If I don't get to see the court papers, there will always be a question. That's why Miss Calhoun called me down here – to get to the bottom of this matter, to lay it to rest once and for all.'

Would this be enough? Could she possibly persuade him? She *had* to get her hands on those grand jury findings. Regina held her breath.

'So you're asking me to do something that's against the law – get you a copy of a document that's officially sealed?' Jackson Blodgett chuckled. 'Few months from now, they'll open it anyway. Why can't you just wait?'

'Because it might be too late.'

Jackson nodded, seemed to consider. And then . . .

'I'll see that you get them,' he said as he slammed both hands on his knees. 'Take care of it myself. What's your plans for tomorrow? You gotta have some – come all this way. Maybe Tom Raspberry? You been at the Duvals, you'll know all about him. He and Forrest. Bed, too – they're all three joined at the hip. But I'll have the reports you want waiting for you in the cabin – the cottage – by noon. That sound good? The sheriff will bring it over himself. You'll like him. He's a talker. Folks feel bad about Joe Howard. They want to help.'

Oh, really?

But what she said was, 'Thank you, Mr Blodgett.'

Jackson shook his head, a man who needed to tell a hard fact. 'Killing a colored man's not the same down here as killing a white man. It may be in other places . . .'

'Not always in other places,' interjected Regina.

'But not here, where we're dealing with a certain history, with a certain way that things have to be done,' said Wynne Blodgett's daddy. 'I'll make sure you get what you're needing. I want this thing cleared up. The town wants to put all this behind us. Right away, too. Before someone gets hurt.'

Regina thought he'd look over at Mary Pickett; after all, she was the one who had – for whatever reason – gotten in touch with Thurgood. But Jackson Blodgett did not look at Mary Pickett Calhoun.

'Thanks for your help,' said Regina.

'Nothing at all. Any man would do all he could for a son that he loves. Willie Willie sure loved Joe Howard.' Jackson got up then, one hand on the newel, leveraging himself. He lifted his hat back onto his head. 'Good day to you, Miss Mary Pickett.'

He started off on the swept gravel that led to the front of the house, but his was a slow progress. One leg moved him forward, one leg limped behind. He'd been standing or sitting all the time Regina had seen him, and so she hadn't noticed the limp.

After a moment, Mary Pickett said, 'Infantile paralysis. It got him when he was four, but nobody noticed right away that he had changed, that he was dragging his foot, that he couldn't run anymore. His mama was long dead. His daddy working hard. Not paying attention. The sickness – when it went, it left him like that. I bet that's something Willie Willie didn't tell you.'

No, Willie Willie had not told Regina that. But she wondered as she heard Jackson Blodgett's halting steps, as she almost unconsciously started to count – one, two, three – the slow progression of them, down the lane, over the sidewalk. As she heard the opening and closing of his big car's door. Limping like that, how on earth had he managed to run with the other children into Willie Willie's forest? Or *had* he done this? Had he even been invited to come along at all?

The telephone was right where Mary Pickett had said it would be, in the kitchen. A big, black, old-fashioned thing, attached to the wall, just inside the door. There was a worn white stool beneath it, a container of kitchen matches hooked just to the right of it on the wall, an open package of Old Gold cigarettes on the linoleum counter. Regina had seen Mary Pickett smoke Chesterfields. She wondered whose cigarettes these were. Little Dinetta's? Surely not.

There didn't seem to be anybody around, not Mary Pickett, not even Dinetta.

Across from Regina, on the other side of the room, there was a double door. The top of it opened to the rest of the house. Regina listened hard. There was no sound from beyond the kitchen, no Dinetta humming as she dusted or swept carpets, no sound of Mary Pickett's typewriter keys. Regina grew curious, or even more curious, since she'd always wondered about this house, what was in here. But the thought that if she peeked through, she might find herself looking straight at Dinetta or, worse, Mary Pickett, kept her firmly in place by the back door. Around her, the kitchen gleamed spotless. The Frigidaire hummed, the clock ticked against its own wall, and the whole place smelled of ammonia. There was no sign of any cooking going on. For the first time she wondered if it was Peach who did the cooking, if she came in, specially, some days to do this. Peach had mentioned she did laundry. Did she do Mary Pickett's, and did she do it here?

Regina picked up the telephone receiver, asked politely for New York, and gave the number, two letters, four digits. She listened for a moment to the click and the static, looking out through the back screen at a different view of Mary Pickett's grounds than what she was used to. From here she could see a few stray carrots, a few leaves of collards, left to decay on the dark earth. She thought these must be the remnants of a Victory Garden, maybe one that was still being nurtured, still going on.

The operator cut in: 'Your connection is ready.'

When Lillian, the receptionist at the Fund, answered, Regina asked for Thurgood.

'Now, weren't you glad about that pillow?' Thurgood enjoyed a good joke, especially when the joke was one of his own. His laughter washed through her, a tonic. 'Nothing like a Southern bus to wake up a colored person's butt. When did they change you over?'

'Richmond.'

'Could have been worse. Sometimes they do it as early as Washington, D.C.' Then, 'What's going on?'

Regina took a deep breath. It was true Thurgood had let her come down here, and alone, but she was thinking now this might have been a snap decision. He'd been tired that day, discouraged. By now he could have changed his mind. He would have had time to go into 'Reggie's Room,' look at the mountain of cases in it, and wonder why on earth he had let Regina out from under them. Was investigating the death of one veteran worth all this?

'You *sure* you don't need Skip to come down?' Thurgood said, maybe reading this into her hesitation. 'Help you out?'

Oh, God. The last thing she wanted!

She let her breath out on a rush of words. 'No, I don't need Skip.'

'Then tell me what you got.'

Not much – even she had to admit this. She didn't mention the shirt – this was a party line, and she'd save that for later. But she told him everything else – about going over to the Duvals', told him about reading Mary Pickett's book on the steps of his law offices in order to get let in. Thurgood laughed. This reassured Regina, at least some. Quickly, she went on to Jackson Blodgett and his offer to get the grand jury proceedings for her.

Thurgood was as curious about this as she had been. 'Why would he do that?'

'He said he wants to cooperate in any way he can in finding out who killed *that boy*.' Imitating Blodgett, Regina drawled the words out. 'He didn't quite call Joe Howard a nigra, but he might have.'

'Oh, so he's Joe Howard now,' said Thurgood. 'You be careful about getting personally involved.'

'He's dead,' said Regina, blushing.

'You know what I mean. You put yourself in it, get emotional, you're going to miss something. You met his daddy?'

Regina told him about Willie Willie. She caught herself looking through the screen door as she talked, half expecting him to come in.

Thurgood said, 'Sounds like a character. Now, what's *she* like?'

'Prim. Proper. All the things you'd expect in an aging Southern belle.' Regina almost told him that Mary Pickett had once been married to Jackson Blodgett, but then changed her mind. Something like that, the bond, just might intrigue Thurgood. But if Thurgood got intrigued, then Skip could get intrigued, too, and somehow or other finagle a way to come down. Even though Thurgood couldn't see her, Regina shook her head to that. She'd call him again when she knew more. There would be time enough to bring up that long-ago marriage then.

'Anything else happen?'

'No,' said Regina. Crossing her fingers.

'Good. But you better tell your client . . .'

They heard a cough.

Oh, God. She'd forgotten to warn him.

'Party line,' she said.

Thurgood seemed to consider this. 'Anything else?'

She thought about telling him about Wynne Blodgett, but remembered that cough.

Regina looked out the window, saw that it was still light. The words seemed to come out of her mouth before she even thought them. 'There's a colored lawyer. Tom Raspberry. At least, I think he's a lawyer. *Everybody's* telling me I should go talk to him.'

'Then do it. Keep in touch.' And with that Thurgood hung up the phone.

In Revere, Regina found Tom Raspberry's office the same way she would have found it in New York. She went up to the first colored person she saw on Main Street and asked him where it was. He was an old black man on a rusted bicycle peddling fresh eggs layered from a wicker basket that had been lashed by a rope onto the front handlebars.

'Tom Raspberry's office? Please.'

The man's reply was slow and specific. He got off his bicycle, took off his hat. His smile was wide and toothless, almost beatific.

'You the lady lawyer come down from New York to help out Willie Willie?'

'Yes, my name is Regina Robichard.' She held out her hand, and he took it. His own hand was hard and work-callused, but it surprised Regina, after days spent introducing herself to wary white folks in Revere, Mississippi, how good it felt to be touching human flesh again.

'And my name's Ben T.'

Ben T. said he'd be glad to help her. Ride her over there on the back of his bike if she wanted him to. Regina thanked him but said no, she didn't want to put him to any trouble.

'No trouble at all,' he said. But in the end he nodded, pointed out the way, and then walked her down two blocks, going out of his way to make sure that she understood it.

'Once you get there, you'll know where you are,' Ben T. told her. 'He's right there on the corner. Tom Raspberry's building himself up a new place.'

She thought about this, three blocks down, when she turned the corner onto what a bright sign told her was Catfish Alley. And Catfish Alley was definitely a jumping place.

One thing Regina suddenly realized she'd missed in Revere were signs of progress. The war was over; the rest of the nation an active hive of rebuilding, of the old going down and the new strutting up. But not in Revere, not from what Regina had seen. Here the houses appeared to be all old Victorians and staid antebellums. Anna Dale Buchanan's bungalow had been surrounded by other bungalows, not one of which looked less than fifty years old. Even the shacks she'd seen out of the corner of her eye on that first night, riding into town with Willie Willie, had been unpainted and crumbling, almost falling-down ancient.

But Catfish Alley wasn't like that at all. It felt like Harlem and smelled like it, too. Good scents of enticing things, fried up and waiting. And it sounded like home. Regina heard Cab Calloway echoing himself, complaining about Minnie the Moocher on two different radios. The stations must have started the same record seconds apart.

Poor Min. Poor Min. Poor Minnie.

People stopped on the street to hum along.

Regina watched and she listened. Just being surrounded by other black folks again was a relief. Her shoulders loosened. Her step lightened. It was a lot of work to become 'American,' like everybody else. You always had to be on your guard. Were you doing things right? Were you ever *American* enough? She wondered if others were like this – the Irish, the Italians, the new immigrants from Eastern Europe; if they felt this way, too. Happy to be back among people that were like them. Happy they'd landed someplace where they could relax, at least for a minute, and that bore a resemblance to home.

The window was there, level with her eyes. You couldn't miss it.

THOMAS BANKS RASPBERRY
LAWYER
REAL ESTATE AND PROPERTY DEVELOPMENT

Under that came

The Revere Fair Dealer

Then

THE PENNYWISE BANK

Then finally, and most exuberantly of all

EVERYBODY WELCOME! COME RIGHT ON UP!

All of this painted black and outlined in gold, on a window so clean and polished that Regina saw everything she had on, down to the pattern on her tortoiseshell sunglasses, mirrored back perfectly to her in its gleam.

The building itself was new, mortar still sticking through the cheerful red brick like ice cream peeking out of an Eskimo Pie. It was a surprise to her, the first new building she'd seen since she'd got to Revere. And owned by a colored man – who might very well possess a great deal more. Two washtubs of red carnations sat before the yet-to-be-painted front door. A breeze touched them, and they waved at her, bright and cheerful and as well tended as anything in Mary Pickett's fine garden. All this encouraged Regina. Tom Raspberry hadn't *seemed* very welcoming when they'd met yesterday, but perhaps she'd been mistaken about him. Back here, on his own turf, so to speak, and among his own kind, he might turn out to be entirely different. When Regina opened the door, it was onto a stairwell filtered in sunlight.

Pine stairs led directly up into a large, open hallway, where the parquet floor was bare, no furniture on it. Four doors lined the right wall. One had Tom Raspberry's name, this time on pebbled glass; others announced *The Revere Fair Dealer* and the Pennywise Bank. They were all closed. She thought of choosing one and knocking on it. But across from them was a row of long windows. Regina hesitated, her hand already bunched. Maybe her conversation with Tom Raspberry could wait for a moment. She walked to the windows.

They faced east, and gave Regina a clear view down to the river. She realized now that Catfish Alley must be on a rise, though she hadn't felt the land mounting as she'd walked here. From this far up, the second story, she was able to see the lazy snake of the Tombigbee's brown waters, could see a trestle bridge spanning it and trees that marched almost to its banks. She splayed her fingers against the windowpane, leaned closer. She wondered if this was the place where they'd found Joe Howard, the very bridge against which his destroyed body had snagged long enough so somebody had finally seen it and been able to drag him up.

A tire hung from a rope that was tied to that trestle, and now there were children – no, maybe not children. Teenagers. All of them white. They were clustered around that place where Joe Howard had lain. Boys and girls both, and they were taking turns on that tire, swinging out, out, out over the muddy water, which must be cold now, this time of year. Holding on to their noses. Jumping into that river. Their mouths wide open. Laughing? Screaming? From this distance, Regina couldn't tell. But they were having fun. She could see that, all right. And the thought stunned her that this thing that had so completely marked her – this death of Joe Howard – had not seemed at all to touch them.

Tom Raspberry leaned expansively back in his chair. 'And it's *known* as Catfish Alley,' he said, 'by everybody in Revere and Jefferson-Lee County and on into Noxubee and Oktibbeha and Clay counties, and even all the way down into Rankin and Scott and Hinds counties, as one of the most *syncopated* parts of the state.'

Out from behind Judge Duval's shadow, Tom Raspberry appeared to become a great deal more syncopated himself. Out had gone the dark tie, the white pocket handkerchief, their places taken by a much livelier set of mixed blues and greens.

'You like?' he said, catching her stare and motioning to his neck with pride. 'I got it in New Orleans, a small shop off Canal Street. Last autumn. You ever heard tell the two capitals of Mississippi?'

'Jackson,' answered Regina promptly. She'd done her homework.

'*Two* capitals.' Tom waited a slow beat, then answered his own question: 'Memphis and New Orleans.'

He leaned back, exploded a cannonball of laughter aimed squarely at his own joke. Like Thurgood.

Regina took the opportunity to dart a quick look around. They were in his private office, but there had been no outer office, no secretary like Miss Tutwiler over at the Duvals'. Regina imagined that folks knocked on Tom Raspberry's door and came right in. Just as she'd done.

As Tom chuckled on, his laughter easing off like the slow put-puts of a train chugging into the distance, Regina's attention shifted to the wall behind him where what looked like the dummy for an upcoming edition of *The Revere Fair Dealer* hung from drying tacks and fluttered against a display of studio portraits.

Quite remarkable photographs, really, and quite precisely composed and just a little bit larger than you'd think a studio portrait should be, as though someone had decided they shouldn't be missed. The first, the center of everything, was of a much younger Tom Raspberry, his arm holding tight to a determined-looking woman, much lighter-skinned than he was and with serious, wide-awake eyes. *His wife.* No doubt about that. And around them, like roots branching out from a main tree, were photographs of three boys, each staring out as purposefully as their mama and daddy. Each was in cap and gown, with various graduation certificates lined up beneath that progressed them through the Rosenwald Colored Children's School and the Revere Colored High School and then into and out of Tougaloo College. Regina leaned closer. One – who looked just like Tom Raspberry, only younger – had recently found himself the proud recipient of a fresh JD degree from Howard Law.

She looked over. Tom had stopped laughing; he was watching her. 'Mighty proud of my family,' he said. 'Fine boys, and none of them married. Sure to have one your age, if you're interested. And you should be, if you're smart. One you're looking at, that's Thomas Banks Raspberry II. We call him Deuce. He's my oldest. Studied up at Howard with Charles Hamilton Houston, just like your Thurgood did.' Tom lowered his voice. 'Guess where he is now?'

Regina shook her head. She couldn't imagine.

'Jackson!' Tom exclaimed. 'He went down to sit for the *bar*.'

'I thought they didn't let Negroes into the Mississippi bar.'

'They don't,' Tom said matter-of-factly.

'Then why's he down there?' She might be wrong, but Tom certainly didn't seem like the type to encourage the wasting of time.

'I sent him on down there for the same reason I'm seeing you now – things are changing. Some deep foundations starting to shake. When the dust settles, I want to make sure it's not covered me over.' Tom stretched out a little, leaned back again in his seat. 'It's the war did it. I graduated Howard Law, too, but there was no chance of me making my living doing lawyering full-time, not if I wanted to come home and live near my people in Mississippi. No way I *could* do it, not with a wife to support and children to educate. If I wanted to go on in the law, I had to find me some way to accommodate myself, and the Duvals have been my accommodation. They're bound and determined to get this judgeship for Little Bed now. Get themselves some real respectability. But you know how they started out?'

Regina didn't.

'Same way as every other lawyer start out in Revere, at least the ones that don't own land.' He let this settle in so she knew he wasn't talking about Judge Calhoun. Clearly, he wanted her to know that Judge Calhoun was an entirely different matter. 'Some poor farmer finds himself in a pinch. Usually, this involves a dispute with some other farmer – or, worse, the bank – and the lawyer goes on out, offers to help him. This is a small place, lots of gossip, so most of the time the lawyer knows what's what before he gets there, has already come up with a neat plan of action – involving the courts. But the farmer's all worried. *How can I pay you?* The lawyer aw-shucks it, insists he don't want no money. He says that right off the bat, first thing. If the farmer wins out, well, they can discuss a fee later. If the farmer doesn't win out – just on one of the very *rare* occasions when this happens . . . well, there are other ways to settle up. The lawyer tells the farmer, "You *still* don't have to worry about a fee. Why, that little piece of bottom forty you got out yonder? I'll be happy to take that off your hands, call it a payment. This here's a little paper you can put your name or your *X* to." Most all the farmers around here are land-poor, anyway. They own the earth, they just don't have money to pull up a crop on it. So the idea sounds all good to the farmer. Besides, everybody thinks they got a good chance of winning their lawsuit when they first get started out. Reality sets in later. Now' – Tom Raspberry leaned further back, still very much enjoying himself, but Regina held her breath; the chair looked like it might be on the verge of tipping over under his weight – 'getting your hand on land's not something particular to color. You can't tell it from his waiting room but Forrest Duval – and his daddy, Forrest III, and his granddaddy, Forrest Junior, before that – none of them had one bit of care about skin color, at least when it comes to taking hold to some land. They'd represent anybody, even if they wouldn't let them sit down in the white folks' waiting room. But black folks feel better dealing with black folks. That's where I come in – or *came* in.'

Regina said, 'I get the picture.'

'Do you, now? I wonder.' He paused. 'I saw Bed Duval run up to you after you got out of ol' Duval's office. Bed's a good man. He knows how things are down here. Old Forrest Duval's his daddy. He knows how things are, too, and much better. But a little lady like you, from the North . . . well, there are many things you might need to learn.'

'And what things might these be, Mr Raspberry?' She leaned forward a bit, very, very careful to keep the irritation out of her voice and off her face. For all she knew he might be *trying* to make her mad.

'There's a hierarchy,' Tom said affably. 'You ever heard the word *oligarchy* before?'

Yes, of course, she had heard the word *oligarchy*. Now she knew he was trying to rile her. *This little lawyerette come down from New York. Let me just show her what's what.* He could have been Forrest Duval or Jackson Blodgett. Sounded just like them.

Tom said, 'What it *means* is some few rule and the rest don't count. You gotta tell them they do. You might even have to pretend that they do, but the world knows they don't. Down here it goes rich over poor. White over black, *but* if you're an enterprising man, there's always the chance for a little overlapping. And in Revere, on the rich black heap, I'm at the tip-top. That's because the Duvals and I have an understanding.'

Regina glanced over at the wall again. There was no certification from the Mississippi bar on it. She remembered what Mary Pickett had said about Willie Willie and her father, the distance that separated them. And she knew that even though Tom Raspberry and Forrest Duval might be good business partners, they didn't meet eye to eye.

'Okay,' said Regina, looking around. 'Things seem to work well for you. Maybe they work less well for someone like Mr Willie Willie.'

'Things work well enough for Willie Willie,' said Raspberry shortly. 'Now, the Duvals been lawyering for generations – mainly penny-ante stuff, like I said. But Bed went to war. He came back and married Mary Alice Mackey. *Her* whole family's been in Revere since Jesus walked the earth, which means not quite as long as the Calhouns and the Mayhews, but almost. The Mackey connection's a prime one down here. Now the Duvals can't just be rich, like the Blodgetts, they got to be dignified. *That's* why Bed's daddy's determined to get that judgeship for him.'

Regina didn't get the connection. She must have looked dubious, because Tom said, 'All this is relevant. But I imagine it's not why you're here.' The leather of his chair popped like a firecracker as he settled back into it. 'Well, what can I do for you, Miss Regina?'

'I was wondering,' she said, 'why Mr Duval recommended I see you about Mr Willie Willie's case.'

Silently she counted slowly to three, an interrogation trick that Thurgood had taught her, before she continued:

'You know, Miss Calhoun sent us a lot of newspaper clippings about Joe Howard's murder. One of them was from *The Revere Fair Dealer*. Yours.' She nodded to the next edition's dummies, tacked up and drying on Tom's wall. 'I think the headline went something like "Can This Go On? Even in Mississippi?" Or words to that effect. I don't imagine a sentiment like that was very welcome here in Revere – at least in certain quarters of it.'

Again, the slow, count-to-three pause.

'I can't imagine that put you in Mr Duval's fine, upstanding Negro book.'

Tom didn't say a word for a moment, but he did lean closer. His mustache was so thick and luxurious that Regina could see the small fan on the side of his desk bristle air through it.

Then he said, 'Robichard,' like the name was dawning on him for the first time. 'Isn't your mama the famous Ida Jane Robichard? And wasn't your daddy, Oscar – the one that got himself lynched?'

She'd never heard it put quite like that before – 'got himself lynched' – but Tom didn't seem to be trying to irritate her anymore.

'Yes,' she answered. The one word came out quickly, more quickly than she was used to it coming out. She hardly ever answered this question so directly, in one syllable. Usually she dodged it, turned away, didn't say anything at all. She'd learned to do this young, when she was five or six, because even then people were asking her about what had happened to her daddy. Everybody she knew back then seemed to know the story, but she had never told *her* story to a living soul.

'Yes,' she repeated.

'Thought so,' said Tom Raspberry. He, too, motioned toward the fluttering dummies of the *Fair Dealer*. 'Like you say, I run a newspaper, and I been writing about Ida Jane Robichard in *my* newspaper for years. Saw her myself once over there in Greenville. God, what a firecracker! Still, you had to admire her; talk about coming down into the belly of the beast.'

'She doesn't think of Mississippi that way. It's part of a larger problem. That's how she sees it. My father "got himself lynched," as you say, in Omaha.'

'During the great race riots,' said Tom. 'Up north. Bright-skinned woman, your mama. I imagine that's the thing got your daddy in trouble. Most whites would have taken her for one of them. Especially in a place like Nebraska, where they don't have that many colored folks to begin with, didn't have the variety of us that we have down here.'

'It didn't have anything to do with my mother,' said Regina quietly.

'Oh, I know all about that other woman,' replied Tom. 'The *real* white woman. How she said your daddy touched her on the street. How she said she'd never been so disgusted in her life. But I imagine people seeing your mama with your daddy – it might have upset them. Let's just say it sure didn't help.'

Regina's first urge, a blind one, was to get up, turn to that new oak door, walk right out of it, down into the street. Keep going. Until she'd walked herself all the way back to New York. Who did this man think he was, saying those things like this about her mother, about the way her daddy'd been killed? Then she looked at him more closely and saw real curiosity in his eyes, on his face. She knew he wanted to know, *Why* had this happened? A young man with a pregnant wife, working two daily shifts of a horrible job at Swift's Packing House so he could save up money for law school. Who'd been walking down a street one day. Who'd seen a lady about to fall. Who'd reached out a hand to keep her from tumbling. And two days later was dead.

She'd been drunk as a skunk, that's what someone had written in an anonymous note to Regina's mother, much later. But by then even Ida Jane had given up hope she'd live to see justice done for her husband.

'I never knew him. He was killed before I was born.'

Of course, if Tom had heard Ida Jane speak, he knew this. It was always one of the first things she said.

My baby never got to meet her own daddy. What he could have done for his people – if he'd been allowed to live – why, we'll never know.

Tom suddenly looked old, and as baffled by all this as Regina was. But what could she tell him that would explain it? There was no explanation. She slipped her hand into her pocket, ran her finger around the edge of the photograph of Joe Howard with his own father. It had become almost a talisman, like, she thought, Joe Howard's medal in Willie Willie's truck must be. Regina had patted the snapshot so many times since she'd got it that the sides had worn down, become as smooth as the picture itself. She transferred it automatically now from pocket to pocket, not even thinking what she was doing but doing it just the same.

The whip of the fan was the only thing slicing the silence. A door closed softly out in the hallway, and Regina thought she heard voices. Tom never took his eyes off her. 'That said, now tell me why you came over here? The real reason.'

How could she say, *Do you think Wynne Blodgett killed Joe Howard Wilson, because I'm starting to?* Blurt it right out like that? Instead, she decided to dodge the question.

'Everybody said you'd be the best one . . . I mean, in Catfish Alley . . . You'd – '

'It's not that everybody told you about me.' An interruption, true, but with it he threw her a lifeline. 'It's more like you got something you want me to do. I've been at this a long time. I recognize a do-something-for-me look when I see one. You seem like you might be willing to add on a please to it – something that doesn't always happen – but you still want something. Why don't you tell me what it is?'

Regina looked at the long lineup of certificates and diplomas behind him.

She said, 'I haven't even been able to see the grand jury docket.'

'That's normal,' said Tom Raspberry. 'It's sealed. Nobody can see it. Once they finished up, foreman handed it over to Judge Timms like he's supposed to. That's that.'

'But,' said Regina, 'Jackson Blodgett said he'd make sure I got a copy. He says he's doing it for the good of the town.'

'Really?' said Tom. He cocked a bushy eyebrow.

'But there's not going to be anything in that grand jury report, at least I'm not counting on it. What I need is for Bed Duval to go to Judge Timms and get him to call out *another* grand jury, one with some clout to it this time. I – we – have to find something that will make him do that.'

'There's nothing gonna make either of them do that,' Tom said matter-of-factly. 'Judge Timms . . . he's the meanest man in Mississippi, which automatically means he's racist to boot. Believe me, it runs like that. Besides, he's up North Carolina duck hunting, and will be there until two days before the election, and that's not 'til November. Win or lose, Judge Timms's not going to let anything interfere with him taking out Dixie and Sugar.'

Regina shook her head, confused.

'His dogs,' Tom clarified. 'Bird dogs. The best in three counties. Judge Timms . . . he's more attached to them than he is to his wife. Besides, only reason Little Bed got him to do anything in the first place was because everybody knows Willie Willie, and Joe Howard was a war hero. And that was *then*, back almost a year ago. They've done what they could for Joe Howard. They're not about to do anything more.'

'Even if we find other witnesses? Other people who were on that bus, saw what happened?'

'And how do you plan to do that?'

'With *flyers*.' Regina nodded to the dummies on his wall. 'You've got a press. If we printed up flyers, put them on all the trees in Revere, in the black parts of town, in the white ones, somebody would come up. I'm sure they would. This woman, Anna Dale Buchanan . . .'

'I know all about Mrs Buchanan.'

'This is the thing about Mrs Buchanan. The reason she got in touch with Miss Calhoun was because she'd read something in the *Times Commercial*. It was just a little something, two, three sentences at most, about the grand jury finding, but Mrs Buchanan was able to put two and two together and come up with Joe Howard. I'm betting if more people heard about what had happened . . .'

Tom interrupted again. 'You talk to Miss Mary Pickett about this?'

'Why should I do that?' snapped Regina. This time she didn't even try to keep the irritation out of her voice. 'What would she care? I mean, I imagine she'd be upset about them. She's just a bundle of good civic pride. She'd probably think they were litter, messing up her pretty little town . . .'

'That's true. She loves her some Revere, all right. But don't you think you owe her that much?'

Regina blinked. 'Why?' she said slowly.

'Because she brought you down. It seems to me this means she wants to see at least some little piece of justice done here.'

'That's not what she said.'

'That might not be what she *said*, but it's what she meant. She knew Joe Howard all his natural life just like Willie Willie's known her for all hers. You don't think she cared he got killed?'

'No, I do not.' Words out before Regina could stop them.

'And why's that?'

Tom's brows knitted, and he looked very much like he'd looked when he'd asked Regina about her father, like he'd asked a genuine question and was curious to hear the genuine response.

Regina said, 'That's obvious enough, isn't it? This is Mississippi. And she's white.'

'Oh,' said Tom, his voice noncommittal. 'So you think a Negro – any Negro, you, for instance, come down days ago from New York – would want to help Willie Willie more than Miss Calhoun does?'

'Of course I do!' Regina was moving into a trap, and she knew it – but what kind of trap? And why would Tom Raspberry lay one for her, anyway? He lived here, for God's sake. He must know how awful it was. 'Don't you?'

'Of course I do,' he echoed. 'No need to take offense. I'm just asking.'

His lips canted upward toward unreadable eyes, but there was the drawl of the South lacing his voice, just like it laced, in different ways, Mary Pickett's voice and Willie Willie's and Forrest Duval's and Bed's and Jackson Blodgett's and Wynne Blodgett's and even that man on the bicycle, Ben T.'s – a cadence that strolled through words and that branded Regina as an outsider here.

And she knew it. Could feel it. But maybe what they *needed* was an outsider.

She hadn't said this aloud, but Tom shook his head, still smiling that sort-of smile. 'Missy, I have an idea you're about to find out life around here's a lot more complicated than you ever imagined.'

Staring over at his face – his *smug*-looking face – she had never in the whole of her life so clearly understood the term *Uncle Tom* as she did at that moment.

You've got yours. Everybody else can just rot in hell. That's what she thought, but aloud she said primly, 'So I presume that's a no to the flyers. You're not going to help.'

Tom threw back his head and laughed again, a very ripe, merry sound. 'After all I said, and you're still asking for me to do this – with my boy down right this very minute in Jackson, sitting for the state bar, and with the Duval blessing so there's a *chance* he might be the first one of us to pass it. Now, why on earth would I jeopardize that?'

Regina opened her hands wide. 'To find out what actually happened?'

'But you already *know* what actually happened.' The look Tom threw her was as shrewd as it was cool. 'Somebody's told you by now or else they've hinted all around it, brought you close up to the point. That's why you come up here, the real reason. You just want me to confirm it, and I will. Wynne Vardaman Blodgett killed Joe Howard Wilson. He *admitted* it. Bragged about it to his friends, and from there, naturally, folks being how they are, it got all over town. Not that this made a scratch worth of difference. In Mississippi, any white man did what he did, they'd still be on the street, too. Don't even need a rich daddy to get away with that; all you got to be is white. But Wynne, he's white, and he's got a rich daddy, too. And that daddy loves him. Gonna look out for him. And Miss Mary Pickett . . . well, she *cares* for Mr Blodgett. This puts her right in the middle of a mess. You want me to put myself right in the middle of it, too? Think I'm a fool? Things might be changing, but they ain't changed that much.'

Regina's eyes narrowed. 'If what you say is true, why didn't Mr Willie Willie tell me all this?'

Tom chuckled, a deep, rich sound, and seemed to feel that was answer enough. Regina gathered up her gloves, her brand-new briefcase, her purse.

A man admits he killed somebody and he's still free to walk the streets, to hang out at the bus depot and the town square, to laugh with his friends, to brag about what he did, and nobody is inclined to do a thing about it. She walked straight to the door.

'I'd watch out for Willie Willie,' said Tom softly from behind her. 'He's a killer, you know.'

Regina turned back. 'You mean his son got killed.'

'No, I mean *he* did some killing. Ask him about it sometime. Ask Peach.'

10

It was dark by the time Regina made her way again to Willie Willie's cottage. Even so, there was enough daylight left for kittens to be still tumbling over one another on Mary Pickett's lawn, for girls to still be playing one last game of hopscotch before dinner, for boys on bicycles, streaking like fallen stars across the streets of Revere, to call back to friends, like they had in *The Secret of Magic*.

'*Come on, now, Booker. Catch up! Catch up!*'

When she opened the door to the cottage, she smelled cigarette smoke and immediately thought, *Wynne Blodgett*. He was that much on her mind.

But the man in the cottage was not Wynne Blodgett.

She realized this as soon as she flicked on the overhead light. For one thing, he was too big, too fleshy. His massive body dwarfed the big magnolia-print easy chair on which it sat gingerly perched.

'Sheriff.' Regina plastered a smile on her face but stayed near the door. 'Good evening.'

'Rand Connelly,' he said. 'We saw each other round the corner other day. With Bed Duval.' He ducked his head slightly but didn't take off his hat or get up.

'Regina Robichard. Nice to meet you.' She inched up her smile, laid her things on the desk by the window, looked over at him. 'I guess you don't need a key to come on in, in Mississippi.'

'No keys,' answered the sheriff, 'because there's no locks.'

She nodded, noticed a brown paper envelope. Small and flimsy, it too had been put on the desk, propped up neatly against the lace curtains at the window. It made her think of the shirt, and she had to fight back a strong urge to check on it, to make sure it was still hidden. She knew the sheriff had caught her looking at the envelope and wondered if he'd also caught her quick, questioning frown before she wiped it off her face. But the sheriff didn't say anything about that, not yet. Instead, he asked her, 'You planning a stay?' which was almost the same thing Willie Willie had said to her at the bus depot when she'd first got here.

'That depends on Miss Calhoun.'

'Miss Mary Pickett?'

'She's the one brought me here.' Echoing Tom Raspberry almost word for word.

'But you're the one made up your mind to stay. That's what I'm hearing.' The sheriff grinned, but Regina couldn't quite tell what kind of grin it was, just interested or maybe malicious.

She chanced a quick glance over to Mary Pickett's house, to the bare light over its back screen door, to its still calm. Quick, true, but the sheriff hadn't missed it. When Regina turned back, he was smiling at her, and she thought that he *could* have been a caricature, the small-town Southern lawman. Mean and menacing. Maybe a bully. But she realized this was a stereotype, and she could almost see Thurgood shaking his head at her, wagging an admonishing finger – 'Don't assume.'

At last, he nodded to the envelope on the desk. 'Mr Blodgett asked me to bring that over to you. To make sure you got it in your hands. I imagine you know what it is.'

She knew. 'The grand jury findings.'

Pop! Pop!

Gunshots. Exploding out, one right on top of the other. Rand Connelly didn't move, didn't utter a syllable, but Regina thought for sure she saw a slow *Gotcha!* grin starting up on his face as he stared at her. As he waited for her, the little slicker from the city, to cry out, to jump. But she did neither.

'Night hunters.' She nodded to the window, to the darkness beyond it. 'Mr Willie Willie explained to me that the deer around here are just starting to see their way back.'

'They've been back some few years,' said Rand Connelly. If he was surprised by her knowledge of animal life in Mississippi, it didn't show. 'Weren't any around here for the longest, not for sport hunting. Had to eat up everything we got. There wasn't a buck roaming for a boy to aim at, the whole of the county was hunted clean out. Now everybody and his son and his cousin and his cousin's cousins think they can shoot anything they want, anytime they want to do it. No respect for the law.'

He heaved himself up from a chair, started toward Regina and the door.

Pop! Pop!

Again. Closer this time. Regina said a silent, quick prayer that the deer got away.

Run, run now! Quick!

'I heard,' she said, moving just slightly enough to block the sheriff's way out, at least for a moment, 'that folks here would have starved for sure if it hadn't been for what they hunted.'

'You got that from Willie Willie, too, I imagine, and he's right. During the Depression, we sure would have. Everybody was poor as spent dirt back then. At least down here we all were,' said Rand Connelly.

'Oh, so you're from here?'

The sheriff nodded. 'Near enough. Out on the prairie, close by Miss Mary Pickett's old plantation place, Magnolia Forest. My daddy sharecropped out there.'

'Not from Carroll County, then.'

'Oh, so you know about Carroll County?'

'I do now,' she said. 'Moonshiners. Rowdy folks.' She and the sheriff shared a quick laugh.

But then Regina saw him look over at her, cock his head, turn wary.

He was curious about her, or so Regina thought, and she wondered what it must be like for him to be in this place, in this little cabin/cottage where colored people lived. She didn't even know if a white sheriff in Mississippi would be called on to go into many Negro houses, to talk to people like he was talking to her.

185

In Harlem, she couldn't recall one white person who had ever come into the apartment that she shared with her mother.

Another spurt of gunfire. *Rat-tat-tat*. Nearer? Farther away? She couldn't tell the direction. It could have come from anywhere.

At the door, the sheriff said, 'Nice meeting you.' Almost tipped his hat, caught himself just in time.

As soon as she heard the last echoes of his boots on the pea gravel, Regina counted to ten – slowly – and then rushed into the kitchen, checked behind the sink for the shirt. It was still there, right where she'd left it. Still wrapped in brown paper. Still with those strange stains around the missing button on its otherwise perfect white front. Suddenly, the whole thing – the brightness of the shirt in the hanging overhead light, the dull brown of stain around the lost button – reminded Regina less of the random smudges of a child's finger painting and more like the free form of a Rorschach test. Something that appeared simple enough on the surface but that hid a whole tangle of meanings, any one of which might call out . . .

Gotcha!

. . . if you didn't understand things just right. And Regina, hunkered down in the bright add-on kitchen of Willie Willie's cottage, had the sinking sensation that she was failing the test.

The file Jack Rand Connelly left was thin and so new that the PROPERTY OF JEFFERSON-LEE COUNTY CIRCUIT COURT looked like it had been stenciled on maybe five minutes before, as an afterthought. When she touched it, ink smudged off on her fingers. The envelope wasn't sealed, and she had the feeling that these particular records might not have been in the files at all. That they had been made up only when she'd asked for them and were pieced together out of whole cloth. Still, Regina was grateful, couldn't help but feel relief that Jackson Blodgett had done what he said he would do and, in turn, given her something *she* could do. But if what Tom Raspberry said was right – that everybody knew Wynne Blodgett had been the one to kill Joe Howard Wilson – then why on earth had his father given her this?

Because there was nothing to it. She found this out soon enough. It was what her mother, Ida Jane, would call a flimflam, something composed of little more than smoke and mirrors. The document contained some names and not much else. The bus driver's, Johnny Ray Dean; a woman, Mrs Paula Peavey (widow), who lived on a rural route in Scooba with her twin boys. There was no mention of Anna Dale Buchanan – but then again, Anna Dale Buchanan, with what she had to say, had never been called. More important, there was no mention of Wynne Vardaman Blodgett here, no record of who exactly had been up for indict-ment at all. This information had disappeared – if, she thought, it had been put in the docket at all.

But there *was* a coroner's report, signed by one Delray Barnes. He was listed as Mr, not Dr. In his sworn deposition, Mr Barnes stated what Regina expected he would. Joe Howard's body had lain long in muddy water. At the time of examination, it was in an advanced state of decomposition and this made it impossible to make a clear determination as to cause of death. No one pressed the point. Three sentences of testimony, and that was that.

Johnny Ray Dean was, if possible, even less forthcoming. He lived just over the state line in Ethelsville, Alabama, and he'd worked driving buses for the Bonnie Blue Line for six years. He hadn't been away to war, hadn't been drafted. That particular October day, so he said in his statement, he'd heard a little rattle in his engine. The Bonnie Blues were old buses. They'd been known to fall apart on you in a minute. All the drivers knew that. Mr Dean had brought his vehicle to a stop on the side of the road, cranked open the door, got out to investigate. Joe Howard had climbed down after him. He said he wanted to smoke him a cigarette. He – Joe Howard – had met up with some friends. He'd gone off with them. And that had been that.

Bob Miller (Foreman): 'What about his things?'

Mr Dean: 'Well, he knowed we'd put them down in Revere. That's where his ticket went to. They'd be there when he turned up to get them.'

This answer seemed to satisfy Bob Miller. At least, after that, no other witnesses were called. On the page was the scrawl of what must be the foreman's initials. He'd okayed this and the case had been dropped. But Regina wondered what had become of Mrs Paula Peavey, the widow. Had she actually been in the courtroom? And if so, why hadn't she been questioned?

Regina caught herself biting on her pencil, staring over at Calhoun Place. A light that had not been on before shone out of an upstairs window. The light and the window and whatever activity was going on behind it surely belonged to Mary Pickett. But what could Mary Pickett possibly be doing up there, in that big house, all by herself so late? She wondered, fleetingly, if Mary Pickett could be working just like she herself was working, and then she turned back to the thin file and reread everything again.

This didn't take long, and once she'd finished, she opened her briefcase and sifted through the newspapers, the old clippings that Mary Pickett had sent to them in New York. With new information, Regina thought she might come up with a fresh idea. She doubted this, but you never knew.

She laid everything out once again in chronological order. After Joe Howard's death, after the inquest and the grand jury, the next significant thing that seemed to have happened was the burning of The Folly, Jackson Blodgett's old family house. His 'home place,' as they all called it. Its torching had been written about in both the white newspapers and the colored ones, though for some reason the story was longer in the colored ones – *The Jackson Afro-American*, *The Revere Fair Dealer* – which went into the placement of the house near the river and its history and with a little extra history of the Blodgetts thrown in for good measure. Poor folks, who had managed to carve out a way upward. Respectful, but by now Regina had heard enough about folks coming down from the hills to be able to read between the lines.

Both articles were long considering their subject – a full column in the *Afro-American*; the one in the *Fair Dealer* continued on to the next page. *Interesting*. Regina wondered about that, and she remembered that Willie Willie had said The Folly was near not only Calhoun Place but the river where they'd found Joe Howard. Regina decided it might be worth her while to go down and have her own look at it.

She was thinking this when she heard . . . *What was that?* The pencil slipped from her hand, bounced against the linoleum floor.

'Shhhh!' she whispered, then realized she was shushing herself. She looked up, listened. Another sound. It seemed to come from right outside her window. A bump. No, not a bump, really; it was more like a rustle.

Silence. Then that rustle again. *Stealthy*, she thought. And a little closer this time.

Boogeyman coming to get you, Collie! Climbing out of the Stink Tree! Watch out! Watch out!

Then a knocking. A pounding. It took Regina a second before she realized that what was pounding was her heart. She patted her chest, tried to calm down.

She looked down at her watch, found it was just past midnight, then raised her gaze to the window, took up her courage, pushed the curtain away, looked out.

Across from her, Calhoun Place was now dark as death, but the night around it sparkled. She had never seen so many stars in her life, a spangle of them, so thick they looked like snow falling upward onto the sky, so plentiful that they almost completely outshone the fat fullness of a chill harvest moon. Regina moved closer to the windowpane, placed her hand on it and squinted her eyes down the driveway. Looking. But, of course, Jackson Blodgett's Buick wouldn't be here so late; he had a family of his own. There was no sign of Willie Willie's truck, either. And the sheriff – he was long gone. Regina held her breath and listened. All she heard now was silence so thick not even a cicada managed to sing through it. Relieved, she was about to move her hand from the window, to close up downstairs, to hurry on up to her safe, warm bed. She was just about to do all this, could even already feel herself snug within sheets, when again she heard the rustle. And this time accompanied by a stealth of footsteps. She was sure about that.

She moved her hand down to ease open the desk's one drawer, but there was little in it, no flashlight, not even a candle. Okay. One more look out the window . . . And that's when she saw him.

The deer.

No, *the buck*.

That's what Willie Willie had called him that first night driving in on the highway, and the way he'd said it had been with a capital *B*. Now he was right smack in the middle of Mary Pickett's garden, daintily picking at the last flowerings of her prized Confederate roses. All the real deer she'd ever seen in her life – *one!* – she'd seen since she'd arrived in Mississippi, but she knew this one. She recognized him in the lift of his head, in the strength of his body, in the flash of his hoary antlers, frosted all over in night light.

He looked up, not toward her but to Calhoun Place. Motionless as a statue for a moment, but alert. The next thing she knew he clattered down the driveway and was gone.

Regina flung open the cottage door. Outside, the world shivered under a new reality. Summer almost over, winter on the way. She pulled her sweater close, was glad she'd not kicked off her shoes as she worked and she looked down the pathway that led to the house and down into the near reach of the forest, but the only thing left of the buck was a strewing of rose petals, pale against the hard ground.

'Did you see him?'

Regina jumped – and bumped hard into Mary Pickett.

Who hissed, 'Ouch. That's my foot.'

'Oh, I am so sorry,' apologized Regina. They might have been in a formal parlor or a drawing room except that Mary Pickett had on a pink cotton bathrobe, bare feet, no slippers. And she held a cocked shotgun in her hand.

'Couldn't shoot him,' she said, breaking it with a sigh. 'Lots of reasons why I should have, though. We're not talking about Bambi. This one's a damn menace. Willie Willie told me he almost got y'all killed. And he would have *expected* me to kill him, Willie Willie would have. He's the one taught me *how* to bring him down, just where to aim for, and maybe if I could have, made him proud of me, things might go back to being the way they've always been.' Mary Pickett shrugged, the barest of movements. 'Doesn't matter, though, 'cause I'm not able to do it, not anymore.'

She turned to Regina. 'You know, when I came out after that deer tonight, this was the first time I ever realized how clearly you can see everything going on at the big house from the cottage. Just goes to show how little I know. I've never actually been in it – the cottage, I mean. Not ever. Not even when it was being fixed up, after the book came out and I was putting in the indoor toilet, building on the kitchen. Willie Willie, Joe Howard – when we needed to see them, they always came to us.'

The two women stood there, looking at each other for a moment, as a float of fallen leaves rose up from the walkway and jitterbugged toward them on a fine breeze.

'I need a drink,' Mary Pickett decided. She motioned over to her big, dark house. 'Bet you do, too. Come on, then.'

She started off, leading the way over the pea-gravel path to the back door. Regina didn't have to think twice; all tiredness vanished. This was *M. P. Calhoun*, after all, not just Mary Pickett, and she was taking her deeper inside, to where *The Secret of Magic* lived, to where it had been created. The author and the book she had written – or, better yet, the new one she had said she was writing – now formed a perfect locus of anticipation in Regina's mind. She even forgot about Joe Howard, Willie Willie, the frustrations of her case. All of it, for the breadth of a moment, because – why, ahead of her, she felt Calhoun Place heaving itself up out of a novel's typeset, made-up pages, and turning into something that was no longer just imagined but was about to be real. Regina had to restrain herself from beating Mary Pickett to the door.

The screen door slammed as Mary Pickett's fingers went to the kitchen switch and flicked on the light. She laid the rifle gently on a white enamel table, shifted it a bit so that it was pointed away from Regina, who suddenly realized that it might actually be loaded. She hadn't thought about that, not really, and she again felt that frisson of fear she'd felt back at the cottage. Mary Pickett disappeared for a moment behind a curtain of barkcloth with palm trees, that looked very much like the one that skirted the sink in Willie Willie's cottage and behind which, she hoped, the shirt was safely hidden. It wasn't something she thought she'd expected to see in an old, built in 1839 *mansion* like this one. But then again, she guessed, a house wasn't a museum. Some fabrics frayed; moths ate at others. You had to be prepared to throw things out, replace them, and move on.

When she brushed into the kitchen proper again, Mary Pickett held a small silver tray on which sat two hefty crystal goblets. She picked up her rifle again, held it loosely under her arm, balancing the gun and the tray. She did not ask Regina to help her, but she did motion for her to follow along. The mistress of Calhoun Place walked over to the split kitchen door. The top half was already ajar; with her hip, she opened the bottom. One after the other, first Mary Pickett, then Regina, passed through.

It wasn't that Regina had never *thought* about Calhoun Place, what might be hidden within it, how it might look, what it might contain. Sitting there at Joe Howard's desk in the cottage, she'd look across and wonder about a house like this in a place like Mississippi, just like she'd wondered, years ago, about Collie's house in *The Secret of Magic*.

'Go on into the hall there,' said Mary Pickett. 'Turn on the switch by the stairs.'

Collie's house was the one thing in Revere that Mary Pickett had not lavished a loving description upon in *The Secret of Magic*.

It had been drawn forth in only one or two quick strokes. The children had run to it; they had run past it. Description had been lavished on the whorls of an oak stump, on the nicks in a red penknife's blade, on a snake of kudzu that Collie and Jack and Booker had tripped across on a back path. As far as Regina could remember, no one actually had ever gone *inside* the big house. No one had asked to, no one had wanted to. In her mind she had always pictured it as a very dark place.

She could not have been more wrong. Calhoun Place only seemed closed from the street, from the sidewalk, when you looked at it from the outside. Once you were actually inside it, even at night, Mary Pickett's house turned out to be wide-open and bright. It smelled of beeswax. It gleamed with lamp-lit silver. The parquetry beneath Regina's feet was as burnished as gold.

Slaves did this. Put it all together. Built it.

A sobering thought, and it sobered Regina Mary Robichard right up.

Not that Mary Pickett noticed. 'Those floors are river oak,' she said with some pride. 'Trees everyplace back in the old days. Jungle thick. My great-grandfather and his Negroes had to cut through them, almost to the bend of the Tombigbee River.'

It was one of the few times Mary Pickett had spoken about race, and Regina would have thought that the mention of it would have distanced the two of them. She had never very much liked talking about race with white people, even the white lawyers who worked in the Fund office. Everyone just seemed so self-conscious. She was, and they were, too. But she found, when Mary Pickett talked about race, really and truly like now, she could have been talking about the weather. Race was just *there*, a fact of life. Black people were everywhere. Here, you couldn't hide from them like white people could in New York.

Mary Pickett handed her the drinks tray, but only long enough for her to lay the rifle on a dove-gray loveseat that fronted the blue silk brocade wall. Regina would have liked to peek into the dim rooms off that hallway. Actually, she was dying to do this, but already she could see this was not to be. Mary Pickett had brought her here for a purpose. Regina could tell this by the set of her shoulders, by her definite tread. The mistress of Calhoun Place took the tray again. She led the way to a needlepoint-carpeted stairway that led upward to a dim landing and then rounded a corner and disappeared.

'My mother did the handwork on this rug,' said Mary Pickett, as she put her foot down firmly upon it. 'She sat in a window at the back parlor, the one that looks over the wisteria arbor and the rose garden, and she worked on this every day of her short life. Stitching bright flowers onto a black background – I always thought this something of an anomaly, even when I was a child and had no earthly idea that a word like *anomaly* existed – but still, I knew exactly what it meant.'

She climbed two more steps, pointed. 'That's her over there.'

Regina's gaze followed the tilt of Mary Pickett's long finger as it pointed along the length of a long wall. The portrait dwarfed the hallway. It stretched up almost from the top of a low green marble-topped table to almost touch the wainscoting above.

Now, *that*, Regina decided, was a true Southern belle.

She thought this even though the woman was dressed in Gay Nineties spangles, not Victorian hoops, her russet hair pillowed up over the swan's reach of an ivory neck, her body facing forward, her head turned back, eyes focused coldly on Regina. At least, that's what it looked like. But still those eyes fascinated her. They were dark as the earth, just like Mary Pickett's, and large like hers were, and sad like them, too.

Mary Pickett said, 'After my mother died, my daddy felt guilty and maybe grief-stricken. He wanted her likeness in this house, and he wanted it big. The portraitist he chose worked out of Memphis. He asked for a photograph, and we sent him some I'd done of her. There weren't many. I thought I'd have all the time in the world to take pictures of my mother, so I took pictures of everything else. Next, he asked for something personal. My father sent the piecework she'd been working on when she died. He couldn't think of anything else. They were married, but I can't say Daddy ever really *understood* Mother that well. On the other hand, the portraitist never came to Revere – at least, he never did until they hung the painting – and, of course, he never knew her but he got her just right. That look on her face, the way it's turned back. That was the soul of my mother, always searching for something she'd left somewhere behind her. I never wanted to be like that, but I guess I am.'

A current of air rustled them, an icy draft forcing its way through some unsealed crack. It shivered crystal in the chandelier in the hallway, tinkled the glasses on Mary Pickett's silver tray. A draft, maybe. But Regina thought it came from the portrait, from the lips of that lifelike, aristocratic, snowy white face, and that it blew straight at her. Determined to whoosh her away.

There was no time to think fancifully, though, because Mary Pickett was off again, almost at the turn of the landing, and Regina found herself hurrying to catch up. Switch after switch was turned, and light sprang up to open a path past velvet curtains and pretty mahogany furniture and ugly ancestral portraits. Past room after shadowed room.

Until they came to the place where Mary Pickett wrote her magic books. Regina knew what it was as soon as she saw it. A small space, not much bigger than a closet. And she would have surely missed it except that a green shaded partner's lamp had been left burning – by mistake? – on the simple square desk. Not much light, really, but still enough for Regina, curious, slowing down, to pick out a Corona typewriter so battered its carriage return was wrapped in hospital adhesive, a glass-and-silver ink stand, a Red Bird school tablet, a dictionary with a crumbling leather spine, a handful of yellow pencils in a Ball canning jar, books tumbling together like Topsy all up the walls. This was Mary Pickett's *personal* place. Regina didn't need to *see* anything to know that. All around her was the scent of cigarette smoke mixed with Shalimar, Mary Pickett's particular perfume, stronger here than Regina had smelled it anywhere else.

'You coming?' From Mary Pickett.

'Yes, here I am.'

Regina turned her head and there it was – the pile of neatly typed pages, weighted in place by a globed glassed-in scene of a forest. A manuscript, that's what it looked like, all right. *Oh, my God! Oh, my God!* Could this be it? She longed to ask, to touch it, feel the onion-skin pages with her fingertips. To read it. A new novel, a sequel to *The Secret of Magic*? A sequel in which she'd finally find out what had happened to Collie and to Jack and to Booker after *The End*. Where you'd learn what had happened to Daddy Lemon and who had killed Peach and Sister's brother, Luther – if he was dead. Regina realized, suddenly, she was dying to know. Had Mary Pickett brought her here to show her this? Would she – Regina Mary Robichard! – be the first one in New York to see this new book? To actually read it?

'If you're coming, come on.'

Mary Pickett opened a door at the far end of the landing.

This room was like the others they'd passed – good furniture, stuffy air, no magic to it – not like that little office at all. An overlay of fading crochet canopied an oak tester bed, with a reproduced Louis XV chair flush beside it, a bare inlaid oak table, no books or mess, no papers, no pencils. It didn't even smell like Mary Pickett smelled. No ghost of Shalimar in here.

Beside her, Mary Pickett put the tray with its glasses and its decanter on a low table, then sat down beside Regina – which came as a shock. She hadn't thought she would sit down this close; she'd thought Mary Pickett would drag that gilt chair over – or order Regina to do it; with Miss Calhoun, you could never be sure – so that the two of them could look at each other and get right to the point. Because, of course, there must be a point to this little excursion. Regina had already realized this. Mary Pickett didn't say a word. She also didn't pour anything from the decanter, either, for Regina or for herself. It just sat there, crystal in the moonlight. But she did fish in her pocket and pull out her Chesterfields. She put one in her mouth, struck a match, flamed the cigarette to life, took a deep pull.

That done, she turned to Regina. 'I imagine it's your mama made you into a lawyer. A strong woman like that, she would have wanted you to go on.'

Said so matter-of-factly that Regina, without thinking, answered right back, 'She didn't care what I did. She wanted me to be happy. She never encouraged me to be a lawyer, but once I decided, she never stood in my way. And she supported me. I mean, she worked. Long hours. But it wasn't something she wanted for me, starting off.'

'What did she want for you?' Words filtering out through a cloud of cigarette smoke.

'I imagine . . .' Regina considered. 'I imagine she wanted for me what she had wanted for herself – back before, I mean. Before my father was . . . before he died. Before what happened had happened.'

'And that was?'

Regina shrugged. 'What everybody wanted back then, what maybe they still want. She loved my father. She wanted to be with him.'

Ida Jane had said this many times, though Regina had never confided this to a soul before – because no one had ever really asked her. Most people just assumed that Ida Jane had wanted her daughter to be a lawyer, that she had determined to make a lawyer out of her. But here was Mary Pickett, in this dark, quiet room, asking for the truth. For a moment, Regina stopped breathing, surprised herself at what she had just so easily said, and to whom.

M. P. Calhoun didn't seem to notice. 'Regina, you ever been in love yourself?'

Ever been in love?

The question came as a shock to Regina, took her aback. And what could she answer? Naturally, in her life, there had been first boys and then men and the kissing and more – all the pleasant physical sensations that came when you were young and involved with first boys and then men.

But love? Love was something else entirely. She had always known this, and that was why kissing and everything else had never led to more. Love had passion to it. Love was something she felt for her mother and the memory of her dead father. Love was something she felt for the law.

Mary Pickett didn't wait for an answer.

'Well, I have been. Still am. I've, let's say, only lately rediscovered that fact.' She made a gesture that swept through the room, reached out the window. 'This is where I first saw Jackson. Sitting right here, exactly where I'm sitting now. I was exactly eleven years, two months, and four days old, and my mother had been dead all of one day, six hours, and fifteen minutes. I had been looking at my watch, which is why I knew all that. When I picked my head up, looked out the window, there was Jackson. He was standing on that rough patch of pavement beneath the magnolia, just outside the gate. It's still rough, that sidewalk, tree roots grown up all through it. City hasn't fixed it in all these years.' She paused for a moment, touched a warm hand onto the windowpane's cold glass. 'Anyway, out I looked, and there he was, looking right straight back at me. Eye to eye. That was when I first *saw* him, if you catch my meaning. Even though, realistically speaking, he'd probably been there, somewhere within the range of my peripheral vision, every single day of my life.

'People like Jackie Earle Blodgett, like what he was, his family . . .' She paused for a moment, seemed to search for a delicate word. 'Your poorer people. Well, they're just there. You catch a glimpse of them sometimes through a car window, in the halls at school, out of the corner of your eye. All they're ever doing is passing by.

'But I didn't *notice* him, as I said, until Mama passed and left me here all by myself to fend off a whole bunch of other people who *weren't* poor people, all Mother's Revere Garden Club friends, who didn't know one little thing about me or my mama

198

and could not have cared less. What mattered to them was what *mattered*. How you looked, what year your people had settled here and where they had come from. How you behaved. All that. The old ways. The Calhoun name. Folks who saved their reverence for what had happened way back in 1861. So they stuffed me into a smocked black velvet dress that made me look like a cased-up sausage, made my bosoms look like something Mae West would have looked on with envy. Then they perched a truly *titanic* black satin mourning bow on my head. Obscene, that's the way they had me looking. I do declare, I could have easily posed for one of those indecent Paris picture postcards.

'But then again, they did the same thing with Mama. They dolled her up in a blue-and-white silk print that had been given to her by her own Virginia grandmother and that my mama always swore made her look fat. They put pink lipstick on her. And pink was a color always made her seem dead, even when she was alive. They said to Daddy, "Judge, I am truly sorry" and "How tragic, Eulalie passing on like that, and *so young*." "Anything I can do to help, you just let me know." Especially the young widows and the still-hopeful spinsters said that. Everybody's always so well bred and *nice*.' Mary Pickett sighed, shook her head, looked over from the window at Regina. 'I never have been able to figure out exactly who it is I can trust.'

'But you still had your daddy,' said Regina, who had never had one, not really, and had to fight a subtle, constant envying of those who did.

Mary Pickett snorted, tossed her head. 'Daddy wasn't one bit of help,' she said, losing her carefully cultivated English. The chintz window-seat cushion shifted beneath her. Her cigarette burned down to ash, she got busy lighting another. 'When I tried talking to Daddy, tried to explain to him how folks were messing things up, all he did was ruffle my hair. Made that bad bow look worse than ever. He said, "Well, Baby Girl, these are your mama's dear *friends*." As though that explained whatever needed explaining, as though it made everything they did all right. The only one

I could ever talk to was Willie Willie. He was the one person I thought knew about the crack Mama had fallen into and that I was fast tumbling into right behind her. But Daddy was sending Willie Willie all over the place. Before the funeral, after the funeral – he and Daddy were just *gone*, mostly every day, mostly into the forest, searching out one thing or another. Deer, possum, squirrel. Aiming at any critter that had the gumption to move. When I asked Daddy about it, he'd only said, "We got to eat." What on earth did he mean by that? *We got to eat*, indeed! It wasn't the Depression yet, for goodness' sake. That was still coming. Willie Willie, shooting, the forest – all these were just Daddy's excuses for running away.'

Mary Pickett blew cigarette smoke through her mouth, through her nose, a cloud of it obscuring her face. But just for a moment. 'So there I was, looking out my window, and there he was, and you know which way he was facing? Jackson, I mean. The first day I saw him?'

Regina, eyes wide, shook her head.

'North,' said Mary Pickett triumphantly, 'toward the big cities. And, just like my mama, I was *dying* to get away. So I got up, ran down the stairs, on out into the street. Called out, "Hey, Jack. Where you heading? Take me with you. I want to go too."'

She took a deep pull on her cigarette and looked out the window, examined her thumbnail, looked everywhere she could, except at Regina.

Regina couldn't help herself, she had to know. 'What happened next?' Impatient as she would be if she were reading through the first pages of a brand-new book.

'With Jack? Why, everything of course! But first off, he taught me what was real and what wasn't. The truth. Sometimes it's a little hard to come by down here. You saw that picture of my mama, the way it rises up out of that gold table? Daddy told me he put it there that way, like it was mounted up on an altar, so it'd always be a memorial to her. Jack told me another reason. The real one, he said.'

They'd gone down to the river together, rolled themselves some cigarettes, had a little talk. After which Mary Pickett had run back into her house, flown up the stairs, hoping to find the words *venereal disease* linked together in her *Webster's Dictionary*. Of course they weren't there, not together. And *clap* had been completely shushed out. But Jackson *had* been there. And when Mary Pickett asked him, as she now told Regina she had, he explained things to her, the source of the venereal disease and the source of the source. Which was, naturally, Mary Pickett's daddy and his running around. 'Up to Memphis. Down to New Orleans. Daddy had it, too, that's what I imagine. It just couldn't kill him before the strokes did.'

'Why, Mary Pickett, didn't you know?' Because, Jackson assured her, everybody else in town did.

'Not that he especially liked being the one to tell me,' Mary Pickett said to Regina. Her face set stubbornly around her words, daring Regina not to believe them. 'There was none of that glee on them that I'd seen on Mother's friends before she died. They'd show up to visit, they'd sit on the wicker porch chairs or in the front parlor and talk all kindly to Mama and then, soon as her back was turned, they'd start up about how drawn Eulalie was looking, and how thin. They'd shake their heads. They'd say, "Now, if Charles Calhoun were my husband . . ." I heard it all. They didn't mind I was there. I was a child, and a child didn't count. They thought I wouldn't understand exactly what they were talking about, and I didn't. Not until Jack told me. "Got to know the truth," he said. "Got to know what you're up against."'

Right at that moment, Regina could have asked her. *You talk about truth, Mary Pickett, and you say Jackson talks about it, too. Well, did Wynne kill Joe Howard? Do you know for a fact that he did, and will you tell? Because if you, Mary Pickett Calhoun of Calhoun Place, Revere, Mississippi, say that he did it, say maybe that you know about the shirt I'm hiding away – why, that would make all the difference. For Willie Willie. For Joe Howard.*

Regina opened her mouth. Around her now, once again, she

felt a shiver. But this time it wasn't the house at all, it was Mary Pickett shaking beside her, her face set, angry and mad. It wasn't the time to ask her anything, not if she wanted the answer, not if she wanted her help.

'But things didn't last long between Jack and me,' said Mary Pickett. 'Even though they lasted years – until we got married – all that time seemed to flit by in a minute. Once Daddy got the annulment, he packed me straight up to Randolph-Macon, where my mama had gone. "Don't know what else to do with her. Can't let her run wild. Why, that Jackie Earle . . . He's Vardaman Blodgett's brother, and we all know what a lowlife he was and what happened to him." That's what he said to anyone who would listen. Not the real reason, mind you, not the truth, but *understandable*, so good enough. By then . . . Well, Daddy, I understood him. It was Willie Willie siding *with* Daddy that tore out my heart.'

Regina leaned closer. She knew she was hearing something important, and as she looked and she listened, she saw the slow transformation of Mary Pickett into M. P. Calhoun, the great storyteller, putting words together in a special way, careful about her verbs and her nouns, her eyebrows knitting together in concentration. All this happening right before Regina's eyes.

Mary Pickett's own eyes narrowed. 'Then when Daddy got so sick and I packed it in and came home, everybody acted like they were pleased as punch. And maybe they were. Folks who've stayed home have a tendency to like it when somebody who thinks they've got away has got to come back. It's what my mother's friends say about me. "Why, Mary Pickett is such an old-fashioned girl, really, a Calhoun to her core. I do declare I always knew it. Down under all that *Magic* nonsense. Glad she got it out of her system. Glad she outgrew all that."'

'But did you? Outgrow it?'

They both looked across the room, out to the hall, to the other small room with the pile of typed pages on its neat desk.

'Too late for all that,' said Mary Pickett briskly. 'I had my chance. Once.'

But still, she'd written that first novel, copying it off, as she now told Regina, 'word for word,' up at Randolph-Macon when she was supposed to be doing her class work. After it sold, she'd planned to head straight for New York, never see Revere again, never see her father, never see Magnolia Forest or Willie Willie, or Joe Howard or Jack. Then her father had a stroke, which was followed quickly by another and then another, each more devastating than the last. After that – or in the middle of it, Mary Pickett couldn't rightly remember – came the Depression. Magnolia Forest had to be sold, Calhoun Place bound to be next, even filled up like it was from rafter to furnace with gently destitute Calhouns and Picketts and all other kinds of cousins. But her little book had turned out to be a success, an unexpected sensation.

'And,' said Mary Pickett in a voice wired with irony, 'we were saved.

'Back here, the first thing I heard was how Jackson had gone on and married Mae Louise Wynne and they'd had them a son. After that, I started doing things I thought I'd never do, *Calhoun* things, like calling on Miss Lilla Raymond – my mother's good friend – to see about taking my mother's place on the board of the Revere Garden Club.' A pause.

'They neither of them remarried.' Mary Pickett's voice got softer, got dreamy. Regina must have looked confused, because Mary Pickett waved smoke at her impatiently. 'I mean Daddy and Willie Willie. I mean Willie Willie after his wife, Florence, died. Years before I left here, there was talk of him and Peach Mottley. Folks said they were sparking each other, but then her brother, Luther, disappeared. After that, nothing seemed to work out.'

'Is all that in your new book?' Regina knew she was pushing too hard, that she was too eager, but it was dark outside and this little room was snug around them, a place for telling secrets. And there was a chance, a little chance, that Mary Pickett might say something. Something important about the book – the new book – that was lying right down the hall from where they now sat. Regina was sure that's what she had seen, and she couldn't understand

Mary Pickett. Didn't she realize how famous she was? That even now, twenty years after *Magic* had come out, the *Herald Tribune* and the *Daily News* and *Look* magazine and *The Saturday Evening Post* would run all over themselves and one another to send reporters and photographers and copyeditors and everything else that was needed down to Revere to interview her if they thought there was a new book? The only reason no one had come before was that Mary Pickett obviously hadn't *wanted* to be found, and the people of Revere had backed her up in this. Maybe because she was a Calhoun and they were used to doing what a Calhoun wanted. Maybe because they respected the fact she just wanted to be left alone and forgotten. Maybe because they were just glad she was back. No matter the reason, the silence around the author of *The Secret of Magic* remained complete.

But there was a world out there that still cared about Peach and Collie and Booker and Jack and shivered when they thought of Luther Mottley crying out, *Gotcha!* from his hidey-hole grave in the hollow of a dead stink tree. And didn't Mary Pickett realize how important Booker had been, and Daddy Lemon, to Regina and to thousands of other little Negro children like her, reading for the first time about spunky black heroes in a white book?

'There is no new book,' said Mary Pickett, 'nor will there be.'

'But what about . . . ?' Thinking, *She told me the first day she was writing a new one. Why, just now, she walked me right past it. She must have known I'd see.* Regina persisted. 'You told me you worked on it, every morning.'

'No. New. Book.' And that was that.

After a moment, Mary Pickett continued. Her voice changed now, brisk and to the point. 'I brought you here to talk about Jackson so you'd understand enough – so I could talk about Wynne. That's what you want, isn't it, to hear something real about Wynne?'

'I'd like to learn the truth about him.'

'The truth?' said Mary Pickett, with a lift of her lips. 'Oh, that again.'

She waved her hand through the spectral smoke of her cigarette, waving it away – and maybe the truth with it.

'I imagine Wynne's attractive enough, but . . . he isn't smart like his daddy, not disciplined, not used to having to work. Nothing like Jackson.' They were sitting so close that Regina could see Mary Pickett's eyes widen with the wonder of this as she continued. 'Wynne didn't go to the war like Joe Howard, even though they were the same age, or near the same age. I imagine he's regretting that now. The not-going-to-war part, I mean. Soldiering's always been an important tradition around here. The honor of it. The medals. And if people thought your mother might have pulled strings, might have been the one . . . Well, you can imagine. Wynne has his failings, his weaknesses. Still, Jackson loves him. How could he not? His own son.' Through the smoke of one cigarette after another, she said all this to Regina.

'But he – Jackson – was wrong to think that Joe Howard's death would just go away, that Willie Willie would let it be forgotten and disappear. I must have thought that, too, and I should have known better. It never happens like that.' She lifted her shoulders, let them slump. 'Down here, in the South, we tell the same stories over and over again, always hoping things will turn out different and better, with just one more telling, with just one more word said a different way. Can you understand?'

What Regina understood was that Mary Pickett was making excuses for Wynne Blodgett. Which meant she must know perfectly well what he'd done. *Everybody* must know it, just like Tom Raspberry had told her they did. Regina reminded herself that this was Revere. Who'd stand up against the son of a rich man who probably owned every mortgage in town?

No one, that's who. She thought of this while Mary Pickett went on talking and talking. Regina waited, not saying a word, as Mary Pickett touched flame to cigarette after cigarette, as she took deep drags on them, as she blew the smoke out. As she told her about all kinds of things that didn't add up. About the town. About the Negroes. About the whites. Explaining, or trying to, at least, about Jackson Blodgett and how poor he'd once been. About the traditions and how they ruled here. This, at last, was something Regina could understand. She'd felt the force of how-things-are-done emanating even from the otherwise progressive soul of Tom Raspberry, even from Willie Willie himself. What an effort it must take to stand up against it. For the first time, Regina realized what a hornet's nest Mary Pickett had stirred up bringing her here.

'But why did you do it?' Regina said.

I already told you.

That's what she thought Mary Pickett would say, and she braced herself for it, not only for the sharpness of the words themselves but for the impatience and the loftiness that always seemed to be the force behind Miss Calhoun speaking her mind.

Instead, Mary Pickett, for a moment, turned quiet as the night around her. Then she said, 'I don't know anymore why I did it. I only know it was something I had to do. And, my God, what a good and right idea it seemed, at least at the time!'

She smiled then, but the smile was a dreamy one not meant for Regina, but aimed past her, out of the room, out the window, to that piece of rutted sidewalk in front of Calhoun Place where, long ago, a young Mary Pickett Calhoun had first *seen* a young Jackson Blodgett.

II.

It was still dark when Regina left Mary Pickett's, but there was a morning's dew already on the ground. She felt the freshness of it as she hurried across and slipped into the cottage, tired and anxious now to climb into her bed.

Once there, though, she couldn't sleep; her mind swirled with what Mary Pickett had told her, the story – Mary Pickett's story – of Jackson Blodgett and Wynne, of Willie Willie, all of them secrets Regina now shared. And the new book itself, the one she'd seen on Mary Pickett's desk, or thought she'd seen, except now she wasn't so certain. Had it really been a book after all?

'Regina, you ever been in love?'

But it was Mary Pickett who was in love and perhaps always had been with Jackson Blodgett, a man who had once been married to her but was now long married to somebody else. Regina turned around, looked back at Calhoun Place's darkened upstairs window. *Poor Mary Pickett*, she thought, and shook her head. Not only had Mary Pickett sided, all those years ago, with Jackson against her father, now she felt called upon to defend his son.

But from what? That's what Regina couldn't understand. It was obvious to her by now that Wynne Blodgett at least knew something about how Joe Howard Wilson had died, if, indeed, he hadn't been the one to kill him. Everything she'd heard, everyone she'd talked to – black or white, obliquely or pointedly – had at least implied this. And, if so, what was the problem? A rich man like Wynne Blodgett, son of a rich man – the law had already proven that he had nothing to fear. Even if she could somehow or other get him to admit what he'd done, brag about it again like Tom Raspberry said he had done in the beginning . . . What good would that do? None whatsoever. *At least, that's what everybody wants me to believe.*

But a man has been killed, and the man who did it – or the one everybody thinks did it, who knows for sure? – is walking around free as any one of the bluebirds that nested out in Mary Pickett's mailbox. But without proof, everybody could just be assuming. Regina thought back to Thurgood, to what he had always told her. Assume *makes an ass out of* u *and* me. Maybe everybody was wrong and Wynne innocent. It was a possibility. But without evidence one way or the other, how on earth could she know?

Regina woke the next morning to the rich and spicy scent of cinnamon. Groggy, she glanced down at her watch, saw she'd taken it off, looked over for it – and there was Peach, the source of the sweetness, dressed bright as a rainbow and sitting snug on the easy chair. Regina blinked, thought she might be still dreaming. But no, it was Peach, all right, what you might call the Real Deal Peach, all decked out in exuberant snatches of paisley, a yellow scarf, blue dress, red fringed Mexican shawl; bright sunlight streaming through the window, flashing at the edges of the sickle-shaped scar that ruined her cheek.

'I called in from downstairs. Didn't hear nothing, so I came on up. Dinetta dropped off your breakfast, but it's got cold,' she added. 'Almost time for lunch.'

'Lunch?' said Regina, instantly wide awake.

'It's a wonder you could sleep, all the racket. Revere Garden Club meeting on Monday. Miss Lilla Raymond – Miss Mary Pickett's dead mama's dear friend, from 'cross the street at Raymond Hall – is going to be speaking on "The Value of Sweet Olive Versus Autumn Clematis as the Basis of the Fall Herbaceous Border." I've heard the title called out so many times, I memorized it myself. Place should be packed. Miss Mary Pickett's working herself into a frenzy.'

Mary Pickett – my employer – is up and I'm not?

'Oh, my God,' Regina said, and scrambled to the bottom of the bed for her robe.

'No hurry,' said Peach. 'Miss Mary Pickett's always in some kind of agitation. It's in her nature. She never was one could just sit down and be happy, even when she gave it her first best try.'

'You know her long?' Regina was dying for coffee, but even more than that, she was dying to talk. To Peach.

'Long enough.' Peach leaned forward. 'I don't *live* here, not like Willie Willie does, or used to at least, but I *work* here. Sometimes. I've got my own independent place. But I *been* here and *was* here the first time Mr Jackson came around for Miss Mary Pickett, back when they were young and called themselves sparking each other.'

'I'm not really that interested in what happened back then,' said Regina, a little too quickly. 'What I wanted to ask you about is Wynne Blodgett. And about something else, something someone left here.' Even with this, Regina thought she might be saying more about the shirt than she should.

But Peach shook her head. 'Oh, Mr Wynne . . . All in good time. Well, you sure should be interested in Miss Mary Pickett, in her ways and her means, since you work for her now, too, don't you? Seems everybody in Revere ends up working for her one way or another, furthering what she got in mind she wants them to do.'

Regina's eyes narrowed. She couldn't tell what Peach meant by this. But she wanted to know. She thought of Peach the first day she saw her, the way she'd gone in the front door of the Old Jail Café, sashayed where she wanted to on the courthouse square. She thought of the two sisters in the forest, their brother, *The Secret of Magic* – and Willie Willie.

If she wanted to, thought Regina, Peach could make a few things very clear.

But Peach seemed to have more important things on her mind than making things clear for Regina Mary Robichard. She reached within the folds of her shawl, pulled out a large paper square.

Peach said, 'I brought you this.'

'This' turned out to be a thin parchment envelope yellowed

with age. The envelope had been addressed to Miss Regina Mary Robichard, Esquire. There was no stamp on it. The envelope had not been sent through the mail. In its lower left-hand corner was a flourished *Courtesy of Myself and Mr Willie Willie*. In fact, all the writing was carefully scripted. Regina recognized the swoop of its swirls and its crosses.

'It was you!'

'Me, all right,' said Peach Mottley, leaning back, a smile on her face. 'Left that shirt here for you to take care of. Did you hide it real good like I told you to?'

Regina nodded, about to say exactly where she'd put it, but Peach clamped her hand over her own mouth, shook her head. 'Don't tell me a thing about it. Don't tell me nothing I don't need to know. And don't bring it with you, neither.' She tapped a light rhythm – tat-tat-tat – on the envelope. 'That is, if you come. But I *would* come, if I were you, you being Willie Willie's lawyer and all. Oh, I'd come, all right. I'd make a way out to Peach's. Now that you've been invited. There's nobody come out to Peach's who don't find what they been looking for.'

She smiled – and her smile was a promise.

Yet it was hard for Regina to hold back a retort. Peach, like Mary Pickett last night, both telling her what they wanted her to hear and not what she needed to know.

Luther Mottley's last still-alive sister was already heaving herself out of the chair, pointing the rainbow of her being toward the stoop door that lay just beyond Regina's bed and led to the stairs.

'The shirt, yes. I understand what you're wanting. But there's other things you need to know, too.' Peach shook her head, did not stop her progression. Regina waited until she heard the downstairs door open and close, and then Peach's footsteps echoing across the pea gravel toward Mary Pickett's, before she opened the envelope.

Inside was what appeared, at first glance, to be a very old, decorated Christmas card with a green fading wreath, tarnished raised gold bow, a charming *Best Wishes*. The works. Regina ran her finger over the wreath, brought the card to her nose. It smelled of faded lavender, though not unpleasantly so. Regina sat silently, waiting until she heard the screen door of Calhoun Place slam before she turned the card over and read.

Miss Peach Mottley
Invites
Miss Regina Robichard
To take tea and cake with her
Sunday
In the Sometime Afternoon
With Mr Willie Willie as Escort

The words had been carefully written, their interweaving ducking into all the nooks and crannies of reverse embossing along the card's back.

You bet she'd be there, but . . . what exactly did 'In the Some-time Afternoon' mean, anyway?

The next day, precisely at noon, Regina found herself sitting out in Willie Willie's little garden plot, waiting. She was dressed in her best gray suit and caramel-colored suede pumps, and wrapped up, she thought, a little like a Christmas present herself in a small cro-cheted afghan she'd found in the old cedar-planked chest that sat at the foot of Willie Willie's bed. The day had turned cold, with gray clouds skittering overhead through a hard-looking, bright sky. Beyond the gates of Calhoun Place, Third Avenue stretched out quiet as a museum; even the shacks that struggled down from it to the river were silent and still. A day like this, with its clean autumn smells and its absolute silence, its majesty of trees stretched so tall you had to shade your eyes from the sun to see the tips of them . . . In a week or two, in New York, when she got back there, where would she ever find so much living quiet again?

She wondered about Mary Pickett: where she was, what she was doing. She'd caught only quick glimpses of her since they'd sat side by side on the window seat and Mary Pickett had poured out her story. About her long-ago love for Jackson, about this town, about Wynne. And maybe that's all it had been – a story. Regina was already lawyer enough to realize how hard it was to get to the truth, how people hid themselves under all sorts of fictions. But Regina believed what Mary Pickett had told her, and this belief had brought with it a strange realization – that she now already knew more about the white Mary Pickett than she knew about any of the black lawyers she worked with in New York.

She was weighing all this in her mind, and counting, at the same time, the spider lilies that seemed to have sprung up everywhere, overnight, and trying to identify the fall fragrance, whether it was sweet olive or autumn clematis, when she heard the gentle rumble that heralded the arrival, in the distance, of Willie Willie's ancient but spiffy Ford pickup.

But once she was settled in beside Willie Willie in his truck, Regina turned seriously scared. Shaking scared. This was Sunday. Already. So far, she'd come up with nothing really substantive, and almost a week of her two had slipped by. Her thoughts flew straight to New York and to Skip Moseley. Saw him as he would be at this very moment, in the first pew at the Abyssinian Baptist Church up there in Harlem, sitting with his nice, pretty mama and his rich lawyer daddy and his two lawyer brothers, and their two nice, pretty, stay-at-home wives.

Yes, there would be Skip, his head lowered reverently in prayer, his perfectly tailored Brooks Brothers suit hiding a heart that was pumping away. *Heh-heh-heh.* Because she had nothing – clouds but no rain, smoke but no meat. And she was going to fail, and already Skip knew it. Had *always* known it, and soon – very soon – Thurgood would know it as well.

'Sunday, all right,' repeated Willie Willie. 'And that means

Church Time, and Church Time – like "In the Sometime After-noon" – means different things in your different places. Around here, it generally means the whole of the day. At least it does in your colored congregations. First off, you got your Sunday school and your choir tune-up, then you got your early-morning prayer for them got to go on to their regular Sunday work, then, about ten-thirty or eleven, they roll out the regular service. After that, there's normally church dinner, one thing or another. Our churches, we'll use any excuse for a meal. Congregants take their trip home after that to check on the livestock, get themselves a little rest, because at six it's straight back for evening worship. Your colored church is a filling station. Folks come in and tank up for their week.'

Regina looked down dubiously at her watch. 'How's Miss Peach gonna fit me in with all this activity?'

'Oh, Peach don't believe in no churching. After Luther got himself disappeared, she decided she was better off just Peach and God on their own.'

Regina glanced across the cracked leather seat to Willie Willie. His clothes were as crisp and immaculate as they always were, a white shirt, dark trousers, spit-shined work boots. It was hard to tell if he'd been to church or not.

They were driving out again over the same road that Regina had originally traveled into town, past the Blodgett/Mayhew house, and the place where the buck had leaped their truck, past the now-deserted bus depot. Once they got out of Revere proper, she saw the houses grow smaller and the land they sat on stretch wider and broader until it reached the red and gold autumn-splashed crouch of the trees. Occasionally, Regina saw a rooster or a pig laid out on flat gravel, its soul making peace with the day.

But that thought of Skip Moseley and their rivalry – or *his* rivalry with *her*; that's how she preferred to think of it – had clinched up her stomach good and tight. She needed to talk to Willie Willie about the case. Did he, too, believe Wynne Blodgett had killed his son? He'd never said it right out, and she needed to know what he thought, there was no more putting it off, so she tried, 'Mr Willie, I went to see Tom Raspberry about your case, and he seems . . .'

But Willie Willie shushed her right up. 'There's no talking of business on the Lord's rest day.' Instead, he pointed out the world to her as she passed through it. 'See those flowers there, that's the spider lily. I already told you about them, the ones at the court-house. They're all over the place back at the house, practically take over Miss Mary Pickett's yard this time of year. That's the sure sign there'll be no more warm weather. You hear that knock-knocking? That's one ornery woodpecker noising away. And that there . . . why, that's a wing-tipped cardinal. And that there – look quick! – that's a little bluebird family.' He stretched out a gnarled, pointing finger. 'Those like the ones make Miss Mary Pickett keep her mailbox empty. Even when she was a little girl, she was always partial to the small creatures, to the ones nobody else wanted.'

'Like Jackson Blodgett?' Regina said softly. She saw him again, limping away from Mary Pickett, up the long driveway that led out of Calhoun Place, and she *knew* that Jackson could never really have been Jack, not Jack as he'd been in *The Secret of Magic*, tramping into the forest, bold as brass, just like the others. He'd not lived *The Secret of Magic*. How could he have? Regina had seen his limp, and Mary Picket had explained it. Polio had grabbed him young, shook him over. After it finished with him, there'd been no way he could run again. Yet, with the stroke of her pen, Mary Pickett had put him where she wanted him to be, gave him the past that perhaps he himself wanted. And who knew, in years to come and in generations, when the folks who knew were all dead but the book lived on, if truth itself would be forgotten and the fiction Mary Pickett had written be believed as what had happened, as what was real?

'Hmmmm,' said Willie Willie. He was pointing out the window again, leading her eye to the bare twigs of an azalea bush and then on from there to the drying kudzu that still strangled an old oak tree, to a burdock. On and on as he pointed out things to her that she would never have seen on her own, marking out a hundred shadings of green, each with its own meaning, his fingers opening a land to her – *abracadabra!* – so glutted with foliage that she wondered how even a rabbit could wiggle through.

Regina checked her watch. They had been driving about twenty minutes now, and had come to the edge of a place that was both strange and wild. She had never seen anything remotely like it before, the lushness of green still everywhere as the calendar bore down heavily toward winter. But there was no mistaking. Willie Willie knew *exactly* where he was. He slowed the truck almost to a standstill and leaned his head close against the windshield with Regina. 'See those trees there, Miss Regina? Look up! See those bare branches touching the sky? See those spiderwebs just barely hanging on at the top? There! There! Look up, then look up again!'

And she saw them! Saw what he meant!

'That's mistletoe,' said Willie Willie, satisfied, 'the best part of the forest. In the winter, when it decides and it's ready, it floats right down on top of you. Caresses you on the cheek, touches you with magic. And when you feel that soft kiss of the mistletoe, you know the time's come to make your wish.'

'Make your wish?'

'Anything you want. It's gonna come true!'

Regina sighed with contentment. Maybe what Willie Willie said wasn't real but it sure sounded good.

'But when will we *get* there? To Magnolia Forest?'

Willie Willie started up again, turned to her and winked. 'We already there.' Regina looked around her. She didn't know how it had happened, but green had snuck up all around her, and now it was everywhere.

'Never *have* left the forest,' Willie Willie continued, 'you been in it since the day you got here, right there where you climbed off the Bonnie Blue bus. Revere *is* the forest. It was carved right out from the middle of it and built up in its midst. It's always been a fight between the town and the trees, which one's gonna win out over the other. My bet's on the forest. Some parts it's wider and thicker, some parts it's thinner. But it's always there, always ready to take back what it knows belongs to it.'

Suddenly, Willie Willie spun his truck so sharply to the left that Regina had to clutch tight to the hanging strap to keep from tipping into him.

And the path he'd turned into was twisted and narrow, the road ahead of them dark, even discreet. Immediately, the smell of the day changed from the soft scent of pine and flowers to that of rich, dark earth. Regina rolled down her window, leaned her head out.

Willie Willie said, 'You gonna like Peach.'

And Regina called out, her eyes on the forest. 'Oh, I already met her.'

'I know you already met her,' Willie Willie said with great patience. 'Now you're gonna get to *like* her. Meeting and liking – that's two different things.'

Peach's house was only a small, sly twinkle at first, but as Willie Willie drove on, it grew larger, took form. Four stout walls, then two great brick chimneys atop a dark roof. Everything coming more and more into focus, like puzzle pieces fitting together. Until suddenly the forest parted. They passed through a small clearing, and were there.

And the house was there, too, the Mottley house, just like it had been in *The Secret of Magic*. It was a *real* house, something that Mary Pickett had obviously seen and not conjured. Behind it lay a garden and a snug brick kitchen that was not attached to the main house, which sat atop a riser of red steps that rose up like a sentry from the circular, pea-gravel drive. In front waved a filigreed sign just like the one at Mary Pickett's, announcing to a visiting world that this was MOTTLEY PLACE, CONSTRUCTED 1901.

Yet even from a distance Regina could see that the paint had peeled off the main walls in strips so wide they only hinted at what once must have been the original, brilliant, bright white. Still, the red geraniums were there, just like they had been in the book, a bright flash of them on each rung of the stairs and lining the path that skirted the house and led to the forest. Geraniums in terracotta, in Maxwell House two-pound coffee tins, in splintery wooden slatted fruit boxes. The house itself was placed at a soft angle slightly off-center of the driveway, making it look something like the top curve of a question mark.

At the apex of which stood Peach, waving to them from the open front door, her free hand shading her eyes.

Regina climbed out of the truck; she didn't wait for Willie Willie. By the time she heard the click of his door, she was already making her way to that house. And there she was right beside her, on the porch, and it was the same porch that Mary Pickett had – green floorboards, a blue-painted ceiling. A combination, according to M. P. Calhoun, that mosquitoes just could not abide.

'Come on in, sugar,' sang out Miss Peach. But she looked at her in a singular way and, for the first time, Regina hesitated. The forest grew still, seemed to hold its breath around her. For a second she was a child again, stealing her mother's sewing flashlight, taking it into her bedroom under her covers so she could read *The Secret of Magic* and find out with the children if Peach was a witch. If she had killed Luther, her brother, and if, after what Raspberry had told her, Willie Willie had helped her.

But that wasn't why she was here, not to solve that long-ago mystery – if it was a mystery, if any of it was true at all – but to unravel a real-life present-day puzzle. To find out who had killed Joe Howard and to get Willie Willie some justice for his son. So in the end, she reached out to Peach, to the warm honey-fruit smell of her, to her flowered apron hanging like a picture over a flower-on-flower silk dress, to her sachet-powdered bosom that looked like a tea cake dusted with sugar, and she kissed her warm, scarred cheek, while around them the forest sighed.

'Thank you for inviting me,' said Regina.

'Glad for the company,' said Miss Peach heartily, sounding like she meant it. *A woman alone, used to being alone. Months, years, decades of loneliness.* The thought sobered Regina.

'Glad for it,' Peach repeated. 'Few are the folks now who turn up out here.'

'I thought she might like going into the house,' Willie Willie said to Peach. He was beside them both, a gentleman opening the faded wooden screen door. 'I thought it would be a treat for her, since she read that Miss Mary Pickett book.'

'But the house wasn't in the book; the inside of it wasn't! At least not like it is,' said Peach, looking pleased yet shaking her head.

'Still, I thought it'd be mighty nice if you showed it.' And then to Regina, 'You're in for a treat. Peach lives in the very best showing place of how things used to be in the South. She worked many a year for Miss Charlotte and Miss Luisa and Miss Hunnicutt Lindleigh, and for their mother before them. Did all their laundry. Other folks', too.' He winked at her. 'Best you remember that. It's part of her story.'

A smile gathered up the wrinkles on Peach's full, biscuit-colored face. 'I was always one for being independent. Independent of Daddy. Independent of Luther. I wanted my own livelihood for myself.'

She laughed at this, and Willie Willie laughed along with her, and then Regina joined in because they seemed to be having a good time. Peach reached over and tenderly ran a finger down the length of Willie Willie's shirt. Touched his hand, as he flourished open the door so she could pass through.

How could anyone describe Peach's house, the absolute profusion of it? The gaudiness, really. It reminded Regina of an overloaded Victorian Christmas tree. Turkey carpets overlapped one another on the floor, sometimes three deep, while up the green brocade walls marched portrait after portrait of gilt-framed American soldiers, some of them old enough that the men were in blue uniform, but the most, and by far the largest of the pictures, memorializing them in gray. One of the pictures had been hung sideways, the only way it could fit. Banners – OUR GLORIOUS CAUSE! HAIL FALLEN HEROES! – waved in a draft from the door. And flags, too, at least two regimental ones, shading down from the ceiling, their colors dim, their edges frayed. But still . . . there.

On Peach's walls, the men were segregated on one side, corseted women hung on the other, the ladies holding tightly on to children or to lace handkerchiefs or to nosegays of African violets. But always clutching at something, at least that's how it looked to Regina, and the children doing it, too, their hands wrapped around a doll, resting small fists on a rocking horse. The only thing they had in common was that they were, all of them, white. Which meant they couldn't have much to do with the Mottleys, so why were they here?

Regina looked over, and there was Peach, with her eyes wary but her head nodding, and behind her, Willie Willie nodding as well. Peach raised her hand.

'Please step into my parlor,' she said with great formality, sounding like the spider in a children's picture book.

Six sofas had found a crowded home in a snug little room with gold-green walls. One a rich burgundy velvet, one a green damask, one filigreed gold on black silk. Regina couldn't tell anything about the other three because these were hidden under scarves so bright they looked like something Peach might wear, and probably did. Chippendale chairs stacked carelessly up one wall and down another.

'Didn't have space to put not one more thing over there. Had to crowd the rest of it here,' said Peach, coming up and throwing a gesture toward a closed door. 'There's two long tables and sixteen high-back chairs in the dining room already. Not to mention the sideboards and the butler tables and the silver flatware and the china plates. My goodness, how those Lindleighs could eat!'

Not everything was in the best of shape, though. Some of the chair cushions were patched with fabric that didn't quite match the green damask on the sofa nearest Regina. Still, what did a patch or a worn spot here or there matter in the face of so much?

In a room with claw-foot tables and brass-legged tables, glass-and marble-topped mahogany, walnut, oak, mother-of-pearl inlaid on ebony tables – an *opulence* of them, an obstacle course! – Regina decided she'd better watch her step.

'My house,' Peach said with a pleased sigh. 'My home. All mine. My very own.'

'This here is Stream Run, the Willman place,' said Willie Willie in dignified explanation. 'Well, technically maybe not Stream Run *itself*.' He took a moment to ponder over this. 'But surely what you might call the idea behind it. You see, Old Mottley, Miss Peach's departed daddy, always hankered after that house. Had a crush on it. *Loved* it. He made all his own store deliveries to Mr Roger Willman's; he wouldn't send one of his working boys. And while he was in the kitchen putting things up, he'd look around a corner, peep on in, see just enough to figure things out.'

'Daddy was good at that,' said Peach, her smile now pouring like sunshine onto Regina. 'I already told you how he built that new jail, put together everything in it, from the foundation up. Even forged the iron for the cells.'

'Good *enough*,' corrected Willie Willie. 'Mottley got his mind around the downstairs, even figured out the wainscoting and the medallions and the brass chandeliers. But there was no way the Willmans were going to let him go up into the bedrooms. No way in this world was that going to happen. That's why the whole of this place is only one story tall.'

He moved aside so that Regina could peek at a curving stair-way, stare at it as it arched gracefully upward, straight to the ceiling and its abrupt end.

Willie Willie continued. 'Good thing, too, as life turned out. Civil War didn't make it to Revere, but the Depressing did. Mr Willman lost his cotton place out there on the prairie back when Judge Calhoun and a lot of other folks did. Mr Roger had to break up Stream Run – the original, real Stream Run, that is – into apartments. Efficiency ones, with no kitchens. He did this during the last war and one of the officers in the Army Air Corps living there called himself cooking on a hot plate, something strictly forbidden. The hot plate overheated, the house caught fire, and the whole thing burned right down clean to the ground. So this little Stream Run out here . . . why, it's the only Stream Run anybody's got left.'

'That's so,' said Peach in confirmation.

'With all this *beauty* added on to it' – a very wide sweep of Willie Willie's hand that took in the surrounding profusion – 'little by little, Miss Peach's folks gave her all this.'

'Her folks?' From Regina. Thinking, *The Mottleys were this rich?*

'The people she worked for. Mostly the Lindleighs, like I said. When the big houses in town broke up, when they were re-inventing themselves into apartments, folks took to giving away all they could. What they couldn't, they burned. Miss Carol Ann McCall, for one. Before they moved her to that rooming house in Aberdeen, she stood over that big lawn at her place and called her working men together and had them spark up the sprawlingest bonfire ever seen in this town. And she, tall and straight, stood out in front of it, burning up every single likeness ever been painted of her family members, tossing them on one after another with her very own lace-mitted hands. Took her half an afternoon and into the night. Miss Carol Ann said she didn't want her people taking up space in some godforsaken auction hall down New Orleans. Miss Carol Ann wasn't the only one to do it, neither. Lindleighs did it, too. I remember when the last three of those sisters were about getting married. One of them moving up to Memphis, one down to Biloxi, one God knows where. You remember where Miss Luisa ended up, Peach?'

'Way, *way* on up north she went,' Peach replied promptly. 'Clear to Nashville.'

'All three of them, during the war, married servicemen and moved into apartments where there probably wasn't gonna be room to turn around in. What they gonna do with all that Lindleigh stuff? They had put all their own family portraits on a mule wagon along with God knows what else and were hauling it all out to some landfill in East Revere when Peach caught sight of them on Main Street. "Why, that's your grandmamma Rosalie," she said to those sisters. "You can't be carrying your grandmamma Rosalie out to the likes of Tom Phinney's dump."'

'True,' said Peach. 'That's what I thought, and that's what I said.'

Willie Willie nodded, went on. 'So they gave her the whole wagonload. That brown sofa there, those mockingbird dishes – that all came from them. And they added on a little bit of this, a whole lot of that. After a while Peach got herself more things that belonged to Lindleighs than Lindleighs got left for themselves. That's how she ended up with everything you see in here. Folks she worked for and their friends, they gave it to her. Little by little. Of course, passing on to coloreds that work for you isn't considered the same thing as selling your fine things or giving your fine things away.'

'That story told,' said Peach, 'let me slip on outside, bring in the tea.'

Regina asked, 'Need any help?'

'No help at all. I got me a *stand*-alone kitchen, and those shoes' – she gestured to Regina's pumps – 'you wouldn't make it there.'

Peach turned to Willie Willie, who nodded. 'Peach's still cooking over an ole-timey stove. Kerosene. Jugs of it out back. Anything sparks, this place'd go up like spit lightning. Dangerous, but she's too old to change her ways now. And, of course, there's no electricity running this far deep in the county, so she needs that oil for everything. I'll help her. You go on in. Seat yourself wherever you want.'

Regina almost tiptoed into the parlor, looked around again, did not sit down. She wondered if Mary Pickett had actually seen the Mottley house, been in it. She wondered if she had kept it out of her book on purpose so that people would leave the Mottleys alone. A mercy. She liked Revere, but she'd already seen enough to know that the elements that ruled it would not easily tolerate a colored person who lived a fine life. This was probably why Old Mr Mottley had decided to build his own Stream Run so deep in the forest. To keep it hidden. To keep his family safe.

Little more than a minute and then Peach came back. She wheeled in an inlaid mahogany butler's tray, Willie Willie pulling back the door. Peach peered around the corner toward the front door, cocked her head, seemed to be listening. Finally, she turned back to Regina. The smile of her lips worked deep crinkles into the scar on her face. She said, 'It's getting late. I guess we better go on and get started.' Peach sat down, motioned for Regina to sit beside her, and then poured tea from Georgian silver into delicate, hand-painted chipped cups. Outside, there was a steady rustle of tree branch against house window, the sound of a forest forever trying to get in.

Across from them, Willie Willie eased himself into a large green velvet chair that sat next to a gold ormolu table, his body fitting comfortably into its depressions, his head the perfect shadow on the ivory lace shawl that covered its back.

Why, Willie Willie comes here often, Regina thought. But of course that was true. It had probably always been true. Hadn't Mary Pickett as much as admitted it? Hadn't Tom Raspberry implied it when he told her about Luther Mottley's death? Maybe, since he'd left the cottage, he actually lived out here now with Peach. Hadn't Mary Picket said something like that?

Regina said, 'Miss Calhoun ever been here?'

'*All* the children came out here,' Peach immediately corrected. 'All with a hankering to see the old witch.'

'They thought Peach killed her brother, just like it says in the book,' said Willie Willie.

They looked at her. They both knew she had read it – Willie Willie because Regina had told him, and then, of course, he'd naturally told Peach.

Well, did you kill him? It was on the tip of Regina's tongue, but she couldn't ask it, not to these two old people who had both been so kind to her.

'Tell her how the Luther part goes,' said Peach quietly. 'You know it better than anybody else.'

Willie Willie leaned back in his chair. He held his head high, almost like he was reading something, a secret scrawled into the delicate wainscoting at the edge of the ceiling – wainscoting that had been carved by free hands, not enslaved hands like the ones that had carved out all that was beautiful in Mary Pickett's house.

'*Mean,*' said Willie Willie. '*That was the word most used to describe Luther Mottley. The word always stayed the same, though what folks signified by it might have shifted some, down through the years. At first mean meant selfish and tightfisted. Somebody who'd never part with anything if he thought it might do somebody else some good. People complained about him, talked about him behind his back, but he couldn't do much real damage, could he? That's all that mattered. A colored man owns a store . . . Want to or not, he has to give credit where credit is due. And down here, credit's due to white people. But he didn't have to like it, did he, now, Luther? Didn't have to like it one bit. And believe me, he didn't. Every chance he got . . .*'

Beside Regina, Peach shuddered.

How good Willie Willie was at his story! Not just with his mouth and his words, but Regina watched his eyes move and a shadow cross his face, then lift, watched his lips purse, his shoulders shift up, slip down, the uh-uh-uh in the shake of his head, his hands a symphony in themselves.

'*He kept the store up. He provided. But Luther was always the type to claw you open if he got scent to your weak side.*'

Regina watched, fascinated, as Willie Willie's body became the *bearer* of his tale, the living platter from which it was lifted. And it was such a simple story, really, all about a thwarted weak man who plucked daily at those he thought weaker than he was. '"*Go on in there, Peach, and iron my britches the way I like 'em this time. You want me to have to lay my strap upside your nappy head again? Want me to match up that scar I already put on your face? Sister? What you mean about Sister? She ain't got no broke hip. She don't need no doctor.*

What she wants is attention. Nobody give it to her, one day she'll heal up, get up, go on about her business!"'

Nothing heroic or noble or even much good lived in the life of Luther Mottley – but, gosh, the way it was told!

'Luther did what he did 'cause he could. This is Mississippi, after all, and a man can do what he wants in his castle. Even a black man, as long as what he's doing doesn't interfere with what the white folks are doing. And Luther made sure what he did didn't interfere; at least he thought that it didn't. Until one day – why, up pops the Devil. Then it's no more Luther owning his badness, it's his badness owning him.'

On and on went Willie Willie as the forest settled around him, as tree limbs brushed against the windows, as Peach refilled tea-cups, as she cut them big slices of Lady Baltimore cake. None of this seemed to matter to Willie Willie. Regina listened, curious, and then she started to shiver. Just as Peach had shivered. She couldn't be certain, not absolutely, and she didn't know quite what to make of it, but it was extraordinary to hear what sounded like Mary Pickett's own story, her *Secret of Magic*, told by Willie Willie exactly as it had been written. Luther's face, thunderous as an accumulating cumulus cloud. His eyes hard as Indian flint. His hands big as bullocks. Word by careful word. And with no real ending to it, just like there'd been no real end to the book. Except, of course, the ending of Sister.

'Luther disappeared, but it was too late for her,' Willie Willie said, shaking his head. 'They got her up, got her on into the buck-board, going to the doctor. William Mills. The colored one that was then. Lived over in Mayhew. By the time we – they – got her there, though, it was too late for Sister. She'd already passed on.'

Regina had been staring at Willie Willie, mesmerized by him, but now she looked up. And there was Peach watching her, eyes big over the rim of her teacup. They were unreadable eyes, really, narrowed by slit lids – but there was something in them that darted Regina's mind back to Mary Pickett's, to Willie Willie's cottage, and to the damaged white shirt hidden there.

12.

When tea was finished and the cups and the cake had been wheeled once again outside to the kitchen, Peach said, 'Mr Willie Willie, you go on out there, bring the truck around closer for Miss Regina. She can't be traipsing around in the dark.'

It wasn't *quite* dark, but Willie Willie said, 'Sure thing, Miss Peach,' and set off. The truck was parked at the end of a dirt-pack drive, a short distance, and Regina could surely have walked it, but she stood beside Peach and watched him from the broad Mottley porch. Around them, the silence was suddenly so thick that Willie Willie's footsteps echoed back to them magnified, as though he might be walking into a megaphone instead of over gravel and then onto solid packed earth. Standing there, brushing up against each other, Regina and Peach heard his truck door slam shut. Regina thought he'd fire the engine, but he didn't. She saw a match flame and then the glowing ember of his cigarette. She smelled its smoke. Peach reached over and took Regina's hand. Peach's hand was warm as cloth cotton, and the air around her smelled like cinnamon toast.

'Let us rest ourselves here for a spell, enjoy this fine moment.'

They eased down, sitting side by side, each looking past Willie Willie, their gazes set deep into the forest. Regina leaned toward Peach and held her breath. She realized she'd been doing this all afternoon, even while Willie Willie was telling his story, and that she'd been moving closer, at least in her mind, so that Peach could tell her *something*.

And Regina knew that that something would be about the shirt. She'd felt a knowledge scintillating around them all afternoon, since before that, even; a feeling that Peach knew secrets, things that might make a difference, could bring them to the tip of her tongue. That is, if she wanted to. And Peach . . . well, Peach knew about the shirt. She'd hinted it earlier, when she'd come to invite Regina out to Mottley Place, out to the forest. Not wanting to push, Regina wished for the calm of one of Mary Pickett's Chesterfield cigarettes. Waited. Yet, for a long time, Peach said not a word.

Then, 'You know about *Gotcha!*, don't you, from in that *Magic* book?'

Regina nodded and Peach nodded with her, the long curved scar on her cheek catching the glow from the kerosene light. 'That *Gotcha!*, it's real, you know, rooted deep. And we all got some of it growing in us; depending on the life, a little or a lot. Something done to us, something done by us; all in there hidden, waiting to pop out. Just like in the book when the magnolia roots break through the sidewalk, and once they broke up, ain't nothing you can do anymore to make things right again, make them pretty, unless you cut down the tree. That's what *Gotcha!* is, Miss Regina, in that book and in the life. What you done, you got to own up to. Things might still look nice on the surface, but it's working its way up. One of these days, you least expect it, it's gonna call *Gotcha!* You gonna get it or it's gonna get you.'

Regina looked up, and for an instant, out there, deep in the trees, she thought she saw her mother, her poor dead father, Joe Howard, all of them together. Honorable people who wanted nothing more than an honorable life. And had been determined to get it, to make something of themselves. Regina squinted closer. Thought for sure, in that instant, she saw a ladybug, bright as hope, flitting around them. Then that same ladybug flying away.

'Yes,' she said. 'I know me some *Gotcha!*'

Peach, too, had been staring at something out into the forest. 'Wynne Blodgett, rich as he is . . . I got the feeling he's about to learn him some *Gotcha!*, too.'

The rest came out as a rushed whisper. 'I'm not good at taletelling, not like Willie Willie is, so I'll get this out as quick as I can.'

After Luther's 'disappearing' and Sister's 'passing on,' Peach had had to get right back to work. No time for mourning. She couldn't hold on to the store, not by herself she couldn't. And she needed the money. Black or white, in the South *everybody* needed money. It would still be some years, she said, before the Great Depressing hit them, but in Mississippi, times were already Depressing enough. But she was a Smart Girl ('At least that's what they called me') and worked hard. Her ironing was good. Her pies much renowned.

'But it's the laundry part I need to go on about here.'

At first Peach worked, like she always had, for people like the Lindleighs and the Mayhews, folks who had taken their trade to the Mottley store and knew all about Luther, ladies Peach had known her whole life. But then, as the years wound on and the old families died off, lost their land, started moving away, Peach had to look around and find, as she now delicately put it, 'Some new sheets that needed washing.

'First one showed up, all smiles, was Mae Louise Wynne. Who'd managed to turn herself into Mae Louise Blodgett. *She* came to *me*. I didn't go to her. Seems her husband had recently bought the old Mayhew house and she needed some help, and with what she was paying, I was happy to oblige. But I never had one bit of delusion about Miss Mae Louise and what it was she was after. I was good at what I did, that's sure enough truth, but it was who I'd done *for* – that's what mattered most to Miss Mae Louise. Lindleighs. Mayhews, even Calhouns. She wanted me working for her because I'd once worked for them.'

But Mae Louise proved easy enough to 'do' for, and Peach ended up working over at the Blodgett house for years. They'd settled into a routine early on. Peach showed up at nine Monday mornings, right after Jackson had gone to the office and Mae Louise had gone back to bed. Peach did the washing. That was that.

'And Wynne?' This from Regina.

Peach shook her head. 'Oh, Wynne could be anyplace, even when he was little and *should* have been in school. But he wasn't. Not always. He had those cousins, you see. His mama's people.

He'd sneak off. Spend time with them. He didn't have much idea what was going on in his house; didn't care, neither. At least, that's how it seemed to me.'

'But didn't his parents *make* him go to school?' said Regina, shocked. She thought her mother would have been, too, and Thurgood and Skip Moseley and almost everybody else she knew, striving away up in Harlem, that somebody who had the chance to go to school didn't. For all them, education was the acme of their world, the heartbeat of its ambition.

'Child,' said Peach, with a shake of her head and a shrug. 'You got to understand. Wynne's mama, his daddy – they *loved* that boy to death. He could do no wrong. Pretty like he is, maybe everything they wanted to be but weren't, Wynne got to do just as he pleased.'

On Mondays, Jackson and Mae Louise would leave their dirty laundry waiting in the hamper in the bathroom, and Wynne's was supposed to be there, too. But usually it wasn't, and Peach would have to go hunting it up. She'd take it down to the cellar, wash it all out, hang it to dry, then iron it in the afternoon and put it where it belonged.

'I hardly ever saw Miss Mae Louise. Once she got up, she was out and about. But she knew how I liked to dress, all patched up and put together. Knew I liked to hold on to things. So, once in a while, she'd sit the sack of clothes, the things she planned to send over to the Salvation Army, at the back door. She told me to take what I wanted and just leave the rest. So, maybe a week after Joe Howard'd gone missing – but before he'd turned up – I sifted through it. And there was the shirt.' A gleam in Peach's eye aimed straight at Regina. 'I didn't go looking for it. It was just there.'

'Maybe put in that sack by Mrs Blodgett?' Regina's voice barely a whisper.

'Maybe,' said Peach. 'Or by Wynne himself. He was that careless, that above-it-all and special. And it was sure his shirt. I could tell that right away. Nobody in that house was fancy like he was.'

But she hadn't realized *exactly* what she'd found, not initially.

The shirt was all smudged up and ruined, but the fabric was good, and almost all the bright, shiny buttons were there, only one of them missing.

'So I put it with the rest, squirreled it away like I'm used to.' Peach gestured behind her to the house. 'Everything I got, I knew I'd pick out a use for it one day. Then things started happening. Joe Howard finally found. Willie Willie beside himself. Miss Mary Pickett looking crushed . . . So much going on, I forgot all about that shirt.'

'Until?' Regina now edged so close, she could feel Peach's warm breath on her cheek.

'Until Willie Willie went tracking, went looking for the place where they killed off his boy and came back with Joe Howard's medal and a button. Said he'd found them together. And I knew right away it was *that* button, the one missing from off of Wynne's shirt.'

'The thing that Willie Willie's always flipping,' said Regina, looking back in her mind, seeing him do it, at the bus depot, on Mary Pickett's street corner. Wherever he'd seen Wynne Blodgett.

Peach nodded. 'And I knew what was around it then, too, that smudgy bad stain where that button had been . . . Why, that was blood. Poor Joe Howard's blood.'

'But . . .' said Regina, shaking her head, a lawyer again, not a friend, and *Where was the proof?*

'I know what it is,' Peach snapped. 'And you know it, too.'

Regina nodded, and Peach went back to her story, whispering that she hadn't told any of this to anyone, not even to Willie Willie, and, above all, she'd not shown anyone the shirt.

'Wynne's mama,' Peach said, 'she'd have forgotten all about it, and Wynne himself would think it long gone. Even if he knew I had it, wouldn't have made one smack piece of difference to him. I'm Negro, he's white – that's the only thing matters. He's not scared one bit. Ain't a jury in the South's gonna go after him. Mr Bed tried, look what it got him.'

'But Mr Willie Willie? Why didn't you show it to him?'

This time Peach did sigh. 'To keep trouble away.'

'How?'

'What you don't know, really *know*, how can it hurt you? And that shirt might not mean anything to a Blodgett-bought judge down here in Mississippi. But to Willie Willie – it's proof.'

Regina closed her eyes, looked back for an instant. Again, saw that slice of bright silver, tossed into the air, throwing back light. Saw Wynne Blodgett staring at it, transfixed. Saw it land again in Willie Willie's dark hand.

'But he knows,' whispered Regina. 'Somehow or other.' *Both of them do.*

'Not got no *proof*, though, without that shirt,' Peach insisted. 'You the lawyer, you know that. That's why I gave it to you. You're Willie Willie's *attorney-at-law*, come down to get him some justice. You'll know just what to do with it, who to give it to. When the time comes, I know you will.'

'Miss Peach, I'm not sure . . .' And for a moment Regina's mind was crawling with fear. That Peach was giving her too much credit. That Skip Moseley was right and she was out of her league.

'No,' insisted Peach. 'You're the one. I thought it out before I gave it to you, and I been thinking about it ever since. You can take that shirt away, use it to get a real trial for Willie Willie. Up there with some fair-minded New York folk.'

'Miss Peach, justice . . . the system . . . it doesn't work like that. What happened here, it's got to be *tried* here. At least at the start.'

Peach looked out toward Willie Willie. 'You'll figure out something.' Then, 'Isn't that what you're supposed to do?'

They sat staring at each other for a moment, each deep in thought, both still as stones. Finally, Peach patted Regina, a soft running of fingers along her arm, then reached into the deep pocket of her apron and brought out something cold and hard, and passed it to Regina. She pressed it deep into the delicate bones and small mounds of tender muscle that made up Regina's hand. Pressed down so hard that Regina cried, 'Ouch,' and would have pulled back, but she couldn't.

What Peach had given her was a key.

She looked over at Peach again, and, for the first time, this close, Regina could see the tracing of fine lines around her new friend's mouth, could almost see Peach's lips clutching tight to cigarette after cigarette. She wondered what life must have been like for her, the witch, living out here all these years after Sister had died and Luther . . . After whatever it was that had happened to Luther. Peach all by herself with the *Gotcha!*

'It's to the jailhouse,' she said. 'The new one my daddy built up with his two hands, from its foundations. Did everything in it. 'Member I told you about that? Now, my daddy was a man given to pondering deeply, and when he finished up the iron work on the windows and the rooms and the lock-ups over there at the jail what he thought to himself was, "Henry Mottley, you go 'head and make yourself an extra one of them cell keys." See, living in Mississippi like we do, you never can tell when a nice set of jail keys might come in right handy. You still can't tell it now.' She took a breath. 'Daddy called it a "just in case."'

Down the path, Willie Willie arched his cigarette out the window. The two women heard his truck door open, heard the rustle of leaves as he ground the cigarette butt carefully into the earth.

Peach said, 'He's always careful about that. "Don't want no fires this deep in the forest." That's what he says.'

He climbed back inside, started up, and they heard the gentle rumble of its engine and the smooth way Willie Willie shifted it into gear.

'Just in case,' Peach repeated. 'Keep hold to it. Don't tell a soul.'

Once she and Willie Willie started off, Regina rolled down the window, looked back. Peach stood on tiptoe on the top step of her porch, as though by stretching tall she might be able to make them out a little while longer before they disappeared. At least, that's what Regina thought. She waved and waved, quick motions, almost urgent in their goodwill, and Regina wanted to tell Willie Willie to stop the truck for a moment. That she needed to run back to Peach and tell her something, or hear something from her. But she realized how silly this sounded.

I still have a week here. I'll see Miss Peach again soon. There'll be plenty of time to come back. Why, when I come back I'll bring my copy of Magic *and I'll get her to sign it. Miss Peach writes as fine a hand as Mary Pickett does. Didn't that invitation she gave me look perfect, and she must have written it out herself. I'll bet she'll like it when I ask for her autograph.*

A crow cawed. An owl hooted. Willie Willie turned out of the forest, onto the main road. And Peach disappeared.

They drove along in silence, the road a ribbon before them, mile after dark mile. And no sound on it except the rattle of the truck, the call of autumn's last lonely cicadas, the soft rustle of the wind as it breathed through the trees. Regina's mind was on what Peach had just told her, on that shirt. She still had no idea what she would do with it. But now that she realized how important it was, she was anxious to get back to the cottage, to check on it, to make sure it had not disappeared.

She was thinking all this when she heard Willie Willie say, 'I do believe you might do it.'

Regina turned toward him. 'Do what?'

'Set things right for Joe Howard. Peach said you would. Told me that the first time she met you. Repeated herself again when the two of us went out back to the kitchen room after the tea.'

Again, Regina thought to the shirt, to what Peach had just told her, but said, 'She thinks I can get us a trial in New York, but I can't. We got to work here, and things don't look good. You got a judge out of town bird hunting, and a district attorney who's washed his hands of the whole thing. Says he's done what he could. Got a *grand jury* called, didn't he? And everybody, himself included, acts like he's some sort of saint.'

'A grand jury *was* something. Nothing like that's ever been done before, at least not in Revere. Not for a Negro man. Got my hopes up with it. If the law worked, then the order behind it might work, too. That's what I thought. But nothing came of it, and before you got here, I swore I'd just . . . Well, I guess you don't need to know what I was planning to do.'

'Did I tell you,' said Regina, brightening some. 'Jackson Blodgett did get the sheriff to get me the grand jury docket – not that they helped all that much. He said you were the one first took him out to the forest.'

'Which one said that – Jackie Earle Blodgett or Rand Connelly? They both could have, you know. *All* the boy children came with me, one time or another. Even the ones I didn't particularly take to, like Rand Connelly. Even the ones came from hardscrabble stock, like Jackie Earle and his wife-stealing brother. We knew each other and I *had* to take them all, me being nothing more than a nigger man and all.'

Regina had never heard him use this word before. The force of it slapped her.

'Don't call yourself that,' she lashed out without thinking. 'Let them do it if they want to, but don't you give them the satisfaction of knowing they can make you do it to. Besides . . .'

'Besides what?' If Willie Willie were astonished by what she'd just said, he didn't show it. 'Why, Miss Regina, that's the whole tragedy of it. Lynching's a terrible thing, that much is for certain, but the judge explained to me once what tragedy *really* is, the literal, old-timey meaning of the word. It's something that might look good outside but inside it's evil. Can't control it. Nothing you can do about it. And, sure enough, Mississippi's a tragedy. The state of it is. These people who won't do a thing about Joe Howard . . . why, I've known them all my life. They've known me. They knew him. A place like Revere – it's not like Memphis or Jackson or New Orleans. Everybody's in everybody else's business here. White ones and black ones, we all played together. Dreamed our little dreams together, concocted our lives. Up until we were ten, that is. After that, we split up. Went our separate ways. White ones going on to school. Black ones mostly out to the fields. White ones sifting themselves into your good folk and your good-for-nothing folks. Sure as black from white, this happened, too. But that didn't stop us from *knowing* each other, if you understand what I mean.'

After that, they drove back to Revere in silence, Willie Willie's truck lights tracing out the road ahead. Regina opened her purse and dropped the key into it. She felt it wedge its way in between her lipstick and compact, her handkerchief and change purse and wallet. She felt it brush against the smooth-sided picture of dead Lieutenant Joe Howard. She rolled her window all the way down. There was pine and the wood smoke on the air, autumn scents, and she wondered what springtime would smell like in a place like this. And she thought about the buck. She wondered if she might see it again before she left, if it might wander one last time out of the forest and into Mary Pickett's garden. She hoped it would.

It was only after they had driven far enough into town that the forest backed off and released them onto a road where light flickered through curtained windows. They were driving down Main Street again, past the big houses Willie Willie had told her about when she'd first come into town, but going by this time he kept his eyes straight ahead. 'A nice place, but still . . . it's best to be careful. Don't let no wayward thing get hold to you.'

'Who would want *me*,' said Regina, and she laughed.

'Maybe nothing . . . But then again, maybe something.'

She didn't know what he meant by this, looked over at him, saw nothing on his face. They turned onto Third Avenue, and there was Calhoun Place. The way Mary Pickett's house was set, close to the street, you could stop at the curb or follow the long brick driveway all the way in and be led right straight through to the rear of the house and the cottage. Since the cottage was near the back door, Regina had always thought the drive was set up this way so that deliveries could be made through the kitchen or that folks could ask questions of the help. But in the time she'd been here, she'd never seen a car pull all the way to the end. Normally, Willie Willie parked at the curb. Mary Pickett kept her Daimler in its own patch of gravel at the side of her house. Dinetta walked wherever she went.

But tonight Willie Willie turned in, drove clear through. Regina peered over at Calhoun Place. There was a light on over the front door and another farther down on the veranda. She saw a silver tray and some glasses. Regina looked around for Jackson Blodgett's blue Buick. *Regina, you ever been in love?* But the Daimler and the slowly moving Ford truck were the only vehicles there.

Calhoun Place itself was brightly illuminated, more brilliant than Regina had ever seen it before. Light poured out like a stream of fresh lemonade from the glass front door and peeked out through cracks around the draperies on the main floor. Mary Pickett getting ready for her garden fete, thought Regina, remembering what Peach had told her. She wondered about that long portrait in the front hall and what Mary Pickett's mother, Miss Eulalie, caught forever looking back, would think about what was happening with Willie Willie, what had happened to Joe Howard.

They were almost at the cottage itself when Willie Willie turned off the engine and let his truck die. He didn't move. That's what got Regina's attention, his absolute stillness, a stillness that drew everything into itself. She swiveled around from looking at Mary Pickett's, speculating about her coming party and her mother's life, so that she could see what Willie Willie was seeing.

The door to the cottage stood open. Behind it, dark rooms yawned, a black gaping hole – except for a light from the bedroom that splashed brightness onto the bricks.

'You leave that bulb on? You leave that door open?'

She thought back. 'It was afternoon when we left. I don't think so.'

Willie Willie's voice calm as the weather. 'Now, what I want you to do, Miss Regina, is reach under your seat, pass me over that shotgun tucked in there. Gentle. It's loaded.'

'It could have flown open. The door, that is. Maybe the wind . . .'

'Nope, no wind. Door's been opened on purpose.'

She didn't know how he knew this, but she believed, right away, that he did. She handed over the gun, gingerly as she could. It was the first one she'd ever handled, and for a moment she was more scared of it than she was of that gaping front door. This feeling didn't last long.

'You think I need to call the sheriff? Mary Pickett's got that phone right there inside the kitchen . . . I know where it is . . . I wouldn't be trespassing. I mean, she *told* me I could just go on right in . . .' Regina realized she was jabbering, and she forced herself to shut up.

Willie Willie said, 'Wait here.'

He left the headlights of the Ford burning and jumped onto the drive. His feet came down so lightly that Regina barely heard them land. She saw him pause at the door, pull something from it. And then watched as he slowly entered his house.

The shirt! Oh, God, I hope nobody found it. I hope Willie Willie doesn't find it now.

Once inside, he turned a flashlight on. It must have been one he kept near the front door, but she'd never seen it. Regina watched its pinpoint reaching into the downstairs corners, disappearing for a moment as Willie Willie went into the kitchen, then becoming visible again as he traced a path up the stairs. She wondered why he didn't turn on the electric lights, but he didn't. Regina had to scoot down a little and wedge herself closer against the windshield in order to see his shadow against the curtain in the bedroom. She heard a door open and then close again. This, she decided, must be the small closet next to the bed. In a minute she saw a faint light seeping out of the bathroom window, a busy piece of brightness, industrious as a firefly. She decided that Willie Willie must be checking behind the shower curtain, looking in the ancient claw-foot bathtub. Making sure everything was safe for her.

After that, one by one, the electric lights flashed to life, first in the bathroom, then in the bedroom, the living room and the kitchen. Willie Willie didn't stop until the whole cottage was lit up, bright as Mary Pickett's. Through the little window, Regina watched him walk back downstairs and out through the front door. She realized she'd been holding her breath but now it gushed out. She scrambled out from the truck before he got to her.

'I guess I didn't close it all the way after all.' She didn't really know which one of them she was reassuring.

'Nothing but this.' He held a sheet out to her. The paper blue and so porous she could see the lights and the outlines of the cottage right through it.

She looked at him quizzically. 'What's it say?'

But Willie Willie shook his head, looked sheepish. 'Can't quite make out the words myself. Ain't got my glasses.' He reached the paper over to her, and she took it.

There were just a few words on the flyer. She sped through them and then smiled over at Willie Willie as she read them again, this time out loud.

INFORMATION WANTED IN THE DEATH
OF LIEUTENANT JOE HOWARD WILSON
Contact
Thomas Banks Raspberry
NAACP
Revere, Mississippi
Cash Reward

When she looked up, Willie Willie was frowning. 'You know anything about this, Miss Regina? These – what did you call them – flyers?'

The look on his face made her own smile falter. 'Well, actually, they were my idea. I thought if we put up something around town, we might generate some interest. Not everybody knew about that grand jury. Anna Dale Buchanan didn't, not 'til she read about it in the paper. There might be other people like her. It's not that the city went out of its way to let folks know what had happened. I asked Tom Raspberry to help because he's got that printing press puts out his paper. At first he laughed, said he wasn't going to do it. I don't know what made him change his mind, but he must have printed these out and left me one to show what he'd done. Put too much pressure on the door and didn't see that it opened.' Regina babbling almost, she was that relieved. That yawning door, so frightening when she'd first seen it, now meant nothing after all.

'Could be,' said Willie Willie, busy breaking the shotgun, but then he stopped what he was doing and gave Regina his full and steady attention. 'Could be Tom Raspberry's just bought himself a whole mess of trouble, and that's his right. Tom's been in trouble before this, lots of it, and he's always managed to wiggle himself free. He's the type attracts fuss like flypaper attracts flies. I just don't want you getting stuck up there beside him. Might not be so easy for you to get yourself off it as it has been for him.'

'Yep, put 'em up all over town,' said Tom Raspberry, already in his office at eight the next morning when Regina came in. He was sipping coffee, in a good mood. Five other people were crowded in there with him. Four men, a woman – they were sipping coffee, too. Regina recognized the mother from the courthouse square, the one who'd stepped off into the street so that white men could pass. The woman smiled at her. Regina smiled back.

'What you see before you are the charter members of the Greater Revere, Mississippi, Branch of the National Association for the Advancement of us Colored People,' said Tom with great dignity, his voice slowly emphasizing each syllable in each word.

'Miss Regina Robichard, I'd like you to meet Mr Curtis Willmon. He took over Mottley's Dry Goods. Mr Leonard Wilson, owner of Wilson Funeral Homes. Mr Methuselah Evans. He's vice president over my own Pennywise Bank. Dr and Mrs Daniel Stillworth. Dr Stillworth, a proud graduate of the Meharry Medical College, takes good care of the dental needs of our colored people in these three adjacent counties, and Mrs Barbara Stillworth takes good care of him.'

Chuckle. Chuckle.

Regina and Barbara Stillworth telegraphed a look to each other. *No use getting upset now, but someday that will have to change, too.* And Regina thinking, *All these people professionals, at least independent. Not working for whites, else how could they do this?*

Tom said, 'Lawyer Robichard, since this is what you might call our inaugural meeting, mind sharing a few words about why the national office sent you here?'

She hadn't expected this, and, unlike her mother, Regina *hated* giving speeches, but she walked farther into the room, took a deep breath, looked into their raised eyes, and began: 'Ten days ago, in New York, Thurgood Marshall received a letter that had been sent to him from Revere, Mississippi, by one M. P. Calhoun . . .'

Afterward, when the others had made their promises, shaken hands, and gone, Regina brought Tom Raspberry around to the blue flyer.

'Sure,' he said. 'I'm your man. I had the boys, the ones who deliver my papers, put them out all over the neighborhoods. The black neighborhoods, that is. I put them around the white neighborhoods myself. *Loved* doing it. See any on your way over?'

Regina shook her head. 'Not a one. On Main Street, or on Third Avenue.'

'That's 'cause they been already pulled down.' He let out a that's-what-we-got-to-deal-with sigh that was almost gleeful. 'First thing this morning, soon as some white somebody one saw one, they'd be at tearing them down. Won't be nothing left of all my hard work but fluttering fragments by now. Still . . . it's a start. Shows we mean business. You betcha. But if there's none of them left around, how'd you come up on this one?'

'It was tacked up on my door last night. I thought you'd left it.'

Tom shook his head, frowned. 'Wasn't me. I was gonna bring you by one later on.' Tom listened as Regina told him all about coming home with Willie Willie. About the open door, the flyer pinned on it.

'You weren't scared, were you, to be there by yourself? I mean . . . door left wide open and all.'

'I wasn't by myself,' said Regina. 'Mr Willie Willie stayed, insisted on it. He slept propped up in a chair all night. I asked him to please come up, take his own bed, and I'd sleep on the couch. He's getting so old, you know?'

'Old? Willie Willie?' Tom considered this. 'Maybe. But he's still strong as an ox. Just last week, I was passing by up there near the courthouse and I saw him lift Peach's pie safe off the wagon and set it down into the street so she could get to it better. All by himself he did this, and that pie safe weighs like a burden.'

Regina nodded. 'He wouldn't switch with me. He said he was used to sitting up through the night. Out in the woods, when it was tracking. "Have to do it, if you want to get hold to your prey." I didn't hear him leave until morning.'

'Well, you wanted to get some attention,' Tom said, nodding to the flyer that had been on her door. He wasn't smiling. 'I guess you did. You be careful. The somebody who put this up on your door, he's the one left it open . . . It was meant as a sign. He knew Willie Willie would see it or at least you would tell him, and Willie Willie would know what it meant. Someone's watching, and they don't approve.'

'I'm always careful,' said Regina. She thought, but didn't add, *Are you forgetting I'm from New York? Are you forgetting my daddy's Oscar Robichard? I know all about bad men. I know all about bad things happening.*

There was silence between them. The dust dancing gold on the sunlight that flooded through Tom's window suddenly seemed to absorb all their attention.

Tom said, 'I suppose this whole thing gave Willie Willie quite the shock. What'd he say last night when he saw it?'

'He said you were fixing to get yourself in a whole mess of trouble.' Regina used Willie Willie's accent. She thought her imitation of him was pretty good. Not as good as his of Mary Pickett's but still . . . coming along. Regina decided not to tell Tom how Willie Willie said he could be getting her into trouble as well.

'He might be right about that, about my raising a ruckus.' Tom chuckled, a wry, clear sound. 'Nothing else might come of it, but that surely will.'

'Then why'd you do it?'

'Because,' said Tom, as he threw a quick glance to the row of diplomas behind him, 'it's time.'

Regina leaned closer. 'Did something happen with your son down in Jackson?' *What was his name?* 'With Tom Junior? Did something happen with him when he was taking the Mississippi bar?'

She thought of Joe Howard. Beaten to death.

'*Nothing* happened,' said Tom. For the first time since Regina'd met him, Tom lost his breeziness. 'Which is the same thing *always* happens. I knew I was sending him down there without a snowball's chance in hell they'd let him in. Even with me working my tail off here, building up my businesses and being a fine, upstanding Negro and an asset to the whole community, being an errand boy for the Duvals, delivering all the few black folks that can vote so they vote the right way – even with all that, you think I thought my son had a chance to join the bar here in Mississippi? No, I didn't.'

Tom's eyes snapped – lightning there, too, and Regina felt the power behind those eyes, felt it electrify her as he went on. 'I sent him on down to Jackson to be turned away because that was the ritual. That's the way we do. If you're a Negro, being turned away from the bar is like being admitted to the bar if you're a white lawyer. At least you tried. It's what you do so that folks think . . . "Well, at least that boy tried his best." But my Tom Junior – he's not having none of it. Not anymore.'

Regina leaned closer. 'What's that mean?' But *knowing* what it meant. In the well-chosen words of Ida Mae Robichard, 'Honey, that young man had had him enough.'

'It means,' said Tom, 'that when he was down Jackson he met himself a man named Medgar Evers. Evers is a made-in-Mississippi boy, like my Tom Junior is, from over there in Decatur. Now, Medgar, he fought in the war, and when he came back, he aimed to vote right here in this state for what he'd seen colored boys killed fighting for over there. *Dying* for. So he got him some folks, his brother Charles among them, and they marched on the court-house last April. They wanted to register for the election coming up. Trouble was, other folks in Decatur, they didn't see things the same way Medgar was now seeing them. He was turned back. Not by strangers but by white boys he'd grown up with, white boys he'd played with and hunted with all of his life. Except now *he* was the one they were hunting. They rode in their pickups and their jalopies around the colored section of Decatur all night long, determined in their minds that Medgar wasn't going to register and be able to vote like *they* were able to vote. There they sat, leaning out their car windows with baseball bats in their hands and 42-caliber shotguns. Tom Junior said, in the end, Medgar gave up. He had to. This time. But he's not turning back. Medgar's going to apply to the University of Mississippi Law School. And one day, he says, he's determined to vote, right there in Decatur, Mississippi, where he was born.' Tom paused, shook his head, no longer angry. 'Well, Medgar, he fired up my boy and then my boy fired me up. I started thinking, *Why* do *I just take it for granted that no colored person can be admitted to the bar?*'

'Mr Duval won't be happy. You bringing up things during an election year.'

'Neither will his son be, Little Bed,' said Tom, and then he shrugged. But his shoulders came down with the weight of the world on them. Regina wondered if he, too, was thinking about that Confederate flag waving in pride of place over the courthouse, because she sure was.

Think you can best me?

'Forrest Duval's got Bed, but I got my son, too,' said Tom. 'When Tom Junior gets home from Jackson, he's got to know his daddy's going to be right here, standing beside him. And that I'll continue to be there for him, no matter what comes up.'

Regina looked around at Tom's office, its dust so new it still smelled of cut trees, the long row of proud pictures and diplomas black-framed and hung so carefully on the main wall. A dynasty – that was what Tom was building, just like Jackson Blodgett was building his and the Duvals had built theirs and the Calhouns before them, all of them putting a greedy hand to whatever they could to get ahead. She liked the fact that Tom was just like they were, trusted him more for his self-interest than she trusted his change of heart. If he'd printed those flyers, tacked them up, then Regina knew a tide might be shifting. Tom Raspberry's interests no longer melded perfectly at the edges of Forrest Duval's interests, at least not anymore.

From the hallway, she heard footsteps, then a knock at the door.

Tom got up as it opened. He was smiling again, first at Regina and then at the man and the young boy that came through. Dressed just the same – white shirts, clean but faded blue pants, dark suspenders – they looked alike, too, the boy a miniature version of the thin, dark-skinned man. The child looked at Regina through eyes round as saucers.

'Reverend Lacey!' Tom was at the door himself now, pumping the older man's hand. 'Good to see you, sir. Thanks for coming in. Thanks for bringing the boy.' Then, to Regina, 'Miss Robichard, I'd like to introduce you to Reverend Charles K. Lacey. He saw one of your flyers down there where he lives near Macon.

Called me up, first thing this morning. Said his grandson Manasseh's got something you might want to hear.'

Manasseh Lacey! She still could barely believe it. It had taken long moments of coaxing – the boy had been holding tight on to his grandfather's hand the whole time – but eventually, slowly at first and then flooding, the words had come out. About the POWs, the Germans, the bus stopping, about a dark car waiting there, and about the men – men wearing hoods. And Regina was thinking, *Nothing new here, nothing I haven't already heard from Anna Dale Buchanan*, when Manasseh said, 'I knew one of them.'

'One of whom?' She leaned closer, took his small hand, thinking at first he might mean one of the Germans – but how could that be?

'One of the men by the big car.' A quick look at his grandfather. 'One of the men waiting for Mr Joe Howard.'

Wynne Blodgett? Was this who Manasseh was talking about? Did Manasseh know him? Could he identify him? But she couldn't say that. Her heart tapped away like thunder, but she couldn't lead him. 'Who was it?'

'Sonny Taggart' came the child's prompt response, and he wasn't looking at his grandfather anymore, he was looking at Regina. 'Lives down from us out in the county. He and his mama, out on Short Cut Road. Aunt Eloise does cleanup for them. Sometimes.'

Manasseh paused, took a deep breath. 'Juicy Fruit,' he whispered. 'Lieutenant Wilson gave me a stick of it. He was nice to me.'

Regina had to look away when he said it, toward Tom Raspberry, who was looking away, too.

Sonny Taggart might not be Wynne Blodgett, but at least he was something. A lead.

Rushing home, Regina weighed exactly what to do next – call Thurgood right now with what she had and see what he said? Or take this new information over to Bed Duval and see what, if anything, he would do? Or should she try to see Judge Timms? Was he even back yet?

She had forgotten about Mary Pickett's garden party, but when she rounded the corner onto Third Avenue she could hear the chatter and the music from it, violins enthusiastically struggling through an early movement of one of the Brandenburg Concertos. Regina paused at the gate, uncertain. Ahead of her stretched a string of linen-covered round tables threaded like fat white pearls through the green grass. Women in hats and flower-print silk dresses, their dimpled hands holding tightly on to glasses of what looked like iced tea – or possibly sherry or bourbon – all of which, Regina had learned, in Revere, was referred to as sweet tea. All white faces, all dimpled white hands – and of course they would be, milling leisurely about Mary Pickett Calhoun's bright garden on a workday afternoon.

Except for Dinetta, of course, though Regina hardly recognized her. She'd been spruced up, her brightness subdued, as it were, into a starched gray uniform, a frilly white apron, and a matching lace cap. Company clothes! But not completely – when Regina looked down she saw Dinetta still wore her normal, everyday, run-down, toe-cut-out oxfords. Company clothes, maybe – but not company shoes.

Mary Pickett was nowhere to be seen in all the day's brightness, but Regina imagined she was hiding out in a flower print somewhere herself. One thing for certain, she surely wasn't there to give Regina direction as to how to get through this party to the cottage. She looked around, and for the first time really noticed the low, lush hedges that bordered Calhoun Place from one end to the other, effectively blocking entrance to the property except from the driveway. Regina decided there was no way around it; this was one party she'd have to crash, at least for a moment.

She started up the driveway, more aware than she'd been since she got here of where she was and of everything around her. Sloping green lawn, a big white house, white tablecloths, white faces. As Regina drew nearer, conversation faltered, then stopped altogether, as though she'd turned into a brown cork that, popping along, plugged cheerful words back up into people's throats.

Somebody called out, 'Hey, girl, fill up my drink.' Answered by titters. Not by everybody, at least it didn't sound that way, but by a few. Regina's hands tightened on her briefcase, her cheeks flamed, but she willed herself to keep moving. Two steps more and she didn't have to force herself hard anymore. What was it Ida Jane always told her? *'Consider the source. Anybody talking like that – tells you all you need to know about the way they were raised.'* Besides, this was a story she could carry to the Fund, something she'd be able to throw into conversation when she got back to her small desk in the office. *'Accent so thick, you could have cut through it with a knife. I felt lucky she didn't call me worse than girl.'* It might not be the *war* story some of the men could tell – no dogs, no guns, no threats of death in it – but at least she had a small tale of battle to tell. The anticipation of this made her feel better.

Relieved, she made it through the cottage door, but she'd barely closed it, hadn't had time to put down her hat and her gloves, when the rapping started up. One sharp knock after the other. Regina bent down, peeked through the window, and there was a woman staring back, right at her, straight in the eye. It was the same woman who had called her girl, and she was clutching a recognizable piece of thin blue paper in her hand.

The flyer.

'Open up and come on out here.'

Regina rolled her eyes heavenward, took a deep breath, but really, what could she do? She pulled at the door.

'I'm Mrs Blodgett,' said the woman. Regina blinked, kept her face carefully impassive. 'Mrs *Jackson* Blodgett.'

Regina nodded. Mrs Blodgett. Mrs *Jackson* Blodgett, quite round, had forced herself or been forced into a dress that was bright yellows and pinks, a flower print meant to stand out from the bouquet with which she had been surrounded on the Calhoun Place south lawn. Everything else about her seemed just as willing to stand out as well, from the piled-high pitch of her blond hair to the way her skin dipped deep into the crevices that surrounded her sharp, seen-it-all eyes.

'Mrs Jackson Blodgett,' the woman repeated. In case Regina had not understood.

'Regina Robichard,' she said, and then, for a moment, became Mary Pickett Calhoun, a woman faced with dilemmas. Should she reach out a hand in greeting to this awful woman? Did courtesy demand that she invite her in?

Mae Louise Blodgett did not appear to have any problem handling good manners as they pertained to race. What might befuddle Regina or even puzzle Mary Pickett Calhoun did not concern her at all. Mae Louise stepped smartly back from the door. No, she would not come inside. She left Regina's hand straggling outward. No, she should not shake hands.

'Don't need to tell me who you are. The whole town knows about you, Missy.'

Regina remembered where she was – Mississippi – and held on to her temper. No need to make a scene. She came out of the cottage, all the time thinking that never in a million years would she have pictured this woman with Jackson Blodgett, his wife. *Uh-uh*, thought Regina, suddenly seeing Mary Pickett's face again as it turned slowly to Jackson. The way it lit up, like a flower taking its life from the sun.

Maybe that's why Mrs Jackson Blodgett had introduced herself twice. Maybe there were other people in Revere who had trouble with the idea of the two of them – her with her husband – together. And yet they *should* have fit just right. They were about the same height and even resembled each other, with their careless way of dressing, their shared keen eyes and sharp features, and the silver that was starting to show in their hair. Looked alike – but maybe they weren't alike. Regina remembered how Willie Willie had imitated this woman and made her laugh with the imitation. 'My name is Mae Louise Wynne, and my father is a gentleman planter from over Carroll County, Alabama.' And she remembered Willie Willie's snort of derision, too.

For a second, she almost felt sorry for this woman, who held tight to Jackson Blodgett's name because, maybe, she might not feel she had a real place in his heart. But that sympathetic feeling was not destined to last.

'And I know who you are,' said Regina, stepping out, closing the door behind her. 'Wynne Blodgett's mother.'

Mae Louise had a carefully defined painted red mouth. She creased it up now. She also had fewer wrinkles than Mary Pickett had but wore a great deal more makeup in an effort to hide the ones she had. Base and powder, rouge and mascara; Regina saw each as a separate, careful delineation upon the geography of Mae Louise's broad face.

For a moment, she and Regina stood on the smoothed cement in front of the cottage, both aware they were being covertly watched by the ladies still out on the lawn, all of them calm as the middle of a hurricane's eye. The scent of Confederate roses and of autumn clematis and sweet olive combined around them, all mixed together, intoxicating and strong.

Mae Louise came right to her point. 'This was found on top that stone nigger boy outside my house, the one with the electric lighted lantern. You've seen him?' A small knowing smirk.

'Yes, *Mr* Willie Willie showed me the statue the first day I got here.'

'I thought he might have. It's a county landmark. He'd be the one to show it off.' Another twitch of her lips. 'Anyhow, this whatever you call it . . .' She waved the paper so close into Regina's face that it almost, not quite, slapped her. Regina narrowed her eyes, folded her arms over her chest, gratified when Mae Louise took the slightest step back.

'This *flyer*,' Wynne's mother continued, 'was glued right top that boy's nappy head when I got up first thing this morning. You got any idea who put it there?'

'No, I do not.' And Regina honestly didn't.

'Well, I do. We been having some trouble over at the house.

Your man Willie Willie, he's the one did this. At least, that's what my boy says. My husband means to take measures.'

Mae Louise spoke quickly, one word flying over the other, fast and high. Regina caught her as she glanced covertly over her shoulder at the others, though by now all the ladies had seen her, had seen where she'd gone and were diligently and earnestly talking to one another or looking down at their tea in a polite attempt not to notice. But Mae Louise Blodgett didn't seem to mind. She knew she had their attention and that what she said now would very shortly be all over town – just as she intended it should, a sly way to embarrass the woman her husband had married first and get some prick of jealous revenge. Regina wondered if this had been going on for years. If there had been moves and countermoves. Regina looked around for Mary Pickett but still didn't see her anywhere.

Making sure her voice carried, Regina said, 'Mrs Blodgett, I have no idea what you mean. But I will say that if you continue to insinuate accusations against my client, we will take appropriate action. In the courts.'

Little good *that* would do, but at least she'd answered something back. She hadn't let herself be rolled over.

The collective gasp from the lawn was quick and precise. Mae Louise Blodgett's face flared a stunning vermilion. Behind her, the stirring of spoons against cups died down. Regina looked over and there was a woman eyeing them, her mouth still caught in a shocked, gaping 'Oh.'

And then there, at last, was Mary Pickett at an out-of-the-way table where she must have been all the time, her eyes fixed not on them but on the rough asphalt sidewalk that ran along the front of her house. The place where Jackson had stood, looking up, on that long-ago day when she'd first seen him. The day he'd been facing north. And away from here.

'Jackson *assured* me,' his wife now said, 'that he means to get us some protection. It's all just a bunch of mess, since that nigger soldier got himself killed over in Alabama.'

Regina's mouth popped indignantly open, but Mae Louise shot her own words out first.

'I know what people are saying about my Wynne, that he had something to do with this. Insinuating things without proof. People maybe jealous of what we got.'

'Somebody would accuse your son of murder because they were jealous?' Regina thought of Peach. She thought of Anna Dale Buchanan. 'That doesn't make much sense.'

'It sure does to a lot of folks living here. That's why the whole thing got thrown out by the grand jury.'

'It got dismissed because of lack of evidence, not because he was innocent. And the right evidence might still be forthcoming.' Regina, almost quaking with anger, managed to keep her voice smooth as silk.

'Really?' said Mae Louise Blodgett, no slouch in the smooth-as-silk department herself. 'I imagine it was niggers told you that.'

'Negroes,' corrected Regina. 'And whites.'

'Niggers.' The word deliberately repeated. 'No matter what all y'all call yourself, you better watch out. There's folks around here knows how to call a spade a spade – and how to lay one out, if you catch my meaning.' She smiled, made sure that Regina knew what she was threatening before she went on. 'Oh, we know all about Anna Dale Buchanan, what she says. But she didn't see anything, and everybody knows she's sure been strange since her boy got *his* self killed. Keeps to herself. Doesn't know what's going on, what went on. Doesn't really care, not anymore.'

The wind picked up, breezing in from the river, scattering leaves off the maple at the entrance to the drive and across the street at Raymond Hall, tearing at the clematis and the last of the roses, whipping the scent of them into the air. It ruffled the blue sheet Mae Louise still clutched, daggerlike, in her hand.

'And as for that ungrateful rascal Tom Raspberry . . . He's got his nerve starting up with that nigger group – yes, of course, I already know all about it – what with all old Mr Forrest Duval did to help him get on and so, and my own Mr Blodgett owning the mortgage on everything that old coon's got . . . I do declare, I can't even begin to cogitate what he's thinking. But when my husband sees this . . .' Again, she waved the flyer, two inches from Regina's nose this time. 'Why, I guess we'll find out.'

Mae Louise Blodgett's voice droned on and on. Regina looked out beyond her and watched as the ladies, Mary Pickett's supposed-to-be good friends in the Revere Garden Club, put down their napkins and gathered up their plant cuttings. They looked at their watches and made discreet noises about husbands and children and dinner. They walked down Mary Pickett's cleanly swept driveway, blew kisses to one another, and disappeared from her life.

13

Gotcha!

Regina was at the end edge of sleep when there she was once again, suddenly, deep, deep within *The Secret of Magic*, hiding out in its pages, safe from the world. She was on the street in front of Mary Pickett's house, the one the young Jackie Earle Blodgett had stood on, the one with the gnarled roots of magnolias that glared out through the broken asphalt of the sidewalk. The roots that looked like alligator eyes, poised ready to spot you.

Ready to call out,

Gotcha!

Right there – with their reptile teeth, sharp as stilettos, ready to bite you and eat you and disappear you right out of this world.

But not one thing got to those charmed children – the two boys, the girl – as they ran past the big house, the three of them charging into the night. Streaking over the rough sidewalks, down past the two big houses and the shacks, bound for the river, where an old man waited for them to show them his tricks, to teach them his knowledge.

> *'You hear that sound?*
> *'It's the king bullfrog.*
> *'He thinks he's alone, but he's ripe for the spearing.*
> *'You see that star?*
> *'It's the north point.'*

The voices, next morning, seemed to come from right outside the cottage window, the murmur of them blended into the general early, coming-to-life sounds Regina was used to by now. Mockingbirds quarreling with starlings in some daily territorial dispute. Ducks, heading south, honked their way through the sky.

Hunting Season! Guns shooting! Time to fly away!

Regina thought if she stuck her head out the window she'd feel the flap of their wings. There was the low rumble of early-morning traffic starting up from over on Main Street. And there was the whispering.

She opened her eyes, pulled on her robe, and went to the window. Fog hung like a curtain over Calhoun Place. Toward the east, bare tree limbs scratched at the sky, and for the first time Regina saw the mistletoe nestled high in them, settling into places where leaves had once been. But once the ducks had echoed off into the morning, Regina was left once again with a subtlety of voices. Her ears and her eyes followed them down from the treetops to the side of Mary Pickett's fine house.

Mary Pickett stood there, along with the sheriff and Jackson Blodgett. Even though his back was to her, Regina recognized him by the tilt of his head, by the way his hand rested on Mary Pickett's shoulder. It was the first time Regina had seen him touch her. And someone *had* been called out. She could tell it.

Instantly wide awake, Regina ran down the stairs and out into the driveway. The others turned toward her in what looked like a synchronized rhythm, Jackson Blodgett and the sheriff with tight, puckered expressions. It was too early for Dinetta, and she was nowhere in sight, but a woman carrying a coffee cup was wandering over from the big house across the street. Looking both ways. And Mary Pickett, fully dressed in a tweed skirt and sweater, a scarf tied around her pin curls, stood there as well, one hand on a hip, one arm spread wide, her face thoughtful, her eyes pinpointed on her house.

Regina followed that stare, and she, too, saw what the others were seeing. What Jackson Blodgett and Rand Connelly were shaking their heads at, what the curious neighbor, shocked, was now moving away from, what Mary Pickett attempted to hide with the outstretch of her arm. Regina, moving closer, saw it, too.

NIGGER LUVER GET THAT NIGGER LAWYER OUT FROM HERE

Misspelled words. Bad grammar. Trashy folks, thought Regina. And that was reassuring, because only people like that used a word like *nigger*, or so she'd been taught. Still, the lawyer in her automatically questioned that misspelling. The correct cipher of 'lover' was not difficult to come by. It was on cards and candy boxes, in flower-shop windows, prominent on the covers of *True Confessions* magazine. *Love* was a word most people knew well. She wondered why it had been so prominently got wrong here, especially when the much less used *lawyer* had been got so perfectly right.

But no one else standing there seemed to notice this, much less think that it mattered. What seemed to count was that Mary Pickett's house had been desecrated by words written so large that Regina did not need her eyeglasses to read them, so big she was sure that if Thurgood had been looking down from New York, he could have read them himself. Splotches of black paint dripped from the letters down the pristine white walls of the house, crystallized on them, shone as darkly as dried blood.

Out of the corner of her eye, Regina watched Jackson edge even closer to Mary Pickett, and she saw Lilla Raymond see this as well. The two of them – Regina and Lilla Raymond – stared at each other for the briefest of minutes. And Regina wondered which would soon enliven Revere's telephone party line more – the fact that Mary Pickett's house had been vandalized or the fact that Jackson Blodgett had touched his once-upon-a-time wife, had comforted her in public, had held her close.

Mary Pickett looked over, her eyes jewel bright and shiny.

Now you know what it feels like. To be singled out. To be cut low. To have people think they can do anything they want to your things and even your life. What it feels like to be black in Mississippi – at least for a minute.

That's what Regina wanted to say, but what she heard herself saying was, 'I am so sorry.' So sorry. Over and over again. Surprising even herself that she was.

Sorry first for this word painted openly on this wall and what this word meant to Willie Willie and to her and to all the other Negroes in Revere. Sorry for her father and for Joe Howard. Sorry for those separate, unequal drinking fountains and the Confederate flag over the courthouse. But sorry for Mary Pickett, too, who maybe hadn't known how things really were but was quickly learning. Regina shook her head like Mary Pickett was now shaking hers. Both of them, maybe, sorry for the whole sorry state of the world.

'I'll take care of it,' Jackson said to Mary Pickett. 'I'll send Wynne over. He'll be honored to put things right.'

Mary Pickett nodded, but she glanced at Regina. And the thought passed wordlessly between them – or maybe Regina just imagined it did – that Wynne Blodgett had already done what he meant to do.

Late that afternoon, when Regina called the Fund, she got her archrival Skip Moseley on Thurgood's phone.

'What's up?' she asked. 'Where's Thurgood?'

Because something had to be up for Skip to be taking Thurgood's calls.

'Man, oh, man,' said Skip, and he was whispering, almost buzzing. 'Is this place in an uproar or what?'

Regina waited. She knew from experience that dead silence on her part would be the best encouragement for whatever it was Skip was dying to tell.

And it was.

'Big changes,' he said.

Skip was what he liked to call 'a natty dresser.' And there, in Mississippi, sitting on a tall red-vinyl-and-aluminum stool in

Mary Pickett's kitchen, and talking into Mary Pickett's heavy old-fashioned wall telephone, Regina saw Skip, in New York, as clearly as though he were right there. He was flicking at his red bow tie, pulling out a perfect silk handkerchief, wiping his brow smooth with it. Preparing to tell all.

'A *huge* project coming up in Jackson, Mississippi. Public school integration. Federal court. Thurgood's finally starting with those big cases he's been after. You know, the effect-the-legislation ones.' Skip did a bad imitation of Thurgood's soft Tidewater accent, then laughed – *tee-hee-hee* – at his own joke.

'Oh, that's interesting,' said Regina, with a great deal more enthusiasm than she actually felt. Her mind had wandered to Mary Pickett's wall with that NIGGER LUVER still painted on it. It was well past noon, and she'd seen neither hide nor hair of Wynne Blodgett and his promised cleanup.

'Which means,' Skip continued, 'that the Fund's finishing up with the kinds of things you're working on down there. You know, those individual litigation cases. *We're* moving on, in a whole different direction. Who knows, you might even be out of a job.'

Tee-hee-hee. Again.

'Is Thurgood there?' Regina asked again. She started hunting through the kitchen cabinet drawers that were near her, searching for a stray pack of Mary Pickett's cigarettes.

Skip ignored that question, asked his own: 'Now, where are you, *exactly*? Down there in Alabama – or is it Georgia?'

It was Mississippi – where *Jackson*, Mississippi, was – and Regina knew that Skip knew this. In fact, he probably had a map of the state hanging in his living room, straight pins pushed in at Revere, right at the spot where he thought her heart beat.

And when he had found out, he'd probably said enough – and just enough – to Thurgood so that a little I-told-you-so could be singled out if she happened to bungle things in the end. Something along the lines of how he understood why Thurgood had done this. Thurgood and Buster and Ida Jane and Dr Sam were all such good friends. If he'd had the courage, that's what Skip would surely have said. Or would say.

And he might be right about her, about how she'd got here. That thought was starting to sink into Regina as she sparred with him, as she hunted through dishtowels and silverware for that stray cigarette. Because, really, what did she have to tell Thurgood? Nothing much. She peeked out the side window, and there were people driving by Calhoun Place now, a steady stream of them. She saw the cars slow up, the people stare out of them and point. She opened another drawer and started rummaging through.

'If Thurgood's there, would you please just put him on the phone?'

'Oh, yeah,' Skip said. 'Sure thing.'

He clattered the receiver onto Thurgood's desk so loudly that Regina had to hold the phone away from her ear. She heard Skip start to whistle and the tap of his shoes against the linoleum floor, not going fast. There was a low murmur of voices and the sound of a woman's laugh. After that, for a while, there were just the muffled, ordinary noises of the office – other telephones ringing, someone calling for a secretary to bring coffee, someone else saying, 'Hey, did you see this?'

It was some moments before Thurgood picked up. 'Reggie, that you?'

'It's me, Thurgood.' She smiled, happy at the sound of his voice. 'How are things?'

'Good. Fine. The question is, What's going on down there? Over a week now. We were starting to worry.' All coming out as one rolling sentence, a quick inhale on his cigarette the only punctuation.

She took a breath, gave him a quick rundown. She ended with what had been painted that morning on the side of Calhoun Place.

'Calhoun Place?'

'M. P. Calhoun's house,' she said.

'Oh, is that what it's called?'

But she'd not been sent down to Revere to learn the name of Mary Pickett's house. Thurgood let out a deep breath. Regina could almost see the cigarette smoke on it, curling up, masking his eyes and his face. 'Any idea who wrote it?'

'They blame everything on kids down here. Outside agitating kids, to be exact.' She thought of herself for a moment. 'That is, when they aren't blaming inside agitating Negroes.'

Thurgood didn't laugh. 'What do you think?'

Regina took a deep breath. 'I think it was Wynne Blodgett.'

'Who's he?'

'The son of the richest man in town, the one who owns half of it, plus the newspaper, the bank.'

'Hmm . . . What makes you think it was him?'

She told him everything she'd got so far, about Bed Duval and Judge Timms and what Anna Dale Buchanan had told her and Peach – told him everything, in fact, except about the secret, hidden shirt. On a party line, in a place as chatty as Revere, Mississippi, she dared not mention that, at least not yet.

'And you say his daddy sent the boy away after Joe Howard was killed – over there somewhere in Alabama.'

'They didn't send him far, and they didn't send him for long. He's back. *Been* back, from what I've seen.'

'What you've *seen*?'

Regina took a quick, shallow breath. 'I mean, it's a small town. He's around.'

'You got anything on him? Found any *real* witnesses? People who actually saw his face? You'll need that.'

'Not yet. But, like I told you, there are some leads.'

A pause. 'Reggie, are you sure it's safe for you down there?'

She closed her eyes. Saw that writing. Saw those words. Then she saw Skip Moseley. Hovering.

'Safe as in church.' She thought of what Mary Pickett had said to her and echoed it in a sweet Southern voice: 'Why, everybody down here's just so *nice* to me.'

A chuckle from Thurgood. 'I'm sure they're nice, all right, but you be careful. Now are you *sure* . . .' But he stopped himself. They both knew he'd been about to suggest Skip yet again.

That was the last thing she wanted. She started vehemently shaking her head. 'No, I can do this. I just need a little more time.'

Thurgood said, 'Well, that's all the time you got left – just a little. A week from now – sooner, even – you got to come home. No extensions. With that word out there on the wall, it's getting dangerous. Maybe it's *already* dangerous. Plus, those veterans' cases are waiting. I need you to finish them off. We're making some changes . . .'

Thurgood went on to repeat to her what Skip Moseley had already said.

Regina eased off the phone as quickly as she decently could. Straight from the kitchen, she went looking for Mary Pickett. She didn't know why, but she went out the back door, around to the side, keeping her eyes averted from that scrawled black paint on the wall. She went through the back gardens; she went out to the sidewalk and looked down the street. The Daimler was there, parked as majestically as ever in the driveway. But there was no sign of Mary Pickett, no hint of her, no whiff of her perfume.

That afternoon, Regina decided it was time to take on the courthouse. She walked in the front door, right under the flutter of the Confederate flag. She could have seen it, but she didn't look up. The courthouse smelled of ammonia, lemon wax, and stale cigar smoke. There was a black man in a corner, passing a mop. He stopped when he saw Regina, stared at her for a moment, no expression on his face, then got right back to work. The directory said Judge Timms's office was on the top floor, which proved to be one story up. There was no elevator, and the steps were crowded, but Regina kept her head down and made her way through.

Judge Timms's clerk, Mrs Hightower, seemed to be the formidable prototype for the Acceptable Law Receptionist here in

Revere. Hers was obviously the demeanor that Forrest Duval's Miss Tutwiler strove hard to emulate. Tiny, fine-boned, blue-suited, high-heeled, icy-eyed – Regina took one look at Mrs Hightower and recognized implacability right away.

Mrs Hightower said, 'He's not here, not been here, and will never *be* here, as far as you're concerned.'

And that was that.

But for the first time since coming to Mississippi, Regina felt like she'd truly accomplished something. She hadn't really expected to be allowed in to see Judge Timms, hadn't even known exactly what she'd have said to him, anyway. *A little colored child can identify someone named Sonny Taggart – who lives down a piece from him out in the county on something called Short Cut Road – and this man, by the way, was one of those waiting for Joe Howard when he got off that bus?* What would Judge Timms say to that? How would it matter?

No, what was important to Regina was that she'd gone into that courthouse. She'd gone up those stairs all by herself and she'd asked for what she wanted. Openly, in plain view of anybody standing there watching, she – Regina Mary Robichard – had defied that Confederate flag.

Think you can best me?

Maybe, Regina thought, exhilarated. Maybe, I *can!*

The courthouse clock struck five as Regina turned the corner toward Mary Pickett's once again. The curious, slow-moving traffic on the street had thinned, but the wall on Calhoun Place was still as damaged as it had been that morning. Regina's steps slowed as she drew near to the gate, as she looked at that word.

Nigger.

The house itself looked empty and dark, closed in onto itself. Ashamed. She wondered why Wynne Blodgett hadn't cleaned the wall yet, why Jackson hadn't made him clean it up. And why hadn't Mary Pickett done something herself?

Quickly, running away from that word, already halfway to the cottage – it was then that Regina decided to go to the river. She wanted, *needed*, to see the place where they'd dragged up Joe Howard's battered body. Willie Willie had pointed out a vague path for her that first day from the window of his truck. Now she thought she might be able to piece together the way on her own.

Beyond the gate at Calhoun Place, the land sloped sharply downward. The few shotgun houses clinging to it looked poised to immediately give up and tumble downhill on the next sharp shiver of wind. Regina saw outhouses. She saw smoke rising from out-back kitchens, and she thought again to how Mary Pickett had modernized the cottage for Willie Willie, thought again to how much she must love him. Just like she said.

Across the street, down from Raymond Hall, a black woman unpinned sheet after startlingly white sheet from clotheslines that stretched from the side of her tarpaper shack to a huge oak tree out front. Regina counted ten of them. That's all she could see, but there might have been more. The woman's hands were misshapen and ashy against so much brilliant whiteness. She smiled brightly when she caught sight of Regina. She called out, 'Hey, there!' She waved, and the brisk sweep of the motion called down a cascade of brightness from the ancient trees overhead. Red and gold leaves, dying already, lost their last hold and showered onto the sheets, onto that dark working female, onto the bare earth of her yard.

Why, she's beautiful, thought Regina, *and so is that tree and all the trees behind it, leading into the forest and the clear sky over them and the birds and the smell – the rich loam of earth meeting with river.* All of it beautiful. All of it new – at least to her.

Regina waved back. Called out, 'Hi, how are you?'

She wondered who the woman was, what she was doing with all these sheets, who they belonged to, who she worked for. She thought that Willie Willie would know, and Dinetta and even Mary Pickett. They'd know just who she was, her name and her nickname, and who her husband was and how they'd ended up in this house and who their parents had been and who their children were, and their cousins. Black or white, all her neighbors would know her whole story because she lived by them, had probably always lived by them, and belonged.

There weren't that many outside electric lights on Mary Pickett's street, and across it, where shacks sloped toward the river, there were none. But a beam from the center of town spangled through the trees. It illuminated the way back to the courthouse and to Calhoun Place – that is, if Regina chose to take it. She didn't. She started on her way again and suddenly the *Magic* kids were there, right beside her. Collie and Booker and Jack, the children who had run out of the cottage, out of the Big House, and maybe down this same street. Pointing out the very things to Regina that Daddy Lemon had once upon a time pointed out to them. And there was Daddy Lemon himself, a sprightly old man who now wore Willie Willie's face and who knew all about magic and might even know – maybe, maybe – about murder. An old man who sang out,

> See that burdock tree – bark's good for toothache
> Sage bush there – good for a blood wound
> Draws out the poison
> Draws it out fine
> And that Dancing Rabbit
> Running
> Running
> Toward the River
> Toward The Folly

Because The Folly was this way, too. Regina remembered. And The Folly was the Blodgett house. Burned – she'd read this in New York – almost down to the ground.

The road got rougher; she felt it through her shoes – pumps, which she now regretted not changing – as it crumbled from poured concrete toward broken asphalt then from gravel to hard-packed mud. She heard electricity sizzle through wire and then watched as a lone streetlight flared to life over her head. It fell on what looked like patches of lace draping from the tree limbs, then spreading out in swatches from branch to branch. They glimmered between the trees like the magic entrance to a fairy tale. It took Regina a closer look and a moment to realize she was staring at spiderwebs, condensation shining like gossamer through them. Around her the forest ruled, its trees rooted to the land, the overarch of its limbs able to hold back the sun. Regina bent close to touch the webbing. It dissolved on her fingers, leaving a gritty, soft residue. She rubbed it together, brought it close to her nose, and sniffed – and smelled Revere. The mud of its river, its sweet flowers, the scent of its dense growing things, all caught and exuded on the remnants of a fragile spider's web. Regina breathed in once, and then again, more deeply. For a moment the way things smelled in Revere absorbed her and she wondered if she would remember it once she left here, if there would be something that would bring it back to her, as she made her quick way up Lexington Avenue or down Fifth, as she got off the subway and hurried through Harlem. She wondered if Joe Howard had been remembering this very scent, the freshness of it, as he made his long way home from the war. Wondering and wondering, smelling her fingers, her mind far away, her eyes toward the forest. Finally, looking up, she saw the dog.

It was a huge thing, and so dark it looked like it could have been sliced from the earth. Or maybe gnawed its way out. Its mouth hung open with visible teeth; its eyes focused on her. And they were live things, so conscious of her and concentrated on her that Regina imagined them counting the breaths as they entered her chest. Numbering them, aware that they had grown shallow and quick, because this was obviously a hunting dog able to sense fear and ferret for it. Regina forced herself to look back at him, to take one deep breath and then another until she felt the pulse at her throat slow.

For a moment, for an instant, everything stilled.

Shhh, Regina, the forest whispered. Quiet, too.

Then a whistle from somewhere deep within the trees, some-place hidden that Regina couldn't see. A high, quick sound, but immediately the dog trotted toward it.

Regina waited until he had completely disappeared, then she looked over her shoulder. She was still near enough to turn back to Calhoun Place, and probably she should do that. She could smell the wood smoke from its chimneys, could see them playing hide and seek through the branches of the trees.

All the matinee movies she'd ever seen flooded back to her now, the ones she'd always thought of as the white-girl pictures. Where the white girl would hear a noise in the basement, would hear a noise in the attic, something tapping away outside, and she would be compelled to go and investigate. Not like a black girl. Regina would laugh about this with friends and with her mother. Black girls had enough trouble on their hands. They didn't need to go seeking it out.

But if she went on, who knew what she might find?

So what choice did she have? She had to push on. And the dog hadn't followed this path. No, he'd disappeared into the forest, been swallowed up by the forest, so really, was there any reason she should not go on the way she'd planned? She couldn't think of one, but her steps slowed anyway and she looked around. Cautious.

Regina had gone on only about fifty feet when she started smelling the river, its dank scent hanging like a dividing curtain on the air. She heard a frog croak behind it, and a splash that might have been some deep-river catfish leaping up to strangle, for a second, on the night air.

If the river was here, she must be near The Folly, but still, when she actually got there, it seemed to jump out of the forest at her, a surprise. Because it hadn't been burned 'down to the ground' like the clipping from Jackson Blodgett's *Times Commercial* had said. The Folly still stood, slabs of it rising like shadows from scorched earth, entire walls even behind the ruin of what once must have been a front porch. The whole thing, the wreck of it hulking up close to the dirt road, a kerosene lamp flickering light onto its burned-out step.

Someone is here.

Regina heard a whisper, then footsteps. She saw a shadow separate itself from the ruined walls and come on out onto the porch – Wynne Blodgett and the dog, the big one from the road, standing there with him. The two of them now motionless as marble. Waiting for her.

14

'Come on up,' Wynne said. 'Join me. Mind the steps, though. Some of them are pretty done in.'

His was 'a refined voice,' as Anna Dale Buchanan had described it, with a different accent, too. Softer than his father's, stronger on the vowels than Mary Pickett's, and not like his mother's high-pitched whine at all. Another of the endless ways of talking Southern that Regina had found in Revere.

It was a young man's voice. And he *was* young, maybe younger than she was. At least that was what Regina speculated, twenty-three, twenty-four at most.

Still sowing wild oats.

Still playing kids' pranks.

That's how they explained away what he did.

Yet Regina listened to him, paid strict attention. She went up to the house slowly, one careful step at a time. It was darker now, shadows playing everywhere, and the dog – big and scary – was free to pull her into any one of them. But she'd deal with him, too, if that became necessary. Because Wynne Blodgett was the one she needed to talk to, and now she had her chance.

'You Mary Pickett's lawyer?'

No 'Miss' before 'Mary Pickett.' He was the first one Regina had heard skip that.

'I'm Mr Willie Willie's lawyer.' Safe on the porch now, Regina turned slowly to face him. 'But we've already met. Remember? That day at Calhoun Place, when you returned my handkerchief. By the way, thank you again.'

'You're welcome.' His smile was easy. 'You interested in the home place?' A shift of his head that took in the ruin behind him. 'Why don't you move in a little closer, look on in over there.'

She glanced quickly around, satisfied herself that the dog hadn't moved, and then once again did as Wynne said. Ash from the burned-out window sash crumbled through her fingers as she peered in.

She saw, right away, that within the shell of this destroyed decaying false antebellum crouched a log cabin, around which the much grander house had been built – or almost built. Because parts of it looked like they'd never been finished. The left side didn't rise to a second story; she could see the remnants of only three columns on the crumbling porch. Looking close, forgetting Wynne Blodgett for a minute, she made out bark that remained, even now attached to its outside walls, the clear outline of still-intact windows, even the fluttering of curtain at one of them. All of this eerie. The new house completely destroyed, the original still right there.

'Interesting, isn't it, the way it burned down. A *set* fire. You can always tell them,' said Wynne. 'Want more light?'

He lifted the kerosene lamp, brought it so close that she felt its heat at her neck.

'No, thank you,' she said, moving slowly away, wondering what exactly he meant by that 'set fire' but saying, 'I've seen enough.'

'Suit yourself.'

She turned around then. Wynne smiled, settled down on one of the lower stairs, reached into his pocket and pulled out a tin of hand-rolled cigarettes. He offered one to Regina, a surprise. When she said no, Wynne shrugged and motioned for her to sit on the step beside him. He laughed when she hesitated. 'It's okay. I *told* you this is our home place. Can't nothing happen to a lady lawyer here. Besides . . .' A grin. A pause. 'I got myself something to tell you.'

So she sat down. And once she did, he moved nearer, positioning himself so he was that little bit too close to her. She tried to edge away, but when she shifted, sharp splinters worked their way through the wool of her skirt. They seemed to tell her she'd better be careful, sit quietly, not fidget around. Or she'd be sorry.

The forest whispered, *You're getting what you came for. Now, listen up!*

She looked out over the trees, and there were Mary Pickett's three brick chimneys rising dark against a sky dying into mockingbird colors – gray, with white clouds and the odd streak of blue.

'New York and all,' said Wynne, dragging at his cigarette. 'At least that's what I heard.'

'I'm from New York.'

'Didn't have to say it, even with that accent. You don't look like anything from around here. Don't act like it, either.' A pause. 'I been watching you.'

He reached up, fanned away smoke from his cigarette before it waved into her face. Another surprise to Regina, but she distrusted all this sudden courtesy, thought it might be the biggest danger of all. In the distance, she heard a dog bark.

'That yours?' she said, looking over at the huge dog he'd brought with him. It still stood at The Folly's edge, hadn't moved. But when Regina moved, the dog's eyes followed her.

Another bark. In the forest. Sounding nearer.

'That yours, too?' she said, motioning toward the trees. 'The dog, I mean.'

Wynne grinned again. 'Not mine. Mine wouldn't waste his time barking. He'd be up on you, teeth in your jugular before you even knew he was there.'

So much for Southern good manners.

'I'll remember that,' Regina said.

She'd never been this close to a white man. Not even to the one white lawyer in her office, a man from upper New Hampshire, son of a Congregationalist minister, who was as determined as the rest of them were to see simple justice and had once stammeringly confided to Regina that her mother had been the inspiration for what he'd done with his life. Regina had nodded, edged back, and studiously avoided him after that. Not that she hated white men, not really. Still . . . after what they'd done to her father . . . she couldn't help herself.

But that had been in New York, and New York, she had to admit, was nothing like Revere – a place where black people and white people were all jumbled together, had built up a land, and still lived, in a sense, right on top of each other, constantly traipsing in and out of one another's lives. So close that they couldn't just naturally be separated, Regina thought now, looking at Wynne Blodgett smoking his cigarette, holding it just like Willie Willie held his, between his thumb and forefinger. No, you needed Jim Crow laws for that, and Confederate flags waving over a courthouse, and separate drinking fountains, and separate schools, and poll taxes and literacy tests for voting, and substandard schools – and in the end a good man like Joe Howard Wilson dead.

And after all that, what was it you got? A bit of air, a bit of smoke, all that separated her from this man. Who smelled of Old Spice cologne, like Willie Willie smelled of it, and of cigarettes and wood and stale whiskey. And kerosene, too. She sniffed that on him, as though the slightest spark could set him off like tinder, because this was a white man who could get away with murder, and probably had.

That was the difference down here. In Omaha, the men who killed her father had not known him, had barely even looked at him before they lynched him up. But everybody knew Joe Howard – they knew Willie Willie – here in Revere.

Something rustled beneath the burned steps, shot out for the underbrush. Made Regina jump. Still, the dog didn't move.

'Wasn't nothing but an ol' critter,' said Wynne Blodgett with a chuckle. 'My dog'd have done with it upside of a minute. If I sent her at it, that is. Probably just a muskrat. Such a little bitty something. Not big enough to hurt you here.'

His voice pushed a little at that one word, *hurt*.

And there was the smallest smile on Wynne's face, the wrinkles it made linking right on up from his lips to his eyes. He nodded her on, and the nod seemed to take them right back to Joe Howard, to the murder, to why she'd come here and why she stayed. She could almost see his words straining out at her about that.

But instead she asked about his strange, ghostly shell of a house. 'What do you think happened? Why did it burn?'

'You mean *who* burned it?'

Wynne looked thoughtful for a moment, regarded her through a cumulus of smoke.

'Willie Willie,' he said at last.

'Really?'

But the pieces were coming together in Regina's mind, a perfect fit. The date on the clipping Mary Pickett had sent to the Fund. She'd have to check it again, make certain, but from what she recalled, The Folly had been torched right after the grand jury had brought back its verdict on Joe Howard's 'accidental death.'

'But why? I mean, why do you believe he did it?'

'Because he *did* do it. Everybody in town knows that.'

Just like they know you killed Joe Howard? But not really knowing it. No evidence to prove it – so far.

Regina was really careful not to move; the step beneath her was a thicket of splinters. 'And if he did, like you say he did . . . and really . . .' She shrugged, shoulders up, down. 'I wonder why your daddy . . . I mean, I wondered why they never just went on and put him in jail. Him being a Negro and all. I was wondering about that.'

Wynne Blodgett stubbed out his cigarette, pulled out another. Again, he offered the tin to Regina first. Again, she shook her head no.

'Mary Pickett.' Her name came out of his mouth on a plume of white smoke. 'That's the plain and simple reason. Willie Willie belongs with Mary Pickett, and my daddy never could force himself to lift a finger against a Calhoun. None of my family could. They . . . *She* treated him like dirt, but my daddy . . . Underneath,

I guess he's still hoping.' The grate of a chuckle. 'At least, that's what my mama always says.'

But he must have thought better about getting into what his mama might have to say on the matter. Instead, he motioned behind them with his cigarette, arching it out, bringing it so close to Regina's cheek that she could feel the heat from its nub. 'You see that little house inside all this, the log cabin? You get close enough at the window you could make it out?'

Regina nodded. She'd seen it.

'That's what you should ask me about sometime. That little house inside, what it means, how it got there. I don't imagine you got anything like this where you come from. Not in New York. But there's a lot of that kind of stuff down here. Big houses sprouting up from what you might call humble beginnings. Calhoun Place started out a log cabin, too, but I don't imagine Mary Pickett's ever let you in it – at least not past the kitchen. Not uppity like she is. A nigra like you.'

He laughed, and Regina didn't correct him.

'Well, I have,' Wynne said. 'Been in it. And you can still see the beams of the old cabin, if you look really hard in the front parlor and in the living room. If you know exactly what you're seeing, you'll recognize it right off. A beam left standing here, a rough wall there. They tell a story, point out a family moving on up, or at least trying to.'

'Why don't you tell me about it?'

'You interested?'

He brushed his pant leg against the silk of her stocking. Her eyes narrowed, but she didn't flinch, move away. She sure couldn't do that. Not if she wanted to find out once and for all what had happened to Joe Howard. Not if she wanted to get this man to tell her the truth. Close now. Too close. And she smelled again that whiff of stale liquor seeping up through the creases of his fine clothes and fine face. She had the strongest urge then, almost a directive, to get up, retrace her steps, walk away from this ruined house, on past the dog on the road and the woman unfurling her laundry, walk back through Revere to New York and the way life had been. Get away from this man and what she knew he was bound to tell her. Run away from what she had come here to hear.

But Wynne Blodgett had no idea the war that was waging inside her. He'd wound himself up now, was talking away.

'I guess you know what happened. Willie Willie, with his gossipy ways, his tale-telling ways. He would have told you.' A chuckle. 'Sure would have.'

So she calmed down, exaggerated a wrinkle into her forehead. 'About what?'

'About my uncle Vardaman,' said Wynne. 'How he got himself killed – one shot right through the middle of his head – by Old Man Coddington Mayhew for messing around with old man Coddington Mayhew's young wife. They called it a suicide. You ever heard a suicide killed himself with a neat little rifle shot through the middle of his forehead? No, I just bet you haven't, even in New York. We were poor then, and Coddington Mayhew was rich. So he could just out and do mur – ' Wynne caught himself. 'Whatever he wanted. But I didn't see no Negro Defense Fund coming down to give us a hand. Didn't see your rich Mary Pickett – related to all those Coddingtons and those Mayhews three ways from Sunday – sending off to get us no justice and relief.'

Regina said, 'I'm sorry about your uncle.' But what she was thinking, though, was how his voice changed when he told this story. How his grammar switched, how he started dropping his g's, started subtly rearranging his words. As though this wasn't his story at all but something he had maybe heard repeated by his daddy, by his mother – rehearsed to him by his family and just taken up.

Wynne said, 'Don't have it on me now, but next time I see you, I'll show you his picture. Think you'd like that?'

Regina said that she would.

'You know the one brought us the news? Told my daddy – nine years old, he was – to come, haul off his big brother's body?'

'No.'

'Willie Willie!' Wynne's voice rose triumphant. 'That uppity nigger always thought he was better than everyone else, and *sure* thought he was better than we were. Curled his fat lips right on up in the air whenever he saw us. Arrogant coon, always doing what the rich white folks wanted him to do. Anybody kin to Judge Calhoun. Anybody who'd help his little nigger kid, Joe Howard, go on.'

Gotcha!

Rising to the surface.

Regina could almost hear Peach whisper the words.

Regina had to force herself to breathe, but still she said nothing. They sat side by side on that porch, the night gathering around them in that magic hour that quieted the day birds and welcomed those that sang in the night. Wynne reached below the porch steps, pulled out a clear jug where something dark and liquid danced. He took a swig, then offered it to Regina. She shook her head no.

And then immediately realized she had made a mistake, because Wynne snapped, 'It's not nice to always say no. Didn't your mama teach you good manners?' Breaking the calm, taking him out of the rhythm of his story, which was where he belonged. Regina jumped, automatically held out her hand, but he laughed. 'Naw. You don't want it. You're not the fun-loving type. But then again' – a thoughtful silence – 'neither was Joe Howard.'

And it became that easy. Peach had been right. Wynne didn't see a reason in the world he should hide what he'd done. Who'd come after him – the judges, the jury, for killing an uppity black man? That had already been tried and Wynne had won. Now he thought he could say anything he wanted to. He was white. He was rich, and he ruled this land because of what his born-poor daddy had become.

The moment now. The point of his story.

No longer afraid, Regina leaned close.

Whispered, 'Mr Blodgett, did you kill Joe Howard Wilson?'

'Yes. Oh, yes, yes, yes!' White lightning flaming out of his mouth. A dragon's breath. And his eyes full on her, searing right through her. 'They all call him a hero – but Regina, honey, you should have heard that nigger scream.'

A Moment in the Magic Forest

October 1945

Gotcha!

He gets off the bus, Joe Howard, counting. One, two, three steps, all down onto dirt and the dry heave of mulch. Onto the dying crunch of an unfortunate bug. Into a familiar scent of forest that's released by the touch of his Army dress shoes. And for an instant he feels safe, is safe. He is home. His feet settled on his earth now, but his mind counting again. Six, seven, eight – a good ten white men.

Because home is also 'Get moving, nigger. Cussing in front of white women. Keeping an officer of the law waiting. You got yourself some manner learning to do.'

Joe Howard, an officer freshly discharged from his nation's army, wants to say, 'Call me sir, you goddamn cracker.' He wants to add, 'And if you want something from me, you better tack on a *please*.' He wants to say these things and swagger out more. But of course he doesn't. He's home, after all. He lost his temper on the bus, and look where it got him.

Gone so many years; so much happened to change him: school, a war, foreign lands. But nothing *had* changed him. A white man tells him to do something, and he does it. His feet are touching Mississippi again before he thinks, *Why, I didn't have to get off that bus. Who compelled me to do that? I didn't have to do what a white man told me to do.* But by then . . . Well, the bus is starting up again. The child Manasseh at the window, his hands splayed like a prayer against its cracked glass. Eyes big as saucers, tears flowing from them. Manasseh, he's looking at something he'll never forget. And from another window there's

Miss Anna Dale. She's shaking her head. Maybe she's crying, too.

Can he *really* see them, Joe Howard, through all the dark and the gloom? Maybe. And maybe that is the best he can do, because there's the bright Bonnie Blue pulling off now. Rumbling away. Going. Going. Gone. Taking the light, leaving the darkness.

Leaving Joe Howard and those men . . . those men, their faces shrouded behind white flour sacks.

Again, that word, *nigger*. Again, that word, *lesson*. And through it all the purposeful rustle of small animals, of little critters, because they know what happens when men show up this late in the forest. Not everything in it is gonna live through it. The animals realize this. They skitter off.

Joe Howard thinks about skittering off, too. After all, this is his forest. He knows every inch of it, its toothache trees, its dancing rabbits, its healing plants. He knows secret river bluffs old as Jesus himself. Where to find arrowheads the Natchez Indians left behind, where the caves are, where to hide – he knows all that.

Trouble is, these white men, the ones hiding out in the white dragon hoods, they grew up here, too. Maybe they grew up *with* him here. Who can tell? So trouble is, this is their forest as well. No hiding away. No thinking you're safe here. Not when his daddy was the one who taught it to them, and now they know every inch of it, too.

Years gone, boys now covered up by the white sheets of dragon men, but still Joe Howard recognizes some things. A cough, particular in the way it rattles upward, goes on and on, doesn't want to stop. He wants to say, 'That you, Sonny?' But they're not boys any longer. He'd have to call him *Mr* Sonny. But with school behind him and a war and foreign lands, Joe Howard is damned if he'll do that now.

'Damn officer. He needs to learn how to take him some orders.'

Take him some orders? What kind of no-account talking is that?

The first blow. Didn't see it coming. He staggers. Another one, harder this time. Joe Howard still standing. Refusing to let himself go down into the dust from someone close up to him. Someone who's taken off his hood. Someone who knows it doesn't matter one bit if Joe Howard can see his face because who's gonna care? Joe Howard squints closer. Young. Clean-looking. Light hair – but those eyes. Doesn't Joe Howard know those eyes? Isn't this someone his daddy warned him about, told him about, told him to keep clear of? *Specially* warned. That's what Joe Howard remembers.

'Y'all ain't nothing but a bunch of poor whites.'

His mouth again. Joe Howard finds himself flying. No way now he's not gonna eat him some dust.

Joe Howard. That you? Hurry up! Catch up!

He's flown so far that . . . Why, he's in Italy. Taking that hill again, killing those Germans, his best friend, L.C., only a little ahead of him now.

'Come on, Joe Howard! Close now. You can catch up. No doubt about it!'

'L.C.,' he whispers in wonder. 'It's good to see you man but . . . aren't you dead?'

'Shut that nigger's mouth up!'

Joe Howard soaring again, and now the Germans are every-place, speaking their English with Southern accents.

'Did you see that coon crawl? Crawl, coon, crawl.' Kicks raining like bullets on him. Joe Howard counting them all. But he picks himself up . . . God, what an effort. Reaches up. Touches himself. Makes sure there's no exploded L.C. on any part of him. Touching himself. Making sure he's all here. He hears laughter. That's how Joe Howard first knows he's still alive, through his hands first and then through his ears. Still alive.

'Come on, catch up! Catch up!' L.C. calling to him – or was it that magic child, Booker?

Teach him a lesson. Well, then, better get on with it now.

He gets up. Daylight in the forest now, sun shining all around him. It takes him a minute to realize what he's looking at is head-lights from a car. A big car, not black but blue. He sees this in torchlight. Who in hard-up Revere could afford a *new* car like that, flashy and bad?

'Aren't you Jackie Earle Blodgett's boy?' Words broken up by broken teeth. *Thackie Earle Throckett.* Pain that he's in, Joe Howard has to stop himself from laughing. Jackie Earle Blodgett's boy doing all this?

'*Mr* Blodgett to you.'

Joe Howard down again, struggling up.

'You'd been a man, you'd have fought a man's war. Not let your mama get you exempted.' This time, every single syllable ringing out of his mouth, clear as a bell. Joe Howard knows the whole story; his daddy has told him. Told him all about silk purses and sow's ears, too.

This boy, this Wynne Blodgett boy, reaches over, pulling at him, yanking him up – with his free hand because he has a tire iron in the other.

'Hey, nigger soldier, what's that you got on your chest?'

Joe Howard looks down in the bright light, in the sunlight from the car, and he sees his own medal. The one he got and that L.C. got, too – once he was dead. And this white boy's got the nerve to be grabbing at it.

'Hey, Wynne, don't you think . . . Man, this here's Willie Wil-lie's boy . . .'

Caution in this voice and maybe a tremor of fear. Yes, fear. Joe Howard recognizes it, because he *knows* it, has always known it, really. Home like he is now, in this dark, dark forest that is his South.

Skittering again. This time men sneaking off. Like the critters before them, they know what's coming next, too.

Now just Joe Howard. Just Wynne. Still reaching for that medal.

And Joe Howard's reaching up to his own medal. Gets his hand around it. Jerks it off. Holds on tight. And now it's more than a lesson. One. Two. Three. Four. His head. His arms. Crack. Splatter. He swallows, and something catches in his throat. He doesn't know if it's soft tears or hard teeth. Oh, yes, this is a very great lesson. Maybe the greatest lesson of all.

Hands okay, though, and that's very important. Fingers still able to slip his medal off. Joe Howard struggles up. Lunges at that white boy, snatches him a button off that once-perfect now blood-splattered white boy's white shirt. Holds it in his hand. Next to his medal. Already braced for what's coming next when it comes.

Somebody's chopping at a tree, bringing it down. Joe Howard hears the dull thudding, feels it too from where he is, his head once again in the dirt, his ear hearing the heartbeat of the forest.

All the time, catching up with L.C. And there – why, it's his daddy off in the woods, coming on, running toward him, shouting, 'Watch out, son. You be careful. It's a strange place you headed for now.'

Joe Howard trying hard to hear him, trying hard not to count what was happening to him anymore and thinking, *I'm done for.* Thinking, *I'm a dead man*, but smiling, too, as he eases the medal and the bright button near to the *Gotcha!* roots of an old burdock tree. His daddy is coming, and he knows his daddy will track it. Won't rest 'til he finds it.

And he wants his daddy to know who did this to him.

15.

Once away from The Folly, Regina ran to Calhoun Place, her heart hitching, looking back once or twice for the dog, for the man, but not stopping. Scared, oh, so scared – but also triumphant. *Wynne had done it. He'd confessed.*

She barely stopped, charged right through the big gate. Someone had switched on the single bulb over the front porch of the cottage, and there was light flooding out in greeting from Mary Pickett's house. Even though it was chilly, the small electric oscillating fan on Mary Pickett's front veranda blew a breeze through the bare azalea bushes that surrounded the wide porch. Regina rushed by, but not before she saw the silver tray perched on the railing with a decanter on it, two glasses, a small silver dish of what looked to be nuts. Regina thought immediately to Jackson Blodgett and looked around, but his big Buick was nowhere in sight. Neither was Willie Willie's green truck parked there – it rarely was, lately – but she realized she'd been hoping to see it. She wanted to talk to Willie Willie first.

Instead, there was Mary Pickett, bent deep into the bushes, but she looked up and smiled at Regina and waved too, her face radiant, her hand filled with the shards of a broken glass.

She said, 'I was worried. Dinetta said you hadn't come home from downtown. I called myself setting out to find you, but then Mr Blodgett came round. He said Wynne was out in the forest all day, but he'll be here tomorrow, to fix up that wall. Make it like before, like nothing has happened.'

The air shimmered between them. Regina looked around at the house – the words on the side of it more vivid than ever in the dusk – at the gardens, at the gracious way one part of Calhoun Place flowed to another.

Mary Pickett was still smiling as Regina walked up to her.

'He did it,' she said. 'Wynne did. He confessed.'

No question about what 'it' was. Instantly, Mary Pickett's face closed down. *Not again.* She sighed, brought out a little exasperated smile, like she didn't understand why they never could move on, always ended up in the same place – a sweet entitled Calhoun place.

'To whom did he confess?'

'To me.'

'That so?'

Mary Pickett's drawl slowed even more. But Regina saw change flare, bright as a comet, across her face, blazing away all its life and its color, leaving nothing behind but a mask of dead white. Paling her skin and lips, etching out the fine line of her nose until the only thing left of the Mary Pickett Regina knew were two fierce eyes. Sparking.

'But you knew that, didn't you?' And as Regina said the words, she realized they were true. 'Maybe you've always known. Still you had to assuage Willie Willie. Isn't that what you said? *Assuage* him. So he would keep working for you.'

'He doesn't work for me anymore. Or hadn't you noticed?'

Each word drawn out, each syllable changed into two, but clean, easily recognizable. The way a well-brought-up Southern lady, Regina thought, might talk to the help. And she, Regina, *was* the help. Brought down, paid for, housed, fed. Maneuvered. Miss Calhoun pulling the strings all the time.

Something was dawning on Regina, and it was a dark something. 'Then why?' she said, her words now just as drawn out as Mary Pickett's had been. Buying time.

'I already told you why. I owed him.'

'Owed him for what?'

And suddenly of course Regina knew. How had she missed it? Willie Willie telling stories. Willie Willie knowing all the tales that made this place tick.

'For *The Secret of Magic*, of course.' Mary Pickett looked right at her. 'It was his, all of it. He's the one made everything up.'

282

Regina shook her head – *No. No. No.* In that short instant before she started to hate her, she realized now how much she'd started to like Mary Pickett, had thought, maybe, she'd met a good white person at last.

'But you made sure you put your name on it? Made sure you got the credit for what he thought up.' It was said so low she didn't know if Mary Pickett had heard her.

But she had. She blushed scarlet. 'I didn't say it was his *book*. I said it was his *story*.'

'You mean you *stole* it from him?'

'There wasn't any stealing to it. Willie Willie can't . . .' But Mary Pickett's mouth clamped down tight as a trap, biting off whatever else she might have said. Regina stood in front of her, almost breathless to hear what it was. Whether it would be an excuse or a defiance. She didn't mind. She could argue with either. And she *wanted* to argue. She was *dying* to put an arrogant white woman like Mary Pickett Calhoun in her place. Pretending to be so good, so interested in Willie Willie and his welfare, in Joe Howard, and all the time keeping the real money and the fame and the power. Fashioning herself the famous M. P. Calhoun, the great storyteller. Using Willie Willie to keep up what her ancestors had used his ancestors to build.

'*Steal*,' Regina repeated. 'His ideas. From Willie Willie. After all he did for you.'

She snapped the words out and was gratified to see Mary Pickett flinch away from them.

Down but not out, Mary Pickett lifted her chin, turned toward the sanctuary of her house. 'They were good stories. But what on earth could Willie Willie ever have done with them? You tell me that?' She flung the words back over her shoulder.

It wasn't going to be that easy. Regina had no intention of letting it be that easy. Before she knew what she was doing, she had reached out and pulled Mary Pickett around.

'Is that it? Is that all you've got to say for yourself? Are you some kind of monster? Aren't you even sorry for how you robbed him?'

Mary Pickett turned, wrenched her arm away, and smacked Regina with the lightning from her fierce eyes.

'*Robbed* him of what? What good would those stories ever have done him?' She paused for a moment, squared her shoulders. 'Don't you pay attention to anything? Willie Willie – he can't read. He can't write.'

The words, rushed out on a deep breath, seemed to deflate Mary Pickett. For a minute, something flickered across her face – entreaty, maybe – but then she stared pointedly down at Regina's dark hand on her light arm, and whatever it had been, the look flashed away.

'You let go of me right this minute,' said the mistress of Calhoun Place, cutting the words out, sharp as a scissors. 'That's all I got to say to you. Take your hands off me and don't you ever touch me again or I will not hesitate to call the sheriff and have you thrown right into the jail. Bury you so deep under it they'll need every lawyer at that Negro Fund down here working before you'll have even a hope of seeing daylight again. This is Mississippi, and you don't understand a *thing* going on down here. What Wynne said to you – it doesn't matter. He was amusing himself, just passing the time. But that doesn't matter because he's just like you, you two could be peas in a pod – both *expert* at getting all the facts straight and all they mean wrong.'

Can't read. Can't write.

Not that it mattered, really, not in her estimation of Willie Willie, but Mary Pickett . . . Mary Pickett was something else. A thief now. A *plagiarist*, even. Seeing nothing bad in what she'd done, and able to get away with it, too. People like Mary Pickett, like Wynne . . . nothing to stop them. Talk about being peas in a pod. Anger sputtered through Regina; a current of it, deeply charged.

Regina tossed and turned the whole night, woke up tired the next morning, her fists clenched tight around the snowy white sheets. She got dressed, drank only the black coffee Dinetta had left in a thermos for her, and stepped out from the cottage. The day was bright and clear, air cool to the touch. She walked to the side of Calhoun Place, to the path where the sidewalk met the street. She saw it again, that NIGGER LUVER, and she marveled that she had passed right by it last night, so angry with Mary Pickett that she'd forgotten to look. But Wynne would come, and the painters with him, just like Jackson Blodgett promised, and they'd scrape it off, cover it over, make sure that it disappeared. And soon everyone would forget what had been written, like they seemed to forget so much else.

Regina was standing on the sidewalk, her hand shielding her eyes, staring up at the wall, when Wynne Blodgett drove up in his daddy's blue Buick. An old Ford truck – not Willie Willie's – turned onto Third Avenue behind him. When Wynne stopped, it stopped, and three men climbed out. They wore everyday clothes – dungarees, wool plaid shirts, heavy mud-spattered lace-up boots – clothes that looked like people actually worked in them. One of them had on an Army jacket, and he resembled Wynne, the same golden hair. They were all of them young. Young and sturdy. Not one of them looked at Regina.

They followed Wynne around to the side of the house, the notorious side. Even now other cars were easing down Third with their windows open so that folks who hadn't already seen could take a look-see. There were no policemen keeping order, no one said anything to them, but when they caught sight of Jackson Blodgett's Buick, the gawkers uniformly quickened their motors and moved on.

The men who'd come with Wynne reached into the back of the truck. They pulled out paint cans, two ladders, brushes. One of them stared over at Mary Pickett's poor, stricken wall and started slowly shaking his head. But he was smiling; a slow, calm smirk that Regina could recognize even from where she stood. If she tried to leave this was a phalanx she'd somehow have to get through. And she just wasn't up to it. Not today. She decided she'd wait here until they were well into their work, then she'd walk out, up the street. She'd go to Tom Raspberry, tell him what Wynne had told her. Mary Pickett said it didn't matter, but maybe Mary Pickett was wrong.

Regina watched Wynne point out the side of Calhoun Place, shake his head. *How could this happen? Who'd have done such a thing?* Now, looking at his son, Regina could imagine what Mary Pickett had seen in Jackson Blodgett – at least, she could almost imagine it. Good girl meets bad boy. Good girl saves bad boy. Good girl runs off with bad boy. No matter what details the plot promised, the story itself always read out the same. The bad boy won. He won because he was stronger. Not only was that the way in Mississippi, it was the way of the world.

But Mary Pickett, *The Secret of Magic* – what good was speculation about any of that now? Wynne Blodgett had confessed. At least, to Regina he had.

Wynne stopped pointing and talking, and he was moving toward her. The sun was behind him, and Regina lifted her hand, shaded her eyes from it, unconsciously mimicking Mary Pickett. She didn't have anything to say to Wynne Blodgett, but she did think it better not to turn and run off, not after what he'd said to her. It had taken all the strength she had to ease herself away from him last night, to get up off that porch, not to throw up in his face.

He didn't seem to expect her to run now either. Last night she'd sat very near to him, but she hadn't seen the color of his eyes, hadn't paid attention if they were dark like his father's or icy light like his mother's. Regina wondered why that should suddenly become important to her, but it had. Maybe because you could see the telltale gleam in them a mile off.

Though Wynne wasn't a mile away from her now. He was close and getting closer.

In all her life, Regina had seen only one photograph of her father. It had sat, prominently displayed, on a mahogany table in her mother's apartment and had followed Ida Jane when she married, to dominate the mantel in Dr Sam's house. The photograph had been a studio shot. In it her daddy looked strong and vital, not the kind of man who would be easy to kill. But he had been killed. Which meant the men who lynched him must be *enormous* – at least, they had always seemed enormous to Regina's child's mind. Mythical in their power, these men who had been able to reach out and take her father's life, and with it her mother's life and her own not-yet-born life – take them up in their hands, crush them to dust, scatter them to the wind.

'Want to sit down.' Wynne's tone was pleasant, but what he said obviously wasn't a question. *Sit down or else.* Regina caught herself looking around for Mary Pickett but then stopped. What help had Mary Pickett ever been?

He said, 'I brought that thing I promised to show you. The picture.'

What picture? She thought he must be talking about something he'd said last night, but he couldn't possibly think she'd be interested in anything else he had to say. Not after he'd admitted killing Joe Howard.

But still . . .

He'd talked to her. He'd told her things he perhaps hadn't meant to. If she got him talking again, who knows what might come out?

He was already cutting across the lawn, and she followed him to the rusted white wrought-iron table and chairs that sat in front of Willie Willie's cottage door.

Settled, Wynne reached into his back pocket, pulled out a wallet, pulled out a snapshot. Leaned closer.

'That's my daddy and my granddaddy and my uncle Vardaman. That's from a long time ago, after we sharecropped and my granddaddy was overseeing out at the old Mayhew Place. Doing a good job of it, too, from what I hear, enough to have high hopes for fixing up the home place. Of course, after Vardaman was killed . . . well, granddaddy and daddy, they got let go.'

Regina glanced down, because this was obviously expected. The photograph was an old-timey black-and-white photograph with people stiff in front of the camera, looking like they half expected getting their picture taken, being captured like that, might do them some harm. Two lean, handsome leathery-looking men and a young boy, all sitting on the porch of a free-standing log cabin. The Blodgett house was smaller than it had seemed last night, but the coating of the photographer's paper had turned its dull unpainted board to silver. Black and white, but Regina had been long enough in Mississippi to know that the color was there. Pink in that corner of hanging crepe myrtle, brown spots on a dog; white and more white in that brush of cotton that grew all the way up to the door. But why was he showing her this? What did it mean? She thought it might have something to do with what he'd told her last night, his confession. That maybe – just maybe – he might think he'd said too much, gone too far.

Again, he leaned close, and again the hard bone of his knee touched her thigh. Beneath the warmth of her cashmere cardigan – the beige one, the one just like Mary Pickett's – she broke out in a cold sweat. And this made her more afraid, that he could see the film of fear on her, could sense it just as Willie Willie would have been able to sense it.

By now great ladders rattled against the side of Calhoun Place. Regina could see them from where she was sitting. She heard the sound of scrapers against wood and men talking in low voices, assessing the damage and, maybe, cleaning it up. She heard distant shots – one, two, three – echoing out at them from the forest. Hunting squirrel. Hunting bird. Hunting deer. Hunting something. Anything. All the time.

Wynne put the picture away now, back in his wallet, and the wallet back in the pocket of snappy pressed jeans. He was still smiling. 'But ain't no niggers ever laughed at us, and I'm not about to let that happen, not now. So you better remind your little friend Willie Willie that his son's dead. Joe Howard's not coming back, and there's not a thing in this world going to be done about it. The grand jury's ruled. What happened was an "unfortunate accident." Not an *incident*, an *accident*. Joe Howard's gone to glory, bit the dust – however you colored folks put it – but Willie Willie's still alive, and he's living a nice life here in this nice town of Revere, Mississippi. His murdering friend, Peach . . . why, she's alive, too. And he needs aim to keep her that way.'

All the nerves in Regina's body jumped to attention.

'Peach?'

'Yes, your good friend Peach. One lives out in the county. All by herself, last time I checked. If I was you, I'd keep my mouth shut I had any notion of protecting her.'

Wynne stopped. He winked. 'Willie Willie comes and goes as he pleases, has a snug little house and all the money he needs. He was the old judge's pet nigger. Now, like everything else that was part of the family, Mary Pickett's taken him up. She may be a Calhoun, but she's got her limits, just like we all have.'

Wynne whistled, looked over at Regina. Repeated, 'A nice life. Willie Willie would do well to leave well enough alone, and he might just do that. That is, if he's got a smart lady lawyer telling him that's what he *ought* to do. For his own sake.'

Wynne reached over. He grabbed her breast through the thin fine weave of her cashmere sweater. She didn't see it coming – he was that sharp and that quick. But the wrench was so hard she almost screamed under it. *Almost* screamed – but not quite.

Instead, a hand came up, and it was her hand and the fingers on it were her fingers and they had formed themselves into a tough little fist.

She aimed square for that smart-aleck look on his face, but at the last second he stepped back and so she missed her aim but her fist smashed into him anyway – at his chest, at his heart.

'You filthy coward.' Spitting the words out. 'You think you can come here and threaten me? Threaten Peach? You think the way things are now – why, it's just going to go on like that forever. You can *kill* folks, a man – beat him to death – and the *Gotcha!*, it's never gonna get you. But Peach knows you did it.

She's got the shirt to prove it. The one with Joe Howard's blood on it? The one with the fancy buttons on it – one button missing? The shirt you thought you'd got rid of way back? Well, she found it, and it *means* something. And what it means is that you're gonna pay.'

For a second, for an instant, Wynne looked genuinely scared. Regina was sure of it, and her heart thudded in triumph as he lost his balance when she hit him, tottered on his feet, almost fell. *Almost* did. Later, when it would play back through her mind, she would see him. The startled look. The hand groping. The breathless moment. All this – before he caught the sharp edge of Willie Willie's table and righted himself once again.

'You black bitch . . . I'll make you sorry for this.'

Now it was her turn to laugh, a loud bark of it that startled the birds in the trees, that hushed the murmur of men talking. That silenced Wynne Blodgett, at least for a minute. She *would* be sorry for this, and she knew it. Was already sorry. Losing her temper like that. And Peach. Telling about Peach. But for a moment none of that mattered, because, right now, the throb of her hand felt so good.

Wynne tucked his picture safely away, straightened his shirt, notched his belt tighter. He started off down the side of the house toward his men, and he was whistling something. His whistling was a little off tune, and the song was something she recognized the melody, she just couldn't place it.

Regina sat back down, her arms wrapped around herself, shaking slightly as she heard his feet beating against the dead leaves on the side of the house and the sound of his hearty laughter, his calling out to someone, his saying, 'Well, hey there, how all y'all doing? How's the work coming along?'

She held her breath. She waited. She listened to see if Wynne would come back to her and bring those other men with him. But he didn't come back. He continued to laugh, to call out his greetings. She imagined him shaking men's hands. Soon enough she heard a car door open and close, and then the sound of an expensive engine first gunned and then purring to moving life. Soon the sound of this died away as well, and Regina was left with the memory of his song.

> *I'll be seeing you*
> *In all the old familiar places . . .*

There. She had it now, putting words with the melody.

> *I'll find you in the morning sun*
> *And when the day is through.*

Except Wynne Blodgett wasn't Frank Sinatra, and when he whistled the tune and the words played in her head they became . . . scary. A promise. Regina shivered. Only then did she realize how much her hand hurt, that it was throbbing, really, and that she should be looking somewhere for some ice. She thought of her own little Willie Willie cottage, but she knew there was nothing there. Then she thought of the kitchen in Mary Pickett's house, where there would surely be something. Hadn't she seen the egg man go into the kitchen that very day? Regina pulled herself up from the step and looked up – directly at Mary Pickett, who stood in her window, still as a stone above that stack of loose papers that Regina had thought was a manuscript but probably wasn't. Not, she thought grimly, unless Willie Willie had come up with a new book.

There was nothing on Mary Pickett's face, no reading of it. Regina couldn't tell how long she'd been there, what she'd seen. The only thing she saw was that it was white, whiter than normal, and with the same dead expression on it – Regina saw this after a moment – that had been on Mae Louise Wynne Blodgett's face when she'd come over to her rival's house, to her husband's fancy lady's house, to *Miss* Mary Pickett's Calhoun Place house to meet with the ladies of the Revere Garden Club, white hands clutched tight around a sheaf of late roses, and a piece of blue paper fresh from Tom Raspberry's printing press.

The same tightness around the mouth, around the eyes, that seemed to be seeping from deep inside, shriveling up everything in its wake. Until it drew in the skin of Mary Pickett's face so that the eyes themselves got smaller and smaller and the vision within them dimmer and dimmer until they were no longer capable of seeing anything she did not want them to see.

16.

'An offer,' said Rand Connelly, the sheriff. 'And this one's not from the district attorney. It came straight up from Judge Timms himself.'

It was late afternoon, and the day had turned cold enough that Tom Raspberry had switched on the small kerosene stove in the corner of his office. Three of them – Regina, Willie Willie, and Tom – were sitting around it. Only the sheriff stood up.

When Connelly had first come in, Regina held out her hand. After a pause, Rand Connelly reached out his own hand and took hers. One quick up-and-down pump and it was over, but the pumping had knocked the sheriff's hat off his head. He bent down and picked it up, kept it in his hand.

'I thought he wouldn't be back until November,' said Regina, but she saw hope flare on Willie Willie's face, a bright flame of it. The first she'd seen there. This was the sheriff, after all, and the circuit court judge. But the sheriff himself did not seem happy. With his hat off, his blond hair hanging into his eyes. He looked like what he was – the errand boy.

'It's a good offer,' he repeated, 'and not just from Judge Timms but from the businessmen in the White Citizens Council and the ladies in the Revere Garden Club.'

Willie Willie's smile faltered. 'What they got to do with anything? They not in the law courts.'

'Now, Willie Willie, you know we already been *through* that,' Connelly rattled out, blushing a little, impatient. 'Justice been done in this case. Poor Joe Howard, bless his heart, he suffered an accidental death. However . . .'

'But Wynne Blodgett did do it.' Regina leaned toward the sheriff. She tried hard to keep her voice from shaking, to sound like

293

the professional woman she was. It was important. 'He told me that he killed Joe Howard. Himself. Besides, I've got . . .'

'Hmmm . . . And when was that?' Talking about the confession and hearing nothing else. Regina half expected him to add 'little lady,' but he didn't.

She said, 'Last night. Down at the Blodgett house. The Folly.' She stopped. For the first time, she wondered if white people called it that, or just Willie Willie.

Connelly's face tightened for a moment. Then it relaxed.

'Wynne talked to you? Lawyer come down from New York for Willie Willie?' He snorted. 'Who's going to believe that?'

'He told me where it happened. Same place Mr Willie Willie said it did. Same place where he found Joe Howard's medal, out there on the state line.'

Willie Willie said, 'And I still got it, hanging on the visor out there in my truck.'

'Not that you *got* it. I'm sure you *got* it. It's where you got it *from*, that's what's gonna be the question. You say one thing. Somebody else – we'll leave names out of it – just gonna deny it. Say it came from someplace else. Folks'll say, "Why, that lying . . ."'

'Mr Connelly, sir. You ever known me to lie?'

The sheriff blushed. 'I wasn't talking about you in particular, Willie Willie. You know that. I was speaking in general.'

'Miss Regina wouldn't lie, neither.'

The sheriff let that pass.

Regina made a great show of fishing through the papers in her open briefcase. 'But we do have new evidence. Mrs Anna Dale Buchanan was on that bus, and she would be happy to testify. She –'

'She didn't actually see a thing,' interrupted the sheriff. 'Don't know nothing . . . anything . . .'

'Well, maybe you should talk to her again. No one called on her to testify, not in front of the grand jury, and she's free to do it,' said Regina. 'Or maybe Mr Duval could speak with her directly. That is if you don't want to do it yourself.'

'If Bed Duval did something like that,' said the sheriff, with a sigh perfectly pitched between patience and aggravation, 'with folks riled up the way they are now, writing things on the side of Miss Mary Pickett Calhoun's house and all – a veritable showplace – and flyers flung up all over town, disfiguring the trees . . . why, Bed could find himself not only losing the judgeship but recalled away from what he's already built up. Those that can vote'll make quick work of him for the good of the community. You best make up your mind to that 'cause he sure has. There's not going to be any more investigating done, and there's an end to it.'

Regina said, 'But there was another white woman on the bus. A widow with twin boys. She was mentioned in the court papers. I think her name was . . .'

'You talking about the new Mrs Johnny Ray Dean?' The sheriff knew the facts of his case, but they did not seem to make him look happy. 'A used-to-be widow. She's married herself to a bus driver now. From what I hear, he's cousin to the Blodgetts on his wife's side. Now I hear *the new* Mrs Dean is working herself; she's a receptionist over at the *Times Commercial*. Moved herself up and her kids up with her; went from staying with her mama in a tiny three-room shotgun in Tupelo to living in a nice brick bungalow with a nice husband near here in New Hope.' The sheriff's sad smile said, *You think she's gonna be any help?*

Connelly shot a quick look at Willie Willie, who was sitting stiffly on one of Tom Raspberry's wooden visitor's chairs.

Quietly, Regina said, 'And I guess Manasseh Lacey . . .'

'A little colored boy? Barely big enough to see out a bus window . . .' The sheriff let out a snort.

'I've got something else.'

A bit more attention, not much.

Regina hurried on, telling him about the shirt Peach had given her, where Peach had found it, the stains around the missing button. She saw Willie Willie stiffen, pay close attention, but none of this mattered to the sheriff. Halfway through, he started shaking his head.

'Means nothing,' he said. 'Could be anything on the front of that shirt. And even if it is blood, what's there connecting it with what happened to Joe Howard? Mr Wynne – he's young. Still sowing his wild oats, and – unfortunately – there's sometimes lots of fighting goes along with that. Now, Regina, you're a lawyer. You know what you got ain't gonna work in any courtroom in the nation, let's not even talk about here. Peach, with her shirt, she knows that, too. And probably a whole lot better than you do.'

'I think we better listen to the offer,' said Tom quietly. It was the first time he'd said a word.

A brief nod his way from the sheriff. 'They want to put his name on the War Memorial. Right up there with all the other World War folks who didn't come back – though actually Joe Howard did come back, in a manner of speaking. The White Citizens Council and the ladies . . . They plan to overlook all that. He'll be the first Nigra writ on it, you know. Alphabetized, along with everybody else.'

Regina shook her head. She couldn't believe it. She opened her mouth, but it was Willie Willie who spoke.

'But you knew Joe Howard. And you already know Wynne Blodgett killed him. You always known it.' He was looking right at Rand Connelly, this man he'd hunted with, this boy he'd shown through the woods. The others disappeared from the room, and it was just Rand and Willie Willie.

He didn't shout, didn't even really raise his voice, but the anger in it rustled through the proofs of the next issue of *The Revere Fair Dealer* that Tom Raspberry had pinned up on his wall. Rand Connelly turned scarlet, his face and neck alive with the bright flush of anger. Obviously hadn't expected Willie Willie's reaction. A black man talking like this to a Mississippi white. Now he glared over at Regina as if this new, no longer docile white-folks-pleasing Willie Willie were all her fault.

'Hold on there now, just one little minute – '

A knock cut Rand Connelly short. Another quick rap, and then a deputy poked his head through Tom's office door. Once he spotted the sheriff he hurried over, his boots heavy on Tom Raspberry's new wooden floor. The deputy whispered something to Rand and the sheriff nodded, looked over at the three Negroes, opened his mouth, shut it again.

He turned to the deputy, 'Tell Ray. I'll get right there.'

Only after the door closed again did he turn to the others. 'Willie Willie, Tom – there's a fire started up out there at Peach's. I guess that old kerosene stove of hers blew like we all been saying it would for years. Jim here says it's looking bad, threatens a good part of the east side of the forest. We can talk about all the rest of this later. I think we all ought to be getting ourselves on out there to help. Quick.'

The men got up and followed the sheriff. At the door, Willie Willie turned back to Regina.

'You get yourself on home now, Miss Regina. Stay inside. Close the door.'

Regina set off briskly for Calhoun Place and the cottage, but she had no intention of staying inside or closing any door. She was going out to Peach's with the rest of them. She couldn't wait here by herself, not knowing what was happening there. Maybe this was her fault. What she'd said to Wynne Blodgett about the shirt, about Peach. My God, a fire!

Regina's heart started to hammer, before she knew it she was running down the street. The Daimler would surely be at the house and the keys in it. She'd ask Mary Pickett if she could use it. Otherwise . . . well, she'd leave a note.

On Main the street was clogged with traffic, black men and white men in all kinds of trucks and buckboards, in jitneys, and some few cars, all headed out toward that dense rimming of trees. She looked up and there was a truck pulled by two mules. It was almost on top of her before she saw it. A man screamed out from the cabin. She got away just in time.

Fifth Street was where she started smelling wood burning.

Regina looked toward the sky, and the first things she saw were the twin chimneys of Mary Pickett's house, stark against a day sky that was purpling slowly to night. Between them, the moon shone faintly already – pale, full, and fat – like a dollop of cream on a mauve tablecloth. But beyond Calhoun Place she was sure she saw a feather of rising smoke, touching the tops of the tall, distant oaks, pluming around the mistletoe that was starting to bud out in the high, bare branches. That made her think even more of Willie Willie and of Peach, and she ran faster, as behind her a siren started its high keening wail.

There were no cars in the drive that led up to Calhoun Place, none parked at the curb on Mary Pickett's part of Third Avenue at all, not even the Daimler, which had not moved from its place at the side of the house since they'd got back from Anna Dale Buchanan's. Regina quickly sketched out a new plan. Instead of driving, she'd change her clothes, go over to Main Street, and start walking. Chances were somebody would stop for her. This was the good part of living in what Mary Pickett called a 'nice' town. *Someone* would stop. They'd shout out to her, ask her if she could do with a lift up. And if they didn't, she'd just keep heading east.

The door to the cottage was slightly ajar. She stopped, listened, remembering the night she'd come back with Willie Willie from Peach's, the way it had stood open then, the way the blue flyer had fluttered on it. But that had been nothing; this was nothing, too.

Regina stepped in, halted, and for some reason she sniffed. Nothing on the air but the smoldering from outside, and around her the small downstairs room was quiet. She heard the ticking of the heavy Bakelite Westclox on the refrigerator in the kitchen, but no bird sang in the overhang of magnolia branches outside the front door. She thought about checking the shirt again but decided she'd do this on her way out. Maybe take it with her. Just in case.

Regina hurried up the stairs to the bedroom, took off her

pumps, pulled on brown-and-white saddle shoes and socks. She grabbed her beige sweater from the hook outside the bathroom door. In less than five minutes she was rocketing back down.

She was on the bottom step when she heard the first growl. It was so low she almost missed it, almost thought that it was part of the general quiet stream of noise that seeped in all the time from outside, a car's engine, maybe. Except there had been no noise coming in from outside. Regina stopped, listened. When she turned toward the kitchen, she knew exactly what she'd see. Wynne Blodgett's hunting dog. Devil black. Eyes cold as stone. She had no doubt at all why this animal was here.

'*I'll make you sorry.*'

If his dog was here, Wynne could be here with him. Hiding in the kitchen. Or even upstairs, where he could have seen her switch out of her clothes. Wynne could be anywhere. With his cousins. Planning something. Ready – always ready – to sow more wild oats.

But it was the dog she had to think about now. He had some-how edged into the small living room, was halfway into it now. She thought he must have come in from the kitchen. His body looked loose enough, no tension in it, but even city-bred Regina knew he was poised for the spring. And his eyes . . . a wild ani-mal's eyes, with no remorse in them. Now that he'd gotten her attention, the dog did not growl again. He sat there motionless, just like he'd sat in the front yard of The Folly, but with his mouth slightly ajar so that now, she could not miss the feral baring of his sharp canine teeth.

Very slowly, Regina pulled her eyes away from him, looked around at her options. She was a good four feet from the door, on a landing, at an angle. The dog was less than five feet away now. Again, she hadn't seen him move, but if *she* moved, he'd be on her. The only thing between them was the wood slats of the stair-way. Nothing to him. Something he could bound over in one easy leap.

Another low growl.

She made up her mind. The only way out was the way she'd come in. She must have moved even as the thought registered, because she'd eased down the last step, was reaching for the doorknob – and it was so close, barely two feet away – when he lunged. And he bit.

Regina screamed.

Over and over again, he lifted her forearm in his teeth, shook his head back and forth with it in there like he was playing with a bone, and maybe he was. All on the arm that she'd thrown over her face. Teeth cracking in, pulling slowly out, and worse when they did come out. Because she knew another bite was coming, and another. And another. Pain so deep she couldn't locate it on her body anymore, just had to let it shriek out from within.

She was screaming so hard that at first she thought the shot was just another thing erupting from her own mouth. Thought the blood flooding over her was her blood. Thought the body slumping over her was her own body, dead.

'Oh, God.' It was Mary Pickett's voice, breathless and shaky as an old lady's.

'Oh, God,' said Mary Pickett's strange new voice again.

But the hands that lifted that dog's body off her were sure, and they were strong. And the feet that clattered into the kitchen hit hard on the floor.

'He's dead. I killed him. I heard you when I drove up. In the driveway, I heard it. The dog, and then you . . . I'd been out to the forest. I had my rifle.'

Mary Pickett was babbling, but the cup of water she held out was cool, and it felt good.

'Got to stop the blood. Got to get that sweater off you. Such a pretty sweater it was. I saw it that first day. The one we both had alike. Got to get burdock root for that wound. That's what Willie Willie would put on it. That, and sage. Must be sage in the kitchen. Got to call Dr Sherrod. Oh, heavens, he'll be out in the forest . . . Peach's already dead, but how will he know? Willie Willie will know, though, and I got to get him.'

300

Mary Pickett moved quickly. She lifted up her skirt, ripped off a piece of her slip, wrapped it around Regina's arm, all the time talking.

'Got to . . .'

'Got to . . .'

'Got to . . .'

Got to run, Collie!

Got to fly, Jack!

Got to hide, Booker!

Way deep in the forest.

Before it's too late.

17.

In the night, when she woke up, Regina thought she saw Mary Pickett still with her. There was a thin patter of rain falling on the tin porch over the cottage columns and the determined sound of squirrels under the roof settling in for the night. But it was Mary Pickett she was most aware of, or thought she was aware of. To the end of her life, Regina would never be able to tell. Because there was Mary Pickett, sitting on the edge of her bed, on the edge of *Willie Willie's* bed. Mary Pickett right there in the cottage, a place so near but one she'd never actually been in before. Regina lay there, unconscious and conscious, hearing or maybe not hearing, feeling safe again, her eyes closed.

'There, there,' crooned Mary Pickett or the dream Mary Pickett. It didn't matter. Regina knew whoever was sitting here with her was someone warm, someone safe. Because Willie Willie was sitting there, too.

'She'll be fine. Doc Sherrod said you did good by her – putting on that burdock right away. Drawing out the poison. She'll bear watching, and they might have to do the rabies. Wynne Blodgett, though . . . At least he's the kind would keep his dog clean.'

'You think he did it?' Again, Mary Pickett's faint whisper.

'I *know* he did it. Dog's not gonna come up here, let his own self into the house. Mr Wynne kept that animal under close watch.' There was a pause. Regina heard rain sheeting harder on the roof, but the squirrels in the attic seemed to have quieted. 'He's the one killed Peach, too.'

No argument, no defense. Only silence now from Mary Pickett. It was Willie Willie who went on.

'I taught all those folks, most of them when they were little more than little. They walked out with me into the forest. Bed

Duval and Rand Connelly, sometimes their daddies with them. Your daddy came. And Jackie Earle Blodgett came, too, at least sometimes. Early on. So they all knew what they were seeing. A blind man could have followed Wynne and those no-account friends of his and his cousin kinfolks, and not even Jackie Earle, his own daddy's that blind. He was right there with us, the whole town was, when we found Peach.

'There was three of them. It was easy tracking three different kinds of boot leather touching the ground. Jackie Earle's Buick Wynne's always going around in . . . No other car here's got wheels that big. Out there – why, they splashed kerosene all around the house and that little out-back kitchen, threw on a match so the whole thing burned up even. No more burn on the kitchen than there was on the house, and there would have been – if it was the kitchen gone up first. Beer bottles every-where. Pabst Blue Ribbon. And Mason jars full of that hooch they brew. It was like Wynne *wanted* folks to know it was him. *Dared* them to know it and be damned.'

His voice broke. For a moment, there was nothing but silence. Regina didn't know how long it lasted, then Willie Willie again: 'They tied her to one of old Miss Lindleigh's best chairs. Thing is, Wynne always hated Peach. Never was scared of him. Regina would stand right on up to him, and he knew it. Hated her all his young life. I just don't know what it was exactly that set him off now. Why he'd come for Peach. Why he'd come for Miss Regina.'

But Regina knew. *The shirt. Wynne thought Peach had the shirt.*

She tried to struggle up, but nothing on her moved, she could only listen. She thought Mary Pickett would start in about The Folly, about how Regina had slugged Wynne, how hopelessly silly and stupid she'd been and a failure. But Mary Pickett just sat there. She didn't say a word.

'They all know who set that fire. I saw them – all of them, start-ing with that timeworn Forrest Duval, and going right on down to the boys, the little twelve-year-olds come out there with the men to help out – all of them looked over at Jack Blodgett quick like.

They're thinking, *He got to get his boy out of here or there's gonna be trouble. Maybe he's gone too far now, killin' an old lady like that.* You could read it on their faces, how they wanted to sweep Wynne under a rug someplace, hide him away. Pretend, *We only dealing with Nigras here and we got our ways and our laws, so it's not really a problem.* But most of these are pretty good people, and inside, down there deep in the dark where they keep things like Wynne Blodgett . . . why, down there what he's done is eatin' 'em up.'

'But there must be some proof. You got to get *proof.*' Mary Pickett was herself again, bossy and in charge.

'You can get all the proof you want to, Miss Mary Pickett,' Willie Willie said slowly. 'They don't want to see it . . . proof's never enough. Not when folks turn scared. And they are scared, frightened what they been hiding from gonna jump out and bite them.'

In the corner of the room, just behind his shadow and Mary Pickett's, were those three *Magic* children. Even through her shut-tight eyelids, Regina saw them quite clearly. And their eyes were wide open. Their hands clamped tight over their mouths.

They were staring at Willie Willie and shaking their heads.

But when Regina woke up the next morning the only person still there was Willie Willie. He was sitting in the barkcloth-covered easy chair that he had drawn up close to her bed and his fingers were playing, again, with that bright spot of silver, just like they had been the first time she'd seen him on the gravel out at the bus depot here in Revere.

'How's Peach?' She winced and looked over to see her arm a mass of white gauze and adhesive bandages, with, at the end, five swollen fingers barely peeking out.

'Ol' Peach, she be off now for Glory.'

'Off for Glory? What's that mean?' But struggling up in the bed, she remembered.

'Peach died, Miss Regina. That fire out there in the forest – she went out with it.'

She looked over at him, then, focused, saw the shirt on his lap.

Of course he had found it. He'd know where to look. It was his cottage, after all. And he'd guess that Peach had given it to her, not like Wynne Blodgett, who didn't know and would think Peach had kept the shirt to herself and – maybe – finally got scared and had killed her to get it. Wynne Blodgett, a man like that, how could you figure out what was going on in his head?

But Willie Willie didn't say anything about Wynne Blodgett, not to her. For a moment, they just sat there, two black people, one old, one young – and Regina wondered where the anger was, where had it disappeared to? Because surely, she thought, she ought to still be angry. Her mother would be mad as hell. Things running on like they were in Mississippi – Ida Jane would be pitching a fit.

Except this was *her* fault. Regina knew it. If she hadn't hit Wynne. If she'd just bided her time, kept hold of her temper. If she hadn't told him about that shirt.

'Mr Willie Willie . . .'

He shushed her. 'Miss Mary Pickett done told me everything. About what you told Wynne. About how you punched him.' A chuckle. 'Anything you could tell me and more. Miss Mary Pickett and me . . . Well, we know each other. Been knowing each other for a mighty long time.'

'Then she told you it was my fault. I'm the one . . .'

'What Miss Mary Pickett said to me, Miss Regina, was that you wanted to help me, get me some justice for my son.' He paused. 'I'm grateful to you for it. I rightly am.'

Regina wasn't convinced, but across from her, Willie Willie still played with his hands, strong, ashy fingers brushing together. If it had rained last night, if she hadn't been dreaming, then the air had been washed clean by it. Sunlight beamed like a searchlight through the open blind, turned the gray in his head into bright molten silver, brightened again the real silver that played in his hand.

'But tell me, now, how you doing?' he said. Now he looked up, and his smile was so quick she almost missed it. Outside, there was the sound of a door slamming, of someone tramping up the back steps over at Mary Pickett's, and going straight in the back door.

'Fine,' Regina said and smiled, but she ached all over, pain pushing tears into her eyes.

'They cleaned up that dog, took him over to the doc. Don't look like he got rabies, though. I wouldn't expect that. You won't have to have those shots. I guess that's something.'

He looked up. 'And I got something to say to you. Miss Mary Pickett told me what you think about that book.' He didn't call it his book or her book, Regina noticed; he just kept talking on.

'How old are you, Miss Regina?'

'Twenty-six.'

'Uh-huh.' Willie Willie seemed to take this in, digesting her age, his eyes making her seem younger than she actually felt. 'Well,' he continued, 'Miss Mary Pickett was twenty when she got called back here. Twenty when she came home at the start up of the Depressing. And to what? To a stroked-out daddy and a house falling down around both of their heads. To a passel of cousins and cousins of cousins, all of them forever needing some help. To the only man she'd ever love – I know that now – married off and father to another woman's child. But she was still my baby girl, and I could see the world on her shoulders. So I'd go over at night into the kitchen, and I'd take Joe Howard with me. She'd help him out with his little schoolwork, and I'd tell her my stories. But they weren't all just *my* stories. I'd heard a lot of them myself – from the Choctaw, from somebody claim he was the last conjuring man survived of the Natchez, from the old-timey folks, some came right down from Miss Mary Pickett's own daddy. People who carried on stories from when the forest began.'

Regina looked past him, out the window, over at a great house that had been built on slave labor.

'So you think what she did – she *stole* from you – you think that was *all right?*'

'No, that's not what I'm saying.' Willie Willie seemed to consider.

'What I'm saying is, it looked right to her then. You know, Miss Regina, once upon a time there was a man named Luther Mottley. He's in that *Magic* book. In a way, it's almost all about him. What he could do. What he could get away with. Now, Luther – he was one right really bad man, and everybody in this town knew it. His daddy, the one built up the house and the shop, had called Luther back from New Orleans to take care of his two sisters. That's how it was back then, that was the custom. But Luther loved New Orleans and he hated it here, and he hated his sisters. Hated and hated – until the day Sister fell down and she broke that hip. Luther'd stand on the porch. Wouldn't let nobody near her. Ol' Doc Sherrod – this Doc Sherrod's daddy, a white man – went out to help, and there's Luther politely holding a rifle in his hand. That's another of the customs. You see, Doc Sherrod was on Luther Mottley's land. Sister so weak now, pulling herself across the floor to do what Luther ordered her to do, moaning but scared to moan too loud because it might upset Luther. He might turn on her. Scared to death he might hurt her again. Until one day – why, Peach and I killed him.'

Just like that, word following word, with as much expression in them as if he'd been telling Regina he'd bought red apples that morning off a truck passing through. Regina sucked in her breath.

'Killed him,' repeated Willie Willie. 'And then disappeared him. Not because of what he'd already done to Sister, not because of revenge – you got to believe that – but because Luther had to be stopped before he did worse. I was a rough young man back then, grown up in a rough young land, a land full of strange stories and customs. Now I ask myself, "Would I do it again?" ' He paused. 'I like to think not.'

He smiled at her then, clapped his hands. She'd seen a magician do this once at the end of his act, almost as though it had come time to break the last spell. When Willie Willie did this, the delicacy of a ladybug spread her wings and floated up from the protection of his old and gnarled hands. He must have been hiding her all along. Regina hadn't seen, but she watched now as the lady-bug spread her wings, fluttered them, and flew straight up. Regina tried following the flight, but she couldn't. She turned her head in the direction of noise, but this turned out to be the scratching of the magnolia limb against the windowpane. This took her eye away from the ladybug just for an instant, but still she lost it.

Beside her, Willie Willie chuckled.

'What you just witnessed,' he said, 'why, that's nothing but the secret of magic. Ol' Man Magic always does that. Makes us forget what we started out after. Makes us look where he wants us to look.' He pointed to a spot on the ceiling, far off in the corner. 'See, there's your good-luck ladybug, big as you please.'

He reached down then, lifted the shirt, brought it over to Regina on the bed. Then he took the silver he had played with his hands and laid it on top, where it fit like a puzzle piece, in with the others.

'The button' she said, and she was on fire with what it meant. Proof. Proof that Wynne Blodgett had done this. Despite the pain, she started struggling up.

Beside her, once again, Willie Willie shaking his head. 'Don't mean a thing. Not even this. Didn't you listen to the sheriff over there at Tom Raspberry's? Didn't you hear what he said? Why, Wynne Blodgett could come right on out and say that he killed my boy. He always did it, always admitted it. To his friends, that is, when he was drunk.' A lift of Willie Willie's shoulders, a smile on his lips that wasn't quite nice. 'Wynne's always been one to talk more than he should. No, this shirt, what happened – it don't mean one thing for this town, for those who own it and rule it. But that don't mean it don't mean nothing to me.'

Willie Willie smiled at her, and his smile was radiant, a *father's* smile. And she loved it.

'You did your best for me, Miss Regina, Esquire, and for my son, Lieutenant Joe Howard. And I thank you for it.'

18

It was going to get worse before it got better. That's what the
new doctor said. This time a black one, a man named Dr Mills,
who came over from Malthorn, a little-bitty town, he told her,
north of Revere. 'But it's home.'

'What's that they say . . . fortunate in your misfortune?' The
doctor had a deep, rich drawl. 'That's you, all right, Miss Robichard. No major veins touched. No real tendon damage. You'll
keep those scars for the rest of your life, but they'll heal clean. In
time, you might even forget they're there.' He tapped her cheek
with his stethoscope. 'At least he didn't have time to get hold of
your face. You can thank Miss Mary Pickett for that.'

'Yes, I should,' she said, but she didn't. No matter what Willie Willie had told her, how he had tried to explain things. Not that she was
angry – about *The Secret of Magic*, about what it had meant to her and
what she now knew. No, not *angry*, really . . . She just didn't want to
have anything more to do with M. P. Calhoun.

The doctor came twice a day at first and then once. He always
told her she was improving, always asked her about her job at the
Fund ('Want to visit New York myself someday'), always said to
convey his kind regards to Miss Mary Pickett. Asked if she –
Regina – saw much of Mr Willie Willie.

'He's the one took us out into the forest,' said the doctor. 'Me
and my brothers. Mr Willie Willie's the one taught us to hunt.'

But Regina did not see Willie Willie. After that first night, he'd
disappeared once again.

Instead, Regina spent those last few days getting better, looking
out the window at Mary Pickett and Dinetta, each in a crocheted
shawl, picking through things left over from the harvest – setting
up collards, canning late tomatoes and lady apples – their heads

bent close together and talking away. Once in a while, Mary Pickett looked up and over at the cottage. Dinetta never did.

But it was Dinetta who brought Regina the news.

She was upstairs, her luggage laid out on the floor, putting the last of her clothes in it – an awkward thing, with her arm still in a sling. But Thurgood wanted her back, and Ida Jane, almost frantic with worry, threatened to come down to Revere *this very minute*. The compromise was that she and Dr Sam would meet Regina in Washington, D.C., the day after tomorrow. Like Thurgood, Ida Jane talked about the dog attack, the death of Peach, all of the violence. Nobody said anything anymore about Joe Howard and the case, because they all understood that the case was all gone.

'You got to see this!' hollered a newly friendly Dinetta from the cottage doorway. Regina paused from folding a blouse and listened to her taking the stairs two at a time. 'Not gonna believe it.'

'Believe what?'

'A black cross flaming bright as day last night over at Mr Jackson's house. You know, the old Mayhew Place where he lives.' Dinetta paused. Dramatic. 'And they say Mr Willie Willie's the one done it.'

'Who says?'

'The newspaper says. Well, it's not exactly *in* the newspaper. Here, read this.'

She held out a special edition of *The Revere Plain Dealer*.

BLACK CROSS BURNED ON BLODGETT LAWN

Local authorities were called to the old Mayhew house yesterday morning at three a.m. by its owner, Mr Jackson Blodgett. Mr Blodgett told them he looked out of his window to see flames coming off an object on his land and immediately called the fire department. Although this reporter was not allowed close enough to assess just what the object was, rumor has it that Mr Blodgett is saying it was a black-painted cross. When questioned further, he stated, 'I guess we all know who's behind this, and it's time to call an end to it. This is no longer a joke. This time I've got the proof.'

The fire – not a large one – was quickly extinguished, and the sheriff was seen accompanying Mr Blodgett into his house, along with some men who were identified as cousins from Alabama of Mrs Mae Louise Wynne Blodgett's. A small crowd gathered but was quickly dispersed.

'I hope Mr Jackson prints something about this himself in the *Times Commercial*; otherwise, Tom Raspberry's gonna find himself in a whole mess of trouble. You been up here, but since Peach died, let's just say things been mighty skittery.' Dinetta looked like skittery was a feeling she might relish. 'Negroes are mumbling down in Catfish Alley; whites mumbling on their side of town, too.' Dinetta nodded, wise – at least to race – beyond her young years.

'So what's going to happen?'

'It's *already* happened.'

Regina read through the paper again. Shook her head, puzzled. 'What about Wynne Blodgett? It doesn't say anything about him. Was he home?'

'That's just it. Wynne's nowhere around. Nobody's seen hide nor hair of him all week. He's probably off with those no-accounts he hangs out with from over Carroll County. His kinfolk, he calls them, and maybe they are. But if he gets wind of this . . . Honey, there's gonna be hell to pay. Sheriff's over here right this minute. He's talking to Miss Mary Pickett. They want to go out to the forest, find Willie Willie. Get to him before that murdering Wynne Blodgett does.'

Regina said to her, 'Quick. Please help me. I got to get dressed.'

Calhoun Place was dark, already in mourning. At least Regina thought this as she hurried by. Hurried by, not ran by it. Her arm under its sling, and its gauze bandages had started to throb even before she'd made it downstairs to the cottage door.

Mary Pickett was already in the Daimler, the windows rolled up, a scarf tied around her hair. She was looking just as frantically as she always did for the car keys, and, like always, they were in the ignition, right in front of her eyes. Regina pointed to them as she rapped on the window.

'I'm coming, too,' she said.

Mary Pickett put her hand on the key, said an automatic thank-you, and then rolled down the window. She looked from Regina's face to her cast and started shaking her head.

'You'll just get in the way. Wynne all liquored up – when he goes out looking for Willie Willie, it's not going to be pretty.'

Regina said, 'But I'm Mr Willie Willie's attorney.'

Mary Pickett looked at Regina closely for a moment, at her face this time, not the cast. Finally, she said, 'Well, I guess you are that. But Willie Willie's not going to need a lawyer. I know Wynne. He's got no intention of bringing him in for trial.'

But without another word, she leaned over and opened the front passenger door.

Regina climbed in, careful not to wince, careful not to show Mary Pickett how much her arm hurt. Once the door slammed, Mary Pickett started up.

The Daimler lurched out onto Third Avenue, the bumper scraping the pavement as Mary Pickett aimed it sharply to the right. She reminded Regina of some kind of big lost bird as she bent over the steering wheel, her arms akimbo in their plaid jacket, her legs long and bony over feet in white socks and old-lady oxfords, her head arched forward as though it were her mind that pulled the car and not the other way around. Behind her lay a rifle on the plush backseat.

Regina didn't have to ask what had happened.

'Duwayne Winters came up on my porch not an hour ago. His people used to sharecrop with my daddy over out there at Magnolia Forest. They're white,' said Mary Pickett, still with her eyes fixed straight ahead. 'He wanted to tell me that he'd heard from a cousin of his who had heard from . . . well, I guess you don't need to know the progression. It was about what they were planning to do to Willie Willie. What they called *teaching a lesson*. It took Duwayne a minute to get up his courage to tell me. I guess he heard them talking days ago, but he didn't say anything to anybody because he didn't want to get his mama's nephew in trouble. That part of the family's been in and out of the Jefferson-Lee County jail for years. But now with this new thing come up . . . with that black cross burning. White folks are not going to put up with that. Willie Willie's out there in the forest, and maybe Wynne's already gone out there after him.'

The rain had started up again, a cold, gray drizzle, and the pavement was thick and bright with it. Mary Pickett careened the Daimler down Main, past the bus depot, where the street gave way to the highway. Regina remembered the day when she'd first arrived in Revere. Willie Willie striding slowly toward her, puzzled, then smiling, then grinning as it started to dawn on him just who she was. A lawyer from New York – but not Thurgood Marshall. What a tease this would be for Miss Mary Pickett! What a tease it would be for the white men so avidly staring out at them from the front of the depot! But today there was nobody sitting on the dilapidated porch, nobody grinning, nobody staring. The white men had all disappeared. They'd gone into the forest.

Once she and Mary Pickett left town, there was snow everywhere. At least, it looked like snow to Regina, as she stared out at it, holding tight on to the strap over the door so that she wouldn't topple over with Mary Pickett's rough driving. Thick and white, but only at the edge of the road. It took Regina a moment to realize she was looking at cotton, rough filaments of it. Cotton that had fallen off trucks and wagons, that had slipped out of burlap bags strapped to mules and dray horses – a harvest of cotton that led to the forest, looking for all the world like – Oh, God, what was it Peach had said? – like something Hansel and Gretel might have sprinkled to find their way back.

Mary Pickett said, 'Near Peach Mottley's. They'll all be there. Out to Peach's, or what's left of it now. That's where things will begin.'

The two of them, Mary Pickett and Regina, reached the part

of the asphalt where the middle line down the center disappeared so you had to watch what was coming, and around them a forest loomed.

'He never could understand Willie Willie – Jackson, I mean. He thought if he could just *own* him like he owns everything else . . . But if Wynne kills Willie Willie, if that happens, it's Willie Willie owns them. That's the way it always is with murder, and with everything else. You think you're getting away with something, but you never are. You think you've covered something up, but it never is. Just when you think you're safe – why, it jumps out to bite you . . . Maybe that's what he wants. I should have paid more attention. I should have tried to explain things better. I should have . . . at the end.'

Who was the *he*? Who was the *him*? Regina, not from Revere, wasn't quite certain, and she felt her strangeness, her isolation from this place and the intricate interweaving of its people. She looked over at Mary Pickett to see if it was Willie Willie or Wynne or Jackson Blodgett. She tried to read the answer in her face, in her eyes. But Mary Pickett had veered off the main road then, and they were traveling on a road leaf-littered and cluttered with scrub pine. Regina turned back to her own window, she rolled it down and let the low-hanging branches brush against her, tangle in her hair, like they had that first time when she'd come out to take tea with Peach. She let the trees try to hold her. For a moment she was back in the cottage, back in the bedroom, the night the dog had come. And she saw three children standing in the corner. She saw them shaking their heads. She felt their dread. She smelled what they smelled – the burn on the forest.

Collie and Jack and Booker crouched at the edge of the forest, frightened by the screech of the hooty owl, by the snake sound the kudzu made as it grew in the night.

But then they saw Daddy Lemon, always just ahead of them. His big arms arching, smiling at his children. Beckoning them on.

19

November, and still fireflies flitted against the magic that had been Peach Mottley's house.

'Sheriff's already here,' said Mary Pickett, as a matter of fact. 'And it appears like he's brought in a posse of folks with him. Rand's gonna need all the help he can get. First Peach, now Willie Willie. Our Negroes were already upset enough about Joe Howard . . .'

Our Negroes.

Mary Pickett realized what she was saying, looked around at Regina and blushed pink but went right on talking anyway. 'Lots of things are changing. Sheriff's scared they might decide to fight back. On the other hand, he's got Jackson. And Jackson . . . Well, he's going to use everything he's got to take care of his son.'

They looked around at a litter of vehicles now jutting out of what had once been open space. Regina recognized the sheriff's Ford, and maybe Bed Duval's Studebaker. She thought she remembered seeing him in a car like this. But these almost got lost in a jumble of others. Old cars, old trucks, many with decals of the Confederate flag pasted on them. Staring out of their back windows. Holding on tight to any bumper they could get.

But Regina hardly paid them attention. She was climbing out of the car. She was staring at what, once upon a time, had been Peach's filled-to-the-brim house.

Burned, now, to the ground.

That's what she'd been expecting. Everything dark and gloaming, smelling of decay. But this place wasn't like that, not really. There was still too much of Peach in it. Regina made out bright shreds left of her shawls and of her velvet sofas, a glint of gold from a splintered gilt mirror, a shred of brocade wallpaper charred around its edges. Red flashed here, yellow there, garnet and purple, a long piece of quilt, shards of white porcelain – small, defiant specks of color making Peach's house glow, still bright.

They stood there for a moment looking around, quiet, and the forest quiet with them. Then Mary Pickett reached into the backseat and pulled out her rifle. She picked up one of the kerosene lamps that winked from steps that had once led up to Peach's house. The two of them set off toward a flicker of lights they could see through the trees.

Mary Pickett was a good tracker, a good nimrod. Even Regina, new to the woods, could see that. Mary Pickett led her around Peach's house, around Peach's kitchen building, around scarlet geraniums, ash on them but somehow saved from destruction and still bobbing away in their rusting coffee cans. Mary Pickett tracking a path that Regina couldn't make out until her feet hit it, but she followed anyway. Behind them, other cars drove up, other car doors slammed, and soon there was a babble of voices, a yelping of dogs. Neither Regina nor Mary Pickett turned back.

Something moved in the bushes over her head, and Regina looked up. For a second she thought she saw a man high above her head, hanging there. And that hanging man became her father, the way she'd always thought of him, swaying back and forth at the end of a rope. She opened her mouth to scream. But she snapped it shut again, because she couldn't do that. Mary Pickett would send her back for sure then, thinking Regina had called out because of the pain in her arm, using its poor, shattered state as her excuse.

And it *would* be an excuse, because even as she said the words Mary Pickett would be thinking, *A Yankee girl, her own father dead, she's not ready for what we'll be seeing.* Regina knew just what that was. *Willie Willie out there somewhere. Dancing at the end of a rope.*

The forest touched her again, sassafras and willow and oak branches caressing her, trying to make it better. Mary Pickett stopped, raised her head, canted it, listened. Regina raised her head, too, and looked up at what she'd first thought was her father. Instead, she saw mistletoe, balls of it everywhere, clinging to the tops of the bare trees, floating in the breeze, silver-green in the soft moonlight and round as a face. But it wasn't a face after all. She looked down and almost screamed again. Little bodies everyplace. Rabbits, birds, a dead possum. All too near Peach's house when it burned, and taken down by surprise with it.

Now the voices and the dogs yelping came from in front of them, not just behind.

'We're on Magnolia Forest land, near the cleared cotton fields,' said Mary Pickett. Regina didn't know how she could tell, but she believed her. Mary Pickett took off running, Regina puffing up behind, and suddenly, around them, the trees pulled back, like a curtain going up, and they were in a cleared field. Regina stopped for a second, caught her breath, her arm throbbing. All around her, white in the reflection of moonlight, was a sprinkling of cotton like the remnant trail they'd seen on the road. A cotton field, she thought, but only for a moment, because Mary Pickett stopped now, too.

Ahead of them, the sheriff was bending over something. And the leashed dogs were going crazy. And someone was vomiting.

And there was the smell.

But there was no other way, they had to keep going forward. They slowed their pace, started walking now, because now they were certain what they'd find in the end. Without thinking, Regina reached out her hand – and just like that, Mary Pickett's was in it.

And then there it was.

Willie Willie was not up in a tree. But he was dead anyway, a circle of men around him as he lay on the ground.

'Holy *shiiit*.'

Rand Connelly didn't look embarrassed about his cussing, even when he saw Mary Pickett. He didn't try to stop her from coming forward. He seemed dazed, confused. All the men did. And scared.

Regina looked down, and again, at first, she didn't recognize it. It was a figure, bloated and dark and burned. It took a moment for her to understand that what she saw was that great buck deer. *Poor thing.* It must have been caught in that fire at Peach's. Burned, too, like everything else had been. But how had it gotten here? What was it doing this far from . . .

It was then she saw the rope holding him together and the human legs sticking out from the bottom of him, and at first she thought it was just an illusion, like the mistletoe faces had been an illusion or like the *Magic* children she'd seen that night had been an illusion. Something made up in her mind. Something not there.

'Miss Mary Pickett, I think you better move off from here. You might want to take that girl with you,' the sheriff said.

That's when Regina realized she must be wobbling. She must look like she was going to faint.

Mary Pickett wasn't paying attention. She bent down beside the men who were working on the ropes, and she took a knife from her pocket and started cutting at them, too. Gently. Gently. All the time whispering, 'Willie Willie.' Over and over again. Sure he'd be in there. All of them preparing themselves for the worst. Only when the last string splayed did Mary Pickett struggle up.

But she didn't take her eyes away. Neither did Regina. They owed it to him to be there as witnesses when they got him out. Strong hands pulled the carcass from around him, and there he was with blood everywhere, covered in the blood of that dead deer and his own blood that had oozed into the ground. That had called creatures out of the forest to scavenge.

'Goddamn! Goddamn!'

The sheriff cursing in earnest now, his hands digging at the body, wiping the blood from the face. Going quicker, getting deeper, cleaning the face, as the white men drew nearer and the black men – the few who had come out – started edging away.

'Goddamn Willie Willie. He's done killed Wynne Blodgett!'

And all around them the forest started to shriek.

'Daddy Lemon! Daddy Lemon! Come quick. There's a toothache tree here and an old creek called Bogue Chitta and an arrowhead big as your fist. And the Dancing Rabbit. Look there! You can just see him! That Rabbit's dance, dance, dancing everywhere!'

They scattered off after him immediately, the sheriff and all the white men and their dogs, but Regina didn't think even they believed Willie Willie would be as easy to find as he turned out to be. But he was. Right there at Peach's still, barely hiding in what remained of her root cellar. Almost, Mary Pickett said to Regina later, as though it was part of his plan to be caught.

'Wanted them to know he was the one who had done it.' Mary Pickett said this quietly. 'Wanted them to know a *Negro* did this, and that maybe justice for Joe Howard had finally been gotten. I don't know why else he would have stayed on.'

All this was said the next afternoon, after Mary Pickett walked back alone from the courthouse. Regina, finished with the telephone calls she had to make and the pleadings, was waiting for her in the driveway of Calhoun Place, anxiously pacing back and forth. She recognized Mary Pickett's return by the way her footsteps echoed hollowly as she made the turn onto Third Avenue. Sleepless, pale as death, Mary Pickett had still dressed up to her Calhoun best, in a suit, gloves, a hat. She'd carried a good pocketbook. All of this done so that, once she got where she was going, they'd remember who she was – the last true Calhoun – and that Willie Willie in a sense belonged to her, as the Willies had belonged with the Calhouns for years.

'It didn't work. They wouldn't let me see him. Sheriff said maybe tonight.' She didn't add, *That is, if he's still alive,* but the words hung there just the same. She slumped into one of the wicker chairs on her back veranda, her face looking as old as the forest itself, red curls a jumble, leaking out of her hat and limping down the side of her cheek. When Regina had first seen her, Regina had thought of Mary Pickett as pretty, but now she doubted she had ever seen a more beautiful woman, not even Ida Jane.

Mary Pickett said, 'Maybe tonight. That's what Rand said, because there's going to be a rally. Speakers. People coming in from other parts of the state. Over from Arkansas, even. Down from Tennessee. And Alabama. Of course Alabama. All those Wynne connections, they'll be here. It is *unbelievable* . . . and women with them. *Ladies*, even, members of the Revere Garden Club. Folks I've known every day of my life. Everybody screaming hate. Everybody so scared.' She shook her head. 'Rand Connelly said it's all he can do to hold the crowd down and keep Willie Willie alive until the state troopers can get here. I think that's why he's letting the rally go on tonight, to buy Willie Willie some time. If there's others coming and all, they won't do anything, at least not right away.'

Suddenly, she turned to Regina, her face fierce. 'You remember that, though. Promise me you'll remember. How the sheriff stopped them stringing up Willie Willie right last night, stood there right in front of him with a shotgun. And Big Tiny Watson, I don't believe you've met him, but he sharecropped for my daddy. He and Willie Willie used to work the same field. Now he's over there, trying to calm things down. All these men know that Willie Willie killed Wynne, and both of them believe that he's going to die and maybe that he *should* die. The times being what they are, and the customs . . . the customs are what they are, too. They're just trying to make sure he goes out with a fair trial and some *justice*. That's all, just a little shred of justice. When all this gets out – and it will – everybody up north's going to say we are monsters. In Omaha, Nebraska, where they killed your daddy, folks will say Mississippi is filled up with monsters. But you'll know different. You'll know there are still some few good white people down here. When you tell this story back in New York, remember them, too. You hear me?'

Mary Pickett was spitting out the words, forgetting all about being a lady. Leaning in so close to Regina that their lips almost touched.

Regina nodded yes. And she would remember. But most of all,

she thought she'd remember Mary Pickett herself, sitting there in the hard sunlight of autumn with her fine felt hat askew and tears leaking like raindrops out of her eyes.

The nod seemed to satisfy Mary Pickett. She sat up straight in her chair with a little bit of the old Miss Mary Pickett vigor. 'There's not a Negro face on the streets, and who could blame them? Not even Dinetta's here, and she never misses a day of work. Wynne Blodgett kills Willie Willie's son. Willie Willie kills Jackson Blodgett's son. Now we got to sure go on and kill Willie Willie. I ask you now, where will it stop?'

A shiver ran through her, light and quick. Regina saw it, and it reminded her of a lone leaf clinging to a bare branch as the first cold winds of winter blasted.

'It's chilly out. You want to go in? Get some coffee?' Regina asked her, but Mary Pickett shook her head. She glanced around at her great white house, her family house, the home place, like this was the first time she saw it.

'No,' she said. 'I don't want to go inside there.'

Regina's eyes followed her, and then she looked over at the cottage, so snug and so pretty, and she thought of Willie Willie and Joe Howard and how they had lived in it and how she, for a little time at least, had lived in it, too.

It occurred to her, *Why, this is the first place I've ever stayed in all by myself.* And even with all the horror behind her and the worse horror she knew was coming, she was grateful to have found, even for this short time, her own home.

Mary Pickett turned to her. 'Did you get anybody?'

Because that's what they'd decided. Mary Pickett would go to the jail, try to see Willie Willie, and Regina would get in touch with New York. The idea that Willie Willie might have a lawyer, they'd both agreed, would only have stirred people up more and made things harder. So Regina was to make the telephone calls. First to the governor's office down in Jackson to try to get protection, and then to Thurgood. There'd been no response at all from the state capital. Thurgood said he'd be on his way first thing in the morning – if they still needed him in the morning. Those had been his exact words. He'd left Regina to catch their clear meaning.

If they hadn't lynched Willie Willie by then.

'Yes,' said Regina. 'I've made them.' And she told Mary Pickett what had been said.

Somebody had gotten loudspeakers, and there was a constant low rumble from the direction of the courthouse, and a progression of cars and trucks and buckboards rolling up Third Avenue toward it. Sometimes they slowed as they passed Calhoun Place, where the NIGGER LUVER still peeked faintly through a badly layered coating of fresh paint. But nobody called anything out at Mary Pickett, and no one stopped a vehicle and got out.

Mary Pickett nodded at Regina's words. She raised her hands, sighed, and said, 'I just will never understand why Willie Willie didn't run on off, cross the forest and the river, get on over into Louisiana quick? He could have done it. He knows the land and the forest . . .'

Regina wondered this as well, but she was reaching some conclusions. Willie Willie was so organized and so tidy. His car, his person, his snug little house . . . all always so methodically arranged. It was the way his mind worked. He left nothing to chance. So if he had stayed on at Peach's, he was looking for something. He must have thought she had something that would help him, something that might be there even after the burning. Something he might need. Maybe just in case what had happened did happen and they caught him.

And then Regina remembered.

'I've got the key.'

20.

Excerpt from

In Magnolia Forest

by M. P. Calhoun

J. B. LIPPINCOTT & CO., NEW YORK, 1948

Grown up now, Collie was the only one left alive in the forest, what with little Booker dead and Jack lost to her, this time forever, like he always had been, really, except in her mind. Daddy Lemon as good as dead and who would soon be dead, at least to her – and yet Daddy Lemon was all she had left. She hurried up streets, all alone now, where always someone whom she loved, who was close to her, had been.

But at least now she had the key. And that key could make at least one thing all right.

She was near enough that she could hear the men speaking into the microphone on the steps in front of the courthouse, one after the other, going on and on. She saw the flicker of strobe lights playing on fear-filled, hate-filled faces. But she turned away from them, and she thought of the forest; thought of its rich, firm goodness everywhere. This was something Daddy Lemon had always insisted they remember. That the forest snuck up on you, reached out to grab you. The roots of it would continually break through. You'd clear seedlings of it from the side of your road; look up and there they'd be all over again. The forest had been here before, and it would be here again.

If Daddy Lemon could just get back there, could hide in the richness of its loam-scented bosom – well, she knew he'd be safe. From here, you could even see the forest, as you could from any spot in Revere, the stretched-out fingers of it reaching clear into the town. Beckoning for Daddy Lemon. Calling him home.

Collie skirted around the men – and the women – on Main Street and went immediately to the back of the jail. She found the door unlocked like she knew it would be. In Revere, the doors were always kept open for tradesmen and friends. People just came and went, dropping off laundry or flower cuttings or their very own special lane cake. And there was no one at this back door. They were all out in front, listening to the speakers, as she had known they would be. In a small town, where so little happened, what little entertainment there was must, of necessity, be shared by them all.

But inside the jailhouse, there was only Daddy Lemon. His eyes were swollen, his face red and bruised. She reached out to him, touched his worn black cheek for the last time, and put her hand into the strong black hand where it had rested – where all of their hands had rested – so long ago. He'd been beaten, and badly, but nothing looked broken. He was still a whole man. She was grateful for that. He could make it to the forest, and once he was there – why, he'd know what to do.

'And always it'll be talking to you. The forest's gonna tell you everything you need to know.'

Tonight she needed to know. So she listened.

What the forest said to her, what it had always said to her, was, Come deeper.

'I'll try to give you a minute.' That's what the sheriff had told her this afternoon. 'That's all the time you got. It's all I can do.'

Just a minute.

But Collie slowed that minute down, she used every second of it, because she had the key.

'I'm sorry,' she said, and she meant it. And wasn't that what we all wanted to hear? From the ones who were close to us. From the ones who had turned on us. From the ones who had hurt us.

'I'm sorry.'

They'd been so close – not just her and Daddy Lemon but the whole town, all of them together, black and white, rich and poor – in a way that was difficult to explain to someone outside but was real.

They smiled at each other, Collie and Daddy Lemon, one last time.

Then Collie said, 'Live me a story.'

And she gave him the key.

21.

The taxi left her off at 69 Fifth Avenue, a place she had never been before. A new land, the woman thought, but she didn't say this out loud. She reached into her crocodile purse – a splurge, but worth it; who knew when she'd get back to New York and Best & Co. again? – and took out money for the taxi driver and gave it to him. On the sidewalk, she looked up at the building and through a canyon of other tall buildings to a luminous sky overhead. Bright as a bluebird's breast, she thought, not a cloud in it. And then she walked in.

The woman at the reception desk was exactly what you would expect: bright-eyed and chipper. Not old, not dour. And with a smile on her face, as she looked up from stabbing wires into a switchboard, which made her look like she might be bursting with hope.

'May I help you?' she said – helpfully. She was very pretty, dark-skinned, dark-eyed and -haired, and she was dressed in a snowy white lace-collared blouse. A very nice blouse; the woman noticed such things.

'I'd like to see Thurgood Marshall,' she said. 'He's expecting me.'

'Your name, please?'

'Mary Pickett Calhoun.'

The receptionist looked down at a ledger beside her, then up again. She squinted a bit and nodded.

'One moment, ma'am,' she said. 'I'll tell Mr Marshall you're here.'

The receptionist got up, started walking, but turned back before she reached the frosted-glass door that led off from the main room into who knew where. She smiled shyly at Mary

Pickett, and the smile took years off her face. Mary Pickett realized she really was quite young. Twenty, at most. A girl with the whole of her life still before her, with the aspirations of it and the disappointments and the mistakes and the changes, all the things you never anticipated – but a *life*, nonetheless. Something that could shine forth, be full.

'Hey, Miss Calhoun,' said the girl-woman. 'I read *The Secret of Magic*, you know. When I was little, ninth grade, I think, and I *loved* Daddy Lemon.'

'I loved him, too,' said Mary Pickett, quietly, and then she added, 'Thank you.'

'Thank *you*,' said the receptionist before she disappeared, 'for writing it. That book meant a lot to me.'

She had a New York accent, syllables all there, sharp vowels. It sounded nothing at all like a voice that had come out of the South. But the 'ma'am' was there, and the 'hey.' Mary Pickett thought this young woman might possibly have what they called in Revere 'antecedents' – a mama from Louisiana, a daddy from Carolina or Georgia, grandparents who had started out in Alabama, then crossed over into Mississippi in order to catch the Illinois Central and start that long, long voyage up to Detroit. Mary Pickett sighed. Good or bad, throughout the nation, it was the South pumped the heartbeat of so much.

She took a moment to look around the office. Dullish green-painted walls with a few ancient-looking palm tree prints nailed up on them. Orange plastic seats with chrome legs. Back issues of magazines – mainly, the NAACP's *Crisis* – scattered on wood-veneer tables. It could have been an office anywhere. Mary Pickett didn't know exactly what she had been expecting, but she decided that this seemed . . . well, right.

She heard the quick tap of high heels, the forceful clomp of a man's sturdy shoe. She turned back to the door, and there was Thurgood Marshall. Immediately he took over the room, the very presence of a man. Lately, his picture seemed to be everyplace. Mary Pickett saw it quite often in the newspapers she read.

But his was the kind of face, she decided, you would remember from the very first sight.

'Mr Thurgood Marshall,' said the receptionist with a flourish. She was proud of him. Proud of what they were doing. Mary Pickett could tell, and she was reminded of something she had once read that had always stayed with her, something somebody had written well before the last war. 'If you find a job you really love, you'll never work again.'

Thurgood Marshall looked like a man who had found his life's work. Mary Pickett had, too – or refound it. This gave them something in common. This made her happy for him.

'*Mr* Marshall,' said Miss Mary Pickett Calhoun. It was a private joke, this salutation, from what seemed like a long time ago now, but still they both smiled. Then she took off her glove. She reached out her hand. The shake that he gave it felt good.

'Come right this way,' said Thurgood Marshall as he held the frosted-glass door open.

On the other side of it – ringing telephones, the clicking of multiple typewriters, the smell of stale coffee and too many cigarettes. She felt herself pulled into a vast forward movement and, without thinking, started putting together images in her mind for a book.

Thurgood Marshall introduced her left and right – to lawyers and secretaries, to the office boy bringing in a bound stack of newspapers, to a visiting member of the NAACP Board of Directors, to W. E. B. Du Bois. He didn't seem to discriminate in the hierarchy of his office. Mary Pickett surprised herself by being gratified by this. She thought that it boded well. There were more white lawyers than she thought there would be, and this boded well, too. Mary Pickett shook hands with everybody. She answered quick questions about *The Secret of Magic*. And she smiled.

'Regina's back here in my personal office. She's waiting,' said Thurgood. 'Place is too small now, and we're so full up in it, they had to stick her with me.'

His personal office was *exactly* like Mary Pickett had expected it to be. Regina had described it more than once. Papers that marched in columns up the wall, half-full cardboard drink cups, a window open to the last of a late-summer breeze. It looked very much like her own office, back home in Revere looked when she had been deep, deep in the writing of her book. A *finished* book, *In Magnolia Forest*. It was in her arms now, one of the things she had brought with her, and for a second she clutched it close to her heart. Finished, that's true, all the way to *The End*. But now Mary Pickett knew there would be another. And then maybe even another. She had only to look around her to know there was no holding life back.

'Mary Pickett,' said Regina, getting up from her desk, coming to the door.

And Mary Pickett said, 'Regina,' still rhyming it with *vagina*. She walked into Thurgood Marshall's office, holding out her hand.

In the months since they'd last seen each other – Mary Pickett dressed in black, standing beside the Daimler at the Bonnie Blue Line depot, waving her off – Regina had changed. Gotten older – Peach must have done that to her, the endless recrimination about what had happened, the death. *What if I hadn't said this? What if I had done that?* Mary Pickett understood that kind of thinking. She'd done enough of it over the years about Willie Willie, about *The Secret of Magic*, their book. Some things you do when you're young, not thinking; you never can change them. Can't make them better. You got to just pick up and go on from there. She hoped Regina realized this. It was important, with all that needed doing, that she not waste the time, that she not waste precious years. Always there were people who needed what you could give them. Who depended on you. Mary Pickett looked over to Regina's small desk, and there was that snapshot on it, the one she'd sent here so long ago in her letter, the one of a grinning, proud Willie Willie and Joe Howard in his new dress uniform. Framed now, holding on to each other forever.

Damn, Mary Pickett thought. *I can't let myself cry.*

She shook her head. This was a happy time, and she didn't want to ruin it with too much serious thinking.

'Nice suit,' said Mary Pickett, about Regina's stylish tweed. 'Hattie Carnegie?'

'Yes, Hattie Carnegie,' answered Regina, and the quickness of her smile said some things would never change. And really – did everything need to?

Thurgood indicated the two client chairs, brought his own massive leather one from behind the desk to face them.

'Coffee, anyone?' he asked. 'A doughnut?'

The women shook their heads. 'No, thank you,' they said together.

Mary Pickett sat down, started opening the smaller of her manila envelopes. 'I brought the clippings with me. There weren't many, and that's a blessing. The hue and cry died down quickly. About Willie Willie, I mean.'

'So he got away,' said Thurgood. He took clippings from Mary Pickett, put on his glasses. 'I'm sorry I never met him, but from what Regina told me, he was an amazing fellow.'

'Yes, amazing,' said Mary Pickett. 'And loved.'

As Thurgood started reading, Mary Pickett turned to Regina. 'All the major newspapers wrote something about his getting away. The white newspapers. Except, of course, *The Revere Times Commercial*, but you wouldn't expect that.'

'You ever see him anymore?' asked Regina. 'Jackson Blodgett? Does he still come over? Maybe once in a while?'

Jackson.

The name brought with it the usual roil of emotions. *What might have been. What could have been.* And then, inevitably, *What had happened.* For a second, tears, the *Gotcha!*, threatened to overwhelm Mary Pickett. But then she lowered her eyes and found what had pulled her through so much in the past, so many losses – the inevitable strong core of her Miss Calhoun self.

'No,' she said quietly. 'I don't imagine I'll see Mr Blodgett ever again, not personally, at least. He's suffered the loss of a son, and he's grieving. His wife, Miss Mae Louise . . . Why, she's stricken. They, the two of them alone, need to hold on tight to each other, get through this terrible time together. I'm sure you understand.'

Regina nodded. She understood.

Thurgood looked up. 'So, from what I'm reading, Willie Willie just *vanished* into thin air?'

Mary Pickett shook her head. 'Not into thin air; he went into the forest.'

She had numbered the clippings like she had done the first time, with blue ink in her perfect Palmer penmanship hand, and just like before, ink had bled into the foolscap. But the bleeding ink couldn't hide, couldn't camouflage what they were all screaming.

BLACK MAN KILLS WHITE MAN, THEN DISAPPEARS

'Except he didn't,' said Mary Pickett.

Thurgood looked up, frowned. 'I thought you said – '

'Oh, he got out of Revere, all right. Physically, that is. First into the forest, then over into Louisiana, probably Texas after that. But he had to leave Mississippi to do it. Leave his *home*, the places he cared for and the people he loved.'

Thurgood was having none of it. 'No offense, Miss Calhoun, but I can't imagine there's a Negro alive not anxious to leave Mississippi. Willie Willie, once out – he probably didn't stop running 'til he reached the Pacific. Besides, from what Regina tells me, the folks you're talking about – Peach and Joe Howard – the people he loved were all dead.'

'Maybe,' said Mary Pickett, tears glistening her eyes, looking right at Regina. 'Maybe they were the only ones he loved. But I like to think not.'

They were all silent for a moment, Thurgood still reading and then passing the clippings one by one to Regina. She didn't look at them now. Mary Pickett imagined she'd wait until later. She'd want to be by herself when she did.

'Well, my goodness, I'd almost forgotten . . .'

She flourished forth another manila envelope, this one marked TOM RASPBERRY. She passed it to Regina, who opened it up. A front-page banner headline from the *Chicago Defender*:

LAWYER SON OF PROMINENT REVERE ATTORNEY TO SIT FOR MISSISSIPPI STATE BAR EXAM NEXT SESSION!

And there he was, smiling away – Tom with his arm wrapped around a younger, spitting image of himself.

Mary Pickett said, 'I thought you might have already seen this, but just in case . . .'

'I had,' said Regina. 'I read it.'

'He won't make it,' Thurgood said matter-of-factly. 'Not in Mississippi. Not yet. They're not ready.'

There was a knock at his door. A woman – a secretary – stuck her head in.

'Mr Wilkins wants to see you,' she said. 'He said it's urgent. Something about Oklahoma.'

'The Rattley case,' mumbled Thurgood. He nodded at Mary Pickett, took the file from the secretary, and followed her out.

Mary Pickett and Regina sat in silence for a moment, listening to Thurgood's footsteps as they blended into the overarching activity of the office. A breeze at the window still flapped at the shade. Regina waited for a moment, then asked, 'You still at Calhoun Place? Jackson Blodgett didn't take it from you, did he? Willie Willie said he held the note on it . . .'

'I'm still there,' said Mary Pickett. 'And he could have. I don't know why he didn't, but he didn't.' They were silent again for a moment, their minds swirling around the contradiction that was the South.

Then, strangely, Mary Pickett whispered, 'Do you miss it?'

And, strangely, Regina answered back, 'Sometimes. Yes, sometimes I do.'

Talking about Revere. They both knew that.

Mary Pickett smiled. 'Bed Duval tells me Tom Raspberry keeps writing you to come down, join Tom Junior and him in their practice. Not a law practice, really, not what you're used to. Maybe not yet, but Tom . . . if things change, he sure can adapt.' They both laughed at this. After a minute, Mary Pickett went on: 'You know how it is in a small town – might as well air all your business on the party line. Bed tells me Tom says you're just what Revere needs. Bed says you might be just what Tom needs. Now, that's just his personal opinion, though he did say that – if you come down – Tom wants to call his new firm Raspberry and Robichard. I told Bed, that it sounds like dessert to me.'

'Me, too,' said Regina.

'But,' said Mary Pickett, looking at her keenly, 'I do declare you look like you might just be in possession of a fine sweet tooth.'

Mary Pickett looked down at her watch then. 'Oh, my!' Started up. 'Gracious, time for me to be going. I've got a train to catch out of Penn Station. But I brought this for you. I wanted you to have it.'

She opened up the last of her manila envelopes, pulled out a thick binding of typeset pages.

'*In Magnolia Forest*,' Regina read. 'Is this your new book?'

'The galleys of it,' said Mary Pickett. 'Lippincott's bringing it out early next year. They did *Magic*, too, way back when. I'm surprised they remembered me, but they did.'

She knew she looked pleased as punch. She couldn't help it. She said, 'Look here.'

And she flipped through pages, to the third one, and there it was:

This book is dedicated to
Mr Willie Willie
My Guide through the Forest

There was a rattle at the window, and both women turned to it as a tiny, good-luck ladybug beat against the glass, trying to get out. They each hurried over to help it, but the ladybug had found its own way, poised on the outside sill for a moment, and then launched itself, flapping, catching the wind when it could, going straight into the immense and unknown freedom of a bright sky.

But Mary Pickett had been taught her directions by Willie Willie.

She knew that ladybug was heading south.

Author's Note

I wrote *The Secret of Magic* with four people in mind.

The first person was my grandfather.

In 1942, my maternal grandfather, Joe Howard Thurman, joined a segregated Army and fought in World War II to liberate the world from the Fascists and the Nazis. At the time he did this, he was still effectively denied the right to vote in his home state here in the United States.

My grandfather joined the Army because he loved his country (he always wore a little flag pin, even before they became politically fashionable) and because he loved us. My three sisters and brother and I knew he'd fought because all his friends had; indeed, almost all the men in his generation had. But my grandfather never discussed the war, never talked about his experiences in the Army. He was a quiet, courteous, diligent black man, always right there when we needed him. He was my hero.

I knew, from the time I was very little, that I wanted to grow up to be a writer and that I wanted to write about my grandfather and what he meant to us, how he kept our family together. He was the one who taught me how to read, spending his hard-earned money to buy me a little Golden Book each week at the Kresge's in downtown Kansas City. My grandfather was the first one to tell me I could be what I wanted to be, do what I wanted to. 'You can do it. You just got to *work* at it,' he said.

But we knew that he'd not been able to do everything he wanted to do. I can remember getting on a bus with my grandmother, going downtown to take sandwiches to my grandfather when he was on the picket line. He and other black construction workers had banded together and demanded to be paid the same amount of money that the white construction workers were paid for doing the same dangerous work. This was well after the world war that my grandfather helped to fight had been won. But, in Missouri, the blacks lost their battle. The union they started was crushed and they scattered. But this didn't stop my grandfather's faith, either in his country or in us. He knew we could do what we wanted to do. Work hard. Don't give up.

The second person who inspired *The Secret of Magic* was my grandfather's hero: Thurgood Marshall. Even though Thurgood Marshall was a lawyer and my grandfather had only graduated high school, as a young girl I imagined them having a great deal in common. They both had a particular kind of 1940s Gotcha! charm. This was back in the day when glamour had a lot more to do with a certain natty style, a way of talking and walking, than it did with having huge amounts of money – which was good because my grandfather never had much of that. But he was cool, just like Thurgood Marshall was, though they didn't look anything alike. My grandfather was trim and tidy and dark-skinned, unlike Mr Marshall, who was taller and fairer and who seemed, in pictures, to have rawer bones. Still, in my mind, I've always put them together, moving along on a trench-coated mid-century noir vibe.

'That Thurgood,' my grandfather would say, looking up from the Kansas City *Call*, where he'd been reading something about him. 'That's one somebody who knows him some law.'

Back then, Thurgood Marshall was like a member of the family – and not just our family but every African-American family. We all knew what was going on with him and with the NAACP Legal Defense and Education Fund over in New York City. That's because this was a heyday not only of the civil rights movement but of the African-American press as a whole and especially of John Johnson's *Ebony* and *Jet* magazines and his *Negro Digest*. Every black person you knew had a subscription to at least one of these and usually all of them; it was just taken for granted. This meant that you could start reading an article in your own house and know, if you had to leave, you would be able to finish it up wherever you happened to be going – to the barbershop or the beauty shop, down the street to your best friend's, over to your teacher's where you went for a little extra help, or all the way up to Chicago for a visit with your second cousin. The latest issues of *Ebony* and *Jet* would be laid out, waiting on a table to greet you. And in those magazines were people who looked like you looked, shared your same interests and ambitions, and weren't just tearing things down but were building them up. *Jet* and *Ebony* were filled with news about Thurgood Marshall.

But I can't remember reading anything about Isaac Woodard in them, though his was one of Thurgood Marshall's cases. Mr Marshall was head of the NAACP Legal Defense Fund during the war, and there had been a rash of suits against the government for discrimination. There were so many of them that they took over an actual room at the Fund offices – 'Reggie's Room' in *The Secret of Magic* – which was stacked floor to ceiling with envelopes stuffed with neatly typed or handwritten grievances against the way things were in the armed forces. Black soldiers were, indeed, routinely imprisoned or dishonorably discharged for doing what white soldiers had been reprimanded or exonerated for doing. But Isaac Woodard's story was not one of these. It was worse.

Like my grandfather, Isaac Woodard was a soldier in the U.S. Army during World War II. Before being honorably discharged from the service in 1946, he had spent the previous fifteen months fighting in the jungles of the Philippines. He told everybody that the first thing he wanted to do once he got out of the military was to visit his mother in Aiken, South Carolina. With that in mind, he boarded an interstate bus. That much is certain; after that testimony varies. Some accounts record that Mr Woodard was disorderly on the bus, that he was intoxicated. I remember reading once that he offended the white ladies riding on it with him by taking his time in the colored restroom during a station stopover. He kept them waiting. Mr Woodard denied all this. But even if he'd done what people said he did, how could anybody justify what happened to him next?

The driver got off the bus, made a call, and alerted the authorities about what he considered to be Mr Woodard's bad behavior. At the next stop two policemen were waiting for him, and they escorted him from the bus. They took him to the jail where they beat him. When Isaac Woodard insisted on his civil rights – that, in America, he should not be beaten – one of the policemen took the end of his billy club and systematically, one by one, used it to punch out both of Mr Woodard's eyes. He was blinded for life. The policeman who did this obviously didn't think there would be any reprisals. He may even have done the same thing before and gotten away with it. This was a man who must have thought he could do whatever he wanted to, and keep on doing it forever. He didn't realize that things had changed, and that the war my grandfather and Isaac Woodard had fought in had helped to change them. Mr Woodard's family and friends did not just disappear. Outraged, they called upon Thurgood Marshall. The NAACP Legal Defense Fund took up the case, making it one of the first civil rights causes in the postwar era.

No wonder my grandfather idolized Thurgood Marshall. He showed that this kind of behavior was not to be tolerated. Slowly but surely, case by case, he, and the many others like him, opened a view for us as Americans that was inclusive, not exclusive, and that showed that all of us – not just white men – have equal rights under the law.

But I didn't learn about Isaac Woodard until 2009, when I started researching this book. It was a pivotal case for both the growth of the NAACP and the LDF, but it's been almost forgotten. The details of the story seared themselves into my brain. Maybe because Mr Woodard could have been my grandfather, maybe because it seemed to me to be a turning of a tide in the civil rights movement. Maybe because, as with all writers, I like to think I know an unforgettable story when I hear one. And so Isaac Woodard was my third person.

My fourth person was Constance Baker Motley, the inspiration for my Regina Mary Robichard.

By the age of eleven I was ready to branch out a bit from *Jet* and *Ebony* – I still loved them but I was a girl, after all, and so I saved up my twenty-five-cent-a-week allowance and got my own subscription to *Vogue* magazine. I can still remember what a thrill that was, seeing clothes and shoes and even makeup that you'd never come across at the department stores in downtown Omaha back then, at Brandeis, or even at Haas-Aquila. *Vogue* made me feel part of a much larger world. Of course there was no one like *me* in it back then, no one who looked like my family – until one day, I opened up an issue and there was this fabulous portrait of Constance Baker Motley, the first woman lawyer hired by Thurgood Marshall at the Legal Defense Fund. She was the one who had organized so many of the veteran cases; she was the one who had actually been in charge of 'Reggie's Room.' Thurgood Marshall had taken her on in 1946 at a time when few women, and even fewer black women, were encouraged to go into the law. In 1949 he sent her down to Jackson, Mississippi, to participate in a court trial concerning teacher-salary parity between blacks and whites. This was the first time, in that century, that blacks in Mississippi had significantly challenged their separate but equal status, which had been established by the *Plessy v. Ferguson* Supreme Court decision in 1896. By doing this, Mrs Motley helped to begin the long slow process that would lead to *Brown v. the Board of Education* and the end of separate but equal school systems. Of course, every African-American in the South knew all about this. She was famous with us, famous in the pages of *Jet* and *Ebony*. But now, I realized, she was famous to the whole world. I remember thinking, Oh, wow! I called my grandfather up, told him all about it. Then I clipped the picture of Constance Baker Motley out and sent it to him. In the photograph she looks like a woman who knew how to fight a just war and to win it.

There is a framed photograph of my grandfather, Joe Howard Thurman, proud in the khaki uniform of a World War II enlisted man, which always sat on the bureau in my grandparents' bedroom.

This picture never seemed to change its position, was not allowed to get dusty. Unlike my grandfather, it never aged. We still have it.

There he is, a man who idolized Thurgood Marshall, who shared his granddaughter's admiration for Constance Baker Motley, who had probably identified with Isaac Woodard, caught in time forever, snazzy in his uniform over the inscription

To my Baby,
Love, your Joe Howard

My grandfather, who fought for dignity and liberty just as surely as his heroes did.

I'm looking at that picture as I write these words now.

Acknowledgments

Thank you to my wonderful agent, Harvey Klinger, who has been with me since well before the beginning and yet is still able to wake up in the middle of the night with the just-right idea. We all need a Harvey in our lives! Amy Einhorn is truly the editor extraordinaire. Not only does she continue to do meticulous line edits, but her advice, her comments, her grace and wisdom were always an inspiration. And I won't even talk about her dedication – she e-mailed me the last of her edits from New York during the midst of Hurricane Sandy! Am I lucky to have her or what? Liz Stein, Amy's assistant, was a godsend. She answered my many questions quickly and completely and always with patient good humor. Thank you, Liz. Lisa Amoroso designed a marvelous jacket, and I thank her for it and thank all the others involved in moving this book forward, especially Amy Brosey, Tony Davis, Nicole Pederson, and Elizabeth Smith – for their careful thought and thoroughness.

Linda Ford Campany read early drafts of the manuscript and offered sage guidance about the novel itself and also about the state of Mississippi immediately after the Second World War. Bob Raymond was a great friend throughout this whole process. In addition, I am grateful to many others in my hometown of Columbus, Mississippi (which is not Revere, Mississippi), for their support during various phases of the research and writing. The list is a long one and includes: Mr John Brown, Beth and Birney Imes, Lane Hardy Pierrot and Ray McIntyre, Wil Colom, Evette Williams, Butch Dollar, Elizabeth and Claude Simpson, Roger Larsen, Beth Chadwick, Roland Colom, Carol and Bill McAnally, William Threadgill, Lisa Younger Neese, Forrest Allgood, Jo Shumake, Qua Austin, Jackie Exum, Karen Winter, and Carolyn and Sam Kaye.

They shared tales and many insights about how things were in Mississippi in 1946 and how they are now. Thank you all so much!

Lynn Johnson Beatty and Merrill Kalb Watrous were always there with encouragement and advice when I needed it.

And finally, as always, I thank Matt Schumaker, Malena Watrous, and Max Watrous-Schumaker – the best of families. Who could ask for anything more?

He just wanted a decent book to read ...

Not too much to ask, is it? It was in 1935 when Allen Lane, Managing Director of Bodley Head Publishers, stood on a platform at Exeter railway station looking for something good to read on his journey back to London. His choice was limited to popular magazines and poor-quality paperbacks – the same choice faced every day by the vast majority of readers, few of whom could afford hardbacks. Lane's disappointment and subsequent anger at the range of books generally available led him to found a company – and change the world.

'We believed in the existence in this country of a vast reading public for intelligent books at a low price, and staked everything on it'
Sir Allen Lane, 1902–1970, founder of Penguin Books

The quality paperback had arrived – and not just in bookshops. Lane was adamant that his Penguins should appear in chain stores and tobacconists, and should cost no more than a packet of cigarettes.

Reading habits (and cigarette prices) have changed since 1935, but Penguin still believes in publishing the best books for everybody to enjoy. We still believe that good design costs no more than bad design, and we still believe that quality books published passionately and responsibly make the world a better place.

So wherever you see the little bird – whether it's on a piece of prize-winning literary fiction or a celebrity autobiography, political tour de force or historical masterpiece, a serial-killer thriller, reference book, world classic or a piece of pure escapism – you can bet that it represents the very best that the genre has to offer.

Whatever you like to read – trust Penguin.